Veiled Memory

by

S.P. Brown

The Stonehenge Chronicles, Book One

The Wild Rose Press, Inc.
PO Box 708
Adams Basin, NY 14410-0708
Visit us at www.thewildrosepress.com

Publishing History
First Edition, 2024
Trade Paperback ISBN 978-1-5092-5730-0
Digital ISBN 978-1-5092-5731-7

The Stonehenge Chronicles, Book One
Published in the United States of America

Dedication

For Yvonne

Prologue

Saturday Night

The technician made it to the observatory on Mount Fowlkes as the last vestiges of sunlight slipped past the western horizon. In the clear skies of southwest Texas, earthbound objects fade into silhouettes, unchained, like wraiths flitting through the deep black expanse.

Those were the times he liked best, the vast unleashed void, the countless points of lights.

Tonight was different though. An unnatural haze suffused the region, blurring the usually bright stars. Confused, Ben gazed into the sky, scratching his head as though the answer to some cosmic mystery could be coaxed from his tangled mass of hair. "If that's not the darnedest thing," he whispered, still perplexed by a nagging feeling that something was off.

Twin white domes of neighboring Mount Locke sat like mute sentinels propped against a black sky that should have been full of star-speckled brilliance. Otherwise, nothing seemed out of place. A slight wind rustled the boughs of Emory and western gray oak sprouting from the stony soil.

Still focused on the stars, Ben jumped when the giant telescope he stood next to creaked and groaned as it began rotating.

"You say something, son?"

Turning, he found his boss standing behind him. "Just wondering who's manning the instruments?"

"A visiting professor. He could use some help calibrating."

"Can't. There's a call up from New York. A student needs lunar ranging data. Routine stuff."

The boss nodded and walked back inside. Ben craned his neck again. Pollution couldn't have caused this haze, not in this unspoiled environment, but the puzzle would have to wait. He walked across the parking lot of the McDonald Observatory complex to a square metal building standing next to the laser station and called Joe Prather, an astrophysics graduate student at Columbia University.

"We're good to go," Ben said. "I'll call back when I have enough valid returns."

"Make sure the feed is correct," Prather said, agitation obvious in his voice. "You screwed it up last time."

Ben took a deep breath before answering. "I'll get your data. Just let me get back to it."

Prather sighed. "The feed to New York has to work. If I don't get good numbers, I won't graduate. You know that, right?"

"Yeah, yeah," Ben muttered, disconnecting the call. He finished selecting his target point on the moon filling his video screen like a gray ghost. Laser pulses would soon flood the targeted portion of the lunar landscape.

He glanced at the window, shocked at the intensity of the moonlight streaming in. "Fuzzy stars," he whispered, then flipped the switch.

A tight emerald laser flashed across the night sky directed at retroreflectors placed near a crater named Luther. Timing the return pulses would provide the data they needed to calculate the earth-moon distance.

It took longer than usual, but when three more valid return signals appeared on his screen as red dots, he turned off the laser and readied his systems to send the data to New York.

Ben pressed an icon on his cell phone. "Transmitting now," he told Prather and hit a button on the control panel. "Have a good one."

Locking down for the night, he had just about made it to his truck when his phone started vibrating in his pocket. It was Prather. "Look, I hate to bother you, but its perigee was supposed to be near—"

"A little over two hundred twenty-one thousand miles." Ben checked his watch. "Is there a problem?"

Prather's whisper grew quieter. "I know what you'll say, but I didn't screw up. Our system's working fine."

"Just tell me what the hell you're talking about."

Prather lowered his voice even more, forcing Ben to press the phone harder to his ear.

"The numbers are way off, man. It's showing two hundred seven thousand miles. If I didn't know better, I'd say the damn thing's spiraling down."

Ben suppressed a laugh, but nearly choked when he glanced up at the moon filling the sky like an enormous silver balloon. He cleared his throat. "The model must've corrupted in transmission. It's moving farther out, very gradually, like only an inch a year. It's not any closer than normal for this time."

Something on the floor of the valley to the east

caught Ben's eye. He jerked his head and saw a coyote scurrying around sage brush. Even during a normal full moon, it would have been too dark to see anything that far away. Then the enormity of what Prather said hit him.

"What's happening?" Prather asked in an anxious voice.

"I'll get back to you."

Cursing, Ben sprinted back to the control building and ran the same procedure four more times using two other retroreflectors located at different Apollo landing sites. The results were the same. Sweating now, he finally called his boss who alerted two other lunar ranging stations around the world. It took a couple more hours, but they were able to confirm the results.

There were too many questions for Ben to sleep that night, so he stayed up, reclined on the hood of his truck, staring at the night sky, wondering the same thing he knew would be plaguing scientists around the world.

How was the moon's inconstant orbit decaying?

Then it dawned on him. The prophecy. It had to be the prophecy. Their prophecy. His people would be ecstatic. Overhead, he imagined Mars appearing in the southwest in a blaze of red fury and Jupiter rising in the east, burning in full conflagration. A falling star dashed across the sky, yet in this strange glow, its flaming trek wasn't as dramatic as usual.

He smiled, realizing that he had just documented the first factor of the prophecy. Soon, all the clans of the Community would know.

He put a shaky finger to his temple and projected his thoughts to the leader of his clan enjoying a vacation somewhere in Europe.

****

The shrill ring of his office phone jolted Steven Dryer from a deep sleep at ABC News headquarters in Manhattan. He fell off the couch and bumped his head on the coffee table. Staggering in the dark, he made it to his desk. "Dammit, what?"

"Mr. Dryer?"

It could have been a bad connection or his half-awake brain, but the caller's voice sounded muffled. Dryer managed to groan, "Yeah, what is it?"

"Great, the operator said you sometimes sleep in your office."

"Why the hell are you calling me at two in the morning?" Dryer growled, making a mental note to chew out the new girl for divulging his habits.

"Our lab has twenty-four/seven call privileges. And I thought—"

"What lab?"

"Astrophysics. Columbia University. I'm Joe Prather, Dr. Duvall's assistant. You'll want to hear this."

Dryer rolled his eyes and almost hung up on another urgent lead that couldn't wait until morning. "Astrophysics, huh. Tell me."

"Your office has a window, right?"

"Yeah, of course." It didn't, but the caller wouldn't know that.

"It'll be west of the city at this hour. Your window faces west?"

Dryer thought of the bank of windows across the way. "Yeah."

"It won't be at the height of its full phase for a

couple more nights."

"Look, if this is some kind of stupid prank, I'll—"

"No, listen, you have my name. I told you where I work. You can verify me later. Just look out the window and tell me what you see."

Dryer gave the caller his cell number and walked through the newsroom to the far wall. He scanned the street below. The usual traffic moved lazily along the wide expanse. He'd made some enemies, but the bullet-proof glass would protect him in case this was an attempt on his life. His gut told him the guy was sincere, though odd.

He looked up as the cell phone vibrated in his hand. The moon loomed huge over the western Manhattan skyline. "Is that all you have…a big moon?"

"Because it's much closer than it should be."

That got Dryer's attention. "How much closer?"

The guy laughed, reminding Dryer of one of those wild-haired, mad scientists, although a student wouldn't have been fully admitted to the club just yet. *Just practicing, I guess*. He rubbed the back of his aching neck and smiled at his own stupid joke.

"Try fourteen thousand miles. We think it's spiraling down, establishing a new orbital trajectory. The place is wild with speculation as to how it could be happening."

"Yeah, well, this is interesting, but there are science reporters for this sort of thing."

"My boss wants to break the story only after he learns more. You know, control the reaction. But it's my discovery. Well, technically, the guy in west Texas made the measurement, but I ran the first calculation."

"Then why call me?"

"I need someone to know my role, understand? This thing's gonna get big, and I'll be pushed aside. I'm not gonna let that happen."

"I see what you mean." Dryer thought a moment. "I'll have to confirm this. My chief won't let me break a story on the word of a student."

"Just don't leave me out when it breaks. The story's big, Mr. Dryer. You make sure my name is mentioned, okay? I made the discovery."

"Sure," Dryer said, without hearing his own voice.

He stared out into the night, mesmerized by a moon that seemed close enough to touch, and as round as time.

Chapter 1

Monday

Madeline Alleyn stood at the filing cabinet, staring out the window that gave her a spectacular view of Ithaca, New York's business district. A frozen haze lay over the valley at the southern tip of Cayuga Lake, nearly obliterating the small town.

She had run up the stairs to her office in record time, anticipating her coming visitor. In minutes, half the contents of the middle drawer lay scattered on the floor, but she hadn't found what she needed.

The papers in these drawers were essential to her ongoing research, but she hadn't bothered with the other files since her days at Columbia University nineteen years earlier. Most of the material chronicled her education in linguistics and archaic languages. Life had taken many twists since those carefree days—marriage, more school, full-time work, a desperate flight to protect the lives of her unborn triplet daughters.

She withdrew two more folders, examined the articles in them, and dropped it all to the floor. They slid a little on the slick tile, the contents of the folders spilling out. With both hands buried in the drawer, she turned and checked the wall clock. Eight thirty. He would arrive any minute.

Gordon Toop had called last night. The subject of the call had been on her mind of late, but that it could also be on his mind stunned her. By the end of the conversation, the reason for his call still eluded her.

But he had prodded her most sensitive nerve, alluding to things he shouldn't have known. The question of how much he knew had kept her up all night. The topic worried her like no other.

She removed a folder titled, *Runic Symbols*. It contained articles on the rune alphabet common to early Britain, circa second century A.D. She'd authored most of these articles but found two her coming visitor had written. She set one aside and began leafing through the other, but before she could make any headway, she heard a distinctive thump—thump—thump. It grew louder, making its way up the corridor. She turned toward the closed office door.

Madeline knew him by reputation through their shared scholarly interest. She owned all his books and had most of his other research papers. She had never met him but knew he was old, nearing eighty, but still working at Northeastern University in Boston.

His call had been unexpected, his offer even more so, an invitation to speak at a conference. She already knew about the venue—Manhattan—and had to respectfully decline. Her reason was personal, as it always was with talk of the city.

Before she knew it, he had talked her into this meeting, said he was in Ithaca anyway on other business. She felt uneasy, almost trapped. Her antennae had gone up and had remained. Why the meeting today? That question dominated her thinking through the long, cold night.

Maybe his English accent and kind voice opened the door of her usual caution. His invitation flattered her. But slipping back into her more natural suspicious nature on the drive over, she could see the subtle manipulation. She had phoned him from the car to cancel, but he couldn't be reached.

Several hard raps on the door startled her. She fussed over the flower vase, and in two quick steps reached the door.

Gordon Toop was the picture-perfect academic in his tweed jacket, a smoking pipe stuck between his teeth. He entered the room, taking the first step with his artificial left leg, tobacco smoke billowing in with him.

Madeline took his arm, but before sitting, he removed his heavy overcoat and flung it over the back of the chair. He then folded into the seat with a groan, his false leg extending out in front at an odd angle.

"Thank you so much, madam, for helping an old warrior like me," Toop said, his voice raspy. He held up his pipe. "Do you mind?"

"Go right ahead."

His eyes strayed to the clutter on the floor. "I must say, I like to see well-worked offices."

"Sorry about the mess. It's not usually like this."

"A sign of a productive mind."

Madeline couldn't help staring at his prosthesis protruding from the end of his trouser.

"I should have explained Cynthia here," he said, grinning, patting it. "It does make a rather distinctive sound. Korean War. Named it after my second wife who died five years ago. I got a new leg to commemorate her. The first one I named Harriet after my first wife. She died in a plane crash transporting some of the wounded boys after the hostilities ended. She was a physiotherapist working with the injured." With difficulty, he held his leg a few inches off the floor. "Met her getting the first one of these. Suspect I won't need another."

Madeline chuckled, some of her tension draining away.

"Anyway, we haven't properly met. Dr. Gordon Toop at your service, but Gordon will do for a colleague as esteemed as yourself."

"Thank you," she said, extending her right hand while rolling her chair toward him. "I'm Madeline." His massive hand swallowed hers. "Your call last night was unexpected. Sorry I had to—"

"Say no more, Dr. Alleyn. It's quite all right. Been turned down before."

"I wanted you to know that my decision wasn't an easy one." She grimaced with the lie. "I have triplet daughters, and their birthday is this week. So, I'm afraid I—"

"All is forgiven, madam."

"Then why—"

"Am I here," he said, interrupting again. "To give it another try, of course."

Madeline opened her mouth to say something, but he went on.

"Please hear me out. I have some information I think just might turn that lovely head of yours enough to change your mind."

Leery now, she said, "I'm listening."

"I've been made privy to some information. An old discovery. Rune stones, my dear, Middle Eastern rune stones."

Madeline blinked at this. "Excuse me? What did you say?"

He leaned forward and removed his pipe from between his teeth. "I'm here to speak with you about an old discovery the natural history museum in Manhattan was once thought to house."

She sat back into her seat, heart pounding.

Toop's bushy eyebrows elevated. "My dear, are you all right?"

She regained enough composure to say, "Why should that be important to me? I mean, besides the obvious anomaly of rune stones found in that part of the world. Do you have a date?"

"We don't have the stones," he said, leaning forward in the chair again, examining her even more closely. "No one knows how many there were, what they looked like, or anything about them. And we don't know where they now are. But good people believe in their existence, and rumor has it they are five thousand years old. Oh yes, I almost forgot another rumor. It seems the glyph 'Thurisaz' is mentioned prominently on them."

Madeline closed her eyes reflexively. She knew the stones existed. Of course, they did. And she knew their age. These were some of her most closely guarded secrets now being talked about openly. It was like this man had taken a lamp and illumined the dark crevices of her mind. No one could possibly know these things, not even the great Gordon Toop.

She opened her eyes and tried to remain calm, tried not to give herself away, but his smile indicated his little fishing expedition had caught her.

"Do you know the glyph?" he asked. "Not many

people in our field understand it properly."

"Yes…yes, I'm vaguely familiar with it. But, these stones…are they lost? I mean, how did you come by your information?"

"Contacts—old friends—long ago memories." He blew smoke into the air. "I left the museum about a year before the stones' supposed discoverer started her work there a little less than forty years ago. I remained in close contact with the curator of the anthropology division. Then some interesting stories started around, stories about an Irish national named Martha McCormick, an employee there. A very striking woman, I'm told—statuesque, bright red hair. The stories are very odd, just rumors really. By now they could almost be classified as urban legends. A few months after this woman started at the museum, she vanished. People became suspicious. Some thought she might have been studying something covertly, outside her official appointment—the rune stones, you see. But no one ever saw them. An oddity, wouldn't you say?"

He waited for an answer but didn't get one, so he cleared his throat and went on.

"It was merely hearsay, a rumor. Strange how she could get away with something like that. Very strange indeed. It's unclear why it never got checked at the time, and when she suddenly vanished the stones vanished also, or so the story goes."

Just hearing the name sent a shock wave through Madeline as fear galloped up and down her spine. Other than hearing it from her father that was the first time she had ever heard anyone say her mother's name. How had Toop found her? It wasn't possible for anyone to know of Madeline's connection to Martha McCormick.

But after a moment, Madeline knew. Her own physical description exactly matched that of her mother. Her father had often talked about her mother, and the details fit Madeline perfectly—statuesque, bright red hair, a dash of freckles across a patrician nose. At thirty-eight, Madeline was older than her mother who had died at twenty-nine, but that would hardly matter. Someone had made the connection and engaged Toop in the search for the stones. And now her response had betrayed her.

She managed to walk over to the file cabinet and close the open drawer. In a near panic, she closed it too hard. A picture of her children toppled over, clattering to the floor and spreading glass shards everywhere.

"Here, let me help you with that," Toop said, hobbling over. "You seem upset."

"No, no. I'm fine—really."

He handed her the damaged frame. "Lovely daughters."

The innocuous mention of her daughters triggered the old reflexive anxiety. They were speaking of her mother's discovery, and now he had mentioned her daughters. It wasn't clear by his obvious close examination of her if he really knew just how important these things being discussed were to her.

She took his hand, and he helped her to the seat. The rune he had mentioned was featured prominently in an item Madeline had in her possession, a brief letter her father had given her when she was a young teenager, something her mother had written to a person neither Madeline nor her father knew. Only her dead father and mother knew about the note. It was a private family heirloom, or was it?

"I-I still don't see how any of this pertains to me. Is someone looking for the stones? Their origin in the Middle East sounds important if they could be found."

"It's an interesting story," Toop said, smiling again. "Something to entice you to come to our conference, give a talk on whatever research you're currently doing. I'm sure you'll have something timely for us. Then we could have a nice dinner and talk about our mutual interests and that old discovery."

Madeline let a long, slow breath escape. This seemed benign after all. He had a kind face, gentle even. A swirl of aromatic pipe smoke floated around the office, making her lightheaded.

But she remained guarded; too many of her old fears had been touched.

"Dr. Toop, all this is quite interesting, but as I said earlier, I really have to pass. My family responsibilities—"

"I understand, of course. I'm disappointed, but I understand," Toop said, shaking his old head, his fat cheeks quivering.

"There are always other meetings."

"Yes, we'll see." He looked at his watch. "Well, look at the time. So good of you to see me on such short notice, but I really must be going now. Good day to you."

She nodded, smiled, and escorted him to the door.

He squeezed her hand, kissed it gently. Genuinely touched, she opened the door for him, but then he abruptly stopped and turned to her.

"My dear, I'm a man of vast experience. I've known many people—the small-minded, the heroic, some brilliant, others of animal intelligence, and some I wouldn't give a farthing for their company. I know what makes many kinds of people tick. If there's one thing my experience has shown me, it's when someone is hiding something, like you are now. You know *far* more than you let on, but hiding your secrets won't get you anywhere. In fact, it could get you hurt."

Madeline gaped at him, at his effrontery, but managed to say, "Is that a threat, Dr. Toop?"

"Threat? Oh, no, no, don't take it that way, my dear. It's merely an observation." He gave her a crooked smile and a little bow. "Good day."

****

Madeline closed the door and planted her back to it, taking several long breaths to clear her head, his thumping gait receding down the corridor.

The last twenty minutes played a circuitous route around her mind—the rune stones, her mother, Manhattan, the museum, her children. How could this man have pinpointed everything so important to her, the things she loved and feared so much? What had he wanted? It wasn't merely an invitation to give a talk in Manhattan.

Her mother must have been careless, must have made a mistake somehow in her secret study of the stones. Totally unlike her, according to her father's old stories.

Her cell phone began playing a new ring tone she'd switched to, an old pop tune from a previous decade. It sang of love lost. She walked over to her desk to retrieve it.

"This is Madeline," she said, thankful for the distraction.

"Still hibernating in that bungalow of yours?"

"Not this morning, Jackie. You actually caught me at the office."

"Oh, good, it's been weeks since you've been around here. I have some great news, but only if you're ready for a little excitement to brighten that dull life. Dr. Harper wants to see you right away."

"Can you tell me why?"

"Yeah, but I'd rather do it in person."

Madeline grew silent, thinking, staring out the window. "Someone is there with him."

Jackie hesitated. "How did you know?"

"An older man with a false leg."

"I don't know. There's another entrance to his office. But I can hear them talking. He sounds British, and his pipe smoke smells nice."

Madeline closed her eyes.

"Are you okay?" Jackie asked. "You sound—"

"I'll be right there."

Madeline let out an exasperated breath, thinking of Harper conspiring against her. Without thinking, she found herself in the corridor, determined to stop this avalanche of fear from taking over her life once again. At the ornate glass window, the outdoor scenery distracted her. The gray bitterness of the morning presaged things she could not let back into her life. She had run from them at great cost to her and her children, and in doing so had gained so much in nearly eighteen years. Yet, life and security were fragile. Even now, she could still lose everything, even her children. She would fight to the death to prevent that from happening.

She gritted her teeth and began a slow walk down the deserted hall. It lay naked before her, stark white walls. She imagined mean, leering faces along the stretch, calling out her name, demanding things of her she couldn't produce, gloved hands clutching her, dread voices cursing.

The job, everything she now was, she would readily give them up for an average life. What were all her accomplishments for when she was lonely most of the time? Ironically, she had forged a life that helped make a connection with her long dead mother, someone she had never known, and worse, knew so little about.

Her drive to become a respected linguist and historian was really all about making something of herself to please her scholar mother. She was grateful to her father for passing on to her this ambition. It helped make her mother real. But now the life she had forged threatened to put her in contact with the very people who had murdered her mother.

Madeline entered the main office complex and acknowledged Jackie with a nod, not intending to go to her, but Jackie wouldn't have any of this. She hurried from around her desk and burst through the glass door to the outer alcove where Madeline stood, steps from Harper's office.

"Wait," Jackie said, in a furious whisper. "I was hoping to catch you. I wanted to tell you the news first."

"I already know it."

"Really, then why are you so glum?"

"He can't force me to give that talk, and I won't be coerced."

Jackie looked confused. "But a free trip to the city—you'll have some fun for a change." She reached out and touched Madeline's arm. "Oh, honey, don't do anything stupid."

"Don't try to stop me."

"He's in a weird mood. I've never seen him so—"
Jackie got a good look at Madeline, and gasped. "Are
you okay?"

"Didn't sleep much last night."

Jackie grabbed Madeline's arm, hurried her to the
lounge area, and poured a glass of water. "You need to
take better care of yourself. You look awful."

"Gee, thanks."

"I didn't mean it like that." Jackie managed to get
Madeline in a chair. "Don't let this business get to you.
It's just a simple trip. All the papers are done. The
meeting is Wednesday, and Dr. Harper said to set you
up through the weekend. Now that's something. Think
about what you're doing."

Madeline tried to smile. "He'll listen. This is such a
minor, stupid thing."

"Then why don't you—"

"But not to me, Jackie. It's too important to me."

"Damn. I hate this."

"Harper will understand."

"I hope so."

****

Madeline turned away from her friend, taking a
deep breath before grabbing the cold doorknob. Her
hand shook. They wanted her at that meeting for some
reason, but how could she explain to Harper her duty,
her solemn vow to her father, her gift of safety to her
children?

Stale pipe smoke floated in the office against the
dim sunlight filtering through the blinds. Harper looked
over his reading glasses and didn't immediately rise
from his desk to greet her. Instead, he pushed back the

writing pad he had been scribbling on—letter combinations, Madeline saw. Many 'MAs' and 'MMs' among them.

His eyes revealed his intention right off, but he shied away from her stare, motioning for her to take a seat in one of the chairs before his desk.

"I expected to find Dr. Toop here," Madeline said.

"We're alone." But he inadvertently glanced at a door leading out the back of his office. He rose and walked around the portentous desk, stopping opposite her. Had she been standing the effect wouldn't have been the same since he was at least two inches shorter. Madeline let him have this position of power. She had no idea how it would play out, but the game was on.

"How have you been?"

"I'm fine, Mark. Getting a lot of work done from home. Thanks again for the light load."

"You shouldn't refer to your load as light, especially around the other faculty. You're amazingly productive in research." He chuckled a little. "The noise in the department was incredible when they found out you wouldn't be teaching this semester."

"I heard the names," Madeline said. "Jackie filled me in."

"I apologize for all that sexist crap about the boss' girl."

"I'll gladly take a little abuse for the chance to do what I really love. I love teaching, too. It's just that this project is taking more time than I thought."

"Do you have more plans to visit Britain?"

"Not after last month."

Harper hesitated before saying, "I've just talked to Gordon Toop. You know him, I think, from

Northeastern."

Madeline stood and walked to the window. She knew what he would say next. "We have some of the same research interests."

"He's desperate to fill that spot at the conference in a couple of days. Said he talked to you about it."

Madeline listened closely for any inflection; any indication Harper knew more than he let on. She detected nothing, but her stomach tightened anyway. "And he just thought he'd get you to twist my arm."

"Why don't you help him out?"

Madeline fought for control of her temper. It was a close call. "I give enough talks already. But this isn't about Dr. Toop, is it?" She stopped and thought carefully about her next words. "I'll begin to take more speaking assignments if that's what you want, but you'll just have to let me choose the venue. Why is this particular conference so important to you that you have to—"

"Not to me, Madeline, to the department. Your appointment to the Rupert Howard Chair requires a certain degree of exposure on your part, and this meeting is perfect for you. You'll get substantial coverage and so will the department. The conference in Manhattan is in line with your current project."

"It's not for me, Mark, sorry," Madeline said flatly.

"We've made the arrangements already. Four days in the city, all expenses paid. There's no point arguing. Just accept it."

Madeline looked up and met his eyes again. "Why are you forcing the issue?"

Frowning, he walked back around his desk, settling into his leather chair. He fingered the brim of his

Chatham hat sitting on the desk. The joke around the office was that he had purchased it to cover his balding pate in the cold weather.

Madeline never engaged in petty office banter. She owed him too much. He'd supported her and she appreciated it, but he could be a self-serving little prick, using other people's talents for his own agenda.

"He understood my explanation, or I thought he did. But the old bas—"

The word was on her lips, but she held it back. She walked over to his bookcase, running her hand over some classic volumes in European history.

"I've decided not to go," Madeline said softly.

Harper stood, spitting the words out in rapid fire. "The hell you aren't. I've just confirmed it with Toop. He's delighted. I've made his day."

"You've made!" The heat rose in her face. "My contract says nothing about being a lackey of the administration. I'm productive. I do my job."

"That's too simplistic. I have some say in this, you know, and I want our department represented at that particular meeting."

"Then get someone else."

"Hell no!"

"The city is not safe for me," she said in a whisper.

"What?"

"That's why I never go there."

"Hell, is it really ever safe for anyone?"

"You don't understand."

"Explain it then. I'm listening."

Madeline shook her head.

"Don't you think there's a certain amount of paranoia going on here?"

She closed her eyes, turning away from him. "Paranoid," she said in barely a whisper. He had a point, but only on the surface. He simply didn't understand, and she would never tell him why.

He made an effort to calm his voice. "Madeline." He walked back to the front of his desk.

She turned to him. "I won't be manipulated. You hear? I won't. You have no right to force this on me, dammit. No right at all. I-I have allies here, people who'll understand what you're trying to do. I won't let you, and neither will they. I'll go to them, make them see how you run things around here. I'll—"

Madeline stopped and stormed over to a more distant chair where she sat. The silence was a thick thing, a miasma floating between them, making it hard to think. Harper cast about, speechless. She had never before raised her voice, never engaged in outbursts of anger.

If he wasn't going to say more, neither would she. She got to her feet and walked to the door.

"Your threats won't work," he said to her back. "I expect you to be there. You won't like the consequences if you aren't."

Madeline stopped. He did have the power to hurt her, but she didn't care. Instead of responding, she opened the door and walked out, closing it gently behind her.

Chapter 2

Reggie and Sarah entered the great hall through one of the tunnel transport terminals carrying two dead bodies, desperately needing to get them to the thirteenth floor before the murmurs started.

In the early morning hour, the entire building was sparsely populated except for the top two floors. There were a few people around, and the sight of Reggie and Sarah carrying the dead Initiates caused an immediate stir.

"Let's get them up," Sarah whispered, "before any more people realize what's happened."

She put a finger to her temple, sending out her thoughts. Two doors opened on either side of the great hall. "*Help us*," she said telepathically to both men exiting.

Reggie found another flux transporter about to open, one of several rectangular receptacles equally spaced around the great hall. Pulses, occurring every two minutes or so, let the Puzur class direct their tunnels through it and out of the building or to another floor.

When the nearest one produced a quantum flux, Reggie provided a tunnel. In the next instant, they found themselves on the thirteenth floor, headquarters for the Bureau of Agent Training.

They carried the bodies of Russ Porter and Crystal

Kornum to one of the holding rooms used for interrogation.

"*Lirim Ne* need direct access clearance to the whole building," Reggie grumbled. "It's too damn hard to get through when something like this happens."

Sarah thanked and dismissed their helpers. She turned quickly to the bodies, examining their minds again, but gave up almost as soon as she had begun.

"Look at them," Reggie said, nearly in shock. "How the hell did they distort their faces like that? I barely recognize them. Damn bastards." His voice shook. "Look what they did to Crystal."

Crystal's normally cheerful blue eyes were frozen in a haunting stare too terrible to look at very long.

"We better tell Dr. Brownedyke before he gets this news from someone else."

Reggie nodded. "Better get Croft here. He'll be knee deep in it anyway. I'll get another trainee to pick him up at his house and tunnel him over."

Sarah's expression cleared. "Director Brownedyke's coming."

A stark tunnel flashing pale green immediately opened and out stepped a distinguished looking gentleman—tall, lean, wearing a Houndstooth fedora, but without his usual necktie in place. He exited his tunnel still buttoning his shirt.

"What's this? What kind of trouble? You said—" He stopped when he saw the bodies. "But, what's wrong with their—Oh, my." He turned on Sarah. "Are they your—"

"Our Initiates, sir. Porter and Kornum—" She turned away and fought back the tears.

"It's Crystal," Reggie said, putting a hand on

Sarah's shoulder.

The bodies were lying on bleak stainless-steel tables, their faces distorted and blotched black and red as if they wore clown masks.

Brownedyke examined them more closely. "I had lunch with his father yesterday. And the girl. Who did this? I wouldn't have recognized her."

"It's her," Sarah said in a weak voice.

Brownedyke's face turned ashen. "Christine—her mother—Lord, and Hector. She'll have to be notified. I believe she's still in the city. And Lucian—she's his godchild." He turned on them, his expression suddenly stone cold. "I want an explanation."

"It happened on Evvoia." Sarah lowered her head as Brownedyke glowered at her.

"What were you doing there? The warnings. The intelligence. Dammit, why didn't you heed them?"

"It wasn't our intention, sir," Reggie said. "We were forced into it when we encountered—"

"It was Primilov, Dr. Brownedyke," Sarah broke in. "We weren't expecting someone so close to Erazmos, someone of his strength."

"Primilov!" Brownedyke began pacing, running his hand through his thick, graying hair. "This was a setup, then. You were on a routine mission, weren't you?"

"We thought so."

"Dammit! Explain!"

Sarah gave Reggie a quick glance then started. "About two hours ago, I met with Gregor, my informant."

"Greek," Brownedyke growled. "Saĝtuku. I warned you about trusting anyone from that clan."

Sarah shook her head. "It wasn't his fault, sir. I'm

sure of it. I think he and his friend were set up. We were supposed to rendezvous with them about an hour after our initial meeting. Gregor said the friend would be coming with the information we needed since he hadn't actually observed Erazmos's displays. They both wanted out. I've never seen Gregor so edgy—obviously frightened."

Brownedyke turned to Reggie for confirmation and received a nod. "Go on."

"The friend wanted to defect with Gregor, but he was to be accompanied by someone else, someone supposedly easy to deal with. It would involve a double capture, a way to make it look real."

Brownedyke nodded. "Excellent training opportunity with only a week left to their year. I see where this is going."

"Except the only one that showed up was Primilov."

Brownedyke had started pacing but then stopped at the bodies. When Sarah tried to start again, he raised his hand. He finally said, "You'll need to get your informant here. Get to the bottom of this."

"He's probably dead," Sarah said.

Brownedyke's head dropped, obviously disappointed. "Yes—yes, I expect so."

Reggie went to the other side of the table. "They must've been onto Gregor. I'm sure of it."

"No other intermediaries involved?"

"Just the friend," Reggie said. "We didn't expect someone of Primilov's power."

Brownedyke nodded. "That door is closed, then. Clan Saĝtuku has been quiet so long. It used to be that Nicholas—the elder Erazmos—would spread his money around very much in the open. It was a show. He clearly reveled in the attention. You knew where he stood, what he was doing, but not the son. Since the father's death, they've been so quiet, secretive even beyond our propensity."

Browndyke looked at the bodies again. "How old were they? Nineteen? Twenty?"

"Both had just turned twenty."

Browndyke smashed his hand on the table then turned to Sarah. "As Crystal's training agent, it's your duty to contact next of kin. Same for you, Reginald." He turned back to the bodies. "Sadistic bastards. Look at what they did. A Sage's daughter—transformed into a hideous—"

"There's something else," Sarah said. "Gregor made it sound like there's going to be an attack on headquarters. He was pretty cryptic about it, though."

Brownedyke looked at her with wide eyes. "Which location?"

Reggie and Sarah glanced at one another. "Manhattan. Not any of the satellites."

"Here?" Brownedyke hesitated. "Did he say when? How?"

Sarah shook her head.

"Brash," Brownedyke said. "We've been following the buildup. It's been slow—small steps. An assault on central is unlikely, but I'll step up security and get the word out to the other clans to ramp up, put feelers out. We'll find out what's going on."

Sarah and Reggie nodded in unison and Brownedyke went on. "Subversive activity's up thirty percent across Southern Europe and South America. Two of the ten clans are implicated in kidnappings, forced indoctrinations. But murdering *Lirim Ne* Initiates who work to protect them is insane." He looked at them again and almost broke down but managed to control himself. "Where were you two when Russ and Crystal—"

"Primilov came in hot," Reggie said. "He, uh, surprised us. Russ and Crystal were on their own. It took only seconds."

"It was long enough," Sarah went on. "He incapacitated Russ and took Crystal. We told Russ to get back to headquarters and alert everyone available, gather ordinary weapons, but he disobeyed a direct order and went for Primilov himself. We had to follow."

"You found them like this."

"Not right away." She glanced at Reggie. "They had us, sir, ten of them." She pointed to the bodies. "That could easily have been us. But they let us go with a message. Said Russ and Crystal were given a chance to turn, but they obviously wouldn't."

"That's all."

Sarah shook her head. "One of his men said it was a declaration to our leaders. I think he meant you and Professor Livingstone. All those who fail to recognize Erazmos as *En Ilu Uraš* could expect a similar fate."

The expression on Brownedyke's face was one of rage. "The narcissistic bastard. Does he really think we'll bow to him as God?"

"Many already do," Reggie said.

The door flew open, and Cyril Croft walked in on his short, fat legs, looking aghast.

"Cyril will assist you with the bodies," Brownedyke said. "We're at a disadvantage now. We still need answers."

"Sir, Primilov—my past—I need to do something, anything."

Reggie tried to redirect her. "Sarah, don't. This wasn't our fault."

"The hell it wasn't. This was my operation. Gregor was my informant—my responsibility, and now he's probably dead, too."

Sarah went to Crystal's body and ran her fingers over her blonde hair. Such a sweet girl. Tears fell. Her husband had also been ambushed by Primilov in much the same way, right under her nose. That was five years ago. Afterward, she had lost her focus, her purpose, and then her nerve. She left the *Lirim Ne*, thought she was through with it all. It had been Reggie who finally coaxed her back, giving her a new reason to live. She had her life together, especially her private life with Jason, a man who knew what it felt like to lose someone. Now, this.

"I agree," Brownedyke said. "These things happen."

"Whose fault was it then?" Sarah shouted. "How did he do this? Look at them. Sir, that's two strikes on me. First Ray and now Crystal. We need answers now more than ever."

Brownedyke said, "Ray was not your fault either, my dear. Put that behind you."

She shuddered and wrapped her arms tightly around herself. "I can't."

"You've got to."

"Maybe I've got to finally face Primilov."

"I can't let you do that," Reggie said.

"And I won't let you." Brownedyke stopped and

gave her a long, intense stare. "But we do need some timely intelligence. What do you have in mind?"

Reggie growled something Sarah couldn't make out and stalked from around the table. "It's way too dangerous."

"There's danger everywhere, son," Browndyke said. "You proved that this morning even in our own city. But I won't force a mission like this on anyone." He gave Sarah another stern look. "What are you thinking?"

"I don't know. I'll come up with something, soon."

Reggie turned away. He couldn't override the boss and expect to keep his job. Her point was a valid one, and she would make Reggie see it. Sometimes action was needed in their business to help validate their worth. Sarah wouldn't withdraw again. She couldn't. It was Reggie who had taught her that.

"We still need evidence of his power," Browndyke said, placing a hand on her shoulder. "Concrete evidence, not rumor. But don't put yourself at too much risk. Leave room for a quick escape."

"Yes, sir."

"You hear me, Sarah," Browndyke went on. "This wasn't your fault, and neither was Ray."

At that moment, Lucian Livingstone—tall, white-haired, and surprisingly fit despite his age—entered through a purplish tunnel.

"Darius, what's this rumor? I've just—"

Brownedyke didn't let him finish. He pulled Livingstone aside, and they engaged in a telepathic exchange before Livingstone walked to the tables, head bent like a tired workhorse at the end of a long day.

Brownedyke turned to Sarah. "Go prepare a

strategy with Reggie and get us that intel, but don't be reckless. You understand? Come back to us." He turned to Reggie. "Help her."

Reggie nodded, and a black hole erupted in the air next to him. Brown electric flashes lashed out from its interior. He motioned for Sarah to follow him into his tunnel. And when she did, it closed, and they disappeared from the room.

Chapter 3

Madeline sank into the seat of her car, wiping tears. The morning had been surreal. Her most closely guarded secrets had all been on public display. But not this one. She pulled an old sheet of stationery from her coat pocket and held it up, examining the faded, handwritten message beneath a row of shamrock serving as a decorative border.

The note was one of only two items she possessed that had great personal significance, the only things linking her to her mother. It had been written by her mother, but not to Madeline. It was addressed to someone named Lucian.

A source of complex emotions, sometimes inspiring, other times driving her to despair, the note was also the very reason for her academic success. A fact she somehow owed entirely to a mother she never knew.

She needed to know her mother through her mother's work. If she could just discover the focus of that work and what this note was really all about. But the note's message was inscrutable.

Madeline laid the letter on her lap and opened one of the files she'd brought from her office. She drew out two sheets, each containing a single rune. The ending of the paper she'd been working on stumped her. She didn't quite know how to finish it, but now she had an idea, something Toop said.

The most important part of her mother's note concerned the rune stones Toop had mentioned. He was right about one thing. The stones were lost, perhaps stolen upon her mother's death, but maybe not. Madeline had her suspicions.

"Thurisaz," she said, pronouncing the glyph better than he had. "Rumored to be mentioned on the stones, but it's not a rumor. I know it. I know they're out there, somewhere."

She quickly grabbed the sheet containing Thurisaz, a thorn on a stick, the thorn rune.

Her master's thesis had been devoted to this one rune, an interest sparked by her mother's mysterious note. The rune was enigmatic. They all were, but this one especially. It could mean so many things depending on one's willingness to spin it either literally or symbolically.

But how did her mother mean it? And more importantly, how did the author of the message engraved on the Stones of Sumer mean it?

"A door or gate, to…to, the future, or seeing the future, or maybe the truth. Symbolic or literal, that's always been the question. What did you believe? What did you know?"

She grabbed the other page and studied the second glyph.

"Uruz," she said, sounding out the name. "Strength, but why in this context?"

There was no doubt about this one. "A forceful, masculine archetype. Power, but also signifying change. This one is clearer."

She suddenly crumpled the paper into her fist and

threw it on the dash, succumbing to the old inner struggle, the queasiness arising from somewhere behind her navel leaching up through her abdomen and thorax, producing a dry throat and ringing in her ears. She had an idea how to get to the bottom of it all, but she always dismissed it. She was terrified to do otherwise.

She reached for the balled-up sheet and unfolded it, laying it beside the other one. She stared at them.

Looking at Thurisaz, she said, "The opposite is also true. Not willing to heed information given, having a stubborn mind set." This was the reversed interpretation depending on how one held the rune. She thought awhile about this. "Why would she put these two together? Why did she focus there?"

She sighed and went over the note again, reading it through two more times. No great insight occurred to her, no bright moment of inspiration, no epiphany—nothing.

She sank into the seat again and just as suddenly something crept to the front of her mind, a different way of viewing things.

These two runes were important, but she now saw that the conspicuous absence in the note of any of the other runes comprising the runic alphabet made these two stand out even more. The two runes were somehow connected in a fundamental sense. Somehow her mother had seen this from the many inscriptions the stones must have contained. She had chosen to highlight in the note only these two, knowing the classical meaning of the two individual runes. Together they might infer something entirely different.

Madeline looked through the window into the silver morning, her resolve growing. Now was the time to put it all behind her. Succeed or fail, she could then turn her back on the city forever, whatever the outcome.

****

Madeline parked her sedan on Cayuga Street just off the Ithaca Commons and walked the remaining block to a quaint Celtic specialty shop.

She loved going there, but it had been a long time. She'd discovered The Green Erin upon arriving in Ithaca nearly eighteen years prior. She'd fallen into a fast friendship with the owner, a woman about ten years older, someone for whom the mysterious was a way of life. Madeline had spent her entire life avoiding mysterious things, but Cailin Faal was different, and it was time to confide in someone, make a connection over the things that held her captive.

Madeline loitered on the front walk, building her courage, when Cailin appeared at the door, key in hand, adorned in a festive Celtic dress, bright red and blue with white decorative sleeves and low cut, showing off the delicate Celtic cross that hung down to her ample cleavage.

"My, my, what a surprise we have here," Cailin said in an Irish accent. "Why not stay away another six months? A year why don't you?" Cailin gave Madeline a huge hug and kissed her on both cheeks.

"I'm sorry, Cailin. My schedule, the kids, but I really have no excuse."

"Me either, my bonny girl. I should have called. Life gets in the way. Come, I have tea brewin' in the back. I see you need to talk." She hooked Madeline's arm and drew her in.

"How did you know that?"

"It's written all over your lovely face, my dear,"

she said, stopping. "You've not been sleepin' either, I can see that clearly enough. Come, tell me what's troublin' you."

They wound through the cramped, unlit shop past tables of various Celtic wear and jewelry. The west-facing store front didn't allow much light to filter in, leaving the interior dusky. Celtic pillar candles scented with balsam fir, cinnamon, lavender, orange clove, and clary sage gave the interior aroma a curious smell like the burning of an herb garden, but without the astringent odor of fire consuming things still alive and growing.

Stained glass hangings embossed with Celtic symbols hung everywhere. Two wood-paneled niches warmed by fireplaces provided a cozy atmosphere for the plush chairs. There were several booths to enjoy the shop's green tea specialty. When they made it to the back kitchen, the smells cleared Madeline's head.

Cailin lived in the back of her shop and slept on a daybed in a far corner. Trinkets in various stages of repair cluttered two worktables. Sausages frying on a small cooking stove gave the room a mouth-watering aroma. Cailin placed a sausage and a blueberry scone in front of Madeline.

"Thank you," Madeline said, as she sipped her hot tea.

"You know," Cailin said, seated across from her, "the Celts had a saying. 'The seeking for one thing will find another.' "

Madeline nodded.

"What do you seek, dear girl? That sad look always puzzled me, but I see more there now—a loneliness that's eatin' at you."

Looking into Cailin's deep green eyes, Madeline found a knowledge of things not found in books. That was what had first attracted her to Cailin. There was a calmness about her, though she had seen much tragedy in her life.

"I need to talk about things I've never mentioned. My past and my mother's work, my work," Madeline said, looking into her hands. "No one else would understand. I-I should have mentioned them years ago."

"What things, dear?"

"Well, you're obviously interested in Celtic culture, and I know you're also interested in rune linguistics."

"Not to your level, though, Dr. Alleyn."

"But that's just it. I'm not after academic understanding, but insight—mystical insight." She almost choked on the word.

"Mystical!" Cailin's bright eyes sharpened even more. "Now that would be my territory. But, if you don't mind me sayin', you've never shown an interest there before."

"Maybe it's time."

"Tell me what you're thinking."

With trembling hands, Madeline withdrew the note. No one had ever seen it besides her father.

Cailin read it through without looking up. She raised her head, gazing past Madeline, a queer look playing around her eyes. She then read it again, glancing up at Madeline, twice this time. "This note is strange, dear—"

"My mother was beyond strange. I don't know what else she might have been. I've never known much about her. She refers to an archeological discovery she made in Mesopotamia forty years ago."

"Yes—yes, five thousand years old, it says, but the Sumerians didn't write in runes. You must know that since I do."

"You're right, they didn't."

"I have my professor friend to thank for that tidbit of knowledge. You encouraged further study, remember?"

Madeline smiled. "Did you notice the other strange thing?"

"Yeah, a group called the *UngKin*." Cailin stopped, expecting a reply, but Madeline only stared down at her hands. "Maddie, do you know anything about these people and their connection to Ireland?"

"I think so, but not much, not nearly enough. But I didn't come here to discuss them. What about the runes?"

Cailin's eyes narrowed. "There is an allusion here to a contest, maybe a fight. She mentions a prophecy, but the Irish have never been devoted to a prophecy concerning runes."

"These people, this *UngKin*, are highly devoted to this prophecy."

"How do you know that? Do you know anything about them?"

"I think they're some kind of secret sect with ancient origins. They somehow remained intact, but clandestine. My mother was born into it."

"Interesting. If birthright provides membership, then that makes you a part of them, too."

Madeline nodded. She had made the connection as a child.

"And what is this prophecy, darlin'?"

"My husband told me once, but I—"

"Your husband! But how did he—" Tears spilled down Madeline's cheeks, so Cailin said, "Of course, if you'd rather not get into that just yet."

Wiping her face, Madeline said, "I promised myself I wouldn't do that again, but I've already cried several times today."

Cailin patted Madeline's folded hands. "A good cry never hurts. Now, let's focus on those runes, shall we? As you know, these two represent the ancient elements: Uruz, earth and Thurisaz, fire. Your mother seems to be saying something about a contest between these two, or what they represent."

"A battle, maybe."

"Maybe, but that could be on several planes, couldn't it? Metaphysical or perhaps elemental forces, as in literal fire from the sky striking the earth as in destruction of biblical proportions. Maybe this prophecy foresees that. Many people believe the Bible teaches such a thing, and these stones were found in a biblical area. The time frame is biblical as well."

"I've thought of that, but I don't believe the answer is that easy."

"You believe a more metaphysical understanding is correct?"

"Perhaps, but perhaps literal in another sense."

"What sense?" Cailin said.

"That's what I've tried to puzzle out for years."

Cailin took a sip of tea and picked up the note again. "Okay, maybe I can help. Let's see what we know. Uruz means strength and power, and also wildness and virility; that much is clear. It's strongly masculine. It also can mean wealth, material power brought to bear over others. As I said, it's the earth rune. Do you agree with all that?"

"Yes."

"Now, why would your mother put these two together?"

"I've asked that hundreds of times."

"Let's keep asking. Thurisaz is also thought to be masculine, but I don't believe it's as strongly so as Uruz. It's the thorn rune. Thorns are defensive and offensive. They grow out of the earth, so there's a connection on at least that point."

"But there's more," Madeline said.

"Yes, let's see. It's also the fire rune, and as such it's associated with anger, uncontrolled emotions, volcanic activity, even—chaos. Now, how could these concepts do battle? Maybe there's a context that's literal, but not in the sense of natural disaster?"

"That may be the heart of it."

"And then there's that prophecy."

"Yes."

"Now, what could this prophecy refer to if not a biblical-sized natural disaster—macro scale?"

"Micro?" Madeline said suddenly, the word popping into her mind unexpectedly.

Cailin gave Madeline a long look. "Where did that come from?"

"I don't know. I've never thought about that before."

"Micro...okay, then...so, let's see...take it way down."

"What do you mean?"

"On a personal level."

"What?" Madeline said, confused.

"The elements—maybe the prophecy refers to personification of these elements. That would have aspects of metaphysics and literalness."

"Personification?" Madeline suddenly gasped, remembering something, a deeply repressed memory of a long-ago conversation.

"Are you okay, dear?"

"Yeah, it's just that—" Madeline looked at her watch. "I really have to go."

Cailin gave her a surprised look. "But we've just started."

Madeline hoped Cailin couldn't hear her heart thumping wildly. "You've helped, believe me."

"Okay, but one more thing. I've read that combining these two runes is dangerous. Of course, I'm speaking now of the magical arts, not this prophecy."

"Magic?" Madeline said, taken aback.

"Could this community be associated in some way with powers, sorcery?"

"I don't know," Madeline said, averting her eyes. "I don't really believe in such things."

"I know, but you wanted mystical insight, remember?"

"Yeah, I did."

"Then I've given you something to think about. By the way, do you know of any world culture or religion that personifies the ancient elements and believes they will somehow do battle?"

"No—none."

"Nor do I, Maddie, nor do I." Cailin took her hands, forced eye contact, and held it. "You're not tellin' me everything, are you? But no need, I'm here when you need me."

"Thank you, Cailin—so much. I can't tell you how much."

"Then don't try. You haven't found what you're seekin', but keep lookin'."

Madeline smiled. "I will."

They rose, embraced, and Cailin saw her friend to the door of her shop, but before leaving Madeline placed an envelope in Cailin's hand.

"Please, I can't tell you anything more than what we've discussed, so don't ask, but if anything should happen to me see that this gets into the right hands. The note explains what to do."

"You're in some kind of trouble, aren't you?"

"I could be."

Cailin's eyes were pits of sorrow as she took the envelope and stared at it. "You know, you've always been mighty secretive. A moment ago was the first real time that you've opened yourself to me. Keep doing that, Maddie, and you'll find that you have allies where you least expect them."

"I need them now. I can't do this alone."

"Let me help."

"I don't know what more you can do. I just need to find those stones. I can't explain it fully. I just know there's something important about her work that's always interested me, but it's more than just curiosity. I feel drawn to it. I've even had recurring dreams about it."

"Dreams?"

"Yeah—for a long time now, at least since my middle teen years. The same one over and over, and they're getting more frequent, over the last week especially. I'm beginning to think I'm losing my mind."

"What you're describing sounds an awful lot like obsession."

Obsession. The word made Madeline flinch.

"Are your dreams somehow connected to the stones and this work you think you have to do?"

"Maybe…it's probably related to that, subconsciously anyway."

Madeline looked through the front of Cailin's store at people going about their business, their breaths frosty puffs of clouds in the cold morning air. Happy people going about their happy lives—shopping, laughing, being normal. It made her envious.

"I'm going to put an end to this one way or the other."

"Determination can be your friend, too," Cailin said. "Stay focused and be careful."

Madeline nodded and left the shop for the last time.

Chapter 4

Skipping the last two classes of the day, Phoebe Alleyn and her sisters made it to the Ithaca Commons in record time, despite the icy roads. Assorted shops, restaurants, and coffeehouses lined the cobblestone street. Round tables littered the walk, deserted now in the cold.

Phoebe had to pull Dione and Rhea along because of what she planned to do. It didn't take much to convince Di to skip class, but Rhea, the milder one of the triplets, only came along to keep them out of trouble. Phoebe had hinted that they were going to The Green Erin, but that wasn't her plan at all. The shop next door interested her much more, but their mother would kill them if they were caught in The Wyrd Emporium.

Phoebe didn't care about petty rules today. Something was up with their mother, some problem she seemed to be having. Phoebe sensed that it was something dangerous. She had been thinking this way since Saturday night when the man who ran The Wyrd Emporium approached her from the audience following her debate win over that college student.

She stopped her sisters two doors down from his shop and hesitated, eyeing the door, remembering the encounter from Saturday night. She could still smell his stinking breath.

****

"Well, now, quite the smarty pants, aren't we?" the old man had taunted, shaking a crooked finger as he approached the stage. "You'll learn soon enough the universe favors them what knows a thing or two 'bout magic."

Phoebe had started to say something, but as he drew closer, the smell of him nearly made her gag.

"Where are your sisters anyway?" He looked around. "I know you're one of the Alleyn triplets. Been watchin' you fer three years." He stared over his shoulder as though expecting someone. "Your mother's s'posed to be some great history professor, ain't she? Got quite a reputation on the Celts. Jist so happens, I've been discussin' her theories with one of ma patrons."

He lowered his voice and bent at the waist to give Phoebe a closer look. "Tell her fer me that she's off base. And as fer you." He came nearer, his nauseating breath filtering up her nose. "That boy had better arguments. Jist ask your leggy mother."

Phoebe's face had grown hot at that point, and she took a step closer, despite his smell. "What are you talking about? What should I ask her?"

To her surprise, her voice had produced a strange ring of authority that somehow affected the old man. His face went slack like he'd been struck dumb. He staggered, forcing Phoebe to steady him with a hand, which seemed to frighten him. Reaching into his scruffy brown jacket, he withdrew a thick, rough-hewn stick, clutching it below some odd symbols etched all over it, symbols Phoebe felt certain she had seen before.

"You tell her fer me that people oughtn't dabble in

things they know nothin' of." He held the stick out in front of him, using it like it could ward off something evil. "Tell her the power of Uruz will find her out."

Before Phoebe could think of something to say, he spun around and darted off through the crowd.

****

Phoebe had relived that moment many times since Saturday night, debating what to do about it. Should she tell her mom about him? Her sisters? Weird dreams had also started followed by voices in her head. It spooked her so much she held her tongue.

The old man seemed to know something about her debate argument. He also seemed to know her mother. But how could her mother know him? He didn't look like someone she would hang with, even on her worst bad hair day. None of it made sense. Then something struck Phoebe, and she knew she was getting close to the truth. Her mother must be keeping something important from them.

The weird things that had happened during and after the debate, and earlier in the day at Rhea's soccer match, forced only one theory to the front of her usually logical mind.

The old man must have put a curse on them using that crooked little stick with the weird writing on it. But that theory had one problem—the timing was wrong. She hadn't seen that grimy man at the soccer field in the morning when the strange things had first started. Thinking harder, she knew the answer was that he must have been somewhere at the soccer game close by, pointing the stick, cursing them with it.

She debated with herself all the next day, but by evening she had finally decided on a course of action.

Maybe there was someone out in the blogosphere who could help. She had wanted to start her own for the longest, and now this was the perfect opportunity. So, after her sisters fell asleep, she grabbed her laptop and created one using a code name, *Charolastra*. Space Cowboy seemed to be a perfect fit. It all came spilling out, a call for help to make sense of it all, her desperation obvious in each sentence. She put it all in, the strange things happening, and especially the dream about that face in the clouds and the birds and that strange guttural language voicing the words—*fire, air, water.* She shouldn't have known the language of her dream, but she did.

Phoebe stared at the door to the man's shop, concentrating so hard her eyes hurt. The lights were on, so she knew he was there. She needed to do some eavesdropping then corner the shopkeeper and get him to talk.

But Rhea finally had enough of the intrigue. "I won't go another step till you tell us what we're doing."

Dione surprised Phoebe by agreeing. "Mind telling me why you're acting like me, all devious?"

They were near the fountain in the center of the outdoor mall, but it was turned off. The water in it had frozen over. Phoebe just shrugged. The irony of the situation wasn't lost on her. She was usually the one trying to get them to listen to reason.

"Let's just walk by and see if he's there," Phoebe said.

"Who?" Di and Rhea asked.

Phoebe figured it was time. She couldn't keep it from them any longer. She told them about the weird things she had noticed at Rhea's soccer match, about that old man and what had happened during the debate later that night, about the suspicions she had of their mother who had to be hiding something. It was all as clear as day.

But they were having a hard time believing any of it.

Rhea turned suspicious eyes to Phoebe. "You proved in the debate that magic isn't real. You won, remember?"

"Really?" Dione broke in. "That's the best you can do, Phoebe? Telepathy? You having a brain fart or something?"

Phoebe sighed and closed her eyes, concentrating extra hard on Rhea. The result was an accident. Saturday night when she'd read her debate opponent's mind totally by accident, surprising her so much she almost fainted on the spot. Doing it again now, Rhea's eyes rolled back in her head, and she almost passed out. Di had to steady her.

"You kissed Will," Phoebe said, shocked.

Rhea turned as red as her tan skin could go. Di was about to spout off something nasty, but before she knew what was happening, Phoebe grabbed her mind, and said, "So that's what all the fuss is with Tracey. You caught her boyfriend with Kitty. You're lucky you only got a black eye for telling."

Rhea and Dione took a step back as though trying to avoid a sudden contagion.

"Believe me now?"

Di nodded, but Rhea grabbed her hand. "And you think this has something to do with me popping those soccer balls? They really weren't defective in some way?"

"I told you, Rhea," Dione blurted out. "You're turning into the Hulk. You even look a little green around the eyes."

"That's because they are green, you idiot!"

Di pushed her. "That's not what I meant!"

Before they could start fighting, Phoebe stepped between them. "That's why we have to go in that shop. I believe that man did something to cause all this."

Rhea shook her head. "That's about the worst idea you ever had. You know how Mom feels about that place."

Phoebe rolled her eyes. "Since when do we listen to everything she says? Anyway, that man threatened her, kind of. We have to find out what he's up to and how he could do this to us."

Di shook her head. "You want to go talk to that old freak? Isn't he the same one who shouted at the moderator from the back of the room?" She cleared her throat. " 'Magic ain't superstitious!' "

Rhea pushed her from behind to stop the cackling. "Okay, so the nut bag harassed you a little. Just forget about it."

"You guys don't understand. He talked about her like he thinks she's connected to—"

"No way, Pheeb," Di interrupted. "If she finds out, we'll be in some serious shit."

Phoebe grabbed Rhea's hand, meaning to pull her into the place, but then a familiar voice called out. A man pushing a huge cart turned onto the Commons from Cayuga Street.

"Gettum hot…right here!"

Dione clenched her fists. "It's Gibbs, the trolley vendor. He cheated us last time, remember? We oughta get our money back and report him."

Phoebe glanced at the squat man who had stopped right outside The Wyrd Emporium. Before she could say they didn't have time to fight with Gibbs, Di grabbed her hand and pulled her to the line forming at his trolley.

They were even with the shop now, the cluttered front drawing Phoebe's gaze.

The windows were messy, as if the owner didn't care about impressing anyone. Old urns, funny-looking symbols, and grotesque totems graced the window display. And were those really shrunken heads?

Phoebe strained to see into the place, but the vendor's booming voice distracted her. A tooth with a gold cap shone through the half-smile he wore. "What'll it be this time?" He grabbed three boxes of red-hot zingers. "I remember you three is mighty partial to these."

"Yeah, about a million years ago, and not at the price we paid last time," Dione said, crossing her arms and glaring at him. "You charged us three bucks a box. Will said they're supposed to be only two."

The man's narrow eyes flitted over her. "You three can afford it, sweetheart."

Rhea stepped to the front. "News flash. We aren't rich."

The man looked skeptical, but Dione wouldn't let him off the hook. She moved up beside Rhea and put her hands on her hips. "Will said you charge more to children of professors. It's true, isn't it?"

"Now that's a serious accusation." He jerked his head toward a policeman turning the corner. "All I've gotta do is call that officer over. Honest shopkeepers don't like being harassed by rich folk." He shoved the boxes in her face. "Now pay up."

A couple of people had come by, but Dione ignored their calls to hurry, and whispered, "Watch this one." She turned back to the vendor. "Like my sister said, we ain't rich, and you ain't honest. Maybe the policeman will listen to you, but maybe he'll listen to us more. You wanna chance it?"

The vendor tensed and looked over his shoulder at the approaching officer. "All right then, damn ya, two dollars it'll be."

Phoebe stepped forward. "You already have an extra dollar from each of us. That overcharge, remember?"

Di gave Gibbs a crooked smile. "My sister's right. One dollar each, or we tell that officer you cheat children of Gownies."

The man's eyes darted over them, but then he grumbled something and pulled on a dilapidated cash drawer that creaked and groaned as it slid open. To Phoebe, it felt like an explosion had gone off. She swayed like a sapling tree in the breeze as the rumble roared through her mind.

Her hands shot to her ears. "*Make it stop!*"

A deep thumping beat a discordant rhythm through her brain, and each time it swelled her head like a billows. She opened her eyes to slits.

What she saw reminded Phoebe of those movie scenes where bullets zip by in slow motion. The whole world had entered some strange dimension existing in the space between waking and dreaming. Everyone was frozen in time. Phoebe turned on her heels, gawking at the meager street traffic stuck in ultra-slow motion.

Then the drawer groaned to a stop and what felt like a rushing wind blew over her.

The world turned normal again with Dione snickering at the vendor.

"Blooming redhead," he muttered back, shoving the boxes at her. "And don't come back!"

Phoebe felt a tug and started gliding along the cobbled street. Rhea and Di had each taken a hand and were pulling her to the nearest storefront where they collided against the wall. Dione's blue eyes darted over the street as if seeing it for the first time. And what was that flash leaping through Rhea's sparkling green eyes? Whatever had happened to Phoebe was affecting them, too.

A tickling in the back of Phoebe's mind caused her to spin back to Gibbs just in time to see an owl and two tiny sparrows swoop over the commons. Instead of disappearing over the buildings as the owl had done, the sparrows circled the vendor and—

"Ugh!"

The vendor ducked, screaming, but poop from the other bird got him right on his head. Gibbs cursed, shook a fist at the darting birds, and scuttled off, slipping and sliding with his cart.

Dione laughed at the sight of him wiping off the mess. "Serves the old buzzard right, getting dive bombed."

Bells jingled as someone left The Wyrd Emporium, and before Rhea and Di could protest, Phoebe pulled them inside.

The man with stringy gray hair was there, the same man who had pulled that stick on her after the debate. He gave a quizzical glance around, but Phoebe had been too fast for him to see. They darted to a hiding spot. He shrugged and turned back to his customer.

"You shouldn't have," Dione whispered.

They were crouching behind a partially unpacked crate of funny-looking pottery.

Phoebe put a finger to her lips. "We won't be long. I just need to ask him about—"

An oily, burning fragrance caught in the back of her throat, gagging her. The light was dull. A smattering of sawdust littered the creaky wood floor. "Let's wait until he's alone."

But bells on the door jingled again and in walked a lanky man with a silver goatee and a checkered hat. It was their mother's colleague from the history department at Cornell.

"If he sees us..." Dione whispered, her bright blue eyes popping.

Phoebe yanked them deeper into the store as the shopkeeper bustled over to where the professor stood admiring knickknacks on a shelf.

"Well, well, Professor Wick." The shopkeeper held out his hand, but Wick ignored it. He glanced back at his other customer and lowered his voice. "I trust what I sold you worked."

"Quite well, in fact, but making this particular bindrune is a complicated process, mystically speaking, of course. One has to be in the right frame of spirit. The aurors must be aligned, if you understand my meaning. For that, I need the item I called about. You said it was in."

"Arrived yesterday." The shopkeeper cleared his throat when his other customer walked out. "Forgive me, Professor, I'm curious 'bout what you're plannin'.

Must be a special purpose. Jist guessin', mind you."

Wick's thin lips produced a mirthless little smirk, stretching his face even thinner, reminding Phoebe of a bearded lizard. "Sometimes one's enemies need to be taught some lessons hard to press upon them otherwise."

The shopkeeper's eyebrows arched. "Them's my sentiments s'actly. But ya know that particular bindrune is meant to—" He caught his breath, and his eyes widened. "Oh, I see now. That's a right powerful method." He wiggled his grimy finger in Wick's face. "Control is the key to bend her will, mind you, but if she finds out, she'll strike like a viper."

Two fingers curled like fangs and struck at Wick, forcing him back a step, but Wick waved his hand dismissively. "Yes, yes—"

"By the way, I saw that redheaded shrew over at the library Saturday night. It was at the debate them fools organized."

Di hiccupped. Phoebe put a hand to Rhea's lips but couldn't stop the "Oh" that had escaped. The two men turned, forcing them to lower their heads even more.

Seconds passed, but the men never moved. "The one the Ithaca Debate Club runs," the shopkeeper went on. "They had them brats this year. Imagine the nerve. Is magic real? Had to control myself durin' the thing. Then I got to thinkin'—"

"Not a good idea, my dear man."

"Wha...oh, yeah, me thinkin'." The shopkeeper cackled. "Good one, Professor." He grabbed Wick's arm and led him over to examine more of his junk. "Anyway, that theory she fancies—the one 'bout Sumerian runes. Don't know much 'bout it myself, me being unlearned and all, but she'd need somethin' to back it up, right? And I thought 'bout artifacts…some kind of discovery."

Wick stroked his goatee, suddenly more interested. "Artifacts, yes, I suppose, but she's not an archeologist. If she has some relic or other, how would she have gotten it?"

"Maybe she knows somethin' you and the others don't. Her idea ain't original, mind you. If you had his old papers, you could—"

But Professor Wick was already shaking his head, bringing the shopkeeper up short. "This theory of Sumerian runes is useless. If she's into that, she'll be laughed off campus like he was decades ago."

Wick stuck a smoking pipe between his teeth. "But I wonder why she's so secretive all the time?" He put the package under his arm and started to turn but seemed to reconsider. "I'd give anything to know her source material if there is any. Too bad nothing was left of his work." Wick examined his fingernails. "I hope to do the ritual in a few days. I'll complete the bindrune tomorrow. It shouldn't look too different from the one you carry. We'll get the information out of her then."

The shopkeeper gave Wick a strange look as if trying to work through a puzzle. He snapped his fingers. "Then you need somethin' important; somethin' to give it the proper context, if you know what I mean, Professor."

Wick nodded. "Something of hers, yes, but how to get it?" Waiting for an answer, he began doodling with a miniature set of stone columns.

"That set is one of the best. You see the detail, the angle of the fallen Sarsen stones they've fixed in place."

"What are those?" Rhea whispered.

Phoebe craned her neck for a better view. "A tiny replica of the Stonehenge ruins."

"Stone what?" Dione said.

"Shhh! I'll explain later—listen."

"They're quite exact." Wick's mustache twitched. "I'll take it."

A cat meowed on a counter above them, making Dione fall to her butt. They ducked, but too late. The stringy haired man leered from around Professor Wick and spotted them.

"Who's there, Zelda?"

The girls sprang for the door, but the shopkeeper dashed down the aisle faster than anything and pounced on them. Di and Phoebe were caught.

"Run!" Phoebe screamed to Rhea.

But Rhea shook her head and stayed in the partially opened doorway.

"You three again! Up to yer usual shenanigans, are ya?"

Phoebe tried to turn away so Professor Wick couldn't see her face, but then his color drained.

He gave the shopkeeper a knowing look. "Alleyn triplets," Wick growled in a menacing voice. "What did you hear?"

"Nothing," Phoebe said, staring right into his narrowing eyes.

"I was gonna tell you 'bout our little junior miss, Professor." His grip tightened on Phoebe's arm, and his breath nearly knocked her out. He wore a gray flannel shirt under that same dirty brown jacket he had been wearing Saturday night. She could see that little stick in his front pocket. It seemed to draw her. She felt herself relaxing, getting closer to him, to it, but then Dione bellowed.

"You have to let us go!" Her face was glowing red in one of her tempers. Phoebe did a double take because Di's red hair seemed to be glowing, too. "We haven't done anything wrong!"

The shopkeeper held Phoebe at arm's length, which made his jacket fall back over his shirt pocket, hiding the stick. Her head cleared.

"This little black-headed one 'ere sure turned the tables on that boy, didn't she? Think you're pretty smart, I bet. All about logic and rational s'plainin', ain't you, sweetie?" He let Dione go and ran a finger around one of Phoebe's black curls. She struggled against his grip, but he was too strong.

"Leave her alone!" Rhea screamed from the door.

Wick jerked his head to her. "Close that door." He adjusted the package under his arm, stood straighter, and cleared his throat. "There's really no need for this, Haldane. Dr. Alleyn will probably be along for her brats any moment."

Haldane, the shopkeeper, leered at Phoebe. "That boy made some fine points you'd be mighty smart to consider when he said it's the qua...quantum nature of the universe what favors magical folk."

"Your ears must have been plugged, because he didn't say it like that."

"Ask your mother, then. Seein' it's she who's studyin' magic."

Phoebe's mouth went slack, and her heart skipped a beat. She suddenly knew where she'd seen that strange word he'd used when he pointed the stick at her. Uruz. Somehow it was connected to the dream she'd started having.

And Haldane hadn't been mistaken about one thing. Phoebe's mother knew a lot about the Celts and the superstitions they believed in. Anyone who cared could read her scholarly articles. But the way Haldane used the word magic, the way he clutched that funny looking stick, brandishing it like some kind of weapon, what did it mean?

Uruz was a rune, one letter of a kind of ancient alphabet. And more than that, it was one of the earth runes, maybe the chief one, and earth was one of the four ancient elements: earth, air, water, fire.

Phoebe had dreamed about three of the four elements, and for the first time while awake she tried to remember more as she stood there stunned at what Haldane had said. None of the runes had been in her dream, and she didn't know which of the other runes represented air, water, and fire. But Phoebe had read some of her mother's papers and knew there were twenty-four runes, each with a basic meaning oriented either male or female, and sometimes both.

Her mind began to race. Why was she dreaming about them? Why now, just when all this crazy crap had started to happen?

Then Phoebe made a leap of logic. There were three important words in the dream—triplets of a sort. Were they connected to runes someway, maybe a magical connection? It was nuts, but the memories of Saturday and what she had suddenly been able to do kept her from dismissing the idea.

The element earth hadn't been in her dream. That was curious. Haldane had used the male oriented earth rune, Uruz, like a curse or an incantation. Why had he used that particular one when he'd cornered her after the debate, threatening her mother?

Suddenly, it all seemed so perfectly logical—the information about runes she knew, the fact that her mother had referenced them in her papers. She was hiding something under the guise of her regular job as a professor, and these men knew it. Phoebe couldn't be certain what it was. She didn't want to believe it, wouldn't believe that it could be what they thought, that she could be like these old, crabby men.

Phoebe tried again to yank her arm free, but he held tight. "It isn't like that!" she screamed. "She's a professor, a-a proper scholar! Her theories aren't weird. You're wrong. She'll show you."

Haldane's eyes crinkled with delight. "Kind of shakes you up, don't it, knowin' and all? She's a runologist. And a good one, I hear."

Phoebe was shaking her head at the spin they were giving to her mother's job. "She's not some kind of…" She looked around the shop but didn't have the right words. "She doesn't dabble in…*this*."

She'd put as much venom in it as she could, and Haldane's grin vanished.

"More lip from this one, Professor."

"That's quite enough," Wick said.

"Nothin' wrong with playin' with what the cat drug in," he cackled, turning back to Phoebe.

Wicked snarled. "Haldane!"

The shopkeeper jerked his hand from her as though it had been shocked. Phoebe rubbed her arm, but instead of shrinking back, she stepped toward him. Haldane shrieked, pulled out the stick Wick had called a bindrune, and started mumbling the names of some of the runes she knew from reading her mother's papers.

Then he collected himself. "Oh, your little family will discover soon enough how very real magic is." Haldane glanced at Professor Wick, smirking. "Ironic, ain't it, Professor, how she thinks she's gone and proved magic ain't real just usin' that tiny little brain of hers? Like I said, your mother knows better."

Phoebe managed to calm herself. "What do you want with my mother?"

Haldane gave Wick a nervous look as he backed even farther away. Professor Wick stepped closer and hissed, "She may not be into the sort of things found here, girl, but I daresay she has various other hobbies to keep her busy."

Then Wick's face softened, if that was possible. "Did you hear the little girl? She's read her mommy's papers." He said it in a sing-song voice. Then his eyes narrowed to two mean slits. "Insolent little bitch, you'd better enjoy your mother's brilliant papers while you can. I daresay she won't be writing any more of them."

"What do you mean?" Phoebe said, still trying to control the shaking that had started.

Wick smiled. "I know where you live. Nice little house. I remember when your mother had you three shortly after coming to Ithaca for the doctoral degree. Lovely place to grow up. You shall be sad to leave it, I should think."

Wick snapped at Haldane, "Put that away before you hurt someone, you fool!"

Haldane stuck the bindrune in his shirt pocket. As if to put an exclamation point on what he'd been saying, he gave Phoebe a little smirk and patted it.

It was clear they weren't going to say more, but that wasn't going to stop Phoebe. She tried to close the distance Haldane had put between them, but Rhea grabbed her arm and pulled her toward the door.

"Oh, no you don't!" Haldane shrieked.

"Hold her tight," Wick ordered him, apparently having changed his mind. "We'll see what their mother has to say about them being in this shop." He gave Phoebe a nasty stare as he whipped out his cell phone. "Probably here to do her bidding, eh?"

Haldane's fingers dug into Phoebe's arm.

"Take your filthy hands off her."

Rhea's voice was cold, totally unlike her, but Haldane only sneered and gave Phoebe a little jerk.

"What do you have against my mother?" Phoebe asked, eye to eye with him now. "Why are you so interested in her theories?"

"Her theories," Haldane snapped. "Why, she's a thief. Them's not her theories, girl, they're—"

Phoebe looked at him, waiting, but he clammed up. Needing to know what the hell was going on, she reached out and grabbed his hand, but when she did, that deep thumping in her head came back, and the universe collapsed around her.

When her stomach settled from its trip to her throat, she found herself surrounded by sparkling white light dancing on and off like mad fireflies. She stood before Haldane, and his thoughts were—visible, twinkling.

Her breath caught as a feeling of power swept over her in a rush of wind. Voices of her sisters, of Professor Wick, of others from down the street streamed through her mind. Then Haldane's thoughts coalesced in a mix of strange words—Ansuz, Thurisaz.

Runes again. Haldane had called her mother a runologist. Was she some kind of rune scientist or rune doctor? The one thing Phoebe did know was that the way he'd used the word didn't have anything to do with being a professor. He'd meant something else by it, deepening Phoebe's suspicions about what her mother had been up to. There were secrets in their house, secrets connected to the way Haldane thought about these things, the way he thought about her mother.

Then Phoebe began to shake.

It was Rhea with a hand on her shoulder, pleading to Haldane, "Let us go, please."

But Phoebe didn't want to be let go any longer. There were too many things she didn't understand.

"He cursed us," Phoebe whispered to Rhea, but everyone else heard.

"Wha—" Dione started to say.

The men were puzzled about something, so Phoebe concentrated harder, and the moment she did—

"Damn you, Gibbs, you have to do it."

"And if I git caught?"

"Fucking coward," Haldane cursed. *"Wick and the others are taking their precious time about it. He'll never git what he needs. What I need. I can't wait no more on 'em."*

"And just what is it you need, Dane?" Gibbs asked.

"'Never mind. You've got your money. We jist need to put one ov'em—I don't care which one now—put 'em in the hospital fer a spell to git the mother out the house so we can have ourselves a good search."

Phoebe straightened. They were planning violence then a break-in. It was a memory of an earlier conversation, one Phoebe couldn't tell if Wick had been privy to, but it didn't matter. He seemed to be the ringleader.

"*Yeah, that might work, but won't she have someone stay with the other two brats?*"

"*Naw, old lady Faal, the one with the sassy daughter what owns that shop next to mine, will probly keep the others at her place.*"

Through his mind, Phoebe could sense Haldane adjusting his thoughts, but then Gibbs spoke up through the memory. "*It'll be dangerous to invade the lair of witches.*"

Phoebe's eyes widened. Was it true? Was this the reason for everything happening? She took a step back, but Haldane's grip only tightened. And this time it really hurt.

"*Not so loud,*" Haldane scolded Gibbs in the memory.

Suddenly Phoebe snapped back to her body. The connection to Haldane broke in a barrage of white fire and a sensation of speed, of spinning, then laughter. Laughter!

But not from Haldane or Wick. She was sure of it. And not from Rhea or Dione. Frantic laughter filled her mind with words—an accented thought, a man's gravelly voice.

"*Expecting you…*"

Phoebe tried to turn and run but couldn't. A stranger was there, someone on the Commons doing to her what she'd done to Haldane and laughing about it. It was a faint, static-filled voice in her head, unlike the clear thoughts from the memory she had just invaded, as if these thoughts were coming from a great distance.

It wanted to hold contact. It needed that.

Phoebe wanted to run from the store and search the streets to find the person putting the horrible pressure inside her head, to rid her mind of him. Something was there, something powerful, opening her mind, probing her thoughts. And more than that, she was slipping away into what seemed to be the edge of something vast and black, a fathomless pit. It was cold and heavy as if a sheet of steel had enfolded her, pulling her to a depth she dared not go. But she'd been challenged before, by teachers, by debate opponents, by her smart mother. She knew how to fight. And with a fluttering heart, she shut her mind against the laughing voice, which flickered like a dying ember, and was gone.

Phoebe came back to herself to the sound of Wick saying, "Hold her up. She's fainted."

Opening her eyes, she said, "Who's Sherman Rasmusun?"

Haldane looked stunned and backed away, but this time she was the one holding him close.

"H-how'd you find that out?" Haldane said. Then he scowled and lunged for her.

Dione kicked his leg, hard.

"Ow! Why, you little shrew!"

With a face twisted in rage, Haldane raised his hand to hit her, but Phoebe stepped in the way. He tried to break free, but she wouldn't let go of him.

Wick joined in and grabbed Phoebe. "Let the others leave. We'll question this one at the back of the store."

But her sisters would have none of that. They grabbed Phoebe's free arm, yanking her this way and that. Then the world went black around the girls, and aqua green electric sparks bit at the two men. Haldane yelped and Wick released his hold on Phoebe.

And just before something grabbed the three girls and sucked them into a black void, Phoebe lunged for Haldane and managed to grab the contents of his shirt pocket as the triplets disappeared before the rounded, shocked eyes of the two rotten old men.

Chapter 5

Prometheus Erazmos stood on the east-facing veranda, watching the moon march slowly toward him over a calm Aegean Sea. The sight of it thrilled the tall, dark-haired man. He gripped the carved, wooden railing as he gazed over the water surrounding the Greek island of Evvoia, his ancestral home.

Sherman Rasmusun had been summoned because of the famous prophecy of Alexander Tarkus, his ancient clansman. That had been made clear by Victor, Erazmos's manservant and lore master of clan Saĝtuku. Rasmusun feared many things in life, but none more than the man standing at the railing.

Victor, the ancient first of the household, had informed Rasmusun that the master had been agitated for days, something about a botched job long ago. Victor turned his old face toward the rising moon, the intensity of it diminishing the vault of stars overhead. Even the whispery clouds struggled to block the luminescent glow.

The moon's craters stood out with deft clarity—the darkness of the seas, the hoary shadows—so close Rasmusun could almost touch them. But Rasmusun could not keep his eyes off the frightening man at the railing very long, not even to gaze at this strange moon. How erect he stood, how regal.

Suddenly, Erazmos raised his arms and began

radiating before them, his glow surpassing the brilliance of the looming moon. The veranda began to vibrate hard enough to produce a curious susurration. Before long Rasmusun's teeth began chattering as the quaking crept up his old legs.

To keep from falling, the two old men walked to the banister for support and were startled to see rocks strewn on the ground below, moving helter-skelter, bouncing and trembling as though the whole earth had become a prospector's pan. Others were suspended at various heights, none more than a few inches off the ground. The effect extended many meters beyond the veranda.

Rasmusun turned to Victor, and whispered, "What does this mean?"

Victor hesitated, scratching his ancient chin. After much contemplation, he said in a shaky voice, "A duel or contest perhaps." He placed a hand on Rasmusun's shoulder, steadying himself on the younger man. "Perhaps family lore explains this."

"Bizarre," Rasmusun said. "A battle for dominance?"

"Earth is always dominant. Of the four elements, earth is superior, and the moon is his mistress."

A smile stretched across Erazmos's face. Rasmusun tried to understand the context of the struggle. Two powers vying—earth and moon—but the more he watched, the more frightened he became. The tremble in Victor's hands wasn't reassuring.

"The struggle is upon us," Victor said, almost reverently.

"What?" Rasmusun said.

Victor frowned at him. "Our brothers will have to

be taught. Tonight means triumph is near."

Rasmusun nodded. The lore master would know many things others wouldn't.

"The final victory," Victor said. "My master will make it possible through his power."

War, always war. Rasmusun wanted to run, but knew he couldn't hide, not from the monster at the railing.

Victor was an old hand in the clan wars. Rasmusun knew all the stories, but he sensed the conflict to come would be different because of the might of Erazmos. Maybe his own insignificance would allow him to hide from the worst of it. He wished it were so.

"Think," Victor said. "Have you forgotten the lessons of how the master's family arrived in Greece?"

Ancient history. Now the old bastard was asking too much of him.

Victor pulled Rasmusun a step or two farther away from their master.

"The whole people as the clans are sometimes called. The *Gu Umia* in ancient Sumerian. Those referred to now most often as the *UngKin*, or Community, reckoned the year of the family's arrival in Greece as 3050.

"They had come as an insignificant family, one of many in the clan. Other families had arrived years before and had already established themselves when his family landed on these shores. Still others of his clan had remained in Turkey or points farther east or spread to Bulgaria or other parts of Eastern Europe."

Rasmusun was too nervous for a damn history lesson, but he knew the Erazmos family had a very humble beginning and had been dominated by others.

He nodded with as much enthusiasm as he could muster.

Victor continued. "But once Tarkus spoke, the Erazmos family rose magnificently. Now, many centuries later, they are at the pinnacle."

He patted Rasmusun on the shoulder, rewarding him for understanding. "Earth will rise, and in that quickening, will conquer." Victor smiled at him. "Such is his legacy, his destiny, and he among all the descendants since his family first came to Greece has the power to claim Tarkus' words as his own."

Rasmusun could only nod to all this, and after what seemed like hours the two men were ready to collapse, barely able to take more of this surreal performance. The constant vibration made their old legs mushy and more than once they almost fell.

"The moon is his mistress," Victor said in a lower whisper, nodding with understanding. "He is welcoming her," he said louder. He turned to Rasmusun. "Perhaps the master is merely welcoming her as one would a lost lover, reveling in her beauty."

Rasmusun thought he had understood earlier, but these words were beyond bizarre.

Finally, the display ended, allowing Rasmusun's frayed nerves to settle. Erazmos lowered his arms and diminished. He remained at the banister a moment longer, still looking out over the sea, then he turned aside and faced his two servants with a knowing smile. They bowed low to him.

Tall and still athletic despite his forty-five years, he pulled back his black hair and wiped sweat from his forehead. His eyeballs were black with granite gray irises and stark white pupils. As Erazmos came toward them he replaced the dark glasses that had become part of his persona, a courtesy for which Rasmusun was extremely grateful.

"Master—the signs. The timing is perfect."

Erazmos didn't answer Victor but paced about as the weak breeze kept the waters of the Aegean unnaturally calm. He stopped suddenly before them; his hands clasped behind him. He was dressed in his customary black, his silk shirt partway open at the chest, sweat glistening on olive skin. Erazmos began fastening the black buttons.

Both men bowed their heads.

"It is as I suspected," Erazmos said. "Tarkus will be proven correct."

"And the others—" Victor began.

"I have their loyalty, my old friend."

"They have already performed the oath?"

Erazmos laughed. "You are getting too old, Victor. It was last week. The subclans performed a *ru namneru* last Tuesday. I did not tell you. You needed your rest."

A tear came to Victor's eye. "But, Master, I wanted—"

"There will be other opportunities with the remaining clans. I assure you."

"Yes, Master."

Erazmos laughed again—a reckless, mirthless laugh. "And this society of theirs has no idea."

Victor and Rasmusun exchanged glances, but movement below on the moonlit grounds startled them.

Victor said in a frightened voice, "The dogs are loose."

It was only a flitting shadow, and now it was gone. Perhaps the master's dogs were chasing the rocks as

71

they bounced around. Or perhaps it was only a shadow cast by moonlight over one of the larger boulders.

To Victor, Erazmos suddenly said, "Heighten security. We have an intruder near and another lurking some distance away on the beach."

"Where…h-how!" Victor stammered.

"Never mind that. It is good that my enemies know some things, but not all. After the incident this morning we should expect more probes near the compound."

He raised his hand, his head cocked curiously for a moment. A tunnel opened, flashing golden electric charges. A woman exited, walking slowly, as if fighting a compelling force drawing her. She stood before the three men, bewildered and mute, sweating, her face fierce in determination, but she couldn't fight his power. Rasmusun thought her pretty—brown hair cut very short. She came to them, wholly docile and unable to do a damn thing about it.

"What do you seek?" Erazmos said, obviously amused.

Great drops of sweat beaded on her forehead and ran down her face as she fought hard to take back control. She obviously would have run, but Rasmusun knew the effort was futile. Erazmos was inside her mind.

"She fights well," Erazmos said.

Rasmusun grimaced because, in the next moment, the master entered her mind with what he knew to be frightening force. He had done the same thing to him many times. Still conscious, she nevertheless collapsed, but Victor stepped forward in time to hold her up. She was only slightly larger than he.

"I recall a Duckworth in recent years," Erazmos

said to Victor, "could this be—"

Victor's eyes widened. "Of course, the husband-and-wife *Lirum Ne*. It was a most unfortunate accident."

****

With an extra effort, Sarah jerked free of the old man's arms, aggravated that they had recognized her and their talk of Ray, her dead husband. She fought harder, turning to run, but it was no use. The monster raised his arm and, without touching her, lifted her head. He twisted his hand, and she rotated for him. He examined her body and smiled.

His face went blank. A pale man with sandy hair and hulking build appeared before Erazmos, dark flashes announcing his presence. He presented himself in a low bow but straightened when he noticed Sarah.

"Dimitri, meet the wife of the man you murdered some years ago. SAL Agent, Sarah Duckworth."

Dimitri Primilov turned his blond head and black eyes to her, his expression lustful.

"May I suggest a use for her, my friend?"

Erazmos removed his dark glasses. His eyes intensified and became black pools. They reminded Sarah of Dante's demon hell, allowing no escape, producing only despair. Primilov received the telepathic communication, careening backward, but he remained erect.

Sarah tried to close her mind, but, before she could release the scream she felt rising inside her, she collapsed, but didn't fall. Instead, Erazmos held her up by his power.

Barely conscious, Sarah heard Primilov say, "What of the black man, her partner? Is he here?"

Amused again, Erazmos said, "I have him whistling a tune I found in his mind. He stands now on the beach, kicking sand. Do not keep him waiting long and do not hurt her...much." He chuckled. "We will send both back to their keepers shortly."

Primilov produced a crooked smile and took Sarah in his arms and into the mansion.

Sarah knew what was coming and wished he would just kill her instead.

****

With a little smile that seemed to indicate how satisfied he was with the world, Erazmos turned to Rasmusun. "Do you know why you are here tonight?"

Rasmusun tried but failed to keep his quivering legs from shaking even harder. He wanted to feel sorry for the woman, but he was too afraid for his own life to worry about a stranger. "Victor told me some of it, but not much."

"It has been quite a while, has it not?"

"Five...no, ten years, I think. Too long, far too long, but I am here now to serve you."

"No need to be nervous. This is old business, something concerning my father when I was but a child."

What could he mean? There were so many opportunities with his father. Some successes, but mostly bungling errors had kept his record far from spotless. Rasmusun wrung his hands, trying to decide whether he should be even more frightened than he already was.

Nicholas Erazmos had provided him a handsome living, perhaps five important jobs per year calling for his talents. What could the son want now after years of hiding only to be summoned by old business? He wiped the sweat from his face, thinking as hard as he could.

"Relax, my friend. You are not here for punishment, though my father was always too lenient with you. Do you see the moon?"

Rasmusun nodded, ready to please.

"But of course," Erazmos said, gazing up into the sky. "How could you miss it? Her brightness is a thing of beauty."

He became quiet, and when Rasmusun couldn't stand the silence any longer, he said in a voice much higher than he would have wished, "Master, it's so unusual."

Erazmos nodded. "It is coming as the prophecy says." He gave a short burst of laughter, but without the slightest hint of merriment to it. "This is merely a prelude to what it will eventually be. But do not concern yourself with that. We will chronicle the signs. Today I need information Victor says you should have.

"I remembered something from my childhood, an agitation of my father concerning you. I suspect the prophecy could be involved, somehow. It came to me quite suddenly yesterday as I contemplated the signs, but not much memory of this incident remains to bring forward, I am afraid. Victor has remembered some things as well, but not much. I was young, and it was well before my *dirig ed*."

Rasmusun turned to Victor at this use of the Sumerian tongue.

Victor frowned. "The turning. The onset. Do you not recall our ancestral language?"

It was small rebuke from the old man, but he didn't like it.

Erazmos continued. "My memory of this is rather incomplete as Victor says the event was nearly forty years ago. It concerned an important discovery that I wish to learn more of now before the coming conflict." Erazmos turned to Victor for confirmation.

Victor bowed his head. "That is correct."

Rasmusun continued to plead with his eyes, begging the old man for help, but Victor merely shrugged his bent shoulders, and said, "Your father asked Rasmusun here to make sure a discovery by another clan would be forgotten."

"Discovery?" Rasmusun began rubbing his forehead and the back of his neck, muttering something barely audible. They were stretching the boundaries of his memory. "Forty years ago. Forgotten."

A long pause ensued, and Rasmusun began sweating even more, but then comprehension dawned as he remembered that dark week and the assignment he had been given, the memory of which he had long since repressed.

"Of course. Nearly forty years ago, you say. Not quite that long. It must be the incident with the stone tablets. The ones we found at the dig in the Middle East. I was brought in to assist. The tablets contained writings, but there was some indication the information on them was sensitive to the purposes of our clan. Your father didn't want it to become known, so he recruited me to help, and I was most happy to do so. It was a frightening task, but I did my duty, Master."

"I am sure you did." But turning to Victor, Erazmos said, "Stones?" Victor shrugged again. "Describe them," he said, turning back to Rasmusun.

"There were several tablets. I-I don't remember the

number. Ordinary in size, some larger than others, the largest maybe twenty inches across, irregularly shaped. They all had runes on them, though. Odd runes, I think, if memory serves. Lots of speculation on what they might say. Your father was angry about this. I remember thinking how strange his reaction was. I'm not sure why he wanted to suppress this information. His source—I remember this part well—his source felt the stones could somehow distract the clans' attention."

"A distraction from what?"

"I didn't understand it at the time, Master."

"And this information, what was its nature?"

"I don't know that either, but for some reason, your father was worried about it."

"Source…Could Hector Kornum have been involved?"

"Kornum…yes, he was among the group before I arrived at the dig, but I am not sure who passed the information along. As I recall, he and I are the only remaining members of the team still alive. Later, I made sure the stones would be forgotten." Rasmusun thought more about this. "Come to think of it, the German may still be alive as well. Strange fellow and even stranger now, I hear."

Erazmos turned to Victor to confirm the story, but Victor merely shrugged. "And where are these stone tablets now?"

"Forgotten, as your father wanted."

Erazmos frowned. "But he is no longer here, as you know. Where are they?" Erazmos repeated.

Rasmusun quaked, a black cloak of terror descending over him. He cursed himself for being flippant. Stammering, he said, "For-forgive m-my disrespect, Master. We were in New York at the natural history museum where the stones were first brought after a short stop in Ireland. I'm not sure they're still there. It was an insignificant find to the ordinary people, and they took no notice of them. My colleague wasn't about to turn them over to her superiors at the museum as she felt they were a matter only for the Community."

"Do you think they could still be at this museum?"

"I don't know, Master. After my task, I was no longer concerned with them. I never returned as I was given no further orders from your father concerning the tablets. Your father was assured then that the information they were thought to contain would not get out."

"Insignificant you say, maybe to the ordinary people, but not to us. Get them if they are there and bring them here at once."

Erazmos summoned Dimitri who appeared dutifully by his side. "The girl?"

"She is prepared, Master."

"We have plans to make, Dimitri. Drop everything else you are doing while we consider the future."

Having said this, Erazmos could no longer contain himself. Merriment, or the rough approximation of it, broke from him. He turned to the west this time and his laughter filled the veranda.

"They are there," he said, pointing.

Rasmusun and the others turned to look, but no one knew who he could be referring to. No one else was on the veranda.

Building slowly, the laughter grew to maniacal dimensions, causing both older men to cover their ears.

They steadied themselves against the railing. The veranda shook again as quantum distortions—stronger now than before—rocked the grounds.

But Dimitri Primilov stood erect, unwavering.

Chapter 6

After driving for hours in aimless circles around Ithaca, Madeline made it back to her West Hill neighborhood, anxiety bubbling over like a boiling cauldron. Her emotions had a strangle hold on her reason and both were held captive by fear. Like her walk down the corridor earlier, she drove through a dreamscape. Nothing seemed real—cars, store fronts, countryside—nothing existed for her, but the word Cailin had used.

Personification.

It put a new light on her thinking about her mother's note.

Her children were the key to Madeline's fears about Manhattan, though her boss didn't know this was the reason she could never return to the city. She would never compromise their safety. Never put herself in a position to be found by those people. This was her one obsession, but one born of necessity, a sacred duty no one else could perform. She'd made the choice long ago.

Her bungalow loomed around the bend, looking forlorn in the frosty afternoon. Green shutters with star and crescent moon cutouts were eerily visible.

Madeline found herself back in her study where she placed the old file folders on her desk and stared at her unfinished paper on the monitor. It was clear to her now. This project, another in a long list of meaningless attempts at connecting with her mother, was a fruitless endeavor. The only way to make sense of any of this was to find the Stones of Sumer, her mother's discovery.

Incredible as it was to believe, Toop and possibly others knew about the rune stones. But how could they? And why now? She pulled the note from her pocket, unfolded it, and placed it down next to an old beige hatbox. The box contained items from her past life with her husband, but nothing much from the time before her marriage. It contained secrets. Her children didn't know about the many inconsistencies it contained, like the fact that their name wasn't really Alleyn.

She glanced up at the many pictures of them at various ages displayed on the walls of her study. Artifacts Madeline had secured because of the nature of her work were everywhere in the room. An exquisite glass case exhibited ancient Irish and Celtic pottery and small figurines of mythic figures like Aife, a semi-immortal warrior woman who became the lover of the demi-god, Cu Chulainn. Less valuable items cluttered two tables bracketing a futon where she sometimes slept.

One piece of treasured art stayed in the girls' room. A four-hundred-year-old Irish Claddagh figurine was the only other item from her mother she still had besides the note. The fist-sized object depicted a heart surrounded by two hands.

May your hands be forever blessed in friendship and your hearts joined forever in love.

Madeline had given the Claddagh to her children when they were old enough to appreciate its sentiment.

Her father had done the same with her.

She went to the window and pulled the drapes aside. Frost blanketed the glass. Madeline removed it with one swipe of her hand, revealing outdoor scenery as gloomy as it had been for months. An uncanny stillness lay over the world of vineyards and deep gorges, frozen over in winter's long grip. She noticed a couple walking a dog on the wooded street, phantoms moving through the world of the living. Mere shadows, as intangible as smoke it seemed in the icy mist, almost nonexistent. Like her past.

Madeline stepped back into the warm embrace of the room, panic rising in her like an erupting volcano. But, in the next moment, she snapped her head around.

Someone had banged on the front door.

****

The triplets crashed to their butts on the icy front stoop, banging hard against the front door of the house, their bodies crumpled together.

Phoebe adjusted her glasses, but before she could gather her senses, the front door opened. Their tall mother stood there, looking down on them with fearful eyes.

It suddenly seemed to Phoebe that all the times she'd noticed her mother worrying over nothing, all the times she'd been overly cautious—their whereabouts, what they were doing, who they were with—had been for a reason she now knew something about. Because of what the old men had said she now had a better understanding of her mother, but what Phoebe desperately needed were answers. Who were they, really? What was her mother up to? And the most important question, what, or maybe who, was she scared of?

They struggled to get to their feet because the trip they had just taken, about two miles in an instant, left them woozy. Phoebe managed to put the bindrune and folded piece of paper she'd snatched from Haldane in the back pocket of her jeans. Her mother didn't notice because she was too busy scanning the street beyond. Phoebe looked, too, but there was no one there.

"What's happened?" their mother asked, as she helped the girls through the door. "Why are you late? Don't you know how busy we'll be in a couple hours?"

The party. Phoebe had totally forgotten. This was the perfect time for partial honesty. "We're on it, Mom, but we had some things to do downtown first."

Their mother looked at her wristwatch, skepticism in her eyes.

"We'd have been much later, so we skipped the last class period...or two."

She gave them all hard looks, then said, "The caterers and wait staff will be here soon. Make yourself useful for them when they come."

****

The thought of that nasty Professor Wick coming to their home was a feeling worse than that bad pudding they'd all eaten two weeks ago. With what had happened today, the surprise run in with Wick, they had to be sharp. They had gotten some useful information; perhaps they could get more tonight.

They debated as they helped prepare for the party. Should they tell her what they'd overheard, what had been happening? Should they call the police? Di said the mayor should know or maybe even the president, but she got eye rolls for that. They decided to play it cool, say nothing, keep her in the dark a little while longer.

By eight, the bungalow was stuffed with boring professors pretending to enjoy themselves. It had been their mother's turn to host. Bad on them, but maybe the timing wasn't terrible.

Phoebe gravitated toward the younger crowd. She spotted a young woman surrounded by a group of men hanging on her every word. She wore a cool leather skirt, and her deep gold hair fell gracefully onto her red silk blouse. Phoebe admired the sophisticated way she held herself, the way she flirted with several men at once. She drew near and realized it was her mother's new teaching assistant they'd met at the beginning of term, Claire Walker.

Claire winked at Phoebe as she joked about a story that had been circulating for years throughout upstate New York. "He lives in the national forest between Cayuga and Seneca Lakes. They say he's wild."

"An urban legend, I'm afraid," a man said.

Claire waved him off with a flick of her hand. "Well, I believe it. My father used to tell my brother and me about him. He's supposed to be some kind of Russian immigrant."

"And how would anyone know that?" someone asked.

Another man stifled a laugh. "And he's living in the forest between the lakes, even in the dead of winter?" They all chuckled at this.

Claire planted her hands on her hips. "It's not like he's supposed to be Bigfoot. He's human, you know. More like an old west mountain man."

"And the rangers can't catch him?" More snickers.

Phoebe waited for her to answer the jerk, but instead Claire gave Phoebe a weak smile of defeat and looked away. Phoebe concentrated and Claire turned back.

"You know the type…a-a…" Claire looked puzzled, like she wanted to say something more, but had misplaced her thought. She looked at her watch. "Gosh, it's late, and I'm supposed to help Dr. Alleyn in the morning. I better go home and make sure I'm prepared."

The men all gave fake yawns. Someone standing next to Phoebe groaned, and said, "It's only nine." But Claire was already halfway to the door.

Then Phoebe heard a loud and pompous, "Preposterous," blast through the room. Somehow, she had missed his arrival. She peeked around the corner and saw Wick's skinny chest puffed out like a blowfish as he repeated the word, flashing his eyes at her mother serving two ladies from a shrimp cocktail platter. It was a look like she didn't even belong in her own house. Phoebe snaked her way around people to hear him better and managed to keep out of sight.

"It's a fairly superficial rearrangement of an old, discarded idea, isn't it?" Wick said to his ready audience. "Unworthy of drawing such high accolades, I should think."

A frumpy looking man with red cheeks said, "It's not even very original. Why, I heard some character in anthropology had the same idea decades ago."

Wick laughed. "His contemporaries ridiculed him so much he left. Good riddance, I say. Such tripe has no place on our campus."

Phoebe muttered under her breath, "Pompous

windbag," but no one heard.

"Now his idea has a new champion," the man continued. "Her talk of Sumerian runes and a Celtic connection is pure hogwash."

The mention of runes sharpened Phoebe's attention.

"It's all laughable," a fat lady said, her backside bobbing. "There simply can't be a tie between runes and ancient Sumer. Your work in this area, Charles, proves that."

"I appreciate your support, Bertha," Wick said, "but I'm afraid our esteemed chairman has been horribly swayed by something besides reason, eh?"

The insinuation was obvious. Phoebe wanted to say something rude, but the fat lady's butt jostled her then the man named Edwards spoke up again.

"Every reputable scholar knows Sumerian writing was in cuneiform. Runes are a strictly northern European invention and appeared much later."

Wick stuck a smoking pipe between his teeth, nodding with an air of approval. "She's secretive about something."

They suddenly went silent as a man appeared in the midst of the group.

"You all must have better things to do than stand around ridiculing one of our own."

Phoebe recognized her mother's boss, Mark Harper. He was short and heavyset and waved a cigar about. He easily overpowered the others, but Wick crossed his arms.

"Is that what we're doing?" Wick said, chuckling. "I'd rather thought the ridicule was aimed at our leader, or did you not hear that too?"

"I heard, but I've got skin as thick as a rhino, hard to penetrate with barbs, you see. Our host hasn't been around the briar patch nearly as long as I have. She's still quite—"

"Her sensitivities don't concern me, and they shouldn't you either. If she and her strange theories can't stand up to objective inspection, she should be replaced."

"So, my appointing her to the academic chair has a ring of bias, does it?"

Wick's pointed eyes sharpened even more. "And something more, eh?"

"Save your accusations for a more appropriate context, Charles. Even you wouldn't—"

"Her theories are groundless," Wick spat out. "Where is the evidence for what she's saying— archeological or linguistic?"

"She's in the process."

"She's chasing phantoms, Mark. You've read her work. It's not up to snuff, as they say."

"Oh, well put, Professor," Harper said.

Wick's paleness had now turned a nasty shade of green as he breathed in the cigar's strong smoke. Some of the others began checking their watches.

Before Wick could retort, Harper continued, his face even redder. "She's published everything she's ever worked on, unlike some of you, and she funds her field work instead of constantly clamoring for the department's money."

"Her theories are borrowed. They were rejected by this very institution long ago."

Harper sent a cloud of smoke in Wick's direction. "Fresh insights are something supple minds give to old ideas."

Wick turned white and spluttered, "Now see here—"

"Why don't you have a brandy or some wine perhaps and calm yourself. Here, one of her daughters will be glad to…"

Harper reached out and pulled Rhea over as she passed. She recognized Wick, too, then spotted Phoebe wedged in the corner.

"*It's okay,*" Phoebe said telepathically.

"Be a good sport," Harper said, "and bring the professor a glass of Pinot noir."

Rhea pleaded with her eyes. "*What am I supposed to do?*"

Phoebe smiled at her for pulling off a perfect bit of telepathy. "*Just do as he says.*"

She scurried off as Professor Wick leered at Harper. "I repeat. The standards of our department have fallen in recent years."

"It was my decision, and I've given her the latitude to follow her ideas. Now why don't you people make nice and mingle. The food's excellent."

Wick lifted his chin. "I haven't spoken the last word on this, I assure you." He spun in a huff and made for the front door.

During all this Phoebe noticed her mother had been trying to free herself from an old drunk professor. She tried to call out to someone in Wick's group, but Mark Harper took her by the arm and turned her away from the door giving Phoebe the chance she needed.

Phoebe faltered when she made it to the porch. Like a ragged bandage unraveling from the head of a mummy, a sliver of cloud slipped from the edge of the moon releasing a glow that cloaked the yard in a silver ring. She searched the gloomy shadows. That same watchful presence she'd felt on the Commons came back like a thick covering, and with it a feeling of hate. She thought of that haunting laughter and let her mind expand. Without warning, the trees began swaying as if in a furious enchantment.

Nearly at the street now, the group noticed the swaying trees. The fat lady clung to Professor Edwards, her throaty voice weak from fright. Wick and his group turned. Moonlight gave their faces a phosphorescent glow.

Phoebe screwed up her courage. "My mother's theories aren't weird. I've read some of her papers. They make sense to me. You're wrong…she'll show you."

Wick separated himself from the others. His sneer got even uglier. "Impertinent little busybody. Why don't you go off and play with your dolls instead of eavesdropping on adult conversation. The second time now you've done tha—"

The word stuck in his throat, making him fall into a fit of coughing.

"Charles!" the fat lady cried out. "Warren, he's…" But Edwards was clutching at his own throat and turning purple.

It took several minutes, but the group of professors finally got Wick and Edwards to their cars. And just as Phoebe turned to go back inside, she noticed someone strolling past the house. She strained to see better, but the person turned and walked off into the gloom.

She stood there a moment longer warring between shame and stubborn pride. What she'd done to Wick must have been some kind of weird instinct, like he had to be stopped. And with hardly a thought, he had because she'd made him.

When Phoebe finally turned toward the door, her mother was suddenly there, placing a tender hand on her shoulder.

"I'm sorry."

"For what, honey?"

"For those people you have to work with. They said awful things about you."

"Did they?" There was a note of sadness in her voice. "Well, I never told you I had my detractors, but they're gone, so let's rejoin the party."

Detractors, more like enemies. Phoebe made up her mind right then to find a way to help her, but the only help she knew was to stop Wick from whatever he meant to do.

"I've been sneaking peeks at your articles."

Her mother stopped short of the door and turned to Phoebe. "Really…which ones?"

"I like reading about the Celts. I liked the part where you explain how they were superstitious and liked magic. How did that work?"

She smiled at Phoebe. "It was a combination of beliefs. I suppose one focal point was their use of runes."

Phoebe perked up. "Did that make their magic real?"

"Now, you know better than that. Why would you ask such a question?"

A gust of cold wind blew Phoebe's hair into her face. Her mother collected the curls and tucked them behind Phoebe's ears.

"I'm just curious about the debate. That boy had some interesting arguments. He could have been right, you know."

"He was good, but you beat him…remember?"

"But that's only because nobody believes in magic anymore, like the Celts did."

"Yes, well, you see, we don't need the mysterious like ancient people did to help them cope. I suppose it provided some comfort to let them feel there were forces they could rely on."

"But, Mom, aren't there still mysteries…some things we don't understand that might seem like magic?"

"You're referring to his argument from quantum mechanics. That was really fanciful."

"But suppose the Celts with their runes found a way to tap into something we've lost over the years. Maybe they really did have a kind of magical power connected to runes."

"Superstition. I wouldn't waste too much energy thinking about it."

"But suppose they *could* do crazy things like cast spells…like, like witches would do. Could they use runes to read minds and make things float?"

Paleness washed over her mother's face. Emotions, raw and fierce, flashed through her mind like twinkling lights, making it hard for Phoebe to pick up her thoughts. Then something she'd never seen before crossed her face, a look of cold hardness.

"Magic isn't real," her mother said in a flat, deadly serious tone. "People can't read minds or carry things about without touching them in some way. I've explained why the Celts and other ancients believed in it, but we have no use for such superstitions in our day."

"I know that, but there seems to be—"

"Look," she said, getting down to eye level with Phoebe. "The party will be over soon. School tomorrow, remember? No more skipping classes. So, let's go back inside and have fun while it lasts. Forget about that bunch. I can handle them."

She framed Phoebe's face in her hands and gave her a gentle kiss on the forehead. But Phoebe felt her tremble and suddenly a strange look came over her mother. She straightened and stared beyond the yard to some distant place: into the past, or was it the future. Then her blue eyes widened and lost focus as the rest of that cloud moved off and moonlight blanketed the front porch.

"You need to be ready…that's why I let you. But I don't know when or how or even if."

She said it in the smallest whisper possible and Phoebe wasn't sure she was even speaking to her. Then her eyes refocused and captured Phoebe once again in that penetrating stare. "You must promise to be watchful when you're out."

"We're careful, Mom, honest." Phoebe took her hand. "Is something wrong?"

"I'm sorry, baby. I should still be mad after last week's fight, but I can't. You three are the best girls in the world." She wiped her eyes. "I'm being silly now…worrying too much."

Phoebe wanted to ask what was so upsetting about her questions, but instead Phoebe let her mother draw her close and together they entered the house and closed the door against the waxing moon.

****

Much later, she found her mother sitting at her desk, pretending to read one of the papers scattered there. When she noticed Phoebe hovering over her, she moved her shaking hand from her forehead and placed it on her lap.

Phoebe asked again, "What's the matter, Mom?" She touched her shoulder.

"Oh, honey—" If there was a thought there somewhere, it didn't come spilling out. Instead, her mother placed her hands on the keyboard as if to start typing again, but she just sat there immobile. Then Phoebe noticed a sheet of stationery. She went to grab it, but her mother was too quick. She lunged for the note, barely snatching it before Phoebe could.

"It's really old. May I see it?"

"It's private," her mother said with a strained smile. She put the note in a beige hatbox. "It wouldn't interest you."

Phoebe nodded, and said, "Still working on that paper, huh?" It was a leading question just to see how she would react, and it wasn't good. Her mother tried hard to keep a pleading note from her voice.

"I'm kind of hung up on it right now, but it's not a problem. I'll be here if you need me, and maybe later we can talk about exactly why you girls were so late earlier."

Phoebe sighed and thought that she could just read her mother's mind like she'd done with her sisters and Haldane, but she wasn't ready for that just yet. What she might find there scared her.

Then her mother turned more fully in her seat and Phoebe felt the weight of those bright, intelligent eyes.

And then a question Phoebe wasn't expecting.

"Honey, have you noticed anything odd happening around you, anything you can't explain?"

The question nearly knocked the breath out of Phoebe. She panicked and said, "No."

"What about Rhea or Di?"

"I'm sure they haven't either."

Phoebe didn't know why she lied. A feeling of secrecy had washed over her as her mother sat there, weak, drawn. Phoebe ached to protect her, to blaze at those people for their mean words, but all she could do was place a hand on her arm, and hope her mother knew how much she loved her.

"You haven't been ill or had any headaches, have you?"

Yeah, like my head nearly exploding, but Phoebe just repeated the same answer and hoped it was enough.

Her mother looked again at Phoebe with those searching eyes, so alert, so similar to hers. Alike, but different. Her mother's eyes were like a vast and inspiring azure-blue sky.

Skies take people away. The eyes of a scholar, but were they also the eyes of a...

She didn't know how to finish that sentence and didn't want to think what that next word might be. Her own eyes were a deep, inky blue, like a bottomless well.

People drown in wells. Different, but alike. She didn't know which fit better.

Her mother stood and gave Phoebe a fierce hug. "Oh, all right, then. Just thought I'd ask."

She seemed to be back to normal, but Phoebe knew better. Phoebe wanted to insist she answer the question of what was really bothering her so much, but fear stopped her—fear of what might be happening, of what she would find out about her own mother, maybe even fear of some truth about her and her sisters. She left the room with that fear hanging over her.

****

Madeline watched Phoebe leave, thankful she didn't have to look again into her penetrating eyes. They weren't kind like Rhea's or quirky as Dione's could sometimes be. They were intense, perceptive, unnerving. It felt as though Phoebe could somehow divine her secrets, that she knew her innermost thoughts, and was judging her. When she was sure Phoebe wouldn't turn back and start questioning her again, Madeline marched the hatbox over to the closet, shoved it with a foot into a far corner, and threw some old sweaters over it.

****

"Where's the bindrune!" Dione bellowed as she and Rhea turned to the opening bedroom door.

Phoebe walked up to them and pulled out the contents of her back pocket.

Di's eyes widened at the sight of it. "You think that curse stick brought us back here?"

It kind of hurt to think, so Phoebe didn't answer. She ran a finger over the strange lettering while telling them what she'd seen in Haldane's mind and the laughter she'd heard when she broke free of him. Then Phoebe thought of that mythology book they had and rushed to the bookcase in the corner. It didn't take long to find what she wanted.

Rhea settled next to Phoebe on the bed. "Rune magic?"

"Maybe."

"Break it," Dione hissed. "That's what the book says to do. Just break the damn thing before it possesses us even more."

Phoebe rolled her eyes. "That's just silly. We aren't possessed." But she put it down next to Rhea and scooted away from it. "What if it just saved us? We need to study it some."

Di groaned. "I can't believe you're gonna keep it in the house."

"It'll be okay, I think. It looks harmless enough."

Phoebe grabbed it and held it out for Di to take, but she backed away.

"You're stupid to be touching it."

Shrugging, Phoebe put it back on the bed and grabbed the crumpled sheet of paper she had also taken from Haldane. It had large block letters written across the top—*SUMERIAN RUNES*. She stared at it, confused, then her mind clicked.

"This is Mom's theory! He's listed the most important points."

Phoebe bent over the page in the dim light. There were several lines printed in Haldane's faint hand—a discovery in Mesopotamia, runes much older, originating from the Middle East, not Northern Europe.

Phoebe looked up at her sisters. It was all pretty much meaningless.

Dione reached over and turned the page in Phoebe's hand. "There's a man's name on it. Sherman Rasmusun." It was the same name Phoebe had plucked out of Haldane's brain.

Rhea snatched the page. "Is this dude important?"

"He must be," Di said. "We know they're obsessed

with something Mom's working on, trying to make her look bad. They're even planning a break in."

Phoebe nodded. "It's because of this. But why?"

"There's a year written down." Rhea pointed to the page. It was a tiny scribble at the bottom.

"Wait a minute," Di said. "Isn't 1986 Mom's birth year?"

Phoebe shook her head. "Eighty-seven. But never mind that. Rasmusun could be someone else interested in Mom's theory. I wonder if this guy—"

Phoebe stopped as something struck her. She folded the sheet and jammed it in her pocket. "How can someone like Haldane know about complicated theories? Whatever he is, he's no scholar. Why would he be scribbling what Mom's working on?"

They both shrugged. Rhea grabbed the stick, turning it, inspecting every inch.

Standing at the mirror, trying to pin her hair, Di kept giving Phoebe aggravated looks. "All I know is, if this thing cursed us, we should break it now."

"If we break it, Dione, I won't be able to do this cool stuff. And we still have to find out what you and Rhea can do."

Di frowned. "Cool stuff? How about dangerous stuff? How did we escape those men?"

Rhea gave Phoebe a look, expecting an answer, but all Phoebe could do was stare at the bindrune as Rhea twirled it with her fingers. She thought of how they'd vanished, about what had happened at Gibbs's cart, how the world had seemed to stop. Maybe it was one more thing they could do—escape when in danger of being cornered by crazy shopkeepers. Whatever it was, it was something powerful.

"Let me see it, Rhea." Phoebe turned some pages in the mythology book, examining the strange carvings etched on the crooked stick, comparing them to the book. "These are runes all right. Funny looking, aren't they?" She gave Rhea a little sideways glance. "Strange, though, to be cursed by magic and find you're able to do these neat things."

"It's hard to figure how that"—Dione pointed to the stick—"can do anything to us."

Rhea traced a finger along the carved edges of the various runes. She took it from Phoebe. "I wonder how they combine to form magic words for curses and such."

She released the stick, and it just hung there, suspended in the air. She yelped and jumped to her feet. The bindrune dropped to the bed.

"Whoa!" Di said.

They both looked at Phoebe. "I didn't do it!"

Rhea stepped closer to the bed and held her hand over the stick, fingers spread. It floated up to her as if drawn by a magnet. Her green eyes were wide and weird, like they had taken on extra color, becoming brighter, greener.

Phoebe nodded to her. "Go ahead."

She released the stick and again it just floated in place. She twisted her hand, and the stick rotated to the left. She flicked a finger, and it rotated to the right.

Phoebe's head began thumping like it had on the Commons and, at the same time, Di stiffened. Her eyes turned from their natural sky blue to an orangey-red glow, a far-away look to them. Her red hair rose like she'd picked up a huge amount of static electricity. Phoebe tried to touch her, but something prevented it, something surrounding her. A kind of barrier had encircled Di, and she looked like she had fallen into a trance.

Rhea grabbed the stick from the air, which made the thumping in Phoebe's head stop. Di swayed and almost fell over onto the bed. Phoebe was able to steady her without the barrier present.

"What happened?" Di said.

Phoebe let her flop down onto the bed. She seemed too weak to stand.

"You okay?"

Di looked up at Phoebe, her red eyes reverting to normal. "I feel…funny."

Phoebe gave Rhea an uneasy look, and before Phoebe could stop her, Rhea hammered the bindrune against the dresser's edge. It split down the middle. She grabbed the split ends and managed to tear the stick into two pieces.

Rhea looked at it like she'd killed a friend. "Sorry, but it's the only way to know for sure what this thing did."

Phoebe's heart sank. "Feel any different?"

Rhea shook her head. She lifted her hand and narrowed her eyes. When the pieces floated to her from the floor, she broke into a wide smile. Relief overwhelmed Phoebe, too, but Dione got up and stormed off to the far side of the room. "That's just great. You two are happy about it."

"Don't you see? This means we weren't really cursed, after all. That's one less thing we have to worry about." Then Phoebe's excitement vanished. "But what *is* happening to us? What did those men mean by their use of a bindrune, or whatever this thing is?"

Di showed that huge frown, which usually indicated that her temper was right on the verge. "We could have still been cursed by it, and now we're stuck with the effects. But I don't really believe that stupid little stick did anything. Something way freakier is happening. Not something like goofy curses and magic words. You said you felt a presence on the Commons, someone laughing."

Phoebe nodded.

"Well?"

It had been a feeling of desperation, the manic laughter sending cold shivers down her spine. A mocking laugh, not friendly at all, full of hate. She hugged herself and turned from Di. Her sister was right. This thing happening to them wasn't as simple as something that could be caused by some sort of magician or sorcerer or whatever.

Rhea put a hand on Phoebe's shoulder. "At least we know now what it isn't."

"Maybe not, like Di said."

Dione gave them a nasty look. "It made about as much sense as a three-sided nickel."

Phoebe went to the window and drew the curtains aside. Two people were walking a dog through the icy street.

Rhea peeked out over her shoulder. "Anyone we know?"

Phoebe shook her head and threw the broken bindrune into the waste basket. "I don't know what to believe. Di may be right. It either cursed us and left a permanent mark, or—"

Phoebe suddenly remembered something Professor Wick said. They were born in Ithaca shortly after their mother came here. That bothered her because she'd always thought their mother had been from Ithaca and had even grown up in this house. Their mother never talked about their extended family, so that assumption, though ignorant, was at least understandable. But it wasn't true. Their mother must have come to Ithaca from someplace else, attended Cornell, been Wick's student. Why hadn't their father come with her? Then Phoebe cringed. Did he even know about them?

"Well?" Rhea said, impatiently.

"There's another explanation. What we can do could be inherited."

"But Mom doesn't—" Di started.

"I agree. I don't believe Mom could hide that from us. And I don't believe she's a witch like those f'ing men think. They don't really know her. It could only be our dad."

"So when are we gonna tell Mom?"

They gawked at Phoebe, but she gave them a shrug. It was too late for any more talk, and she was too sleepy. They put on nightclothes and Phoebe told them about the blog entry she'd made.

Grabbing her laptop, they sat on Phoebe's bed and their hearts raced when they saw that she had a couple of responses. One was rude, but the other…

"SurferDude?" Di snickered and punched Phoebe's shoulder.

"Listen," she said, and read his response.

Hi, Charolastra. Strange username. I like it. I found your blog doing a search of blogs from Ithaca, New York. I'm from Ithaca, too. Correction, my parents are from here. They just moved us back from California. I'm at Ithaca High. You sound pretty spaced out. Dreams, weird things happening. Cool stuff, really. Why don't you explain more? Maybe I can help.

"He's at our school," Rhea said. "You're gonna answer him?"

Phoebe was thinking, then she started typing:

Yeah, spaced out, you got me on that one. Now don't laugh when I say this, but do you think I could be a witch?

His response was immediate:

Hey, you can't be that bad.

Phoebe rolled her eyes and answered:

Very funny. You know what I mean. Magic...sorcery...how about reading people's minds, levitating things?

Reply:

You serious about that? From your first message you think your mother is hiding something?

Phoebe:

We went through with the plan I mentioned. More weird things. Teleportation was a trip. And now I know Mom is hiding something.

SurferDude:

A mystery coupled with some serious shit. Maybe you are a witch. Try casting a spell.

Phoebe:

I'll pass. Getting late. Bye.

SurferDude:

K

Phoebe snapped the laptop shut and waited for her sisters to respond but all she got were yawns.

"Dead end there," Rhea said, collapsing into bed, pulling the covers to her neck.

"Maybe," Phoebe answered. "We'll see."

Soon she could hear their deep breathing in the black room.

Something was happening to them, making them feel like they'd put in a week's worth of PE classes in one hour. As Phoebe settled in, the chatter of her sisters' quieting thoughts hummed through her brain. Though soothing, it couldn't keep out the same fear she had felt earlier in the shop when that man's laughter filled her mind. She lay still, but the feeling of being watched was so strong she felt like running, hiding. Wind howled past the window, and there was a crack. She sat bolt upright.

Her shaking hand parted the curtains enough for her to press her nose against the chilled glass. Nothing was out there in the front yard, no strange presence, no dirty man digging inside his coat for a stick he could wield as a magical weapon. Yet, a fearsome shadow filled her mind, its dark shape driving out the echo of her sisters' distant thoughts, clouding her own thoughts with…

Not words. This was more like emotions—hate, malice, and something like desire was there, a strong need to possess, or maybe conquer. The words from her dream came back. *Earth*, the missing element. Why wasn't it in the dream? What was her subconscious trying to say? Then she made another leap in understanding. Was Earth the enemy of *Air, Water, Fire*?

Realizing she could be right, a terrible weight pushed against her mind. She had a sense of looking into a black pit, of writhing phantoms, of despair. She turned from the window and closed the curtains with a rattle and switched off the lamp. Terror jumped at her like a great cat springing upon its prey. Phoebe couldn't help the scream that escaped her.

Quick steps. Light warming the room. Rhea and Di were at her bedside, dazed with sleep.

"Are you all right?" Rhea asked.

There was concern in those green eyes, something she usually reserved only for Dione. Phoebe was always too much in control for them to be worried about her.

A stirring at the door brought Phoebe's head up higher. Her mother framed the entrance.

"It's all right," Phoebe said. "Just a bad dream."

Their mother entered and stood between Rhea and Dione, the three of them watching over Phoebe like mourners might on the day of her funeral. In another moment, Di and Rhea went off to their own beds, but their mother lingered, fussing about the bedspread, tension drawing her beautiful eyes closer together. Phoebe had never seen her look so strained. And she'd been crying again.

"Don't be sad, Mom. Whatever's bothering you will go away. You'll see."

Madeline bent down and kissed Phoebe on the cheek. "Go to sleep now." She clicked on a nightlight and glanced back. A flicker of fear crossed her mother's face. Phoebe raised her head higher, but her mother had already closed the door.

For a long while afterward, Phoebe lay awake, an empty feeling deepening in her chest as she tried to wrap her mind around everything they'd learned. Their mother had enemies. That in itself was a real shocker. But why did her colleagues want to hurt them and search the house? What were they after? And what was her mother so afraid of? Could it be this other enemy Phoebe suspected was out there somewhere?

Phoebe thought of her mom and how she had always seemed. Always there for them, steady, dependable, but deprived of a full life, like being stuck in a perpetual winter with no chance of spring. She couldn't remember when her mother ever had time to herself or had ever really been away from them other than for work. She knew her mom loved them, too much maybe, and she knew her mom needed companionship. She had that at one time with their father, of course, but those days were never mentioned. There were no stories from that time in her mother's life, which had always puzzled Phoebe. It was like there was a locked door. No questions about what secrets it guarded were ever allowed. The door to their past was closed, and Phoebe had plenty of questions about it, but the answers lay with her mother.

"*Earth*," she said in a low, halting voice.

Then that word from the debate entered her thoughts—quantum—followed closely by another word she didn't want to think about. As much as she tried to avoid it, the word kept popping up—magic. The two together—quantum magic. The words rang ominously through her mind.

Before she nodded off, thinking of crazy professors with runes written on their foreheads and old shopkeepers with crooked sticks tucked up their sleeves, ranting about earth and moon and goodness knows what else, lightning flashed around the edges of her curtain, a moment's strange, orange glow. She lifted her head and waited, but no thunder came, not even the smallest hint. She pulled the covers higher, closed her eyes, and waited for sleep to come.

Sleep did come, and later she remembered having a dream, but it wasn't one of those safe dreams, like stopping Rhea from stuffing extra cafeteria fries in her coat pocket to snack on or keeping Di from fighting with Tracey's cheerleader troop.

In her dream, she slept, and, while she slept, that same shadow she'd felt at her window descended on her like a thick veil, covering her not so much in darkness as in hopelessness, in a black despair that made it hard to breathe. And in her misery, she panicked, and, still in the dream, she woke with a start and sat up, reaching with flailing arms, trying to escape whatever it was that had her trapped.

That strange laughter started again, but, lucky for her, the veil was flimsy, and she tore through it. With a catch in her breath and a racing heart, Phoebe rose up and up until she found her dream-self floating off her bed, rising until she penetrated the ceiling and the roof of the house. From there she flew into the cold night sky.

A cloud formed into a face, frowning, speaking words in a foreign, guttural tongue she could somehow understand.

Air. Water. Fire.

Then the birds came, their wings so close they must have been brushing her body, though she couldn't feel them. Higher and higher Phoebe flew over the neighborhood. The woods beyond her backyard stretched for miles. She could see Ma Faal's place on the other end of this familiar territory. She let herself relax, and ecstasy rolled over her like a spring breeze after a long Ithaca winter.

But where the wind should have been on her face, cold and crisp, she couldn't sense anything like that. She looked to see what her arms were doing, but they were gone. More birds crowded around, and if they hit her, she couldn't feel it, because she didn't even have a body.

Phoebe shifted one way then the other, flying high over Ithaca now. She could see the city rolling out between the three distinct hills—east, west, and south—forming the great horseshoe bowl surrounding the town at the southern tip of Cayuga Lake. Black water broke into frothy clips throughout the slender, shimmering finger.

An enormous moon above her created a silver haze that she now flew through. She was part of that ghostly luminescence, part of…

Air.

She woke then, sweating, her heart pounding in her ears.

"What's that?" Dione yawned, sitting up on her elbows in her bed across the large room.

"Mom's crying again," Phoebe answered after gathering her senses.

They listened for a while, and soon her sisters fell back asleep. Phoebe stayed awake, thinking of what the day had been like and how they had escaped those men. It was magic, but she wasn't sure any more about runes and the like. Instead, she focused on Rhea's green eyes, the same color those electric flashes had been before that black thing whisked them away.

Was it a coincidence? She was sure it wasn't.

Chapter 7

Two doors down the hall, Madeline couldn't sleep, so she turned on the small TV set sitting on her dresser. There was a roving reporter who had been conducting random interviews earlier in the day in Central Park, New York.

"Sir, may I interrupt your chess game for a moment?"

A pair of old men, obviously wanting to be left alone, leered up at the reporter.

Undaunted, the reporter stuck a microphone in one man's face, and asked, "Have you heard the news of the disturbance with the moon? What do you think about it?"

"We heard on the radio this morning—early. Has my Dorothy pretty worked up. All she wants to talk about now is that old prediction from that ancient Greek fella. Ya know the one, Frankie. What was that loon called again, Tuchuss? Yeah, that's it."

The reporter looked confused as the camera panned to him, but before he could redirect with another question the other old man chimed in.

Frank moved his pawn with a trembling hand. "Charlie, you got it all wrong. He wasn't Greek. He was Italian. And he said something about Jupiter, too, I think."

"Didn't he say something about the moon jumping

around and Mars jiggling? Is that what the news says is happening?"

The reporter tried to jump in, but Frank wouldn't let him.

"Whatever he said, I tell ya, people are scared again and talking all over the place like the last time there was trouble in the Community." He shook his finger at the reporter as if to warn him. Turning again to his friend, Frank said, "You know, like the time when our great grandpas were boys in the old country. It's got me worried, but I don't believe in that other nonsense about the moon and that Tuchuss fella. Is that his name? I'm too old to remember. Anyway, what worries me most is that the young fellas believe it, and they got the energy to get carried away."

The reporter finally broke into the conversation. "Yes, yes...well, obviously there are some strong opinions out here." Trying to regain control over the situation, he raised his voice as Charlie grabbed at the microphone, obviously not done. "And, it seems, everyone's a little agitated around here. Now, back to Diane."

Madeline had been transfixed by this exchange, mortified that what these men had been saying could have gone out to the entire nation. Somehow, call it coincidence or fate, the reporter had stumbled upon the group. Two innocent old men perhaps, but things could be deceiving with these people. She quickly switched off the TV when her phone rang.

"How did you find me?" she whispered after the caller identified himself. "And it's way too late for this."

"You know this news has taken a bizarre turn," the

person on the other end of the line said instead of apologizing. "There are reports of ritual activity at Stonehenge, just past dawn this morning, London time. People in white robes. We don't know how they got word so quickly of what was happening with the moon as the news just broke this morning. Of course, there may not be a connection. We naturally thought Druids might be involved, as they seem to like Stonehenge quite a lot. We'd like to air a brief segment on that and some other strange occurrences. But we need an expert."

"What…on strangeness?" Madeline asked, not intending to make a joke.

The caller chuckled. "Oh—no, no, forgive me. I didn't mean that. Naturally, your name came up after a quick search for an expert on Celtic history and runology—am I pronouncing that right? We thought you were the most likely expert to help us out on what has been observed. Your area is Celtic history, isn't it?"

"Yes, but—"

"We want to know if this activity could have been sparked by the sudden disturbance with the moon. Sort of a human-interest piece to balance all the science reporting. Anyway, we'd like to fly you to the city tomorrow to tape your answers to some questions. It'll air either tomorrow or the next day."

During all this, Madeline had been pacing, holding the phone in a trembling hand. "That's impossible. I mean, such short notice. I'll have to decline the offer. But perhaps I could recommend—"

"You're the top expert we could find, and at an Ivy League school, no less. Frankly, you're perfect. Please reconsider."

Madeline let her arm fall and nearly dropped the phone. Putting it back to her ear, she said, "No, sorry, I can't possibly do it."

"But—"

"I really have to go."

"All right, Dr. Alleyn, but don't go. If we could quote you on air, would you answer a few questions for us right now—over the phone? That would give us something, at least."

Madeline struggled with the decision. She had already been arm twisted into giving the talk at the conference in Manhattan. She could be available for this reporter, but not to be splattered all over television. It was one thing to be in the city and remain anonymous, but quite another thing to tell the world, "Here I am." Especially when she was supposed to be dead.

She had gauged well the notoriety she could achieve and still remain hidden. But now she was beginning to regret all her hard work, her struggle to achieve. She didn't want her face plastered across television like the parade of professors had been doing all day, eating up the spotlight.

But a couple of quotes seemed harmless, so she relented.

"Great, thank you so much. My name's Steven Dryer, by the way. I think first we could start with a little history…"

Madeline talked about the ancient history of Stonehenge and some current day problems the site had with visitors, the fact that for much of the last several decades there had been exclusion zone fences placed around it, controlled by a group called English

Heritage.

"But what of the Druids?" Dryer asked. "Could these people this morning even *be* Druids?"

"Yes, the modern-day version, at least."

"And what would be their interest in all this?"

"Well, none at this time of year, really. They would normally be there for the summer and winter solstices and the equinoxes, and possibly for any eclipses that were scheduled. But none of these are currently occurring, which leads me to believe it may have been some kind of initiation rite."

"You think that with the moon so full, this somehow made the rite more meaningful?"

"Your guess is as good as mine, Mr. Dryer. It was probably something hastily called because of the disturbance, you know, to take advantage of the sudden increase in size that had been so obvious all night. They can be very mystical, you know. I wouldn't make too much of it. But there's one thing. The new distance between the earth and moon in its elliptical orbit—the new perigee. If it's permanent, it will create some different lunations and upset some of the computations people have made via the geometric construction of Stonehenge. You may want to ask an astronomer who has an interest in such things."

"Right, thanks, but one more thing, if I may. Could any other group besides the Druids be interested in Stonehenge because of what's happened?"

Madeline paused at the question, suddenly more nervous, her voice suddenly shaky. "Various other pagan groups, but none so well known as the Druids—" And then she hesitated again. "Listen, I have only one stipulation when you quote me, besides being accurate.

I want you to use my middle name—Gail. Under no circumstances are you to use my first name. Understood? You're not to use Madeline. Dr. Alleyn would be all right, but don't give out my first name."

"Yes, of course. Whatever you want."

"And no picture of me," she added quickly.

He hesitated, just a moment, but it was enough for Madeline to call the whole thing off and retract her comments, when he said, "But may I ask why?"

"I have my reasons," she said, and when he relented and agreed, she quickly ended the conversation.

Madeline sat on her bed and wondered if she'd made a mistake in agreeing to be quoted. And for a long while afterward, she dwelled on the last eighteen difficult years.

****

Madeline dreamed that night the same recurring dream. She'd been having it for as long as she could remember, a woman's hand passing her a simple piece of pottery. Delicately made and intricately carved, beautiful in appearance, a heart held by fragile hands. In the dream, Madeline would take it and look up expectantly, but she could never see the woman's face. There was something familiar about her—a soothing voice comforting her, speaking secrets to her. Upon waking, Madeline never remembered much about the dream, but there was one thing. Each time she took the figurine a word would enter her mind, a word wrapped in shadow, veiled from her and just beyond remembrance in the morning.

As she lay on the futon in the early morning hours before the red sun brought another gloomy day through the window, she thought of Cailin Faal's insight and the other significant word her friend had used.

Obsession.

The word frightened her. It was too much like her father, but she knew Cailin was right. She was obsessed, but how did she get that way? She'd felt haunted for years, something from within, something striving to control her, but what was it and to what end?

Thinking of these things, half asleep, Madeline became aware of movement in the gloomy morning light, a voice whispering words in an alien language. She opened her eyes and saw miasmic shadows gently undulating in patterns of light and dark.

Madeline raised her head from the pillow. She could feel her neck muscles straining to maintain the position. This couldn't be a dream then. She sat up and could make out detail.

She closed her eyes, rubbed them, opened them again. She was not dreaming—tactile sense, spatial awareness—but the ghostly display still danced before her.

The languid light revealed ghost forms, and she knew they were glyphs. Dancing letters flowed around her as if part of the cast of some fantasy video. Madeline almost laughed at the irony of it all—her work had become her nightmare.

Seemingly energized by her alertness, the vaporous symbols began undulating more wildly, as though her conscious awareness of the entity...could this thing be alive...had given the display more intensity. Panicked by this change, she threw off the bed covers and ran out of the room.

Madeline knew nothing of psychology, abnormal

or otherwise. She tended to be secular in all things. To her, visions and other such paranormal phenomena were indicative of a mind bordering on insanity. What she experienced now put her squarely in that category.

She lingered a long time, not daring to retrace her steps, terrified to do so, but calm overtook her when she realized the vision hadn't followed her. Apparently, her panic had broken the spell or whatever it was she had experienced.

Then a suitable explanation dawned on her. Had she experienced a partial sleep-like state based entirely on fatigue produced by overwork and anxiety? She knew she was lucid, and she knew her own mind. Rationality controlled her thoughts, not wild hallucinations. She wasn't insane at all. The apparition must have been an aspect of her recurring dreams, dreams suddenly altered by the distressing events of the last day.

She waited a while longer and tried to calm herself for her children's sake. Her galloping heart quieted. She looked down the hall to their room. The faint murmur of an alien tongue, her waking nightmare, stubbornly persisted.

Madeline walked past the pictures of her children. Following the sound, she stopped at her bedroom door, looking inside, listening. The entities were not there, but she could still hear the whispering murmur, stronger now at this end of the hall. Her children's bedroom door was closed, but the barrier had not reduced the sound coming from the room. Her mind became a pinwheel of fear.

She ran to their door, but she didn't enter. She grabbed the knob, turned it, put her ear to the door. Her heart sank. A woman's voice. The voice of an intruder.

Madeline had always been good with languages, even from her earliest days. She had picked up French and Spanish quite easily as a schoolgirl and had double majored in linguistics and history in her undergraduate days. She'd gathered many other tongues along the way, a smattering of one, fluency in others.

Her master's degree in linguistics had been easy. At that point, she had gone for the hard stuff—the archaic languages, dead and long gone from common human speech. These efforts had been inspired by her mother with her father's encouragement. That was the one thing they both knew about her mother. Madeline had apparently inherited a talent for languages.

Though she had never heard these guttural pronunciations before, she knew these words. She didn't know how, but she knew them. From deep within her, she knew the language of the intruder.

Madeline stood at the door, the strange words filling her mind. She looked around, her heart pounding. There was nothing she could use as a weapon, but the whispering voice seemed pleasant and unthreatening, strangely familiar.

Her hand trembled as she held the doorknob. Wishing to surprise whatever this was, Madeline flung the door open. It rebounded off the doorstop with a loud thud, and she caught it midway before it closed.

The same miasmic display she had seen earlier danced before her, but it had thickened. Like a fog, it would engulf her completely if she entered. A quick scan revealed no one, yet a disembodied voice continued to whisper the alien tongue.

She stepped into a dreamscape. She could barely

make out her girls on their individual beds. As before when she had first reacted to the display, the quietly flowing shapes began to gather intensity as if welcoming her.

Then everything happened at once. The buzzing sound that had first burst upon her consciousness as she lay on the futon grew stronger, drowning out the intruder's whispers. Madeline covered her ears and wondered how her children could remain asleep.

She walked to the dresser and reached for the Claddagh figurine, the point from which it seemed the sounds were emanating. As Madeline placed her right hand on it, pulses of red, green, and blue light cleared the room of the images floating within the miasmic thickness. Everything vanished—color, movement, voice.

And with gut wrenching quickness, Madeline found herself out of their bedroom and back in her study, the Claddagh still in hand. She would have screamed if she could. Rushing back to the girls' room, she found them still sleeping, apparently safe.

She stopped at each bed and touched them, satisfying herself that no harm had come to them.

Chapter 8

Tuesday, Just After Midnight

Steven Dryer sat at his desk at ABC headquarters at Lincoln Square in Manhattan, computer on, mouse in hand. He'd been brooding over Madeline's interview, the one now dead in the water. Though it was late, he knew Sturgis was still in the building, so he'd called him about the bad news.

Of course, Sturgis had yanked it when Dryer told him he had only a taped audio spot. He wouldn't have the video they wanted, not a good situation for a network broadcast. No actual person to look at meant no interview. Joe Sturgis, the news director, didn't want quotes or a pretty voice. He wanted a pretty face attached to a smart voice.

He threw his note tablet against the far wall of his tiny office.

After a tense waiting period for new data from the three principle lunar ranging stations, when all their measurements and calculations were as consistent as the sun rising in the east, leading scientists had finally settled on a definitive report of the weekend's frantic activity. Only then did they issue the report to an unsuspecting world.

Now that the word was officially out, no one knew why or how or when the moon was being drawn closer to the earth in its elliptical orbit. The only indisputable fact was that the moon was indeed closer than it should be—much closer. Its perigee was the closest it had ever been since such precise measures had been made possible, and no one had a clue how it could have happened.

Phone lines buzzed. Heads of state received notice. Computers zinged off word of the discovery to major news bureaus around the world. The halls of academia where researchers involved in the discovery sat ensconced since late Saturday night prepared to be invaded by journalistic hordes.

Television talking heads blathered on about what it could all mean. Then came the experts, frantically called to make sense of the reports. Astronomers, astrophysicists, and exogeologists happily considered all questions, eagerly giving their considered opinions to an audience anxious to know everything. Media stars were suddenly born from the ranks of boring academia. And by the evening news cycle end-of-the-world enthusiasts had staked out street corners in all major cities. To any objective observer, they appeared to be the happiest lot of all.

As Dryer contemplated his future, a colleague from operations walked into his bleak office. He propped his squat form on a corner of Dryer's desk, reached over, and turned the flat screen to get a good view of it. It had been much too long a day for both men. His face registered surprise, which quickly melted into a knowing smirk.

Dryer groaned. "What the hell are you still doing here, Jimmy?"

"No life, same as you." Jimmy looked closer at the

screen. "Nice features, lovely complexion."

"She's very telegenic," Dryer said, still focusing hard on the picture, but not wanting to say what he really thought.

Jimmy laughed. "Telegenic, hell, she's gorgeous. But you know that already. Don't you, buddy?"

"Don't start with me, Jimmy." Dryer gave him a warning look then turned back to the monitor. "She's hiding something, you know. That's why she isn't coming in. You've seen all those academic types we've been parading in and out of segments. They're all eating up the attention, loving the limelight. They want the exposure." He turned to Jimmy again. "What makes her different?"

Jimmy leaned in. "Who says she is?"

"Oh, she's different, all right."

"Maybe she's fulfilled without the spotlight. Some people aren't narcissistic, you know. Good job, family, significant other they're satisfied with, even in love with, you know, the usual fulfillment outside oneself scenario." He slapped Dryer on the back as if to personalize that last point.

Dryer expected as much, but his expression soured anyway. "You're kidding, right? Biggest news story in history, and she gets a chance to be associated with a little piece of it, just a tiny fraction, and she doesn't take it. What's she playing at?"

"That's your trouble, Stevie, you think everyone's made the same way. She isn't, that's all. You're right about one thing, though. It seems pretty benign. Why wouldn't she come on air? Shame to waste such a telegenic face, right, buddy?" He shoved Dryer at the shoulder.

Dryer nodded absentmindedly. "Look at those eyes. Can you imagine those piercing you in class?"

"And the red hair," Jimmy said, chuckling. "I wouldn't be able to concentrate." He tore away from the screen and focused on his friend. "Sounds like you got her figured out, but don't you start obsessing again."

Dryer cursed and pushed his friend's leg off his desk. He stared at Madeline's picture. Stunning, but he would never tell Jimmy how he really felt. Jimmy knew him too well, his obsessions with beautiful, smart women. Smart, hell, she was brilliant, judging by the partial record listed for her on the history department's website. "I have a feeling there's a story somewhere apart from the obvious one, you know, the science angle."

"Dude, this one's all about the science, no more, and it's big. What else could there be?"

"I don't know," Dryer mumbled, running his hand through his hair. "Something, nothing...I don't know, but I'm not giving up quite yet." He opened the desk drawer and withdrew an airline boarding pass for a flight to Ithaca, tossing it to his friend. "I'll be there early tomorrow. I've already made a reservation for lunch at a bistro on the Commons."

"Smooth, and she doesn't know yet, I bet. How are you getting her there?"

"I made a call to her Department Chair soon as she turned me down, a Dr. Harper. Got his home phone from a contact. Assured me she'd cooperate."

Jimmy tossed the boarding pass back. "You're serious about this aren't you?"

"I can smell a story, Jimmy. There's something

she's hiding, and I'm gonna find it."

His friend walked to the door. "Look, last year was tough losing out the way you did on the Pulitzer, but this story—whatever you think you have—is probably not gonna get that back. No matter how bad you want it. There's no prize here."

"There might have been if I hadn't been undercut and stabbed in the back. I knew about this story early Sunday morning. Did I tell you that? But no one would say a thing. They clammed up. Then my hands were tied, and the next thing I know the news is breaking all over the fucking place. Now, all I'm left with is this soft angle. But I have a feeling. Anyway, I've convinced the boss to give me a couple days to go fishing up in Ithaca."

"Fishing?" Jimmy looked at him with skeptical eyes. "It better be just the story."

"I'm through with all that, okay?"

"Yeah, right. If you're that sure, just think about that award you want so bad."

"My head's on straight this time. This angle I'm on, it smells so strong my nose is itching."

"Better be the only thing itching."

Dryer threw the telephone book at him, but Jimmy caught it, chuckling.

"Okay, smart ass, let me tell you why. You know that group the English authorities almost caught yesterday morning at Stonehenge? I told you about it, remember?"

"Yeah."

"Why the hell were they there at this time of year when nothing's happening? The news hadn't even broken yet and there they were."

"Could be a coincidence."

"I don't think so, and I think my Dr. Gail Alleyn—Madeline—is holding something back."

Jimmy laughed. "All we need around here is a conspiracy theory. How would you possibly know if she's hiding something?"

"Her reaction. I'd asked about others besides Druids who could have been there doing what they appeared to be doing. She became, I don't know, nervous, I guess. Her voice tensed. She became..." He let the thought die. "It was embarrassing almost. And then, out of the blue, she refuses to let her picture be seen or for us to use her first name. I have a sixth sense playing the bongos around my brain. I'm following up. She just doesn't know it yet."

"Call when you get back, okay? This ought to be interesting."

When his friend left, Dryer turned back to the monitor and focused on Madeline's sky-blue eyes, brilliantly intelligent, but enigmatic. She looked professional, well put together, her bright red hair falling gently on white shoulders. But there was something else about her, something mysterious, a strange sadness that ate at his imagination. Mysterious women appealed to him, but a mixture of sadness...well, that was just too damn much. He had to know why, but he had to be careful. She was someone who in a former life he could obsess over then the trouble would start. But that was then, and this was business, and his career. It meant that he might have to destroy her to get this story.

He folded his laptop and flipped the TV on.

"...scientists at Columbia University's Department

of Astronomy discovered that the moon slipped another half percent off its normal orbit. That puts it now an additional twelve hundred miles closer to earth from where it would normally be.

"Together with the change in orbit discovered earlier, the moon is now slightly over fifteen thousand miles closer to the earth. There is only a slight rise in the height of the oceans, but that will change for the worse if the moon's orbit continues to deviate in this way, say scientists at Columbia University. Meanwhile, scientists around the world are monitoring the oceans' tides closely for further fluctuations. Flooding in some places is already occurring.

"The orbital acceleration of both the earth and the moon has slowed. Scientists also note that the fading of Jupiter's red spot should not be cause for alarm as this is considered a normal variation. The over bright display on Mars, however, that first began two weeks ago, despite no apparent change in its weather pattern, is probably unrelated to the current moon phenomenon. We'll keep you abreast of the latest news if the situation worsens."

Dryer's boss, Joe Sturgis, a major player in the ratings wars, had dubbed the recently discovered astronomical phenomena, Mars Wars, knowing full well the term was utter nonsense. It caught on big time. It was catchy, and Sturgis loved it, therefore, so did his many minions. Mars Wars would win Sturgis this week's ratings battle and his ace investigative reporter would make sure the ratings were there.

No doubt, Sturgis would lean toward the new girl in their shop, Linda Wheil, to deliver his ratings, and Dryer knew the reason. She was young and pretty, but not without some on-air talent.

And it didn't hurt that she could bring some needed technical understanding to the report, having studied astronomy in the very university department that had announced the discovery. The fact that she had other physical attributes had Sturgis salivating over the expected ratings.

Dryer had to admit she seemed perfect for the story. He could already taste this week's victory in the ratings wars, but only if he had a part to play. He feared being left out of the broadcast team. The boss owed him, and Dryer planned to make sure he paid up.

Dryer marched to Sturgis' office only to find Wheil already there with her cameraman. The story had made everyone night owls. He'd met her once or twice. She had shoulder length blonde hair and a petite build. She wasn't his type, mainly because she worked for the company and had been elevated to his level, more or less. He rarely mixed socially with company talent; the last time had almost cost him his job.

Sturgis glanced at him from his desk. "I'm giving this one to Linda."

Dryer decided to play it cool and not make an issue of Sturgis's betrayal, especially since he had two job offers from their closest competitors. "Figured as much."

Sturgis leaned back. "Good to see you're a team player. I'll—"

Dryer held up a hand. "Just give me a part of the broadcast."

Sturgis looked at Wheil who shrugged and turned back to her notes.

"She's my science gal, Steve, that's why she has to

lead. And—"

Dryer raised his hand again. "I'm with you. But I want in, or I'm walking."

Sturgis slowly stood. "You're bluffing."

"Nope. Got two better deals, and they really like my new slant on this thing."

This got Linda's attention. "What sort of slant?"

"Don't worry. I won't steal your thunder."

"Good," Sturgis said, beating her to the punch. "You can work together. Hell, maybe two different takes will complement one another." He leaned over his desk, both hands flat. "The whole world's gone fucking nuts. People are snapping up telescopes. Hell, I even bought one." He bent over and picked it up. It was still boxed. "Plan to use it right through there." He pointed to the window. "I hope you're up on your cosmology?"

Linda broke into a wide smile. "Don't worry, I know what questions to ask."

"Okay, so go after that hotshot astrophysicist at Columbia, and don't softball him. Let's give the people a report the big boys would envy."

"Right, boss, you can count on—"

"But you have to get this one right," Sturgis continued over her. "We'll have a ton of viewers. We need to win the special report slot this week and this story ought to do it, but you've got to spin it right. Use the Mars Wars angle. Make it juicy. And wear something more revealing."

Linda rolled her eyes. "I won't," she said flatly. "And forget about the Mars Wars crap. That's nonsense. This has to be a real exposé. Get to the meat of what's happening. I've got a feeling they've been holding back. Don't you think that—"

"I'm paid to think," Sturgis fired back, "not you. So yeah, ask the tough questions, but keep the angle where I want it."

Linda sighed. "I'll look silly doing that. It's not right, anyway. I've heard grumblings from the scientists over that bullshit. They're trying to correct it already."

Dryer pulled up a chair, and Sturgis turned to him. "I'm staying out of that one, boss. All I need is ten minutes airtime on an angle no one else has seen. She can say whatever she likes the rest of the half hour."

Turning back to Linda Wheil, Sturgis said, "Correct my line? They can't do that. I want it in. Keep it nice and dramatic. It'll have people on the edge of their seats."

Linda shook her head. "No, it won't. They'll see right through that kind of meaningless bull."

"Do it," Sturgis said, "or don't bother coming back." He sat back down and picked up a bagel he'd been eating. "If this turns out good, you'll have more special assignments."

She couldn't keep the disgust from her face, but Sturgis just smiled. Turning on a dime, she beckoned to her cameraman.

Sturgis returned to his telescope, shaking his head. "We'll run CBS into the ground with this one."

"Maybe," Dryer said, "but it has to be right. They have the science, too, you know."

Sturgis swallowed hard. Apparently, he hadn't thought of that. "Yeah, you're right. Dammit, okay, I'll call Linda later and defer to her judgment." He held up his hand to hold Dryer from speaking and turned to the window, looking at the huge moon. He turned back. "You think you have something?"

Dryer gave him a big smile. "You're gonna like this one."

Chapter 9

Three anxious occupants fidgeted in the richly paneled gathering room of Clan Abgal, located on the tenth floor of the headquarters for SAL—the Society of Advanced Leaning. The fourteen-story building housed other rooms much like this, nine others to be exact, each floor serving as world headquarters for each of the ten clans.

Brownedyke and Livingstone paced the room in the early morning hours, but Christine Kornum sat somberly, waiting for word. Sarah and Reggie were overdue. They should have completed their special assignment hours ago. In the interim, there had been two funerals—quickly planned and quiet affairs, customary for the Community.

Cyril Croft burst through the doors, gasping for breath. "They've been spotted in the building."

"Dammit, why aren't they answering our summons?" Brownedyke bellowed.

"No idea, Darius."

"Lucian?"

Livingstone held two fingers of his right hand to his temple. "It's unlike Sarah to ignore an attempt at communication. I can't get through to her."

"Cyril, find them and get them here."

"Right away, Dr. Browndyke." He rushed out the way he'd entered.

Minutes later, a tunnel opened in the room. Sarah and Reggie exited, looking strangely disinterested. Sarah nodded once to those present, and a small smile graced her lips as she looked at Livingstone. Her eyes brightened when she saw Christine Kornum.

Livingstone approached them. "You look well, Sarah. How was your mission?" His telepathic probe was as gentle as running his finger lightly over still water, but the mental ripples revealed nothing.

"Professor?" she said, a queer look falling on her.

His probe had touched something. Livingstone could tell her mind was struggling to regain independence. Suddenly her eyes became pools of terror.

Sarah screamed, and the moment she did, Reggie collapsed to his knees.

Livingstone quickly rendered her unconscious with an intrusive probe, ending her scream. He caught her as she fell and propped her up in a chair. Reggie struggled to rise. With help from Brownedyke, he made it to another chair at the conference table.

"Tell us what happened," Brownedyke said to Reggie.

"I-I—"

"Take your time, son," Livingstone said. "Think back. What do you remember?"

Reggie stared off at something beyond them. "I was whistling some stupid song. I remember the beach, the Aegean, water shimmering brightly even at night. The moon—so big."

"Did you notice any trouble?" Livingstone asked. "What did Sarah do?"

"Trouble? None—sh—she left. We decided she

would infiltrate close up, alone, not far off the east porch. She insisted on that. You know how she is. We remained linked, though. Then that tune popped into my head, and I don't really remember much else."

"Popped?" Brownedyke said, turning to Lucian. "Popped, how?"

Livingstone turned him around in his chair. "Look at me, Reggie."

Reggie's eyes rolled up into his skull, and Livingstone saw the moment on the beach, his waiting, whistling. The probe stalled at that point, but Livingstone fought through to a deeper layer of Reggie's mind.

"Him!" Livingstone gasped. Sweating now, he grabbed Reggie's shoulders, his face inches from the agent's face, both men battling some unseen force. Reggie nearly collapsed again, but, in the next moment, he slumped onto the table.

Livingstone's breathing returned to normal. "He's clear now. I've removed the trace planted by Erazmos."

"Damn." Browndyke pounded a fist. "They were captured. But why are they here now? Did they escape or were they released?"

"Released, I believe."

"To what end, Lucian?" Christine asked.

Livingstone turned to Sarah and slowly brought her back to consciousness.

"Sarah," he said calmly.

"Yes, professor?"

"You seemed to have had a difficult night."

His earlier probe had already touched something fundamental. She didn't answer, but tears began, slowly at first, then she buried her face in her hands and sobbed, rocking back and forth in her seat. Christine rushed over and comforted her clanswoman until she quieted.

"Don't press her just yet, Lucian," Christine said. "Give her time."

Sarah looked up at Livingstone, at Reggie who sat nearby. "I'm sorry," she said, "I-I can't talk about it just yet, but I have what you wanted."

Livingstone nodded. He already knew what her fate had been.

Sarah stood, wiping away tears.

"You don't have to do this just yet," Brownedyke said.

Sarah shook her head. "I'm ready, sir."

After a moment's concentration, Sarah's facial expression became blank, and an assortment of variously colored vapors accumulated in the room. They gathered around her head then began to stream away from her, whirling and rotating, mixing in odd ways until they congealed into three-dimensional, almost life-sized shapes representative of the objects of her gaze.

A tall, dark-haired man hovered before them. An expansive porch stretched out on either side of him. The man raised both arms and radiated energy, causing the black night to become almost as bright as day. Various earth shades beamed from his body as his eyes grew more veiled, appearing to them as deep black orbs. The display lasted several minutes. Finally, he smiled and lowered his arms. The vapors disorganized again and the picture dissolved.

"You saw this firsthand?" Christine Kornum asked, before she realized the stupidity of her question.

"Forgive me, of course, you did."

"There were actually three of them there. Erazmos was agitated the whole time, staring at the moon and speaking to his servants alternately in Greek and English. I hid behind a rock outcropping."

"Fascinating," Kornum said. "Power such as this corroborates my own sources quite well, led by Hector, of course. But I had no idea of the extent until now. Did you see the quantum distortions being produced? Quite amazing."

"Rocks were floating. I even had trouble keeping my feet. The effect radiated quite a distance from the epicenter where he stood. When he stopped, we were about to leave when I was taken."

"Couldn't you get away?"

"No time, Dr. Brownedyke. I felt him first, and then—m-my own tunnel opened before me. I didn't produce it. How could he do that, Professor? Isn't that supposed to be impossible?"

Livingstone stopped at this and turned to her. "It was, apparently, until now."

"I fought, but I had no chance. I was suddenly walking out onto his porch. I tried to resist."

Livingstone came to her. "He was in your mind, so there was a connection. Did you pick up anything? Impressions, information that might be useful?"

Sarah looked at him. "He seemed…I don't know…light-hearted for a while, toying with me. Two older men were there. I think he was after information from one of them."

"Which one?" Livingstone asked.

"I didn't get their names." Sarah became quiet as the others stared at her. "Rocks bouncing…no, that's only what I saw, not heard in his mind." She turned away from them and went to the window. "He had been contemplative. Seeking information...something about his father."

"Think, Sarah. Search your mind."

"I'm trying, Dr. Brownedyke. He was agitated—his father, not him—years ago. That's it! He had summoned one of the older men for what the man could possibly tell him about an incident."

Livingstone approached her. "What incident?"

"It was a long time ago...maybe forty years."

"Is that all?" Livingstone asked. "There's no more?"

"No, Professor. A moment later Primilov came."

Reggie cursed something and jumped to his feet.

"I've only just realized, Reggie. I'm sorry. From that moment on I was in and out of consciousness. I think Erazmos had weakened my defenses, and he—he—"

"Please, Lucian, let's end this now," Christine urged. "We have what we sent her for. Thank God you're back safe."

They all became quiet as they took in her words. After a moment, Brownedyke spoke up. "Good work, Sarah, very good. You and Reggie go rest. Take all the time you need."

Before leaving, Sarah walked over to Christine Kornum, took her hand, and kissed it gently. "I'm sorry," she said. "I wish it had been me who died instead of Crystal."

"My daughter knew the risks. We had many long talks on the subject. It couldn't be helped." Sage Kornum took Sarah's hand. "You're not at fault."

"Thank you," Sarah said, tears running again.

A fissure opened in the air next to Sarah as she kissed her Sage's hand again, and in the next moment, it became a round black tunnel she could enter at full height. Electric flashes of a deep rich golden color danced around the edges of the tunnel. As she stepped in, her hair sprang alive, charged with static electricity. The tunnel then closed with a slight pop. Tendrils of electric flashes flickered momentarily, but they were also gone in the next instant. Brownedyke dismissed Reggie, and the three of them were alone once again.

"We can confirm that he has the full support of two of the ten clans, the most militant," Brownedyke assured them. "And that may be enough."

Livingstone nodded his agreement. "Nearly forty years ago." He looked at Darius Brownedyke. "Martha's time. Do you remember?"

"Come again, Lucian?"

"That information he was after, an inquiry into a time period I know too well."

"You think it's important?" Christine asked.

Livingstone nodded. "The moon discovery, Erazmos's growing power. Yes, I think so. We need to bring them back here soon. Darius, Christine, very soon."

****

Livingstone entered Christine Kornum's office a half hour later, sure she was still around. As he exited his tunnel, she walked from around her mahogany desk, and they embraced as father and daughter would.

She looked exhausted—dark circles surrounding sad eyes, gray streaks more prominent than ever in unkempt, blonde hair.

She yawned as she sat. "Thank you so much for coming again."

Livingstone took the seat next to her. "I'm always here for you and Hector. No word yet from him?"

"None since the funeral."

"Perhaps staying busy is best. You should go home and rest."

She shook her head. "Hector and I have no choice in the matter. Withdrawing would be all too easy. That's what Erazmos would like, but we can't wallow in pity, or he wins. Perhaps that was his motivation after all. Anyway, too many things are in play now to be distracted, even by this tragedy. I-I just can't believe the maliciousness and after all these years."

"Maybe he didn't know who she was."

"You don't believe that any more than I do. He knew her through her mind if by no other way. It appears the whole damn thing was planned, but how? How did he know Crystal would be there in that alley as a training agent? We don't publicize who the Initiates are."

"Darius is working on that."

"It was really a strike at Hector more than me, but why did he have to do such an evil thing as that? Why did he have to murder my baby?" Her calm exterior melted as sobs escaped her.

Livingstone reached over and took her hand, and she quieted a moment later. "I promised myself I wouldn't do that, and I won't again. I'll see him dead first, and then I'll have a good cry. I'll be all right now."

He admired his good friend, over twenty years his junior. One of his best students when he taught quantum neuroscience at the New York school, now she served as the leader of his clan, his most trusted ally. He had hand-picked her for the position, but she was no puppet.

"I'm tired, Lucian. It's been a hard three years. And now this buildup in hostilities and Crystal gone."

"Take some time; we'll understand. You've created a fine structure with good people in place. Use them and rest, if only for a short while. We can't afford to lose you entirely."

"Sometimes I wonder. The responsibility is so great. Am I really enough for it? And the times we're in and what's coming." She shook her head. "I don't know."

"The subclans would have no other leader, I assure you, Christine. There is no one else."

She fixed her hazel eyes on Livingstone and spoke without the benefit of her vocal cords.

"*It will not be hard to unite the eight remaining clans, but you must lead us. I've been thinking about this for some time. I know you're up to the task. The Sages will all step aside, as will I.*"

Livingstone closed his eyes, not wanting to hear the words planted in his mind. "*That may be true, Christine, but I would rather not. Each clan has a leader, and you're the best of the ten. We don't need a supreme leader to supersede our normal lines of authority. I have a more urgent task to complete in this struggle, but I have only a slight understanding of what it is at the moment. If the third factor reveals itself, my task will be more urgent still. If that moment comes, I will have a clearer picture of what I'm to do.*"

Christine started to argue with him, but he raised

his hand, smiling, which she returned eagerly. He sat there rubbing his temples with the tips of his long fingers, glad to have ended the conversation. Needing a long rest himself, the last thing he wanted was added responsibility and power.

She continued in a more somber fashion and in audible speech, her voice more soothing than the darkness of the room.

"Let me help you clarify things, then, my friend. I feel that we are in great, but dangerous times. We can't afford more mistakes. If these signs are truly part of Tarkus' vision, your task will be to find the third factor and protect it or them as best you can. We have a balance of power now, but after that demonstration, it's obvious his power is rising exponentially. He may be able to succeed even with no further help."

Livingstone looked at her as if for the first time today, a piercing look of understanding. She was right.

"The third factor—fact or fable," he said, more to himself. "After what we saw this morning, I don't doubt the fulfillment of the prophecy is upon us. We're all in limbo, aren't we? We can do nothing in a combative way without the third factor. But there is another avenue."

"The Stones of Sumer," she said, sitting beside him.

"Precisely. Through Martha's discovery, we can rally the clans and try to keep any more from joining him. We can make it harder on him than he realizes. What does Hector know of the stones?"

"He believes she hid them until after the birth and a short period of recuperation. She didn't trust anyone she worked with. Not even Hector. His search for them all those years ago after her death was obviously fruitless. Her family in Ireland knew nothing. He believes she was protecting them by keeping everyone ignorant."

"Her friends too, no doubt," Livingstone said.

"Unfortunately, you're right."

"I haven't been able to contact Hector. Does he know anything at all of their content?"

"Nothing—the note you have tells more than he knows."

"Less than nothing then."

"Lucian, one more thing, these news reports that have cropped up since yesterday seem a bit off. They run to the extreme. Everything is either very bad, or there is nothing at all to worry about with the moon."

"What is your point, my dear?"

"I know that my people are confused. The number of queries to this office and our satellite offices in Europe is enormous. I was thinking. We need a report from someone who can make it more balanced. Someone we can control. Perhaps someone you know."

Livingstone nodded. "I see your point." After a moment, he smiled. "There is someone."

With that he stood, and said, *"Adhal Saĝĝal,"* and was gone, his tunnel leaving purple flashes. A moment later he planted a message in her mind.

"Give Hector my regards. Tell him he owes me a rematch anytime he's ready. The competition will help us both relieve some stress. And, oh, Christine, thank you."

Chapter 10

The girls complained about being driven to school, but Madeline wouldn't have it any other way. Her hackles were on full alert after the supernatural experience the night before convinced her she was on the verge of a complete breakdown. Half an hour after dropping them off, she sat by the window inside a coffee shop on the Ithaca Commons. A storm had rolled through an hour before and pounded the melting ice into slush. She watched Gordon Toop stomp slowly to the door. She had called him only fifteen minutes before coming here, still a little shaky by that reporter's phone call and that conversation she'd seen on TV between those old men playing chess in Central Park. Luckily, Toop hadn't left town yet.

Her decision to call had not been hard. With the sudden threat foisted upon her and the morning's paranormal episode, she needed to somehow make an adjustment in a life careening out of control.

Madeline had known her daughters would endure disadvantages. They would be isolated and know nothing of their past. They would never know the sacrifices their mother had made to keep out the mysterious element, those things her father had incessantly warned her about. Her father had endured the vigil, and now it was her turn. No amount of job responsibility would persuade her to put them at risk.

But he had never experienced what she saw this morning. If he did, he had never mentioned it.

She had to act, so she conquered her internal struggle, that part of her that always cautioned against recklessness, and decided to confront Dr. Toop.

He entered the shop, the pipe stuck between his teeth, and spotted her straight away. His gait was painful to watch. He would lift his right leg in an exaggerated movement and bring it down hard, pivoting on it as the left leg swung forward.

"It's my turn to be surprised by a call," he said, grimacing in obvious pain as he sat down.

Madeline examined him closely. There was no indication he knew of her predicament. The charm was still there, but she felt in control this time.

"I know Harper put you up to this," she said calmly, but with a determined edge to her voice. "You were in his office yesterday. I smelled your foul smoke."

"No need to be angry, my dear."

"Oh, I'm not angry. I just want to know why."

"How do you know I didn't put him up to something, used him to get my way? After all, I've now got you at my conference."

"I don't think so," she said. "You've been in charge of that conference for years, and I've never gone once, though I've been involved in the same research all this time. What are you two after?"

He didn't answer either question, just kept smiling like a damn Cheshire cat.

"That won't work, Dr. Toop. Tell me."

"I won't betray a trust," he said. "I've known Mark since he was a young boy. His grandfather and I were friends—met in the war. In fact, I'm largely to blame for Mark turning to history instead of anthropology."

"What has all that got to do with—"

"His grandfather was curator of anthropology for decades at the American Museum of Natural History. Did you know that?"

"No."

"And, as I said yesterday, I worked there a couple of years. I got to know William's family. Young Mark took a liking to me straight off, because of my war stories."

"Are you saying all the rumors about the stones and my mo—"

"So it's true. She was your mother."

Madeline straightened with the slip. "Yes, but I don't know anything about the stones."

"No, maybe you don't, but why wouldn't she tell her daughter about something like that?"

"I never knew my mother. She died in childbirth."

His eyes widened. "Oh, so sorry to hear that, but your father—"

"Didn't know a thing. Neither one of us knew much about her."

His bushy eyebrows arched. "Really, I find that hard to believe."

"It's not. He knew her less than a year. He was just a working man—a carpenter. He had no interest in scholarly pursuit."

"Quite a mismatch, weren't they?"

"Actually, they were deeply in love."

"I'm sure."

Madeline put down her coffee cup. "Listen, you tell your protégée what I've told you. There is nothing to learn from me. I've wondered about my mother from my earliest years from the tidbits my father knew. I don't know what she was up to in the museum, if anything. She died unexpectedly, nothing more than that. No mystery. If she had these stones, then she must have sent them on somewhere since they've never been found at the museum."

"Then why are you deathly afraid to go to Manhattan?"

Madeline grimaced at his perceptivity. "It's personal."

"Well, that may be, and what you've just said sounds plausible."

"It's also the truth. Tell Mark that he'll have to create his own research agenda. He can't piggyback onto something that may never have existed at the museum. You said it. It's an urban legend. In fact, the stones probably never existed."

"So, you think that's his motivation, self-serving, seeking gain from someone else's work."

"If you know him, you know that to be the truth."

Toop glowered at her and then he chuckled. "You do know him, then."

"Yes, very well, the little prick."

A hearty laugh blew from his round belly, shaking the table.

"I am sorry, my dear. He'd told me how timid you were and, after our little visit yesterday morning, I had to confess that he was right. But then that performance in his office and now—"

"You were there? You heard my—"

"Every word—and you're right, he's desperate for advancement. You know he came to Cornell thirteen years ago as associate professor and hasn't been promoted to full yet. Oh, they're satisfied with his running of the department, but without a strong research background there's no way he'll make full professor."

"How did he know about my mother, and why did he suspect me?"

"Afraid I won't answer that. Loyalty, you know. But really, I don't know much myself. You're right about him, though. A very conniving fellow, indeed. You'll have to find out about the rest."

She thought a while, staring blankly out the window, then said, "You shocked me yesterday with that veiled threat."

"But it wasn't a threat."

"That's not the way it sounded. Listen."

She pulled a micro recorder out of her purse and played a ten second audio segment, his voice easily recognizable.

Toop cringed. "I'm too old for this."

"Then why did you come? Why are you involving yourself in Harper's games?"

"I believe the stones are real, and if they are, I want them as badly as Mark does, for different reasons, perhaps, but my reputation is made. I'm set to retire next year. Yet—" He stopped and looked out at the day. "Being the old war horse that I am, I couldn't resist."

"I'm going to tell you something I've never told anyone. Never." She hesitated, looking down at her hands. "I believe the stones are real, too, and I want them desperately. I won't see them in Harper's hands. They were my mother's work, and they rightfully belong in the hands of her university in Ireland. But I want to study them first, finish what she was doing, somehow get to the bottom of—of—"

She shook as she said all this.

"So, you do know something."

Madeline controlled herself, and said, "Actually, very little. But I'm not above playing hardball, just like I've been played." She patted the recording device with her left hand. "Your threat would be highly embarrassing for you at Northeastern."

"It would indeed."

"Then let's work together."

He reached across, enfolding her hands in his. "I like you. And I like your reputation and work. Forgive my part in this and forget about Mark. He can't hurt you. I shouldn't have agreed to this. I have so little time left to me. It's far too late in life to make new enemies, and I don't wish to be your enemy, Dr. Alleyn."

"Then don't tell him about this meeting, or what I've told you."

"Agreed, and not to worry. I keep my word. So, will you have dinner with me in Manhattan?"

Madeline blew on her coffee, looking him in the eye. "Afraid I'll be too busy. Anyway, I've got to punish you somehow for starting all this."

He laughed heartily again. "Touché, my dear, touché."

"And you owe me something beyond that."

"How may I quickly repay this debt?"

"With information. Your subfield is pre-Christian religions of Northern Europe."

"You've checked on me."

"It's good to know your friends *and* enemies."

"I'm only a friend now, madam, a deeply ashamed

friend."

"Okay, we're over that. But know that I have a copy of this tape elsewhere."

"Of course," he said, "I would expect nothing else."

"I lied yesterday when I said I didn't know much about rune Thurisaz."

"I know," he said, smiling again.

Madeline looked surprised.

"I checked you out thoroughly before coming. Your master's thesis from Columbia covered that quite thoroughly."

"Okay, my turn to say touché. I need to know if you've ever heard of a prophecy from one of the religions connected to the ancient elements, maybe in a way that personifies them."

"Personifies? You mean the elements—water or fire, for instance, being anthropomorphized, springing to life, taking physical form?"

"Yes, that's it."

"Can't say that I have. Why do you ask?"

"A lead I'm following. It concerns the runes Thurisaz and Uruz, a metaphysical or perhaps literal clash among anthropomorphized characters." She looked at him over her cup, sipping. "People clashing."

"People?" He gave her an intense stare. "Are you sure you're telling me the truth about your knowledge of the Stones of Sumer?"

"I know a tad more, but I'm not telling you."

This didn't seem to satisfy him, but he went on anyway. "A distinct prophecy like that would be well known by historians in the field today. There is nothing of that nature."

"I thought so," she said. She held her hand out, and he took it. "I'm glad we understand each other now, and that you're not my enemy. Our interests are similar. It would be a shame if we couldn't work together because of Mark's antics."

"Quite," he said and planted a gentle kiss on the back of her hand.

Chapter 11

The Cascadilla Creek Gorge cut a jagged swath through Ithaca, creating in places an ever-present cacophony of rushing water that had been frozen over only yesterday. Madeline decided to do the fifteen-minute walk from McGraw Hall on Cornell University's campus to meet the persistent reporter who had somehow convinced her boss she should have lunch with him. Following her meeting with Toop earlier that morning, she had wanted to tell Mark Harper she'd decided to go to Manhattan. He'd surprised her with news that Steven Dryer was in town and that she had no choice but to meet with him.

She didn't fight it, but the time would come to take a stand against this kind of administrative tyranny.

In a quick pace, Madeline crossed the bridge spanning the gorge and followed the easiest route from the crown of East Hill to the Ithaca Commons. She relished the time to clear her head and make sure her defenses were properly in place. His phone call last night had touched some of the nerves Toop had failed to reach.

The Commons, and all of downtown, were bustling with activity because of the sudden change of weather. It had taken Madeline years to regain a certain level of ease in crowds since abandoning Manhattan for Ithaca. She was much better these days, but now this pesky reporter and his questions about Stonehenge threatened to reverse the decision she'd made to attend the conference in Manhattan. The moon and that interview with those old men in Central Park cast a pall over her.

Madeline reached Simeon's Bistro at the easternmost corner of the Commons and took a steadying breath. She glanced over her shoulder knowing she could escape back up the hill if needed, but the better route might be to Cailin's shop at the other end of the Commons.

"To hell with it," she whispered.

She pulled on the glass door. The bistro was overflowing with the usual crowd—college kids mostly, but also a healthy smattering of people from town and university. A stereo played a muffled version of some song her daughters could have identified.

She felt someone grab her arm and jumped away from the grip of a man she didn't know. Tall, black hair, nicely dressed, but with a face she somehow knew she couldn't trust.

"I'm sorry…didn't mean to startle you." He hesitated, looking her over, then held out his hand. "Steven Dryer."

Madeline took it briefly. "No…no, not your fault." She turned, looking for a place to sit. The wait staff seemed very busy.

"My booth's over here," Dryer said.

They sat opposite one another at a window with an easy view of the street traffic. After an obligatory exchange of pleasantries and more than one strained moment of silence, Dryer got to the point of why he'd made such a useless trip to talk to her in person.

"You know that group I mentioned, the one spotted

at Stonehenge. Well, the English authorities couldn't make contact with any of them to find out what they were up to."

She looked steadily at him. This was her second unexpected visitor in as many days, broaching a topic close to her mother. "No? Is that what you came all this way to tell me?"

He ignored the question. "It's as if they just disappeared. One moment they were there, the next moment they weren't. Odd, isn't it?"

"They must have driven off quickly."

He shook his head and sipped his glass of Chardonnay. "That's just it. I've talked to the people involved, and no, it wasn't quite as ordinary as turning tail and running. This one guy closest to the scene says they simply vanished. There were no extra cars parked. And there were some sort of electrical phenomena at the site. He swears by his story, but we can't corroborate it because the others were farther away and hadn't seen anything."

Madeline stared at him.

"I didn't mention it in my report this morning. You know...the one you could have been on."

"Too sensational."

"Exactly right, Dr. Alleyn. I'm a first-class reporter, and I couldn't verify this fanciful story, so I let it drop."

She nodded.

"This whole thing with the moon is a bit surreal. Scientists haven't a clue what's causing it. They're scrambling for answers."

"What do you want with me, Mr. Dryer? When Dr. Harper told me about this so-called meeting, I thought there must be some mistake, that I'd already talked to you, had given you my quotes. But then he said you'd called him, and now I'm forced to meet with you. Why would you do such a thing?"

He held her stare, but when she finished, she turned away.

"I just think there's more to the story at Stonehenge, and, well, I wanted to meet you."

"You could have called me again. I might have been open to a meeting here in Ithaca to discuss this further, without cameras, of course."

"That's just it. I don't understand your shyness."

She glanced at the street, watching the crowd swell at lunchtime. When she turned back, the waiter was there with their sandwiches.

"I'm not shy, but I'm not a media hound either." Then she had it. "You don't think I could have something to do with those people spotted at Stonehenge."

"Do you?"

"Of course not. How could you even suspect that? I'm a professor of history, nothing more. Not a cultist or an adherent to some strange religion. I teach classes, do research, lead a quiet life with three perfect daughters. I almost never leave Ithaca, Mr. Dryer. I—"

"Please, call me Steven." He held up his glass. "More wine?"

Madeline cut her eyes from him and looked at her watch. She searched the restaurant with a quick turn of her head.

"You were just in England, weren't you?"

The question startled her. "How did you— Oh, Harper again."

"He has been helpful."

"Look, thank you for lunch, but I really need to—"

"Afraid there's nothing to get back to. The meeting with your doctoral student, Claire, I think, has been canceled."

Madeline held her composure, but it was a close call. "Harper," she said, too loud. She got smaller in the seat as heads turned.

"He likes the publicity for his department, and he wants your cooperation."

"Of course."

"Don't be too hard on him. Plenty of professors are becoming media darlings over this story. They're giving their departments a lot of recognition, but not you. Why?"

Madeline turned away again. Pedestrians ambled by. A student waved, and Madeline smiled back. She didn't answer his question, but then she said in a voice that left no doubt where she stood. "Look, I've told you all I know. I'm not holding back any information. I'm just camera shy. I don't like the spotlight. I don't even like to do public speaking at conferences. I won't appear with you. Dr. Harper is way off base if he thinks he can force me."

"Okay, point well made, Madeline. May I call you by your first name?"

"What? Oh, yes…sure…whatever you like." She hesitated. "This whole thing is pointless, you know."

His little smile aggravated her, and she decided then to straighten Harper out on his view of administration.

"Sandwiches are good, aren't they?"

"Yes."

He followed her gaze through the window. "The place hasn't changed that much."

She turned back to him, surprised.

"Ithaca is one of a kind. I was a student here. I miss the small-town life, the slower pace, a more normal schedule. Please, why don't you tell me a little about yourself?"

"Sounds like you know all about me already."

"I'm sure there are many things I don't know. While we're here, we might as well enjoy the meal. Look, I'll start. I come from a long line of New York journalists. All serious people, print media—hard core. It angered them when I went into broadcasting. They think I sold out for money. I have a brother who works for the New York Times, very successful, well known around the world. And what's worse, he's five years younger than me. That really sucks."

Madeline couldn't help a small smile. "Did you?"

"Did I what?"

"Sell out."

"Yeah, I suppose I did, but I do good work all the same. I inherited their zeal for investigation you might say."

"Is that what you're doing here—investigating?"

"No, honestly, I'm enjoying a lovely meal with a beautiful lady."

Madeline felt the heat rise in her face. "You've come a long way for lunch."

"It was worth it, though," he said.

She looked down, aggravated with her own juvenile response, but more that it seemed to amuse him.

"Harper said you have triplet daughters. What does

their father do?"

"Afraid that's off limits."

"Okay, but I didn't notice a ring and thought—"

"Strike two, Mr. Dryer," she said, placing her hand in her lap.

"Okay—safer territory. Let's see. Runology—that's an archaic field."

"How would you know that?"

"Oh, I did some preliminary reading to prepare for this meeting."

Impressed, she said, "Okay, I'll go along for a while. Just keep the questions on track." She sipped her wine. "You know, I'm not very interesting. I'm not a Druid or any other strange thing if that's what you're searching for. I'm just a dull university professor who happens to be a scholar of Celtic history and well versed in the time period when there was a great migration to the British Isles. As for the viability of Runology, as a field of linguistics, it does have its usage today, especially since I also study the time period when runes were widely used. The field is pretty much dead, at least from a scholarly standpoint."

"But there are those esotericists who still dabble."

"True, but for someone like me, a historian with a broad interest in dead languages, it combines well with my concentration in the Celtic peoples of Britain, since runes were once used a great deal."

Scribbling notes, he said, "But it's still fascinating—the history of these things. I mean, like Stonehenge and some of the other sites. We know so little about them."

"Practically nothing."

"Then the moon suddenly begins to act strangely

and, boom, we see an increased activity around this ancient site we know very little about. And then this unexplained sighting. I'd like to know why."

"So would I, but I can't help you, I'm afraid."

He looked up from his pad and held her gaze. "When did you first get interested in your field?"

"Way back. My mother inspired me, or rather her work did. She died after I was born, within minutes."

"Sorry to hear that."

"My father made sure I knew as much about her as possible, and later I discovered some of the same talents she had. She was a linguist and an archeologist."

"Archeologist? Interested in Stonehenge?"

"Sure, but other things as well. The Middle East, for example, but my father didn't know much about her work." Madeline hesitated. He didn't appear to be working for anyone. That admission had genuinely surprised him. But just to be safe, she said, "I don't know much either."

"So, you come from a family of scholars."

"Actually, no. My father was a carpenter, but, by all accounts, my mother was a brilliant scholar."

"And you're like her."

Madeline felt herself blush again. "I'm flattered you'd say that. She was the real thing. I try to be, with some success, but I have some of my father in me too. Many scholars would never get dirty working in an old woodshed."

He laughed but stayed focused. "The site itself—Stonehenge—was really an impressive feat, wasn't it? How could those people have erected such large pillars, not to mention carry them, what, from Wales?"

"It was remarkable."

"Aren't there wild theories about its construction and who built it? I've read theories about the Druids, maybe the Greeks, even that Native Americans built it. Now that was a strange one. But even stranger was the idea about aliens building it—space aliens."

"A couple of my colleagues might agree with some of that, but—"

"Who might they be?"

"Dr. Wick for one, but he's wrong."

Dryer's eyes darted when Madeline said the name. He seemed to recognize it.

"Do you know him?"

"Just from the department's website. That checking I did before calling you, remember?"

Madeline nodded.

He looked down at his notes. "So, you were about to say something about the builders."

Madeline gave him a steady look and decided it was nothing. "We simply don't know who built it. There were no written records, only the stones themselves. Can you imagine recreating a theology, a cosmology—a coherent theory—from a heap of rocks?"

"What's your guess, then?"

"Oh, its construction, its orientation to the sun would suggest a form of religious worship. It was possibly a sun temple, a monument to a religion that failed. There's evidence of human sacrifice, which surely indicates some form of religious practice. There's even evidence it was used as a place of healing because the blue stones had attributed to them a form of curative."

"By Druids?"

"No, they came much later. They had no role in

building it, but they used the site, and still use it as much as they can. It's heavily regulated."

He thought awhile. "Getting back to the visitors spotted at the site. All indications are there would be no reason for them to be there and how would they have known about the moon when the story hadn't yet broken? The abrupt disappearing act is hard to explain."

"You believe your source on that?"

"My gut tells me he saw something strange. He checks out. He's not a nut. When I asked you on the phone if there could be any other group involved…well, let me just say you sounded evasive, and as an investigative reporter my suspicions were aroused. I was tingling all over."

"Sixth sense."

"Something like that."

"I told you the truth, Mr. Dryer."

He looked at her a long time, stared straight into her eyes, and said, "I don't believe you, Madeline. In fact, I believe you know much more than you're saying."

Chapter 12

Dryer left Simeon's Bistro and followed Madeline up the hill to Cornell University, the academic behemoth sitting astride East Hill like a feudal castle. He needed to clear his head, to think, to assess the damage he'd done, but most of all he didn't want their conversation to end on such a sour note. His comments had angered her in a way he couldn't understand. Blood had drained from her face so completely, so suddenly, he thought she would faint, but instead she merely stood and left without a word, though he knew there must have been a thousand choice ones bubbling just under the surface.

Why had he made the crack? What had he hoped to gain from the smart-ass remark? He walked, taking care to remain well behind and out of sight, and played their conversation over in his head. Each time, her face intruded on his thinking. Hell, he couldn't think. He had a story; he just had to find the particulars and connect them to Madeline. But the more he thought of her, the more the story, or the promise of one, got pushed aside. Story or no story, he wanted to be near her again even if she was furious with him. For now, he kept his distance, without the slightest hint of what he was going to say or do next.

Suddenly, Jimmy's round face popped into his brain with that I-told-you-so look plastered all over it.

He knew his friend was right. Jimmy was always right about his foibles with women, especially when he tried to mix pleasure with work. Things usually got explosive, but he didn't care. As he walked, he forced that part of his conscience aside as McGraw Hall loomed directly ahead.

Dryer took the stairs with the vague impression he should go to her and apologize. Reaching the fourth floor, he turned onto the first corridor he came to and stopped abruptly. Several professors were leaving their offices. The odd student strolled by carrying their cellphones, oblivious to him.

When the hallway finally cleared, he stopped pretending to care about the bulletin board messages and looked around the corner where Madeline had turned. Her office was the last one on the left where an ornate window with a view out over Ithaca dominated the wall. He'd been there earlier just to get his bearings and could see from this distance that her door was open just a bit.

Screwing up his courage, he took a step or two but stopped again when he suddenly heard angry voices from another open doorway close by. One of the men had spoken her name. Dryer moved closer, stopped just outside the door, and looked through the crack to find Mark Harper speaking to some skinny professor. The sign on the door read, Dr. Charles Wick.

"She looked pretty upset when she passed me in the hall just now. Didn't speak a word. I don't even think she saw me. Tell me you didn't have anything to do with that."

"I assure you, Mark. That was none of my doing. Now, if you don't mind, I have work to do."

"Actually, I do mind, Wick. It's one thing to be jealous of someone's success, but to hound her like you have."

"You dare assume that!" Wick said, eyes bulging. "Me—jealous—of her!"

"I won't have you bullying my faculty, and if I ever get one shred of solid evidence of what I already know to be fact, I'll come against you—hard."

Wick straightened himself to his full height, looking more defiant. He took a step toward Harper, but the stone look on Harper's face stopped him. Instead, he turned and began fingering a miniature replica of Stonehenge, or some other such monument, sitting on one of his bookcases.

"You are quite blinded, Mark. Can't you see that she's playing you for a fool—for financial gain? Her theories are not credible, and they will ultimately bring derision to this venerable department."

Harper leered at Wick and his toys. "Which you want to control, I know. You'll recall that I was given this position, not you. That should have settled it, but no, you have to actively oppose me at every turn, don't you?" Harper took a step closer to him and stuck his finger into Wick's bony chest as Wick turned to face him. "It's my choice whose career I promote, not yours."

Wick turned pale but didn't back away as Harper withdrew his hand. "Yes, as Head, you are quite right." He rubbed his chest and looked as though he wanted to retreat, but there was nowhere to go.

"But I'm no fool," Harper said a little less belligerently. "If what she's doing doesn't produce credible results and if her funding dries up, so will my support."

"That day has long passed, I assure you."

Harper took another step toward Wick. Very close now, he looked up at the tall professor. "And that's where you're wrong. There's plenty of time for her to work out her theories. All the time in the world. She claims to have proof that her ideas are correct."

"Proof!" Wick spat the word out, not bothering to hide his contempt.

"Don't get involved, Charles. I'm warning you. This is none of your affair."

Wick suddenly sneered in triumph, his face flush now where a moment ago it had been pallid. "From your own mouth!" He let out a cackle.

"What are you talking about?"

"Was it a Freudian slip, Mark? Affair."

The two men stood face to face like snarling dogs. Harper grabbed Wick's lapel with one hand and forced him back onto the display case. Several items crashed inside.

Wick gasped, and said weakly, "Is this part of your management strategy, threatening your faculty?" Wick had gone wobbly, but his face still shown triumphant.

"In this case—yes." But in the next instant, an astonished look crossed Harper's face as if he'd recognized the impropriety of his rage. He backed away, staring at his hands in disgust, then up at Wick, sneering down at him. He appeared embarrassed, apparently not wanting things to escalate more than they had. He said, almost apologetically, "Maybe I've jumped to the wrong conclusion."

Wick straightened his coat. "As wrong as you've ever been."

"And so have you," Harper added defensively. "I don't want to ever hear that accusation again, because it isn't true."

"Isn't it?" Wick said, still straightening his coat.

Straining to control himself, Harper said, "Look, you overblown bastard, if it's any consolation, I do share some of your concern about her work. But I have reasons you know nothing about. I assure you, I'm watching her closely, and so far, the money she's earning from the chaired position and the budget I gave her are being well spent. If she's right, the gain to the department will be immeasurable."

There was a desperation in Harper's eyes. Dryer had seen it before in his own mirror. Wick seemed to gain a measure of strength from it. *What's going on between these two?*

Calming rapidly, Mark Harper hesitated then turned and walked a little awkwardly to the office door as Dryer retreated around the corner. He watched as Harper marched away from him down the adjacent corridor, apparently heading for his office. Intrigued by what he'd just seen, Dryer debated whether to call out to Harper. He needed more leverage on Madeline and knew Harper would comply. The man lusted for notoriety all right, and if he couldn't have it personally, he was sure to do whatever it took to promote his department. Dryer felt pulled in both directions but finally decided to see him later.

As Harper turned again and vanished around another corner, Dryer crept to Wick's open door and peeked in. Wick stood by the display case, as engrossed in the model of Stonehenge as a boy might be with toy soldiers. Dryer halted, unsure of what to do next, but then he let instinct guide him, as always. Maybe this odd-looking older man would prove useful.

Wick spun to the door and looked ready to launch into another retort when he stopped short at the sight of someone other than Mark Harper. Wick closed his mouth and leered at Dryer.

Not waiting to be greeted, Dryer stuck his hand out and barged into the office. "Forgive the intrusion, Dr. Wick, but we may have a mutual interest in Madeline Alleyn's work."

Wick's eyes narrowed immediately. "Who are you, where did you come from, and what could we possibly have in common that would involve my colleague?"

Dryer smiled at Wick's insincere use of the word colleague. "My name is Steven Dryer—of ABC News." He let the words settle on Wick, whose demeanor changed in an instant. A narrow smile stretched his thin lips to a line. He'd seen these media hungry academicians too often. Wick would be as pliable as putty now.

Looking around, he noted the office seemed like a museum exhibit with artifacts neatly displayed in every conceivable spot—ancient pottery, coins, masks with grotesque faces.

"I'm following up on a lead for a story about Stonehenge."

Dryer's comment startled Wick into wide-eyed wonder. Changing course rapidly, Wick said, "Is that right? And why here?" He offered Dryer a chair and a cookie from a tin container.

"The story is sort of an offshoot of the larger events happening now. You know, the sudden decrease in the moon's orbit."

Confusion washed over Wick's face. "And what, pray tell, has that got to do with Dr. Alleyn?"

"Nothing, really. I've got a lead on a potential story. I think she could give me some expert guidance." Dryer continued to cut his eyes here and there around the office, fascinated with all the memorabilia.

Wick let out a little exasperated hiss. "And you think she's the expert, do you?"

"Of course, if you know anything about the subject of Druids and Stonehenge—"

"My dear boy, I practically breathe information on those topics, unlike some of my...well, lesser-known colleagues." Wick swept his arm in an arc as if to say, *isn't it obvious? Don't you see all this neat stuff?*

"Good, I was hoping you'd say that. But I'm curious about something." Dryer hesitated, debating whether to bring in the fact that he had overheard their fight. "Forgive me, but that argument just now as I approached your office, was that Dr. Harper, your chairman?"

Wick turned red and rose from his seat. He walked around to the right corner of his desk, retrieved a pipe, and scooped some tobacco from a pouch. "I suppose you couldn't avoid it. We have had running disagreements."

Wick was smoking now, a minty aroma wafting over to Dryer.

"About her work?"

"Yes, but other things as well. Tell me, what is this about?"

"I've had a couple of conversations with Dr. Alleyn about this story of mine, and..." Dryer hesitated again, unsure of where to explore, unsure of Wick.

"Let me guess—she's been evasive, less than forthcoming, skirting the issue, but always very nice about it. Am I right?"

Dryer couldn't help nodding to all of that. "Exactly. I'm puzzled by it. She agreed to speak to me on the subject, but then she became reluctant, nervous even. I can't really put my finger on what it is."

Wick smiled and sat down. "Go on."

"Yeah, well, let's see. She wouldn't come on air or allow us to use her picture, or her first name even."

"Sounds like she's hiding something. Unless—" Wick stopped, looking thoughtful. That long stretch of a smile slowly developed. "Yes, that could be it. Her theories—you probably overheard that much—her work, you know, is not very well received in the academic community." Wick then exploded off his chair, as happy as if he'd been given a new model to play with. "Oh, this is too good!" He stalked about the room, pounding his fist into his palm. "She knows. She knows she hasn't got anything credible. And she's scared of being exposed." Then he grew darker. "She's willingly taking the money when she should have resigned her chaired appointment. Why, the little shrew."

"I don't quite understand. I mean, she seems brilliant."

"Oh, she is smart—brilliant as you say, but misguided. She's boxed herself into a corner. She's being paid quite a lot you know. Harper has lavished this endowed position on her. The Rupert Howard Chair in Celtic Culture triples her regular salary, and Cornell's base pay is none too shabby."

Dryer let out a soft whistle. "From what I

overheard; I take it you two are rivals."

"Rivals? Oh, my dear boy, that would presume equality on some level, wouldn't it? No—no, we aren't rivals. She's an interloper!" Wick seemed just then like a school kid who had gotten the right answer, but then he caught himself and glanced over to Dryer. "Sometimes that happens in academics, you know."

"Yeah—and in other fields."

"Yes, well, it's more critical when dealing with young minds, don't you think? Persons of her questionable character should be ferreted out and exposed. Here in the academy, we are about truth, quite an ideal to uphold. To teach the next generation what is fact must be grounded in rigorous science and sound theory. I am afraid our Dr. Madeline Alleyn has bitten off quite a lot in her pursuits."

"More than she can handle?"

Wick turned to him and stopped his pacing. "Oh, yes. Quite a lot more. I've been dealing with this for years, but our esteemed chairman…well, let's just say his judgment is clouded."

Dryer wasn't interested in Wick's accusations concerning Madeline's relationship with Harper. He knew women, and Madeline didn't fit that particular bill. "Tell me, she says that Stonehenge's origin is unknown. Is that generally taken as true?"

Wick sat down and took on an air of the clear-thinking scholar. "Oh, my no. Is that what she said? My boy, I've been around for decades longer than she. There is mystery there, yes, but it is generally understood that the ancient Druids began and completed the work. What is needed is more proof, yes, but that is the accepted fact."

"And they are still around today, the Druids I mean. Do you suppose Druids are still interested in Stonehenge?"

"Of course."

"And are there any others?"

"I suppose there are scattered nuts around. But the Druids are the builders, after all, and the largest group, and quite—" He stopped abruptly.

"You were saying?"

"Well, they are the largest and most respected."

"Respected by whom?"

"Well, other naturalist groups, I suppose. It's undoubtedly because of their ancient history."

"Then, the other night—the sightings at Stonehenge—"

"What sightings?"

"There were people dressed in white at about the same time the moon story broke. Early in the morning…say, four a.m. London time."

"I see," Wick said, leaning closer in.

"It really hasn't caused much of a stir, but I suspect there is something ominous happening at the site. You see—"

Wick moved to the edge of his seat and stared intently at Dryer, waiting for him to continue.

"—I just get the feeling the two are connected."

Wick dismissed it with a shrug. "Stonehenge and the moon. How many times have I heard it, Mr. Dryer?"

"This is different, though. Obviously, there's something to the moon thing."

"Yes, but Druids wouldn't be—"

"I know." Dryer lowered his voice because of the

opened door, suddenly mindful that Madeline might walk by and catch him talking to Wick. "Do you mind if I close the door?"

Wick shook his head.

Dryer walked back to his chair and pulled it closer to the lanky professor. Wick bent forward, forearms resting on his bony legs. "I have the impression that Dr. Alleyn knows something about this, but she isn't talking. Tell me, how well do you know her?"

"Quite well. She was a student with us, you know. Got her doctorate here. Like I said, I obviously have issues with her brand of scholarship. I don't think she is very good there—too unorthodox."

"My gut tells me something's going on, something sinister."

Wick's eyes widened even more, and a look of hopeful glee brightened his face. "Sinister, you say." Then, so low that Dryer could barely hear him. "If it could just be proven, then I'd have her."

Dryer sat up straighter. "Look, I just want a good story. I don't want to get her in trouble. I was talking about her knowledge of a group that seems to be stalking about Stonehenge. People the authorities can't seem to catch."

"Yes, yes, Mr. Dryer. But if she is hiding something, we must know. After all, we have a duty."

"What are you going to do?"

"Nothing—for now, but someone should watch her." He eyed Dryer, closely examining him. "You could do it. She might respond to a good-looking professional such as yourself. And she *is* unmarried."

"What?"

"You must get closer to her."

"Actually, that might be a little difficult now. I kind of insulted her today."

"Well, with your looks and charm, I'm sure you'll get back in her good graces soon. Start off by watching the house, her comings and goings."

"And what exactly am I looking for?"

Wick thought for a moment. "You can start by monitoring her three brats while I do some snooping around here."

"Her children?"

Wick was up again and standing at the door. "It'll give you a purpose while I latch onto something more promising. Then I'll re-direct you." He stopped, thoughtful again. "If only I could get to her files."

"What was that?"

"Her files. It would be impossible here—too many people around." He began pacing again. Wringing his hands like a mad scientist. "She works quite a lot from home. I think everything we need will be there. You may be able to do it. Catch the house when she's away, and the brats are in school."

"A break in!" Dryer said incredulously. "Look, there appears to be something here, but breaking and entering? I don't know."

"I'm sure a man of your talents and drive can accomplish a little thing like that, Mr. Dryer." Wick put a hand on Dryer's shoulder. "The story awaits. You'll get what you want, and I'll be able to confront that ass Harper with something more than conjecture."

Wick's eyes were sparkling with hateful glee. Dryer tore away from his hand and paced the office, trying to think. He'd never envisioned having to go in this direction.

"Start with the children," Wick said. "The little busybodies probably skip school a lot. She's less than a model parent in that regard. Why, they may even know something, especially that little smarty pants—the one with the glasses." He stopped, thinking. "Harper said Madeline will be in Manhattan tomorrow at a conference." He smiled. "Perfect timing."

Dryer stopped pacing, stared up into Wick's thin face, and felt his stomach take a nauseating turn.

Chapter 13

Wednesday

Phoebe had been anxious all morning, waiting for her mother to leave for Manhattan. She had found it hard to remain silent, everything that had been happening weighing on her mind. Then there was that new dream, weirder than the one that had started over the weekend. More strange words that seemed to take form, floating like phantoms. And that haunting voice speaking in a language reminiscent of the one from the other dream. It couldn't be a coincidence. Phoebe didn't believe in ghosts, but with what she could now do, with the revelation that they might be witches, she didn't know what to believe or where to turn. Her sisters couldn't help her understand what might be happening any more than that stranger could, the one who had responded to her blog post.

Phoebe had managed to post again late Tuesday night while her sisters slept. Opening the site, she discovered another response from SurferDude espousing a theory connecting what was happening to them with this strange big moon. She had overheard at school some kids and teachers discussing how big the moon suddenly seemed to be now. It was interesting but not convincing. SurferDude seemed adamant though, which prompted her to keep him on track, reminding him that she may be a witch but definitely not a werewolf. When she mentioned her theory of the four elemental principles or powers or something like that out of mythology connected to runes, his response was:

You've read your mother's papers, right? This whole thing could be just something you've repressed, and it came out in a weird dream. That might be the only thing happening here.

After calming her anger, she answered him:

Listen, I expected more from you. That's not it at all. There HAS to be something to it. I can do things with my mind and so can Rhea and Di. I'm NOT crazy, SD. This stuff is real!

It was obvious to her now, reaching out this way was going to be fruitless, so she snapped her computed shut again, went to sleep, and dreamed the same weird shit.

Her mother fussed over them before leaving, but when she did leave Phoebe could finally enact another plan she had cooked up based on that page she had stolen from the smelly shopkeeper.

She had been anxious to spring her theory on Rhea of how they had escaped Wick and had come back home in that strange darkness. She had watched Rhea all day Tuesday while they practiced their new skills. Had Rhea caused it to happen? She needed to know for sure.

"We're going to Cornell to find whatever information we can on Sherman Rasmusun," Phoebe announced as soon as her mother pulled out of the drive.

Dione turned to her with a big smile.

Phoebe sighed. "We're skipping, but just this

once."

At seventeen, they all had driving privileges, but their mother had taken the keys to their car. So, they hit the street. Phoebe led them away from their usual route and turned them toward a busy commercial section. Twenty minutes later, they found a doughnut shop and an empty table in a corner. It was time to implement phase two.

"I thought we were going to try to find out who SurferDude is at school?" Rhea asked.

"This is more important."

"How are we supposed to get all the way over to East Hill from here?" Dione said. "That's loads of walking."

Phoebe bit into a cream filled pastry. "There's an alley behind this place. Rhea can practice there until she gets it right, then she'll get us to the Commons just like she got us home from Haldane's shop."

Rhea and Di exchanged nervous glances like they thought Phoebe had lost her mind. "What are you talking about?"

Phoebe smiled at them. "We have to figure out how you did it first, but that shouldn't be hard."

Dione slumped back into the chair. "I think you're cracking up. Did what?"

"Wait," Rhea whispered, turning her chair away from an old lady who'd taken exception to Di's comment. "What are you saying?"

"It happened when Haldane and Wick were about to haul me to the back of the shop. Remember those flashes?"

"What about them?"

"What color were they?"

Rhea and Di eyed each other again like Phoebe really was losing it. "Kinda green, I guess."

"Not just any old green. Aqua green."

"So?"

"Look at Rhea's eyes."

Dione jerked Rhea's chair around and leered at her.

"Stop!" Rhea yelled. Two old men turned to them, so Rhea lowered her voice. "My eyes don't have anything to do with it."

"Not your eyes, exactly. The color's the same. That's no coincidence."

Rhea looked at Di. Dione looked back, but neither understood what Phoebe had been trying to say.

"It's you, Rhea. Those flashes when Haldane held me were the exact color of your eyes. You got us back in that black thing, and now you'll get us to Cornell."

"Wait a minute," Rhea said. "Say I can do all that, why are we going there anyway?"

"I can't just go to Mom accusing these men of plotting something. She'll get suspicious of us. We need evidence and data. Facts. We have that paper Haldane doodled on. I need to know who Sherman Rasmusun is and find out why he's important to Mom's theory. I think he's who mom's 'buddies' were talking about Monday night. Then maybe we can tell her, and she can confront them or maybe get her boss to do something that'll keep her safe. Wick made it sound like they're after her job." Phoebe grabbed Rhea's arm to make her understand. "But first I have to know how you got us back home."

They went outside and skirted along the side of the building to the deserted alley in the rear. "You teleported us, Rhea. I know I didn't do it and neither did Dione. Those flashes were the color of your eyes. You produced that black thing."

Rhea's eyes sparkled bright green again. "The only thing," Phoebe went on, "I don't know how. Can you remember what happened at that exact moment?"

Rhea's eyes narrowed. "Well...I remember being really scared..." She stopped. A faraway look came over her. "We needed to run...fast...needed to get away." She focused on Phoebe. "That's all there is...and then...and then..."

She was struggling with things new to her. Phoebe had been locked into her mind the whole time, but it didn't help. The experience was something Rhea hadn't thought about. Instinct must've been working. There was no memory, nothing that could help Phoebe understand it better and help Rhea think it through.

Her eyes brightened even more. "Haldane's angry face, his fist, I-I didn't want you to get flattened." Rhea looked at Phoebe, desperation twisting her beautiful face. "I remember my head feeling like it might explode. It—it kind of thumped, swelled, sizzled. I don't know, then those flashes, that blackness, and we were gone, taken away. It surprised me when we ended up at our house."

"We have to get up East Hill. We can't walk all the way." Phoebe had her attention now. Rhea nodded once, twice. "It's important. If you can't do this now, we'll have to go home and find another way to get to Cornell. It's like we'll all be in trouble if we don't go— now." Phoebe hesitated. "And it'll help Mom."

That did it. Rhea's attention focused to a pinpoint, and a black hole erupted next to them. It hung there with green electric flashes springing out of the interior.

Rhea yelped and fell over, and as quickly as the hole had opened, it closed off again.

"That was so cool," Phoebe said. "Now bring it back!"

Rhea thought about it a second then raised her hand. Her face looked like it did before one of her vicious soccer kicks. She pushed at the shoulder with an outstretched arm, and the hole popped open again. This time it didn't go away. A wind from it blew into their faces, and electric flashes bit their arms and made their hair come alive.

Dione took tiny steps around it, rubbing her arms and face in the static charge and crackle of energy. "There's no sides."

"It's two-dimensional." Phoebe put her hand in it at the edge. The charge inched up her arm. She tried to reach around outside with her other arm to clasp hands, but they couldn't connect.

"What is it?" Dione said. "When you go around it the edge isn't there." She looked at Rhea. "Is it safe? I-I mean, I'm not scared or anything."

"You've been in it before. It captured all three of us, remember?"

"I know," Dione said, "but that was an accident."

Phoebe pulled them farther away from the building. "We should practice a bit then make for Cornell."

Over the next half hour, they did just that. They didn't mind the static that erupted from the total blackness, tickling their skin, or the faint crackling in their ears. It felt like riding on an escalator, moving without really moving.

Rhea found that she could open it while running.

She would sprint, thinking about it extra hard. It never failed to pop open or stay close as she ran into it, letting it collapse around her and take her to any spot on the street. Or she could enter it and stop, letting it enfold her, making her invisible. And the coolest thing of all was that it could go through solid objects. Rhea had accidentally popped back inside the doughnut shop, causing the matron to send up a cloud of powdery sugar. The second time was no accident.

"I don't know if this is a good idea," Di said. "I mean, flying around in that contraption. What if it dissolves with my head on the inside and my body out?"

"It seems safe." But the words had hardly left Phoebe's mouth when the hole appeared again and took Rhea and Dione away.

A moment later, Rhea came back. "It was best to just do it rather than argue with her. She's mad, but she's smiling a bit, standing next to the fountain on the Commons."

The hole popped open again next to Dione who screamed and nearly fell into the water as Phoebe and Rhea appeared from nowhere, whooping and hollering. No one on the street seemed to notice.

"It might be hard to find what we're after," Phoebe said when they settled, "and we don't have much time. You think you can—"

A flashing blackness choked out her next words. When the hole opened again a moment later, Phoebe oriented herself and recognized right off the deserted stretch of sidewalk running between Uris and Ives Hall on Cornell's campus. "It's nine o'clock. It might take hours to find something, so we need to start right away."

"But what are we doing?" Dione said.

"The big library is close to Mom's building." Phoebe looked around. "Over in that direction. The archives should be stored there."

Dione looked doubtful. "And we're gonna just waltz in and say, 'Hi, we're high school seniors trying to look like college students, and we have to spy on someone who worked here decades ago. Mind telling us where the records are so we can poke around in his business?' "

"Very funny, Di," Phoebe said, "but I have a simpler plan."

Dione's eyes narrowed. "That mind stuff is gonna backfire on you one day, and you'll be in big trouble."

Phoebe ignored her. She ushered them up the street and through the front doors of Olin Library.

"What if they ask for our IDs?" Rhea asked.

"They will," Phoebe said, looking around, "but that won't be a problem."

They walked up to a humongous counter and were directed to the basement by a friendly student worker. After several flights down they entered a dingy space, poorly lit with few workers who all looked like they'd been confined to Hades. Phoebe walked up to a large girl who scowled back.

"We need to check the anthropology department archives. We have a class project." Phoebe smiled her best, but it didn't seem to impress the girl.

"Names and IDs," she said bluntly.

She turned a signup sheet around for them. They wrote bogus names and made-up numbers like what had been written by others on the list.

The large girl scanned the sheet then looked and narrowed her eyes, hesitating. "Something doesn't—"

Phoebe blinked, and the girl changed direction in mid-thought.

"Uh…Mrs. Cousins personally approves all entries. How far back do you need to go? There's usually lots of boxes for each department."

"From the eighties," Phoebe said.

"I'll be back."

Minutes later, a gloomy-looking librarian followed on her heels. Her beady eyes examined the sheet they'd signed then swept over them, not liking this obvious attempt to get to her precious archives. She carried a clipboard with another signup sheet on it. "Class project? What professor might that be?"

Her hands had gone to her hips, the scowl worsening. Rhea suggested telepathically that they run for it, but then Phoebe made eye contact with the librarian. The lady's arms fell to her side, and her face seemed to relax a bit.

"Um," Phoebe said, "would you mind telling me who last viewed these?"

Phoebe felt resistance. The lady's eyes darted about as if searching for some misplaced thought, but in a moment, she turned away and walked over to the student's work area where she consulted a computer. "Madeline Alleyn," she called out. "Sixteen years ago."

Phoebe and her sisters exchanged knowing looks. "No one before her?"

"Not more recent than, oh…" She looked closely at the screen. "…looks like about fifty years back. How far back are you looking?"

"We'll have all the boxes from the eighties and

early nineties, and we can't be disturbed."

"Gotcha," the lady said and spun on the spot.

Dione flopped down at a table across from Phoebe and shook her head.

"I'll stop when we clear a few things up, okay?"

She didn't get to give Phoebe her usual comeback, because the student worker opened the door for the librarian who walked in pushing a dolly with four big boxes stacked high.

She gave them a strained smile. "I'll be back with three more loads. What you're after should be here. Call if you need me."

There were thirteen boxes in all with what must have been hundreds of files arranged in no particular order. They needed help, but Phoebe didn't want any more contact than necessary, so they plowed in. After an hour of digging through poorly marked files, they were ready to call the lady when Rhea said, "Look," and pulled the thick file of Sherman F. Rasmusun from a box marked G.

In the late eighties, he'd been in his early thirties when the university dismissed him. A letter confirmed that. He'd been on the archeology faculty, was of Romanian descent, nineteen-seventy graduate of Queen's University Belfast. A Cornell University publication mentioned in an off-handed way a theory he'd been working on related to an archeological dig in Mesopotamia. No details. They flipped through lots of pages in the folder, but they weren't helpful.

Then Rhea found written on the back, *continued to next folder*. They searched through every box, but no other folder contained his name, which meant the contents of each folder had to be checked.

"Only look at the unmarked ones for now."

But there were lots of these. Finally, nearing one o'clock Phoebe found a folder unlike any other because all it contained were about twenty handwritten pages. It seemed to be some personal notes chronicling an archeological dig.

The ink was worn and in a bad hand. Phoebe had to skip words and whole sentences and sections. Then her heart began to race. "Look at this section."

She read out loud. " ""We'd been on the dig two months with...to go on, Martha becoming more restless each day. We had only the barest of information from which to start, but she felt...valid, and none would dare question...There were only four of us from university, the rest being local help hired to...about ten in all. We...to be...as these...ordinary people.

" 'She was so beautiful, brilliant red hair flowing so lovely even in these...sand covering her...to toe. We would have all died for her in that Persian hell hole. Of course, we had to endure the hardship alongside the help. It wouldn't work for them to see us...clean and well...We ate with them, drank with them, went off into the desert to relieve ourselves in their manner. Very primitive conditions made...students wonder why we ever took up archeology. But we knew why. It was Dr. Alleyn. She was our...' "

Phoebe put the paper down and looked at Rhea and Dione.

"He's talking about our grandmother, isn't he?" Dione said.

"But why would she be mentioned?"

"She was an archeologist, Rhea, remember?" Phoebe said. "We know that much. This was her project. Rasmusun was her student. Mom must be working on her theory."

Phoebe read on. " 'Toward the end of the ninth week, our fortune changed. We found the fabled encampment sight, the…Of course, the…in Belfast wouldn't be interested…only just the beginning. I won't say here how we knew for sure. We had our proof. That find would have been enough, mind you, to make a legend out of Martha within the *UngKin*, but for what came next. But…getting ahead. We redoubled our efforts, and in just two…just…more days…digging we had them, the culmination of many…of her brilliant…The rune stones were ours. We were back in civilization mere days…back in Belfast, but Martha became frightened. Those loons from the Grecian part of Clan *Saĝtuku* were threatening. She confided in me, only me. And the greatest honor, she selected me…assistant at the…Museum of…History when she accepted the appointment. And why not…After all, I was senior among the four. I still remember the look on the German's face. Of course, I knew why she wanted to come to America. It was safer in Manhattan. She…support from the organization, plenty of our kind around.' "

"Our kind?" Rhea said.

Phoebe shook her head and began reading again. " 'The work continued right under the noses of the ordinaries at the museum. They never knew she'd brought the rune stones in and began studying them, never knew the…work. But after six months, she…'

"It's badly broken up here. I can't tell a thing." Phoebe flipped a page, then another.

" 'She became Mrs. McCormick after that. She'd

laughed at my advances, said I should concentrate on our work, that I would be rewarded. But I wanted her, not some sort of promotion, just her. But it was too late. I'd been contacted, told to bring the stones to Greece…to do away with…' "

There were whole sentences in a terrible hand, then, " 'It wasn't my fault, not my fault.' "

Phoebe put the pages down and looked up to her sisters' wide eyes.

"What happened then?"

"There's no more," Phoebe said.

"But what does he mean, not his fault?"

Phoebe collected the pages. "We're leaving and taking these."

****

Rhea's tunnel took them directly into the kitchen of their house. Phoebe got the milk from the fridge, and Dione retrieved the cookies, but before they could start eating, the floorboards in the living room creaked.

Rapid steps. Someone running. The front door opened and banged shut. They ran to the sidelights at the door and pulled the curtains aside. A black-haired man sprinted across the street, scrambled into a parked car, and peeled away.

"We have to stop him!" Phoebe cried.

It was too late. They could hear his tires screeching down the road, but the few moments of contact Phoebe managed had been enough.

His thoughts screamed out to her—*I've got it*.

Dryer was his name, and he was working with Professor Wick. She knew exactly where he was headed.

Chapter 14

The moderator called for everyone's attention and glanced toward Madeline. "Our first speaker is the holder of the Rupert Howard Chair in Celtic Culture from Cornell University's Department of History, Dr. Madeline Alleyn."

With Toop's brief introduction, Madeline took a deep breath and a gulp of water and rose to modest applause from a couple hundred or so attendees. She walked to the podium, acknowledging the audience while gazing around the dark, spacious room.

She had prepared a talk on the writing practices of Bronze Age tribes in Britain. After about twenty minutes, she concluded.

"As most of you know, the word runa, from which we get rune, means secret or mystery and is based on pictorial symbols rather than a truly phonetic alphabet, as you can tell by this next slide. To the ancients who used them, runes symbolized secret knowledge and were often tied to magical powers or otherworld experience, often involving secret rituals and outright divination. The exact age of runic usage is unknown. We do know they spread throughout Europe early in the Christian era, but in fact, runic symbols may have been in use much earlier throughout northern Europe. The practice may be quite ancient, even extending to the second millennium BC. As far as we know, though, there is not a common thread between European runic development and that from other geographic locations, like the Middle East for instance, where the writing was in cuneiform.

"I've been investigating a possible link but have not had much success establishing it. And without runes traceable to the area, a link would be impossible to find. Thank you very much."

Madeline nodded to polite applause and took her seat as Toop announced the next speaker. After several excruciating minutes, checking her watch often, she decided to skip the rest of the program. It was now four-forty, and she had arranged an early dinner engagement with a former colleague. She hurried out through a side door with the speaker only five minutes into his address. Toop gave her a nervous stare, but she pointed to her watch and gave him a weak smile and what she hoped were apologetic eyes.

At the front entrance, she pulled a large, crushable hat and dark sunglasses out of a shoulder carry bag. Feeling appropriately disguised, she strode down the sidewalk energized by the warm air. But after five minutes the innocuous glances from others became malevolent stares. People seemed to know her, knew why she was here, what she had done, where she was going. Unable to cope, she ducked into a store to get away from the crowd, reminding herself that no one could recognize her. There were too many people. The city was too large, and large numbers meant safety.

Minutes later, breathing more easily, Madeline mastered herself. She could still be on time. She quickened her pace and walked straight to Café Bosche, one of her old haunts. She had a singular purpose, to meet an old friend, and through her, take the first step in confronting a past from which she couldn't quite escape.

With troubling thoughts cascading through her mind like white-water torrents, she arrived on time at the sidewalk café. Her friend wasn't there, so she sat, eyes still darting about as she tried to conceal all of her face. She pulled the hat lower.

People were coming and going. A stocky man, also in a hat and sunglasses, came alongside and sat behind her at another table. Gradually her nervousness waned. Two men sitting at the table to her left began talking in tones not meant to be overheard. She inclined her head and immediately wished she hadn't. The strangeness of their topic was bad enough, but it was the familiarity that truly frightened her.

"I had a feeling the prophecy would be fulfilled in my lifetime," a thirty-something man said. "But the news reports on the Mars phenomenon are just media flubber if you ask me. The real action is with the moon, and no one knows yet what effects there are likely to be on earth."

"Any official word yet out of SAL?"

"Not that I've heard."

"Everyone is being cautious. After all, it's been, what, four hundred years since any discernable phenomena could implicate the prophecy. Everyone at the bank is pretty hyped about it, except the skeptics, but many of them are rethinking their position, Wight for one and Raknisson."

Madeline gasped when she heard these names from her past. The two men stopped talking. Without knowing it, she had turned more fully to them, exposing her face.

She spun back around. They continued a little quieter.

"It's pretty compelling. All of SAL's top brass are convinced already. But the conflict the prophecy predicts hasn't really started yet, except for those two young agents who were murdered."

Madeline's throat suddenly became dry.

"The Sages of the ten clans are probably on board with the signs and most of SAL's scientists, like Livingstone and Turly. Our clan better get charged if it hopes to hold off *Saĝtuku* and the other one. It's likely to get very ugly."

They were quiet for a while, then: "What does your wife make of all the astronomical disturbances?"

"She's so excited she took the kids to SAL's planetarium last night to celebrate. They manipulated the image of Mars and had it emitting red sparks directed at earth's moon. The words of the prophecy were streaming across the night sky. The kids loved it."

"My sister even named her first child after the first born of Tarkus. Hell of a way to commemorate what's happening."

"There'll probably be lots of baby girls named Prisca in a few months!" Both laughed and, after lingering a moment longer, left the café.

Madeline had been fighting an overwhelming desire to sneak away, but the conversation held her in place. It was the first time in nearly two decades that she had been near this group. She glared at them as they walked off, their casual change from dread to joviality sending a cold rush down her spine. Not really wanting it to, another conversation popped up in her head as the years melted away and the present congealed with the past. Almost eighteen years ago now her young husband had joked about this same prophecy.

He had tried to lighten her mood when he told her who and what he was, demonstrating telepathy and other abilities. Madeline had kept a stone face. She could hear her dead father screaming in her ear to run. In a strange twist of fate, her husband couldn't have known that she had been carrying her own secret into their marriage. She already knew about this group because of her father's fear. They had murdered her mother, after all. Her husband couldn't have known that she, too, had been born into this awful group and that she would never have come within a mile of him had she known he had the same heritage.

By then it was too late. After six months of marriage, she was deeply in love, was already carrying his triplet girls. He was everything her father wasn't, but her father had done an excellent job of it, planting his paranoia deeply into her soul.

Her husband had tried awfully hard that night to lessen the shock of his confession, trying to convince her that he wasn't a believer in this prophecy of theirs, that his clan wasn't dangerous like some of the others, that he wasn't a radical. And she knew she could trust him because, in the months she had known him before and during their short marriage, she knew him to be kind and gentle and sweet. She couldn't have known how inbred this group's propensity toward secrecy was, that these people did sometimes marry outside the group as he thought he had done. If he had only known of Madeline's family, he would have been surprised. But Madeline had remained quiet. She hadn't revealed her secret.

She left the next day without a word, without telling him she was pregnant, without telling him she really did love him, but that they had been a mistake. She'd done it so as to leave no doubt that something horrific had befallen her. No indication that she had planned it because she really hadn't.

Tears cascaded down both cheeks as she sat there absorbed in her thoughts. Apparently, he still wasn't a believer in the prophecy if what these two men had said was true about Jason Wight.

But it didn't matter. All that mattered was the safety of her children. She shook her head as if arguing with someone. She had once learned more than she wanted to know about this prophecy and had been trying to forget it ever since. But that was impossible when it was mentioned so prominently in her mother's note.

Madeline jumped when Charlotte Gentry placed a gentle hand on her shoulder. She bent down and gave Madeline a brief hug. "Gosh, I almost didn't recognize you in that hat and those glasses."

Madeline got up and returned her friend's gentle embrace. She removed the hat and glasses, embarrassed by her paranoia, but glad the disguise had worked.

"You look wonderful, Charlotte. Thanks so much for agreeing to see me."

Charlotte gave Madeline a close look. "Have you been crying?"

"I'm fine, just a bit of a mess today. It's the city— all the memories. I'm glad you were still at the museum."

"That's me, always right here. And look at you.

You look great—still thin but talk about a summons from the dead. I nearly had a heart attack when you called yesterday. I couldn't believe it. When I put the phone down, I sat there and cried. Then I got really angry. Where did you go? Where have you been all these years? Why didn't you tell me where you'd run off to?"

Madeline could see the hurt in Charlotte's eyes. "You have a right to be angry."

"You owe me an explanation."

A waiter startled them by making little coughing sounds. They ordered sandwiches, and the tension subsided a bit.

In a weak voice, Madeline said, "You deserve an explanation, but I can't explain it all right now. Maybe later, I promise." Madeline reached out with a tentative hand. "I never intended to come back, but I had to. I couldn't get out of it this time. Things are happening, things I need your help with. I have no one else to turn to."

"Why the hell now? What's going on?"

Madeline took a deep breath. "I'm a professor, you know, at Cornell."

"So, you went through with it. I'm very proud of you, Madeline, but—" Charlotte leaned in closer. "—we thought you were dead. I mean, Jason had every reason to believe you'd been murdered the way you just disappeared."

Madeline averted her eyes. "I wanted everyone to think that. I guess it worked pretty well."

"Yeah, it really did." Charlotte stopped. "Wow, you're actually here, and I'm still having trouble believing it. Your husband looked for you so long. I kind of kept track for a while. I even talked to him once when he was still searching."

"Please, Charlotte," Madeline said, her voice barely a whisper. "I know I hurt him."

Charlotte said more somberly, "Why in the world would you do something like that to him—to everyone who loved you?"

Madeline examined her hands. "I had my reasons."

"Reasons? Hell!" Heads turned, so she lowered her voice. "I'd like to hear them."

Madeline shook her head.

"Okay," Charlotte finally said, "maybe later." She took a deep breath and sat back in her chair. "I'll get over my anger. I meant it when I said it's good to see you again. But what did you come back for?" She paused. "Oh, I almost forgot. You were pregnant, or thought you were. Did you have a baby?"

"Triplets—girls. I only found out that day."

Charlotte's eyes widened. "Madeline—how are they? It must have been so hard. You don't even have a family."

"Some old friends helped. Jason knew nothing about them. They were still in graduate school at the time. I couldn't have done it without them."

"And Jason?"

Madeline shook her head again and couldn't help the tears that welled up. "I've been so lonely. And the guilt over the children, keeping them from him, sometimes I can't bear it. I feel so alone. It's like I have no past." She put her face in her hands and started to sob, her shoulders heaving.

Charlotte moved her chair closer and put an arm over her shoulders. It only made it worse. Despair like she had never known erupted from her.

She fought to conquer herself, to stop herself from making a spectacle in public. "I've been a real mess, and the girls are starting to notice."

"I'm glad you finally called." Charlotte pulled back a little. "I take it you're not remarried."

"How could I be? We're not legally divorced. Anyway, I have no life other than my children and my job. I don't even know what the legal ramifications are of what I did. I don't know if he declared me dead. I changed my surname to my mother's maiden name. I never talked about her, so he wouldn't know to look for that name if he suspected something. I couldn't bear leaving her name behind as I'd left everything else from my past."

"Do you want me to find out about him?"

"I know he's still around. I've checked."

"You have? Look, nearly eighteen years is so long. Whatever Jason did or said—" Charlotte hesitated. "Maybe I could make contact for you."

"You don't understand. I had to leave. He can't be allowed to find me. It's the children, you see, but I can't explain it more than that."

"The children? What do you mean?"

"Charlotte, please, I'd rather not right now."

"Okay, but remember, I know you. You love him still. What could he possibly have done?"

"I was scared for me and my kids, but not of Jason. I never told you about my mother. How she died. How my father warned me about *those* people."

"What people?"

Madeline shook her head. "I-I can't get into it now. I've said too much already. Maybe later when I feel more comfortable. Now that I've made contact with you, we can have a longer talk. But you must not seek him out. Promise me that. I didn't intend that by coming here. You have to promise." She clutched Charlotte's hands.

"Okay, but what are you going to do, disappear again?"

"No. I'd like to keep in touch with you now that I've made the first step. You know where I live and work. It's still dangerous for me to be here. I don't want to come back to the city again if I can help it. Maybe you can visit me in Ithaca. Here's my address."

She handed Charlotte a slip of paper.

"For now, I just wanted to talk and maybe take a walk and catch up with you. I plan to be back in Ithaca later tonight; their birthday is tomorrow. I wish you could see them, such smart girls. Do you have time for a walk? It's such a nice day for a change."

Madeline's pleading eyes softened Charlotte further. "After eighteen years of thinking you were dead, I have at least an hour."

****

They finished eating and began to stroll the crowded streets. Madeline intended to stay within easy reach of her hotel. She was nervous to bring up the real reason for wanting to see her old friend. Charlotte helped by bringing it up herself.

"You said on the phone you needed a favor."

"I feel like such a heel asking." Madeline sighed. "You know I never knew my mother. I only have a couple of her things with me—an old Irish figurine, a handwritten note. The note is what I wanted to talk to you about."

"What kind of note?"

"Only a personal note to someone who was evidently a friend of hers, an old fling, I think. My father gave it to me when I was thirteen, and I took it with me when I left Jason. He had never seen it so I felt comfortable doing that, because its absence wouldn't hurt the pretense of my death."

"Very smart."

"Horribly devious. I couldn't bear to leave it. It mentions prominently her work at the Natural History Museum."

"Our museum?" Charlotte said, pausing for a moment. "But you said she was from Ireland."

"She was here a short while. I don't know how long, but I do know the year she left because she was still there when she died giving birth to me."

Charlotte stopped walking. "I never knew that. I'm so sorry."

"The thing is she was an archeologist and worked—I'm sure of it—in the Anthropology Division."

Madeline grabbed her friend's arm. "Her name was Martha Alleyn. I was born in May, 1987. She must have started there somewhere early to midsummer of the previous year. I'd say June or July, nineteen-eighty-six. She hadn't been in the states long prior to starting and then she had a whirlwind romance and got married and then got pregnant. I'd like to know if there's a record of her bringing anything with her, a—a finding from a dig she had been on."

"Artifacts? What kind?"

"Ten stone tablets. I think she snuck them in. They still may be there. No mention of them has ever been made on any official announcement from the museum. I've checked. I need you to help me if there's a chance they're there. I need those artifacts, Charlotte, th—this connection to her. I think it'll bring me closer to my past, give me some closure. I-I feel compelled, somehow." Madeline's voice was growing faint again. "Please," she said desperately.

"Oh, honey, of course, I will." Then Charlotte paused, thinking. "You know, there was someone at the museum yesterday morning asking about a Martha McCormick, not Alleyn. There was no reason to make a connection to you."

Madeline suddenly felt faint. The crowd pressed in on them so much Charlotte had to grab her arm and pull her from the middle of the walk where they had stopped. They backed up against a storefront.

"He was inquiring about my mother." She turned to look around, searching for enemies in a hundred passing faces. "You didn't help him, did you?"

"Well, yeah, I did. He's a prominent archeologist. He showed me his credentials, said he was a colleague of hers, worked with her at the museum thirty-seven years ago. He was asking some strange questions about their workspace. You know, how the renovations had changed things, and if their storage cabinets still existed. A very odd-looking old man, very small, grungy, had a nervous tic."

Madeline held tight to her. "You have to be careful. He may be dangerous. Did he—did he seem odd in other ways. Did he do anything strange, or did you get any odd feelings talking to him?"

Charlotte shook her head, eyes wide. "I showed him around. The museum is vastly changed from that period. I told him those labs don't exist any longer. He asked for help, but he wasn't as specific as you've been. I half expected him to show up again today, but he hasn't. Tell you the truth, he seemed more pathetic than strange."

"Don't help him, Charlotte, but don't lie to him either."

"You think he's really dangerous?"

"I'm sure of it. It could be about the stones. Why else would he be around? I kind of knew all along that my mother's find was important, but maybe it's more important than I thought. There are some interesting inconsistencies, like the fact that they are rune stones, but they were evidently found near ancient Ur, in the Middle East, where rune writing of any variety has never been used. That alone would be significant. My gut tells me there's more."

"He's such a tiny little feeble thing, really."

"Just be careful."

"Oh, honey, now you're spooking me. Who the hell are these people?"

"I really don't know, but my husband was one of them."

"But he's so nice."

"I know, Charlotte, he is, but I couldn't trust who he was associated with."

"Why?"

"Please, I can't just yet."

"Okay, I'll wait until you're more comfortable, but what makes you think the stones would still be around? Nearly forty years—they would have been found by now and moved."

"I have a hunch. I've checked, and no mention of

anything similar to this type of artifact has ever been announced. I think she hid them there, and she died before she could finish her work with them."

"Yeah," Charlotte said, thinking, "you may be right, but it'll be a miracle. I'll have to find her workspace, you know, lockers she may have stored them in. If they even still exist. I'll do some digging."

"Thank you."

Charlotte took Madeline's hands. "I'll do it, but you promised to tell me everything, and not run again."

"I promise. My life is in Ithaca now, and that's where I plan to stay." She couldn't help it. She started crying, softly this time, but more from gratitude than grief. "I'm sorry. I've been doing that entirely too much lately. Let's keep walking. That'll make me feel better. Then I've got to get back to Ithaca and start putting in more regular hours at my campus office. I promised Dr. Harper."

"Harper," Charlotte said, astonished, "not Mark Harper."

"You know him?"

"His father and grandfather were former curators in anthropology at Natural History. You didn't know that?"

"Actually, I just found out, but Mark—"

"He must know you used to work there."

"Actually, no, I took it off my CV so no one would know. I wanted a complete break."

"You got one all right." Charlotte hesitated. "Wait a minute. You worked there—what—six months to a year or so. Why didn't you try to find the stones?"

"I did, Charlotte, believe me, I did. But then shortly after I started searching, I got married, remember? In all the excitement I lost interest for a while. I didn't get too far into the search, and then six months later I had to leave Manhattan."

"Had to?"

Madeline turned away from Charlotte's expectant gaze, not wanting to travel down that road again. "What of Mark?"

"He's in the division several times a year pestering the hell out of people."

"Oh?"

"Yeah, he's a real joke around there, but no one says anything because he managed to get on the board. I think he wants the curator's job in Anthropology." Charlotte suddenly looked thoughtful. "You know, instead of that walk, we could go to the museum and have a look around."

Fighting back sudden queasiness, Madeline said, "That's a great idea."

****

Madeline and Charlotte made it to the museum in minutes. With each step, a flood of emotions washed over Madeline, and with each step, she found it harder to continue as she drew closer to the epicenter of her fear.

Before long they were walking up the steps to the front entrance—then someone shouted her name from the street, and the pleasant walk changed to something else entirely.

Her progress up the steps halted. For many hours now panic had been a faithful, if unwanted, companion, lying just beneath the surface of her falsely calm exterior.

Charlotte seemed to sense panic overcoming

Madeline's control. She gripped her arm and pulled her close before the beast claimed her entirely.

They turned to see Gordon Toop, the familiar pipe stuck between his teeth. The picture of a smiling Winston Churchill flashed through Madeline's history professor mind, and, in the next instant, they found themselves rushing back down the front steps to meet him struggling to get out of his cab.

"My dear," he said, "I suspected you would come here, but I thought I'd at least be able to accompany you."

"I should have told you I couldn't stay for the whole session. I had an early dinner meeting."

"With me, I'm afraid," Charlotte said, holding out her hand.

He took her long fingers into his meaty palm. "Quite all right, ladies. Well now, what are we doing here, or should I guess?"

Charlotte looked quizzically at Madeline.

"It's all right, Charlotte. He knows about my mother's work and that I'm looking for the stones." To Toop, she said, "We're going to have a look around."

Two male strangers passed too close to Madeline. She reached up and pulled the hat a little lower, shading her face with the wide brim.

"Nice disguise," Toop said, "but the red hair and your stature easily give you away if someone was looking for you."

"I know. Let's get inside."

Avoiding the front steps for Toop's comfort, Charlotte led them to a side entrance unused by the public, gaining admittance with a passkey. The room they entered resembled a maintenance department as people in janitorial uniforms milled about, a shift change in the offing.

"Our storage rooms are over there," Charlotte said, moving them quickly along. "If those lockers or cabinets and whatever else we're looking for are stored, one of those rooms is the best bet for finding them."

Making it through the gawking workmen, she led them down a long corridor, at the end of which were wide metal doors. They entered a cavernous room, the ceiling at least thirty feet high.

"There are three of these filled with accumulated acquisitions spanning the entire existence of the nearly one-hundred-sixty-year-old museum."

The stuffed skins of exotic animals inhabited whole corners of the room. Lockers, some wood, some metal, lined the walls. Cabinets formed long lines within the room separated by wide aisles. All were marked with code designations for easy identification.

"Don't let our marking system fool you," Charlotte said in response to Toop's question about the tags. "We aren't exactly as organized as the Library of Congress or, for that matter, any old county library."

"So, you don't think it's as easy as going into the files, finding the codes, and checking the contents listed," Madeline said.

"I wish it were. I've checked the system already. None are dated. Some of the files indicate there's no content in some lockers, but I can't believe that. All of these must contain something, or there would be no need to keep them."

Toop scratched his stubbly cheek. "Some of these look older than others, and they appear to be grouped by age. Decades grouped together perhaps."

Charlotte nodded. "That's possible."

"Do you recognize any from your period, Dr. Toop?" Madeline asked him.

He moved slowly down one aisle, running his hand along the cabinets. "These are newer than my period, much newer." They walked along behind him, his mechanical leg thumping softly, then: "These, however...yes. I remember this style. Here—look, and there." He pointed to another adjacent aisle.

Charlotte nodded. "I see what you mean, but there looks to be such a mixture all throughout the room, probably not in any orderly fashion."

"They are grouped though," he said, continuing to look around.

"And then there are the other rooms," Madeline said.

"We have a lot to do."

Toop let out an exasperated breath. "And all locked up tighter than a drum."

"You'll have to check all of them from the era," Madeline said. "Remember, my mother probably smuggled them in. They probably wouldn't be in the records."

"But could she have hidden them that effectively in these lockers?" Toop asked.

Charlotte placed a gentle hand on Madeline's shoulder. "That's what we have to find out."

They stood there a moment, contemplating their predicament, checking several of the closest lockers and their locks, when the light of the room flickered, was steady, then flickered off.

The room went pitch black. Instinctively, Madeline moved closer to Charlotte and found her hand. Electric flashes played off the walls and ceiling in a far corner where more of the stuffed animals were. Dancing shadows, a faint crackling sound. The room became black again when the flashes died out.

Toop said, "There's an electrical problem apparently. The door we came through should provide some light."

They turned in that direction and could see the trace of light at the floor coming from the hallway. "I'll go open it so we can see." Just as he got there, the lights in the room flickered on.

Madeline looked up at the ceiling, waiting, wondering what would happen next. A man's voice came from around the corner where the flashes had occurred. They looked in that direction and saw no one, but the disembodied voice, speaking in frenzied tones, got louder, nearer.

"It's him," Charlotte whispered, recognition dawning on her face, "the man you warned me of."

Madeline looked around for a way to escape, but Charlotte touched her arm and whispered, "It'll be all right."

****

"Who's there!" Rasmusun's voice pierced the room, echoing off the walls.

Two women and a tall, fat man turned their heads and saw him at the other end of the long aisle. Rasmusun advanced on them as quickly as he could, mindful of the fact that he wasn't supposed to be here. Then he recognized the attractive blonde. There was a taller woman behind her wearing a frumpy hat. The fat man came limping up.

"Oh, Miss Gentry, so nice to see you again. I

suppose you're wondering what I'm doing."

"That had crossed my mind."

"I was just up to your office and found the receptionist—lovely girl—she said you were out and to go right ahead and have a look."

The beautiful blonde had an irritated look to her, but he didn't care.

"She doesn't have that authority."

"No?" Rasmusun said, looking up at her. "Well, you must question her about it then. She gave excellent directions to this room."

"I'll have to do that."

"I appreciate the help you gave me yesterday." Rasmusun gave her a little dramatic bow. "But this is proving so much more rewarding. All of this seems so familiar to me." He stopped momentarily, eyeing Charlotte's guests. "I see you're busy."

"I was just showing some friends around. We keep our inventory in rooms like this until they're needed again for study or display. We were just leaving. I'm afraid my assistant misspoke earlier. This is not a public access level. You'll—have—to…"

Her words were forced, and they began to fade as Rasmusun opened her mind as easily as a door might swing on well-oiled hinges. She perceived nothing because his penetration was gentle.

"Search for the stones—good lady," he said a little above a whisper. "When I return, you'll inform me if you have them."

"Yes, I will," Charlotte said in a weak voice.

His eyes were for Charlotte only, her rich blonde hair especially enticing to him. Maybe later, if he could find the time, if he could somehow get Erazmos what he wanted, he might pay her a little private visit. Having entered her mind, he now knew where she lived.

He gave her one last look, lingering at the gentle curve of her hips, and moved past the other two people without so much as a nod, heading for the corridor.

****

"What a rude little twerp," Toop said.

Madeline had quickly donned the hat and glasses again to hide herself as best she could. And now her palms were wet. As the man passed, a ringing in her ears began, and a pressure filled her head. She'd felt it before when those strange apparitions had inundated her bedroom. She thought she recognized his voice, though she had never seen this man before. Inexplicably, she loathed him. If she'd had a gun, she would have instantly murdered him, stomped and cursed his corpse. She wanted a knife to carve the bastard's heart out. Her breathing, heavy and fast in the surge of raw emotion flooding her, began to lighten as he swept down the corridor. With effort, she controlled herself, stunned at these insane thoughts.

The doors through which the man departed closed, and they heard again the faint, unmistakable crackle of energy. The light flickered then became steady again.

"Charlotte, are you okay?" Madeline asked, her panic rising in realization of what had just happened.

"Yes—yes, why sh—shouldn't I be?"

"You seemed to blank out on your feet," Toop said.

"Maybe it's the temperature. It does seem a little warm in here, don't you think?"

Madeline thought nothing of the sort.

"Who was that man?" Toop asked Madeline. "And

how many more people know of your mother's discovery?"

They had overheard what the man told Charlotte, though he had tried to keep his voice low. When Madeline didn't answer, Charlotte said, "I'm going to get my assistant and some student interns on this right away. We have to find those stones."

Madeline knew instantly that Charlotte's sudden urgency had nothing to do with helping her. There were other motivations now, placed in her by that strange little man.

Chapter 15

Walking as fast as his short legs could take him, Mark Harper had been struggling to keep up with Madeline and Charlotte Gentry. He began falling rapidly behind. By the time he spotted them again at the front of the museum he was breathing heavily and sweating. He stopped a moment to recover and took his cell phone out. But they were off again, moving to the side of the building and then out of sight accompanied by someone he could spot a mile off.

Staggering up the steps to the museum, he found his way to the offices of the Division of Anthropology. He had removed the dark glasses he wore while eating an early dinner at a sidewalk café a few blocks away and listening to the very enlightening conversation between one of his faculty members and the executive secretary of this very division. He smiled. He might like the life of espionage. He obviously had some talent for it.

He walked through the door of the main offices of the division and past the receptionist working late, not stopping as she tried to get his attention. Without knocking, he burst into the office of Dr. Samuel LaPierre, Chair and Curator of the Division of Anthropology.

Startled while standing at his bookcase, LaPierre spun around as the door closed, the receptionist blurting over the intercom that Harper had entered unannounced.

"Oh, Mark, it's only you. You could have knocked."

"No time for politeness, Sam. Thanks for staying over on such short notice. I've got to talk to you about something important."

"So I gathered by your call, but why all the damn urgency and intrigue. I've got a dinner engagement with some contributors."

"Yes, yes, it's always about money, isn't it? That can wait—this can't."

"I can give you fifteen minutes, then I've—"

"You'll stay longer if needed, I assure you. Now, where do I start?" Harper had too much sudden energy to sit. Instead, he stalked the huge office, talking rapidly. "Almost got run over by these damn crazy drivers." He eyed the wet bar in a far corner.

"Care for a brandy?" LaPierre asked. "It'll calm you."

"Yes, perfect, that'll be nice. Listen, I might as well go back to my grandfather's day since that's where all this starts."

"William Harper? But that was sixty years ago."

A picture of stern William, as he was called, hung in the foyer of the division along with Mark's father who also had a stint as curator. Mark Harper had grown up roaming the halls of the old museum in the days before the massive renovations that began after Spence Harper's tenure as curator.

Stern William ran the division with efficiency if not kindness and that attribute had come through in his portrait. The scowl he wore perpetually in life was painted there as well. Spence had been just the opposite and a much better fundraiser, but the old man was renowned, almost venerated.

Mark had interned in the division as a student while pursuing his master's degree at Columbia. He was well known at the museum because of his family connections and had once harbored a secret ambition to rise to the curator's position himself, but the doctorate in history had effectively blocked any chance of that.

The degree was not right for the job, nor was his professional stature great enough. That second fact was open to debate as far as he was concerned and he was currently in the process of trying to reverse his fortunes in that area, but he needed help from the man sitting across from him.

"Yes, incredibly, it's almost that old. It was actually near the end of Grandpa's reign here. He was in his last year when he sponsored an Irish national by the name of Martha McCormick. And that's why I'm here. Grandpa suspected that she smuggled in some kind of important find, but he was somehow never able to verify it while she worked here. Very mysterious."

"You're saying she did that under William's nose," LaPierre said with an incredulous look. "I doubt that."

"It's true, though. I was thirteen at the time, and he used to tell me these stories of a Martha Alleyn. Her name became McCormick when she married shortly after she started here. Anyway, she was distinctive in appearance and apparently a talented linguist and archeologist—a tall redhead. I've got one of those on my faculty, by the way, with the same initials, but her name's Madeline, Madeline Alleyn. Same weird spelling, too. She looks exactly like Granddad's description of the mysterious Martha Alleyn. And what's interesting is, I've just learned that Martha was her mother."

"Why was this Martha so mysterious?" LaPierre asked, pouring the drink.

"That's where my grandfather's stories get a little eccentric. He swore to me and my father that Martha and her assistant would communicate without speaking."

"Signing?"

"Telepathy."

The comment brought LaPierre up short, causing him to miss the glass. He grabbed a paper towel to clean up the mess. "You can't be serious!" He looked at his watch. "Listen, I've got better—"

"You've heard all the stories of William Harper. He was many things, but not a jokester."

"That does seem out of character, but telepathy, surely you—"

"That's what he said, and thinking back to those talks we had I think he believed it. Anyway, Sam, you ought to know that I just overheard a conversation between Madeline and your executive secretary, Charlotte Gentry, about the activity of Martha Alleyn at the museum thirty-seven years ago."

LaPierre was all ears now. "Overheard, how?"

"Well, suffice it to say I've had my reasons to suspect that my mysterious redhead was connected to Martha—you know, same name, identical looks—so I contacted Gordon Toop—you know him, I think—and I used him as leverage to force her to take this speaking engagement in the city today, knowing she usually avoided coming here. I followed her, and she met with

Charlotte."

"But how? Didn't they recognize you?"

He held his hat up and pulled his sunglasses out of his shirt pocket and placed both on.

"Ah…an effective disguise. I didn't know doctoral training in history included espionage."

"Funny, Sam. Also, these clothes are not my usual attire. I learned some interesting things that proved I was right to hire Madeline seven years ago out of our own doctoral program. The department about went apoplectic on me. She's a hard worker, but standoffish. A real bore, but very talented, apparently like her mother in many ways."

"So why did you hire her? Surely you didn't know these things years ago."

"My grandfather's description, her name…I don't know…the initials MA stuck out, and I just knew there was a connection because of her looks. The old guy really nailed Martha's description to me in his stories, and it always stuck, so when Madeline came along, well. Turns out I was right. I've waited a long time to attempt something like this, and the right opportunity presented itself."

LaPierre smiled and tried to move Harper toward the door. "I'm sure all of this is of interest to you. Maybe you have a thing for this Madeline. I'd encourage you to—"

"She's attractive all right, but no, well, I-I might— no, that would never—never mind. There's more I haven't gotten to yet. Apparently, Martha brought some artifacts into the museum that weren't cataloged. Ten stone tablets purportedly found near Ur in Mesopotamia."

"Pretty old…stone you say?"

"With runes on them, not hieroglyphs."

A surprised look came across his face. "Are you sure? That would be a first. But, wait, you've been on the advisory board for years. Why didn't you search or get the previous curator involved?"

"I tried. We even searched once, years ago—no luck."

"Maybe they're no longer here."

"Maybe, but it's worth another try. Your own executive assistant promised to help find them, apart from any official search."

LaPiere's eyes narrowed. "Yeah, well, we'll see about that. I'll have a talk with her Monday when she returns. I'll get to the bottom of this."

"I think they're here now. I followed them."

"It'll have to wait, but I'll check on this, Mark. Thanks for the heads up."

"From their conversation, I gather there's a good chance the stones have remained undetected for almost four decades, hidden somehow. If they're found, I'd like to be included in whatever team effort is undertaken and be given some sort of credit."

"But isn't your expertise European history around the Middle Ages?"

"Yeah, well, I'll expand."

"Just like that, huh." LaPierere checked his watch again. "I have to go, but I'll make some inquiries. We'll find the tablets if they're still here, and I'll call you when we do."

"I'll be waiting."

Chapter 16

The cell phone rang four times before Wick answered.

"Got something you ought to see," Dryer said.

"You got into the house?"

"Yeah, but I think they spotted me. Had to get out fast. Don't know why I didn't hear any doors opening and closing. But I don't think they got a good look at me."

There was a brief silence. "Tell me what you have."

"An unfinished paper. Very current. It was open on her computer. The date of the last activity indicates she'd been working on it last night. But that's not all. I did some looking around and found an old piece of stationery. Just a small letter, really. Handwritten. I can't tell how important it might be, but it makes some interesting connections you alerted me to."

"Bring it right over. I'm on my way home."

"Just tell me where."

"Good man," Wick said.

Around six in the afternoon patches of deep, shadowy spaces spotted the yard around Wick's house. Dryer had driven to the village of Cayuga Heights, a neighborhood in the hills just northeast of Ithaca. He turned onto the driveway and parked at a building behind the house. By the looks of the place, it had once been a substantial barn, but now it appeared to be converted into something else.

Walking on a stone path, he rounded the rear of the building and found himself in a garden area surrounding a small porch. One knock and the ornate door carved with rectangular symbols and grotesque gothic faces opened to a well-lit foyer. A wood bench decorated in the same symbols sat against the wall to his right. Two full-length gilded mirrors stood on either side of the entrance to a wide hall.

A fat lady he'd never seen before closed the door behind him.

"This way, Mr. Dryer. Charles is expecting you."

He walked down the corridor behind the waddling lady and entered the sparse light of a firelit room. His eyes refocused as flames cast shadows throughout the vast space. Following the lady, he turned left and walked toward two men turned in their seats, watching him.

Wick stood at the fire, pipe in hand. In the gloom Dryer recognized one man he'd seen briefly in McGraw Hall.

"I've just been telling my friends here that I've found an ally to help us in our work," Wick said, his mustache twitching as he smiled. "I had a feeling you would be productive today, Mr. Dryer." Wick turned and put the pipe on the mantel.

"I got lucky, I guess." The two men leered at him, giving him an uneasy feeling. The fat lady sat close to the fire and began eating some kind of cake, or was it a cookie. "Here, this is her current paper." One of the seated men passed it to Wick who briefly scanned it with those soupy eyes. The half-smile came back.

"Yes, yes," Wick said, his eyes darting over the pages. He finally looked over to his companions. "As I thought—more drivel." The others burst into loud cackling. The fat lady nearly fell out of her seat trying to recover half a cookie that had tumbled to the floor.

"Wait a minute. I thought this was what you wanted?"

"Oh, don't get me wrong, Mr. Dryer. You've done well. It's just that—" Wick couldn't suppress a snigger. "Her work is so incredibly banal. I can't for the life of me see how these things get published. Why, Edwards here is even on the editorial board of one journal she enters with regularity."

"I've tried," the man named Edwards said, wagging his head. "Oh, how I've tried to make them see."

Wick scanned the paper again. His smile faded. He cleared his throat. "Of course, I'll have to examine this in more detail at a later time. Take a much closer look." He continued to read, and his expression soured. "Yes, well…" Wick placed the paper on the mantelpiece and turned back to Dryer. "You said something about a note."

All eyes on him again, Dryer pulled the stationery from his lapel pocket and unfolded it. "It's very personal, some parts anyway. Appears old, too, but it's not dated with the year." He handed it over.

Wick began reading, his eyes moving rhythmically left to right. He scanned it three times maybe, but no smile reappeared. Wick turned his back on them and faced a fireplace so large a grown man could stand in it. Dryer took an anxious step forward, thinking any moment the note might ignite, it was so close to the flame. He wanted it back when this was over. Somehow, he meant to sneak back into the house and return it to that hatbox he'd found it in.

Thinking of Madeline, her beauty, her sincerity, guilt rose in him, tightening his throat. Was this thievery he'd done really necessary? He looked at the others waiting at the edges of their seats and knew he was being used. It was a first. He'd used so many others to get what he wanted.

These men, the fat lady, Wick. The hairs on the back of his neck prickled. He didn't trust them. He looked around the room. The place was even more cluttered than Wick's office. Ornate glass cases stood in the gloom against the far wall. More artifacts there, books strewn about, shelves filled to popping. Totems sat solemnly against another wall. Photos of Stonehenge placed here and there—some aerial shots, others from different perspectives. Wick seemed obsessed with it.

History professors. A bunch of collecting pack rats.

Wick finally broke the silence by reading words Dryer had never before heard spoken. They had a strange sound, something like Thurisaz and Uruz. They were meaningless when he had read them earlier in Madeline's closet, but now in this room, surrounded by these odd artifacts, Wick's pronunciation of them produced a chill down his back, and his mind seemed to go numb. The place was way too warm.

Then he remembered that Madeline was a linguist. But what of the author of this note? They had the same last name, which triggered something else in Dryer's memory. The author mentioned the coming birth of her child.

Then his guilt turned to shame. Her mother, dead only weeks after writing it, dead moments after giving birth to her. His hands balled into fists as he stared at it, hot now to have it back.

Wick swung around, and Dryer could have sworn the note passed through the flames. He caught his breath, but Wick raised the fragile sheet triumphantly out in front of him.

"Here is the origin of her strange theories," Wick shouted. "This short, hand-written message from..." He looked at it. "It appears to be a relative...Martha Alleyn. An archeologist, I think, judging by the contents." He pierced his companions with those limpid eyes, shining now with a ferocity Dryer didn't think possible in the man. "Claiming a discovery of no mean proportion, my friends, if it's real."

"What is it, Charles?" The fat lady had bounced up.

"Rune stones—"

The man seated next to Edwards slumped in his chair. "Just what I told ya, professor. She has somethin', and she's hidin' it."

"It does seem that way, Haldane." Wick scanned the note again.

The fat lady sat down, looking disappointed. "Rune stones are, as a whole, pretty insignificant, Charles. Surely, her theories can't be based on this alone."

Dryer could tell something more was there. He tried to remember what the note said, but none of it seemed important to him, and, for the first time, he wondered why he'd even brought it.

"Yes, Bertha, but they were discovered during a dig in Mesopotamia."

The fat lady choked.

Edwards exploded from his seat. "Meso—but, Charles, does the note give the stones' age?"

"It does."

"Well?"

Wick seemed to relish the suspense he'd created. He strolled to the end of the hearth. "Dated at five thousand years."

"But...but that's impossible," Edwards said. "Runes aren't that old and definitely aren't from that part of the world." He stalked at Wick. "And where are those phantom stones now? I've never heard of such a find."

"Nor have I," Wick said. He held the letter up, reading it yet again in the sparse light of the fire. "But this little note reads very convincingly. Have any of you heard of a Martha Alleyn?" They all shook their heads. "No?"

Wick looked at the grimy man, Haldane. "Suddenly so quiet, Brian? I must admit, you were certainly right."

Haldane looked up at him. "Sumerian runes, then. That's her thing, is it? And these stones she has are the key to some greater discovery."

Wick suddenly looked puzzled. "How would you know that?"

"Oh...huh, well, I don't...not my place to say. I'm just rememberin' an old friend, what he—"

"Ah, yes, I'd forgotten how long you've been in Ithaca."

Haldane nodded. "Born jist up the east shore of Cayuga."

Wick now looked agitated, like Haldane had opened his mouth once too often. "And you knew him,

I take it. Why have you never said so before?"

"He weren't liked much, was he? Got the same treatment she's gettin' now. Anyway, he left long before you got here, Professor, and I ain't heard from him since."

"We can only hope the same thing happens to her."

Edwards cleared his throat. "Why make a discovery of this magnitude and not publish?"

Dryer's eyes widened at that. Only he knew what Madeline had told him in passing. Her mother was pregnant, then died unexpectedly after giving birth. *Unexpectedly.* He swallowed hard. Died before she could present her findings to the world. This *must* be her mother. It was obvious to him. But where could her archeological find—these stones—be now? Did Madeline have them? He looked at the group talking in hushed tones.

Dryer cleared his throat. "Listen, Dr. Wick, if I could just have the note back. It's obviously a cherished item of hers. I'd like to return it if I can. I mean, I'm gonna find a way to—"

"My dear man, that is quite impossible." Wick folded the note and put it in his lapel pocket, patting it with his hand as if to emphasize the point that it was now his to keep. "You've done very well. Been of great service. But this note is enigmatic." He turned to the others. "It makes some strange allusions, my friends, interesting allusions." He looked at Dryer again. "I can't just give it back. It must be studied further. Things must be checked. For the sake of truth, you understand."

"Yes," Dryer said, his heart pounding in his throat. "I understand you've got what you want. A way to smear her." He was bristling now. "Ruin her reputation. Destroy her. That's what you want, isn't it? You don't care about truth."

"Don't presume to lecture me on morality, thief! You have your story to pursue. This note alludes to something she knows—something important she's keeping from you. Think about that. That pretty head of hers is full of knowledge she won't share. Now you have a basis to pursue her more vigorously."

"You have no right to it!" Dryer spat. He looked at the other men, on their feet now. He could take it from Wick by force, but not if he had to wade through the others if they wanted to put up a fight. "I'll go to her. Tell her what I've done."

"And what—confess to being a robber, have your reputation ruined, be thrown in jail. I think I know you better than that, Mr. Dryer. I assure you this piece will be well hidden even if you did somehow convince the authorities to conduct a search. You're compromised, Mr. Dryer. I suggest you go make the best of your story and leave us to our important work." Wick turned to his friends. "Edwards and Haldane here will show you out."

The other two men stepped forward, but Dryer didn't move. He probably couldn't reach Wick before one of his goons, probably that fat ass lady, called the police. She smirked as she fingered a cell phone. The idea of a night or two in jail, even in Ithaca, didn't appeal to him. "This isn't over, Wick." He pointed to the others. "Stay where you are. I can let myself out."

****

Dryer slammed the door and hesitated. Their haughty laughter coming through the walls felt like something physical, entwining him in their derisive pride. "Who are you to question us? The intelligentsia. And you, just a common journalist." He would have struck the wall with his fist, but he didn't want to advertise that he hadn't left.

He had to make this damn situation right. It was always like this, the hard-nosed persistence, his obsessions masquerading as good journalism. But this time the story he'd been in such hot pursuit of had left him like a bad joke, and he wasn't sure he cared. All he saw was her sincere face, and all he wanted to do was strike back at these four, especially at that skinny bastard.

The note was the key. He'd have to get it back, then he would go to her and tell her she had no idea what these people were capable of doing. She could be in danger. If she wanted nothing to do with him afterward, he could live with that, but he couldn't live with himself if something happened to her.

Dryer slipped into another room close at hand and waited. He kept the door ajar to listen. The shuffling steps were those of the fat lady waddling down the corridor. She called out, "He's gone, Charles."

"Come back and let's begin," was the muffled reply.

The fat lady retraced her steps. Light in the hall dimmed as she closed the door. Dryer left his hiding place and turned toward the door she had just entered, curiosity gnawing at him. It was something in Wick's tone. What were they beginning?

He crept to the door she'd come through, opened it to a crack, and gasped when he saw how they were now dressed. The four of them looked like monks in white, hooded robes. Wick struck a delicate instrument, producing a piercing ring. Light from the glowing fire danced on the metallic skin of the chime, making it sparkle red and blue. Then Wick shouted.

"We are here to honor the gods."

The fat lady bent over and lifted an urn from the hearth. Each of them stuck a hand in it and rubbed what looked like dirt on their forehead and cheeks. She put the urn down and did the same. An eerie silence ensued, punctuated by the constant crackle of flames and the slip of a burning log.

Wick's voice rose again. "Where persuasion, logic, and reason could not cause our enemy to do our bidding, this magical rite *will* bring about her destruction." Their heads nodded in disgusting agreement.

Wick described landmarks around Ithaca, its main gorge, Cayuga Lake, a river in the east, a town to the west, another farther up Cayuga's eastern shore, hills and small mountains elsewhere. He described the location in Ithaca of his property, this converted barn, and then he said, "Where we stand is the center of all things. Here the magic is worked upon our enemy, and out of this sacred space our will flows so that no matter where she is on mother earth the magic will not fail to find her."

Wick raised his arms. "Down through earth. Up through the heavens. Well and fire and tree that bind the universe above and below and roundabout. Hear and see and obey our wishes. Strike now at our enemy."

The dry air felt thick, beating at his face as he crouched in the darkened hall at the crack in the doorway. The heat flowing through seemed to be sapping Dryer's will, leaving him with little strength to retrieve the note by cunning or force. His only motivation now was to protect her from these madmen. He made himself small and continued to listen.

The four crazies yelled, "Let the gates be opened—well, fire, tree."

Wick raised his hand above his head as if to strike at something. He held what looked like a short, branched stick. "Let the power of Nauthiz, Ansuz, and Tiwaz compel her to obey our words."

The others started a chant, saying, "Nauthiz, we invoke your burning need. Ansuz, we summon your power over language. Tiwaz, we petition your power of truth."

Over and over they chanted it, circling Wick, his hand still uplifted, ready to strike. Then, in a moment that struck with clarifying reality, they invoked Madeline's name and Wick drove the strange little stick into the delicate sheet Dryer had stolen.

He hadn't seen that hand, hadn't seen the note it held, but now he saw the stick grinding into the fragile page with sickening force. He couldn't help gasping, "No." He would have shouted out if his throat hadn't seized. He almost fell through the door, but he caught himself on the frame.

Wick and his bunch were too intent to hear him. Dryer could only stare at the note as Wick continued to force the stick into his palm with a mean sneer like he meant to puncture his own hand. If Wick made the slightest move toward the fire, he would be forced to act.

But the four suddenly broke out in raucous laughter, and the rite, or whatever the hell it had been, abruptly ended. They removed their robes, suddenly back to normal as if what they'd just performed had been a skit they'd been practicing for weeks. Wick put the note back in his breast pocket, and they all plopped into chairs, apparently exhausted.

"That should do it, I think," Wick said. "Now we'll have to pay her a little visit."

Haldane got up in a huff. "After I get my bindrune back from those damn girls. Mark my word. They know somethin', and they got some powerful magic. You saw how they 'scaped us." He turned for the door but hesitated when Wick called him back.

"I thought all the formaldehyde you handle had addled your brain when you first told me your suspicions of Madeline. But now that I've seen the children up close…"

Haldane nodded. "Safe bet her kids are witches or maybe somethin' worse. We gotta work together. Only way we stand a chance." He turned and swept from the room with surprising speed.

Dryer just managed to anticipate Haldane and made it out of the converted barn and to his car without being seen. They were even implicating her children in some strange way. He wanted nothing more than to clear his mind of everything he'd heard in the barn, but he would never be able to rid himself of the hostility exuded by those people. He drove a mile or two before pulling the car over onto the shoulder.

Think, you stupid bastard.

Chapter 17

"The house is there," Vivian Turnpike said to her assistant.

They were standing on Woodlawn Drive a short way from the residence in question and had exited Vivian's tunnel a moment before at a well-concealed spot. She moved strands of graying brown hair behind her ear as the two of them observed the bungalow they had been watching off and on all day, making repeated visits to Ithaca from SAL headquarters. She adjusted the wool shawl wrapped around her shoulders. A scruffy, sandy-haired man stood next to her, unshaven and disreputable-looking in ill-fitting, baggy clothing. She wouldn't admit it, but she enjoyed his presence, though he smelled of old cigars.

"Think she's in there, Miss Vivian?" Bert asked.

Vivian Turnpike preferred genteel politeness in speech and loved it when people referred to her as Miss Vivian.

"If you halfway try, you can sense that she's there." Vivian gave him an aggravated look. "That thing's not lit, is it? It must be addling your abilities." He shook his head. "Good. We were finally able to get the blasted machine's resolution fine-tuned enough to pinpoint new activity. It went on the blink after we recorded the quantum distortions from Greece."

"We finally found a new one, then?"

"Yes, yes—oh, my yes!" Vivian said. "Brownedyke will be absolutely ecstatic. This is only the second one since Livingstone's contraption came online two months ago. It's a marvelous device, but it cost us two new satellites and three new stations.

"Oh, and that reminds me. Harold says he also spotted some quantum signatures in southern Europe. Not Greece, mind you. This appears to be new. He's there investigating."

Bert nodded. "Imagine being able to find them all now."

"A magnificent leap forward, isn't it?" she said, clasping her hands. "Brilliant man that Livingstone. This should garner him his second Golden Star, this time in a completely different category."

"And what of this girl's tunnel? Anything interesting, configuration wise, I mean?"

Vivian smiled at him. "Oh, if you only saw. I couldn't believe how young she was. I had no idea before coming here. Tunnels don't indicate age per se, except those learning are usually young and their tunnels have ill-formed morphologies and can't be used much. But this little rascal is different. The quantum flux detector shows a tunnel that's peculiarly strong and a perfect shape. Young *Puzurs* take years of intense practice to get it right, but not this one. I've never seen one better."

Bert kept chomping on his cigar, nodding. "How do we proceed then?"

"Diplomatically, to not scare them off. So many of these poor souls will be found and helped now, but it's difficult to convince them to join us. We'll carry on same as usual and submit the paperwork. Either

Brownedyke or I, maybe both of us, will have to visit the family."

"Should I adjust the data base?"

"You enter this one under the *barakara umia bar* category. If they accept, we can move them over when we identify their ancestry and clan. It can be quite a mess to sort out, but it'll happen. Clan officials will see to that even if they have to resort to DNA tests."

Bert pulled the cigar out of his mouth and spat.

Miss Vivian gave him a disapproving look, but then her head snapped toward the house. She put a finger to her temple. "She just tunneled to the backyard. Let's find a better location."

Vivian's tunnel took her and Bert to a spot in the woods behind a large oak about thirty yards from an old cypress board shed. It gave them a direct line of sight to three teenaged girls dressed in jeans and colored blouses, sitting on a rickety bench and eating cookies.

"She's the darkest of the three," Vivian whispered. "The one with the shiny, long black hair."

"T'ain't good that she got her friends with her. Means they know. How do we deal with that?"

"We don't for now."

"Don't seem right."

"Shush," Vivian said. "My, my, she's quite the beauty, don't you think?"

Bert took the cigar from his clenched teeth, spat out more residue, and peeked out from the undergrowth to get a better view. "She'll be a right beautiful woman in a few years." He hesitated. "Say, that other dark one, the little one with glasses, she looks a lot like the long-haired beauty."

Vivian nodded. "We'll have to welcome her

properly into the Community and teach her not to reveal her powers to outsiders."

"Secrecy code enforcement…yeah. But say, could these kids be sisters?"

He finally got Vivvy's attention with that. "What?" She put on the glasses hanging from her neck. "Sisters?"

"I don't mean twins."

Vivian was silent a moment, thinking about it. "The little one does look a bit younger but notice how the other two are listening to her jabber on like she's instructing them or something." Vivian then stared at the redhead. "The tall fiery-haired one must be a friend. She looks nothing like the others."

Vivian was about to duck back behind the tree when there was a sudden onset of multiple quantum distortions. "Bert?"

"I feel them."

The girl with long black hair lifted her arms and the bench rose off the ground, came away from the shed, spun around once, and slowly returned to its original place.

Vivian swallowed hard and felt Bert's hand on her shoulder. His cigar had fallen from his lips. "I see it," Vivian whispered, "but I don't know how she could be doing it."

At first Vivian didn't know what it was she was looking at, but then it clicked in her mind. She gasped, because the redhead was now throwing off visible quantum distortions similar to those Erazmos produced. Sarah Duckworth had captured them in a holotrace at great cost to herself. The girl's red hair seemed to be on fire, waving about wildly. Sticks and rocks and small branches were floating everywhere, even as far off as where Vivian and Bert stood. Wave after wave of distortions rocked the trees standing about fifteen feet away from the bench at the edge of the woods, buffeted as though by repeated bursts of gale force winds.

Vivian tried a weak penetration of the redhead's mind but couldn't break through some kind of barrier that had been thrown up. The barrier surrounded the girls, the shed, and extended out to within a few feet of the tree line. She tried harder to make contact, but her thought worm snapped back to her, nearly knocking her to the ground. Bert steadied her as they watched several tendrils of some unknown substance emanate from the barrier. They were bright, multicolored, and threw off sparkling red energy waves different from the main quantum distortions still buffeting the trees. The tendrils snaked into the woods as if probing, but in the next moment the barrier—a kind of quantum field similar to tunnels—disappeared. The redheaded girl swooned where she sat.

Vivian whispered, "Her lips weren't moving."

"What?" Bert said. He hadn't let go of her shoulder and had in fact drawn closer. Vivian could feel him trembling.

"Earlier when I said the little one was jabbering on about something. Well, she was, but she was using telepathy."

"We have two *Puzur* kids here?"

Vivian looked at the redhead. "No, Bert…three."

"And they can't be sisters," Bert said, looking at Vivvy.

"The two black headed ones sure do look alike,

though. Cousins maybe?"

"Got to be," Bert said. "Can't be sisters. How old might these kids be and when was their *dirig ed*, you think?"

Vivian knew what he was getting at. *Puzurs* experiencing the change, if not in the Community, could never have mastered what she had just witnessed. They would need years of intense instruction. So that meant these kids had been taught or else they were quite unusual because the timing was off. They looked too old for the *dirig ed*, but it was not unusual for the onset to be delayed some. Yet, to do what they just witnessed would even take mature *Puzur* class individuals years to master, but Vivian doubted anyone she knew could exhibit that kind of power.

"She doesn't look older than sixteen to me." Bert looked at the others. "Same for the other two. And definitely not sisters."

"No," Vivian said, still in a whisper though there was no longer anyone around who could hear because a tunnel had taken the girls away. "The *Puzur* birth principal discounts more than one per family and no multiples. That's a biological fact."

"So, we have at least three families in this area, undocumented. And well beyond the *dirig ed.*"

Vivian nodded, agreeing with his assessment for the most part. "Judging by the perfection of the tunnel, and what we just witnessed, and the way the little one was communicating with the others, their transformation is beyond complete and quite unusual."

"Hell, Vivvy, what did we just witness the redhead doing?"

Vivian thought a second. "They must be receiving

training. That's the only thing that explains it."

Bert was shaking his head. "We would've known, Vivvy. And if we had, we wouldn't be here right now. And what was that thing the redhead did?"

Vivian shrugged. "This doesn't make sense." Then she gasped as another thought rocketed through her brain. She turned to Bert.

"Are you okay?" Bert asked.

She shook her head, unable to say it, but felt it when Bert plucked the thought right out of her mind. He lost color and fell against the tree. Reaching into his back pocket, he pulled out a flask and took a huge gulp.

"Bert!" Vivian retorted. "You're on duty, man."

"Sorry, Miss Vivvy, it soothes the nerves, ya know. Bless me. It can't be."

Without answering, Vivvy went still and in the next moment, there was a faint crackling of electricity and a weak pop as a small tunnel opened and dropped a newspaper onto her upturned palms. She scanned the front page of the Community Daily International.

"Two more deaths," Vivvy said. "Their training agents don't know how it happened."

The headlined article read, *SAL In Uproar As More Lirim Ne Initiates Turn Up Dead.*

"Bastards!" Bert said. "To think that we've allowed his clan all this freedom with what he's done."

"It's not like SAL can go in and just remove them. I mean, the second factor and all. His powers are off the scales."

Vivian turned back to where the teenage girls had sat. "SAL lost another one today. Hasn't made the paper yet. This one had a young family. What an awful, awful time."

Bert nodded.

"I don't want to have to report this to Browndyke, but I must."

"Damn war. It's comin'."

She kept scanning the article. "Brains oozing out of their eyes, ears. No apparent trauma to the skulls. Imagine that. Too much power in that one—that Erazmos fellow."

"Second factor," Bert said in a faint, reverent whisper.

"The second factor indeed."

"Did you see the moon when it was full two nights ago?"

"Enormous. Ordinary people haven't the foggiest what it means. Their scientists are gearing up. No one knows how close it'll likely get."

"I've seen it in their papers," Bert said. "They're studyin' it mighty hard. Could even be of some help to us. First factor that is. Yeah, I believe it too. All of it."

"And the third factor?"

As Vivian said it, she and Bert turned back to the shed and stared at the bench, remembering the display of power they had just witnessed, the precision.

"You don't think…" Bert said.

Vivian shook her head. "I'm not paid to think such deep thoughts. The idea of triplet Puzurs in one family. Maybe it isn't allegorical after all."

"Allegor…what?"

"Symbolic, Bert—non-literal. The third factor won't be personified."

"Oh, yeah. Right, well, I've never been one to get all brainy about them things, ya know."

"Yes, I've known that too well about you, Bert."

They said a silent goodbye and left the woods, parting in separate tunnels. Miss Vivian's next destination was a little village in Bulgaria. She sent Bert to SAL headquarters in Manhattan, a few blocks from the American Museum of Natural History, to report to Darius Browndyke one startling fact. They'd found in upstate New York three young *Puzurs* of unknown clan ancestry. Vivian instructed him not to speculate to Dr. Browndyke the possibility that these kids could be siblings and for heaven's sake not to bring up the third factor. That was well above his pay grade. She would have to do it herself.

Chapter 18

The intruder had spooked them, but with their mother in Manhattan, they didn't have anyone to turn to except the Faals or the police, and Phoebe had nixed both ideas. She needed to think, so they went to the bench out back behind the old shed, eating a few cookies, practicing telepathy, talking about who the intruder could have been, about Sherman Rasmusun, and about their grandmother's discovery.

Rhea suddenly screwed up her eyes as though squinting directly into the sun. The rickety wood bench spluttered and creaked, wavered a bit, then rose in the air, their legs dangling some four feet off the ground. Rhea spun the bench around once and placed it back on the ground, smirking.

"Show off," Dione grumbled, coming out of that weird state she fell into when they were in the midst of doing some serious shit. She received an elbow to the ribs for the crack.

Phoebe looked over at Di. This time the swoon didn't seem to affect her as much. She still didn't understand her sister's part in all this, but there was one sure thing. Each time Rhea or Phoebe did something particularly powerful, it affected Di and, in turn, made what they could do even stronger. It felt like a surge of energy had coursed through Phoebe, making her think she could read hundreds of minds at once, no matter how distant. And that was just the start of it.

"You don't understand," Phoebe said, as if they hadn't been in the process of defying Newtonian physics. "I know what we can do. I just don't know how we do it. And I'm not sure anymore it's magic."

"What is it then?" Dione blurted out. "Are we back to aliens?"

Phoebe sighed at the stupid remark. "Yesterday I found an Internet site about incantations, spells, and charms. Stupid stuff." She glanced at the others. "We don't have to say words or use a bindrune like a bunch of dumb witches."

Rhea shrugged. "What's your point? How do we do it then?"

"I sort of asked Mom without giving anything away, and she nearly fainted. Then she turned..." Phoebe remembered how cold and distant her mother had become, not like her at all. "...almost angry that I would dare ask her a question like that."

Rhea nodded. "We figured she was hiding something."

"It's related to her work," Di said.

That much Phoebe knew for sure. She was researching magic related to runes, but to what end?

"How can Mom read those stupid letters?" Di asked.

Phoebe squinted at her. "I'd like to learn, if she'd ever teach me."

Di snorted. "Don't hold your breath on that one."

"Let's go have a look at some right now."

"Got nothing better to do."

Thanks to Rhea's talents, a moment later they were standing in their mother's study, poring over one of her papers.

"She says runes were connected to magic and secret arts. People used these symbols to mean something different, trying to tap into a source of power. You needed knowledge of runes to read what they were really saying in the secret writing."

Rhea said, "Do you think Mom's really a witch? You heard those men. Maybe she is and never told us."

Phoebe reached across the desk and pulled to her a thick binder she'd found yesterday. "It's called a lexicon. I found the language we heard in our dreams. It's Sumerian."

"How do you know for sure?"

"'Cause I found the words we heard, that's how. They're all in here, Rhea."

They thumbed through it looking at the odd words and rough English equivalents.

"*Dimma*, means instructions or directions, like how to build something. Why would we have heard that?"

"And why Sumerian?" Dione said. "How would that get in our heads?"

"That's what I'd like to know, but there's something else."

Phoebe disappeared into the closet at the far side of the room and came out holding a hatbox containing some of their mother's official papers. All had been addressed to Madeline Wight, Forest Hills neighborhood in Queens, New York, or to Madeline McCormick of a different address in Queens.

"This looks old," Rhea said. "I've never seen it before."

"Mom keeps it hidden for a reason. Just now when Dione read from that paper, it connected with something I found in here." She rummaged through the box, but the note on the old sheet of stationery was gone.

Then Phoebe lifted her head, her heart speeding up. She sensed the intruder's mind.

Following Phoebe's silent command, Rhea took them to their backyard.

Phoebe exited from the blackness behind Rhea, her head snapping side to side ready for anything. She ran to the shed and flung open the door. Empty. "Quick, take us to the front yard."

"But we'll be seen if I do that."

"Just do it!"

Aqua green flashes erupted from the black opening and Rhea turned on the spot, searching the yard. Phoebe ran to the street and recognized his car parked fifty yards away.

Another tunnel took them into the house, where they made a quick search, straining with all their senses for the intruder. No one. No time for anything else, they went back to the edge of the woods and searched the perimeter of the shed before entering the woods.

****

Earlier, Madeline's daughters had probably heard him in the house. He'd felt their racing steps as he blasted through the front door, but he felt sure they hadn't seen his face and maybe wouldn't recognize the car. He wouldn't chance that now. He parked well up the street, quickly removed the light jacket, and fast walked to the corner of the property.

From there Dryer sprinted for the shabby old shack and rounded the corner just as two tanned-skinned girls and one redhead disappeared into thin air. A crackling wind hit his face, the static charge making his hair jump. The dancing electric display vanished, but his eyes were fixed on the maple trees twenty yards away between which three teenagers had simply run from this world and into some realm beyond.

Dryer walked through the brush as fast as his legs could take him and was now well within the canopy, but he still hadn't found them or seen anything stranger than a soccer ball lying against a giant oak. He'd picked it up meaning to take it back to their yard to do what, he didn't know. Maybe use it as a peace offering if they recognized him as the man who had burgled their house.

He had to talk to these girls. He knew now his instincts had been spot on. What he'd just seen corroborated the eyewitness account from Stonehenge about a strange electrical phenomenon he wouldn't report until he had all the facts. That time had arrived. Madeline had a lot of explaining to do.

But how did they do it? How could they simply disappear like that? Or did he imagine the whole thing? Dryer stopped his march and wiped sweat from his face. No. He'd seen it.

He made it perhaps fifty yards into the woods, searching, calling, when he came upon a small gorge about ten feet wide and a little deeper. But it was the crackle of electric energy across the way that got his attention. His head snapped up. They were there, and then they weren't.

****

"Where's Mom's letter!" Phoebe screamed, anger seething in her voice like a physical presence.

The man spun in surprise and backed away from

237

Phoebe, mere feet from the precipice of the gorge. "How'd you—"

"Don't talk!" Phoebe screamed, and his face distorted as he tried to reply, but couldn't. Phoebe took a step closer. "Who are you?"

The more he tried to talk, the redder he became.

"Is he the one?" Dione said.

Phoebe cocked her head. "He's a reporter."

"Maybe you better release him before his head pops," Di said.

His breath exploded from him as Phoebe released her mental hold. He slumped over and nearly fell to his knees. "How'd you do that?" he managed to spit out.

Phoebe moved farther away as nearby trees started thrashing and swaying. Startled, she directed Rhea telepathically to do the same. "We'll ask the questions."

He held a cautious hand out and stepped toward them. "Listen—I-I'm a friend of your mother."

"Liar!" Phoebe screamed again, and she closed on him. His hands shot to his head as he recoiled from her.

He nearly stumbled over the edge of the gorge, but Rhea extended her hand and stopped him from tumbling over the precipice without touching him. "You stole from us?"

He shook his head.

This time he did fall, hard, as Rhea flicked her hand, and his legs were swept out from under him. He hit the ground with a grunt and cowered even closer to the edge. He rolled onto his stomach and managed to make it to his knees. "I don't have it."

Phoebe reentered his mind with force.

Dryer stiffened and groaned.

"He's telling the truth," Phoebe said, looking at the

others.

"Please," he said, both hands flat against his temples. "Please stop." He bent over and wiped a small trickle of blood oozing from his nose. "What's going on? How are you doing this?" He gagged and spat as if he were ready to vomit.

"Phoebe," Rhea said, "you better take it easy."

Phoebe had never done anything malicious in her life before controlling those two people at the library. But this power she now had seemed to be building in her, making her want to do things she shouldn't do. Di was right. She shouldn't be using her powers this way. She would have to control herself…somehow.

She felt a little better now that the man wasn't lying anymore. "Get to your feet. You're coming with us."

"Where?"

But darkness had already enclosed them, sweeping up from behind.

The inside of their tiny shed pulsed in an aqua green glow. Phoebe flipped the light switch.

Dryer stumbled to his knees, his hands flailing out before him like a blind man. "How the hell did we get here?"

He backpedaled when Phoebe stepped closer, and fell on his butt, knocking over assorted garden tools in the process. They would have crashed down on his head if Rhea hadn't been there to hold them with a look.

The vision of rakes and shears floating above his head left his face stricken as they floated to a far corner. "What *are* you?"

Phoebe turned to the window facing out to their yard.

"Is this the shed in your yard?" he said, looking around.

"Shut up!"

"It's our clubhouse," Di said.

Phoebe huffed. "Don't be so nice to him."

"Why not—he's harmless," Rhea said, eyeing him.

"No, he isn't. He broke into our house, remember. And he has something that belongs to Mom."

Phoebe looked at Dryer and stuck out her hand. "Give the note back."

"I told you. I don't have it any longer. Professor Wick—"

Phoebe stalked at him again. "Why'd you give it to him?" And then it dawned on her. "You're working for him."

Dryer put both arms up as if to ward off a charging bull. "Don't—please don't." But it was too late. He stiffened against the closed door as Phoebe entered his mind.

"You were, but not now. Why?" She released him.

He clenched his teeth. "I-I got in over my head. I didn't know who I was dealing with. I came back here to talk to you three. I know Madeline's in Manhattan. I don't mean her any harm. Please stop!" Sweat ran down his face.

"Is he telling the truth, Phoebe?"

Phoebe relented and walked back to the window.

"Wick suggested I break in. I know I shouldn't have listened. I came by the house and on a hunch checked the flowerpot at the front door. Bad idea to keep a key there. I saw an opportunity. But I'm not like them. I want to help your mother now."

Phoebe scanned him from head to feet then cut her

eyes away. "He can help, but we'll have to kill him after. He knows too much now."

Di snorted, but Dryer shrank back against the door, stammering, "You don't mean…You wouldn't…"

"She's kidding, mister," Rhea said, "I think." She looked at Phoebe who hadn't smiled. Rhea's eyes widened. "Phoebe?"

"We can't trust him. He broke into our house. Who knows what other things he has of ours?" She stared a hole in him.

"No—wait! I haven't. I'm not a thief. I'm a reporter, trying to do my job. I-I do know things, but it was only because of contacts I have in London, and their story of strange phenomena at Stonehenge."

Stonehenge. Wick. Phoebe's throat went dry. She sat down at the tiny table they used to play at. "What sort of phenomena?"

"Exactly what I saw you do. The disappearing act, the flashes, the static charges. What is that?"

"Never mind," Phoebe said. "Mom's got nothing to do with Stonehenge. She doesn't know about any of this other stuff either."

"I find that hard to believe. Anyway, I came back to warn your mother. They have the note. I'm not proud I gave it to them. I plan to get it back."

"How?" Di asked.

"I'll think of something." He was quiet a moment. "How is it possible that your mother doesn't know about these things you can do?"

"We're careful around her," Phoebe said, but Dryer's look demanded an additional explanation. "It's complicated. You wouldn't understand."

"I understand that what those people saw at

Stonehenge, what I thought must have been some kind of mistake or some sort of perfectly explainable phenomenon is now really—"

"Magic," Rhea said.

A look of amazement fell on him. "Well, yeah, I suppose magic would fit. People can't disappear, but you did, and they did at Stonehenge."

Phoebe cringed at the word again. Without even trying, Dryer's mind suddenly opened to her. Her eyes widened. "You read my mother's note?"

He hesitated but seemed to think better of lying, so he nodded.

Phoebe came closer to him. He tried to back away, but there was nowhere to run. "You better sit, but I won't hurt you this time—promise."

The images came at once and there he was in her mother's closet. He was staring down at the frayed sheet of stationery. It was very old and fading. Phoebe had discovered it yesterday and had scanned it quickly then. This would be her first thorough reading. She began out loud.

" 'March sixteen:

" 'Dear Lucian,

" 'Sorry it's been so long since I've written. Since my marriage I've felt it would be inappropriate to stay in close contact with you. I know you had hopes for us, but I'm happy now. John is a good man, and he needs me. Please forgive my schoolgirl antics in the way I ran off to get married. These past months, I should have had my old friends with me, but I knew I had hurt you terribly and I thought it best...

" 'The point of my letter is my work at the museum, my real work. That work has been quite other than what I made it out to be, for safety reasons. I thought I could trust the people who helped me on the dig, but I'm not sure any longer. You know some things, my friend, but not everything. I brought with me to America ten stone tablets of the most extraordinary construction. The tablets were uncovered near Ur, an unprecedented find for anyone in or out of the Community.

" 'What's really remarkable about these tablets is what's on them. Runes, Lucian, wonderful, incredible runes, the most unusual I have ever seen, some type of hybrid as there is nothing like them from northern Europe, in either Celtic, Anglo-Saxon, or any of the other indigenous groups.

" 'I've made a cursory reading, very partial, nothing extensive, but I can confirm they're from the fathers, incredible as that sounds. Two runes seem to have significant meaning—Thurisaz and Uruz—though I can't yet make much sense of them. There seems to be a notion of conflict. I also think I've made a cursory connection to the site in Britain, as incredible as that may sound. Imagine that. Lucian, the fathers may have actually built it!

" 'The dating of the tablets has already been validated at nearly five thousand years. Of course, that's our time frame, isn't it? All the discussions you and I had in Ireland over the problems our people have had and their inordinate devotion to the prophecy may be in play here. I believe these stones will prove to be relevant, but I need to start on a proper translation as soon as I can.

" 'My pregnancy has slowed me. I've cut back drastically at the museum. I'm due toward the end of

May. We'll need to talk because I'm getting paranoid about the safety of the stones. I've taken some precautions to assure their survival. The stones are hidden for now, in a safe place. Love, Martha' "

Phoebe lowered her hand and Dryer sagged a little.

"Why does Mom have this?" Rhea asked. "Was it never sent to this Lucian guy, whoever he is?"

"Maybe she made another copy and sent that one. But remember what it says. She definitely made an important discovery, didn't she? Mom never said she was famous. Why not, I wonder?"

"The note says something about a dig," Di said.

"She was an archeologist," Rhea said, "but maybe a witch, too."

"Don't know about that."

Dryer moaned and lowered his head to the table. The girls looked at him, but Phoebe went on.

"They were made for a reason…to communicate something, but why runes? And why does she allude to Stonehenge?"

Dryer lifted his head a bit, but Phoebe ignored him. "The five-thousand-year time frame would put it at the time of the Sumerians."

Rhea's eyes widened. "The language in our dream."

"Wonder what museum she was talking about and if those stones are still there. Aren't you curious about that?" Dione said.

Phoebe nodded. "The other day, I saw Mom looking at the website of the American Museum of Natural History."

"Our grandmother worked there?" Rhea said.

"It's not a coincidence that Mom was looking at

this note and the website. They're connected."

Dione said, "The stones are hidden for now, in a safe place, according to the note."

Phoebe thought about that one. "She must mean a safe place at the museum, where she did her real work, remember?"

They nodded.

"She must've lied when she came over from Ireland and snuck the tablets in."

"I like her already," Di said with a little smirk.

Rhea put a hand on Dryer's shoulder, checking him. "But why'd she do that?"

"She was afraid of something. The note seems to point to that, some danger that made her keep the tablets hidden. She talks about trusting people and making sure the stones would survive."

"She didn't though," Dione said.

"You don't think—" Rhea started.

"Maybe the stones were stolen from her, and she was killed."

"You mean murdered, don't you?" Dione whispered.

"But, how can that be, Phoebe?" Rhea asked. "Just for something that's thousands of years old."

Phoebe shook her head. "The older, the more valuable. Think about it. She clearly says in the note that she was worried about the safety of the stones. Maybe someone got to her. She had enemies. But it was obviously after our mother was born. Her birthday is May twentieth, and the note is addressed March sixteenth."

Rhea nodded. "So, if she was murdered, maybe the stones are no longer there."

Phoebe looked at Dryer, still groggy. "We have a lot to find out about."

Chapter 19

Thursday

The girls waited all afternoon and into the night for their mother to come home. She had called and said she'd decided to cut her trip way short. There would be a few surprises for her when she got back, like the fact that they had taken that reporter hostage. He couldn't be released, not until Phoebe figured out a way to tame him without seriously injuring his mind. He would make things worse if he were let go and allowed to write about them.

Phoebe was pretty sure their whole life now revolved around their mother's problem. In fact, she was pretty sure their little family was in hiding. Someone had murdered their grandmother, and she could count on one hand the number of times her mother had ever talked about her family and never their father.

When she finally walked through the door from the carport, Phoebe knew right away that something was wrong. The three of them had been sitting in the kitchen, waiting.

"How was your friend?" Phoebe said before her mother could even put her things down.

She stopped and dropped her luggage. "How did…" The silent stares seemed to make her reconsider asking the question. "She's an old friend I once worked with. She's fine. Tell me about your day." She grabbed a water bottle from the fridge.

Phoebe decided to push things. "You first."

"What do you want to know?"

With everything Phoebe had learned over the last few days, with what Wick and Haldane had said, the things she suspected were true, she knew her mother had been living a lie. Even without their new abilities, it was easy to see how tense she had become even with a simple question. Phoebe had enough of the lies and secrecy and was ready to unfold her mother like a filleted piece of fish.

"Not much to tell."

It was a lie, and her obfuscation didn't help.

"I just have some sad memories from the city, okay?"

"About our father?"

The few freckles their mother had to go with her bright red hair grew even more prominent as her skin blanched with the question. Phoebe had always been so proud of her mother's beauty—her porcelain skin, graceful brow, high cheekbones, sculpted nose, gentle mouth—yet, now, living a life of grinding fear, it tainted her natural beauty.

"That's why we never go to the city, isn't it?" Rhea asked.

Rhea's green eyes were probing, a new look for her, and now the look she just gave their mother seemed to open her from head to feet. Phoebe couldn't help being proud of her.

"I promise one day I'll take you for a whole week, maybe next summer. We can go there instead of to the national park. But right now, you three should go to bed—it's late. No more talk for now."

The moment Phoebe relented she could feel the tension flow out of her mother. They had struck a nerve with their harmless questions. This thing wasn't over, not by a long shot.

There were too many unanswered questions, and their mother should know what had been happening to them, that she had enemies in Ithaca, not just in Manhattan. And then there was Dryer, locked away in their shed under one of Phoebe's mind holds. He wouldn't be doing any reporting anytime soon.

****

It was an hour later when Phoebe decided to act. They had been debating the ethics of going inside their own mother's head for the information they needed. Phoebe would have access to everything, even private moments their mother had likely had, especially with their father. Phoebe gawked at them and assured them she would stay away from such things.

"This is different, guys," she said. "How else are we gonna find out if we don't use these things we can do now, especially since Mom is in some kind of trouble?"

"You think that makes it right," Dione said, "controlling people like you did with the librarian? And now Dryer. You can't just keep mucking with people's heads, Pheeb." She gave Phoebe a serious look. "It's not gonna end well. You're a bit trigger happy with this stuff, and I'm not gonna lie. It's not okay."

But Phoebe was shaking her head the whole time. "Maybe it does make it right. You ever thought of that? To find information that would keep Mom safe. And I am not trigger happy. I use my powers when we need them." Phoebe noticed their doubting looks and rolled her eyes like the only way she would see any sense was inside her own skull. "I'm gonna help Mom, and that's final."

Phoebe left them in their bedroom and found her mother at the computer. She was able to distract her with a gentle mind probe as she walked up from behind. Phoebe placed a hand on her mother's shoulder. The effect was immediate. Her mother sank into the chair. In a moment as brief as a flickering thought, Phoebe saw things that puzzled her. There was a handsome, dark-haired man with tanned skin. He was pleading with their mother about a prophecy, pacing, waving his arms.

"Madeline, it's not what you think." His eyes were familiar, his voice kind. His name was Jason Wight.

The scene spun to an old man handing her mother an important document. The surroundings looked official, like Ithaca's downtown courthouse Phoebe had been to a couple of times. Phoebe looked at the paper and heard the man say, *"Alleyn, with a 'y,' an unusual spelling."*

"A variant spelling, yes," her mother said in a cold voice. *"Distinctly Irish."* Then she seemed to grow nervous and quickly left the building, paper in hand.

A tendril of thought congealed into white walls, diplomas spread about, tongue depressors in round glass containers, cotton balls in others. There was an antiseptic odor Phoebe had never liked. Her mother seemed anxious as she learned of her pregnancy, but the doctor, an attractive lady with flowing black hair, was wild with excitement for the news of triplets.

Images wafted like smoke in a breeze. Phoebe was able to grab hold of one—a beige hatbox—and from it a strong memory of two pale hands holding a yellowing piece of stationery with beautiful, flowing script. They were her mother's hands. It was the same note Dryer had stolen. The memory was very strong, as though her mother had held this letter countless times.

Running through her mind were thoughts of ancient ruins and stone tablets with runic symbols etched on them. Phoebe bent closer as though she could see more detail of her grandmother's discovery that way. She pierced to the heart of the memory, but her mother had never seen these artifacts. There was longing there, deep longing for her grandmother's discovery, but her mother didn't have the stones. This relieved and saddened Phoebe.

Of course, Phoebe had already seen the note, but here, as part of her mother's memory, it struck a chord. She cocked her head and confirmed that the memory had something to do with ancient Sumer, the place mentioned by Wick and the others, the place where her grandmother had made the discovery. She delved deeper and more information from the note poured into her mind—Sarsen pillars, equinox, moon, runes, origin, circle. Her mother had spent countless hours pondering the meaning of these things.

Not satisfied and getting impatient, Phoebe unfolded the layers of her mother's mind as carefully as she might unwrap delicate crystal until at last other things resolved into a clearer picture. Her name at birth had been McCormick and Alleyn had been her grandmother's maiden name, a family detail the hatbox had revealed. But more recently her name had been

Wight, her married name. So that dark-haired man from the memory must be their father. Phoebe's hand shook when she realized she'd seen her father's face for the first time. Their house was void of any of the trappings of her mother's former life with him—no pictures—nothing.

"That's my dad…"

She needed to stay calm, but she couldn't help it. Her mother's memories sped through her mind in torrents: places she'd lived, people she knew, and one memory in particular of Grandpa John yelling at her in a horrible, ranting way. Other things Phoebe knew nothing about were revealed to her in a moment. There was a two-story brownstone in Queens and the museum where her mother had worked.

Hungry now for more about her mother's past, Phoebe went deeper still, and a feeling of power washed over her. She smiled in the rush of it, a familiar tingle better than riding a rollercoaster. Then a voice came to her, and she remembered that strange laughter in her head the day she met Wick and Haldane in the shop. But it wasn't a man's voice this time filling her mind with intonations and inflections, and this was no memory. It was something else entirely, something alien speaking in an Irish brogue, saying, *"Tell me what you seek…"*

The phantom's words echoed into silence, but other words were suddenly there, reverberating in strange, guttural sounds, the same tongue she'd heard in the dreamscape that had filled their bedroom—Sumerian.

When the words stopped, an eerie paranoia welled up in Phoebe so thick she wanted to shut her eyes against it. She couldn't prevent the panic that sprang up in her, causing her hands to fly to her mouth. And in that moment she lost control of the probe. It surged like a dagger, slashing at her mother's mind, snapping her head back as whirls of memories resolved then dissolved like billows of smoke into a cloudless sky.

Wary of shattering her mother like a hammer might smash pottery, she retreated slowly as from a dark, spooky room. She took a step back. Her mother started crying, shoulders quaking. A stab of regret pierced Phoebe's heart. "Are you okay?" she asked, stroking her mother's hair.

Her mother didn't answer right away, but soon she stopped crying and turned to face Phoebe. "I felt dizzy for a second, but it's better now." She looked away, staring out of the window at the dark, clear night.

"I don't know why I was thinking about those things again." It was a sad, frail voice, and she said it more to herself. "I shouldn't have gone to Manhattan." Then in a whisper, "I won't ever again."

Phoebe stood there, wide-eyed, when her mother turned her face up to her. "Oh, honey, it's late. Go back to your room and get to bed."

Phoebe nodded, bent down to kiss her cheek, and walked slowly out of the room, a creepy chill washing over her.

Chapter 20

Another special report on the moon aired in the five p.m. time slot. The moon getting nearer each day seemed to indicate the obvious. The Prophecy of Tarkus must be taken seriously. It all seemed ready to happen.

Everyone, including the most ardent skeptics, was now inclined to believe Tarkus's words. Even members of the strange sect, the Kentaurasians, were slowly coming around. They, unlike most others in the Community, had always been disinclined to be followers of Alexander Tarkus, who, in all his writings, had said nothing about the Alpha Centauri system as potentially explaining the origin on earth of the Community, a particular obsession of the Kentaurasians, and their namesake. Now, however, the evidence validating Tarkus seemed incontrovertible.

But the third factor had not yet arrived, nor was it any clearer what its nature was likely to be. Livingstone and Browndyke were in the director's spacious office complex on the second floor of SAL headquarters. They sat on leather armchairs, sipping cognacs around six o'clock.

Brownedyke's lit pipe sent gray smoke curling into the air, giving the room the aroma of Colombia's finest blend. An anthology of the works of T. S. Eliot sat on a nearby table. Deep in thought, Livingstone examined

Brownedyke's excellent landscape and seascape paintings near them, some of his finest work. Like master chess players working an invisible board, they were thinking many moves ahead, anticipating several variables at once. Brownedyke's short-haired dachshund trotted over to him, begging to be picked up. His large brown eyes stared impassively at Livingstone.

A crackle of static electric energy suddenly filled the office, accompanied by a scarlet glow that dissipated immediately.

"Paper's arrived," Brownedyke said. He got up and carried Buster with him to the receptacle next to his desk. He walked back slowly, scanning the front page and took his seat.

"Here's an article on detecting quantum fluxes. It seems you've made the paper again."

Livingstone shrugged modestly.

"I forgot to tell you that Miss Vivian spotted two additional people we need to introduce to the Community," Brownedyke said as he blew out a smoke ring while scanning the front page. "That project is going quite well."

"Better to get them before the bad element does."

"Oh, here it is. This should also help. I knew it was coming, but not this soon. Sarah must have given that interview right after the demonstration she gave us. A full-length article as promised. Do you like the headline?" He handed the paper over to Livingstone.

" 'Threat from Greece Has Community in Uproar.' Yes, quite effective I should think. This should raise everyone's hackles nicely. The picture of him in the act is a good addition." Livingstone sighed and handed the paper back. "This kind of reporting is good, but we must retrieve the rune stones. That's much more vital to our mission."

"I agree, but no word yet, my friend. We're searching hard for Martha's associate. We believe it's someone named Rasmusun. Our research turned him up and we've found no indication that he's dead. There were two older men standing with Erazmos when Sarah captured the phenomena. The older one we know, but Sarah didn't have a clear view of the other. If it's Rasmusun, he's obviously holed up on Evvoia and under the protection of Erazmos. He'll be very hard to retrieve in that case. Oh, and we found out he disappeared shortly after Martha's death. Quite a coincidence, eh."

Livingstone's eyes burned with anticipation as he listened. "There is absolutely no one else I can think of besides Hector who was involved and who is still alive. We have to find him." He took another sip of his drink and rolled it around his mouth, deep in thought about a matter that had come to him.

"Martha had given birth to a baby girl. I never saw the child myself, as I didn't hear about Martha's death until two days later." He gave Brownedyke a tentative look. "Martha had only been married a little over nine months. She seemed happy, though I remember a change in her after she arrived in America. I think it was shortly after she started her work with the museum that she met this fellow. I never met him myself. Never got the chance."

Livingstone had first met Martha two years prior to her coming to America and had fallen deeply in love with her over the course of a six-month stay in Ireland where he was engaged in research collaborations with members of her clan. That the matter did not progress was to his everlasting sorrow, but he had accepted her decision.

"Nor did I, Lucian, but I do remember that after she married she withdrew from her friends."

"She was with child her entire short-lived marriage. I did see her from time to time, and I do remember thinking she seemed happy."

Brownedyke nodded his agreement. "When I found out she had died, I never could find the husband or the child. They just vanished."

"Nor could I," Livingstone said, sipping again, and lowering his gaze to the floor. "Nor could I."

"I had Cyril do some searching through clan records. I couldn't remember her husband's name, which is understandable since I don't think anyone in the Community ever met him. They eloped, as I recall, so I had Cyril find the old marriage record. That was easy enough since she filed her marriage with her clan. His name was John McCormick. Cyril also found the record of the birth, first born."

"Was there a name?" Livingstone asked, coming quickly back to life from his thoughts and sitting up straighter.

"No—none, which is strange. I don't know why there wouldn't be one in our records. They do show the death as that of natural causes due to complications of childbirth. It seems that he just took the baby and disappeared without leaving a name."

"We know that he was not in the Community. The girl would be thirty-eight now, and for all we know is *Puzur* class."

"Well, that's a thought. If she is *Puzur* class, her

father could have placed her in one of the schools or else she would be *barakara umia bar*. How many McCormicks could there be in our records?"

Brownedyke's face went blank and, moments later, Cyril Croft entered the office. He looked like a bowling ball with a head and legs. He was Brownedyke's chief assistant, an *Atah* class member of the Community, being second born and without the unique abilities of the protectors.

"Cyril, Lucian and I would like to examine the records of all seven schools. Look for a McCormick girl entering about twenty-six years ago. Please do it from my terminal."

The answer came almost immediately. "Nothing, sir," Croft said. "I checked two years on either side of the date you indicated."

"That confirms that. If the child lived to be of age, she either entered school under a different name, which is unlikely, or she wasn't *Puzur* class, or she became *barakara umia bar*. We have no way of knowing the truth."

"But we should keep looking," Livingstone said, "and see if providence shines on us."

The men became silent, and Croft knew better than to interrupt as more often than not they were still conversing. He started to hum softly his favorite tune and fidget with a thread at his cuff.

"Cyril, look in the marriage records of all the clans for anyone in the Community marrying by that same name," Brownedyke said. "Scan about twenty years ago to the present day."

It came immediately. "We have one man named Sean McCormick fifteen years ago."

"No, we need a woman," Brownedyke said. "But, of course, if she was *barakara umia bar* there would be no record. *Atah* class individuals would leave a record, but since there's none that's a dead end."

They declined again into thought, sipping their drinks, and then Livingstone said, "We know that Martha's husband was not in the Community. We also suspect strongly that Martha's daughter, if she lived, was *barakara umia bar*, a *Puzur* class outsider and with the birthright, or maybe she was *Atah* class. There is also the possibility that she never married. This next thought is a long shot. Cyril, search any clan record for a male Community member marrying a woman named McCormick who is not in the Community." It took only seconds.

"Got it...a little over eighteen years ago!" Croft said excitedly.

"Ha!" Livingstone shot up from his seat and took long strides around the room. Brownedyke's dog barked and ran under the huge desk at the other end of the office. "Give us the name, man!"

"Says here, Jason Wight married Madeline McCormick."

"The time frame is right, Lucian," Brownedyke said. "Wait a second. Jason Wight...Wight, yes I know him, *Puzur* class. He's worked down below at the bank for at least twelve years!"

Brownedyke went silent again and, about a minute later, a man with a tan complexion, late-thirties, stepped out of a black tunnel that showed deep blue flashes around the edges. He had black hair and the powerful build typical of the founding father of Clan *Atuku*. He wore a three-piece suit.

"Darius, you called," Jason said, smiling. "Hey, thanks again for allowing me the security clearance to enter directly here. It's a real pain to go through the portals, however necessary..." He stopped suddenly, his voice trailing as he noticed Croft who he acknowledged with a nod. He then turned and seemed surprised to see Lucian Livingstone.

"Oh, Professor Livingstone, I've wanted to meet you for some time." He extended his hand and the men sat down, beckoned by Brownedyke as he pulled an extra chair close to them.

"Jason, we've been discussing some matters that, it seems, intersect with your life. These matters are of utmost importance. We think you can shed some light on a puzzle that concerns your wife, Madeline."

Jason bolted to the edge of his seat, fists clenched, charged with expectation. "My wife—you've found her—where?"

Livingstone and Brownedyke exchanged startled looks. Cyril Croft nearly dropped his glass of cognac. Buster ran back to Brownedyke barking wildly.

"Hold on now," Livingstone said. "We've only been discussing her, and her mother, or the woman we think is her mother. We need some information. Are you saying your wife is missing?"

"She disappeared six months after we married."

"But why didn't we know of this, son?" Brownedyke asked.

"She wasn't a member and I—at the time it seemed a good idea. Not many members knew about what happened. I didn't publicize it much through the Community. I relied pretty much on the outside authorities in a search, and I dropped it after two years.

I just wanted to forget. Dr. Brownedyke, I think you and Mr. Croft came to SAL after I started at the bank."

"You don't know what happened?"

"No, sir, I don't. I've presumed her to be dead."

Sitting in the chair next to Jason, Livingstone reached out and placed a gentle hand on his arm. "Jason, we want to pursue this a bit. Will you help us?"

"What do you need?"

"We want answers to some questions we have about a woman named Martha McCormick. Her maiden name was Alleyn, spelled with a 'y' thrown in."

"Alleyn, that was her mother's maiden name," Jason said, puzzled.

"And her first name?" Brownedyke said.

"I...I can't remember that. It could be Martha. I don't think I ever knew it. We didn't really talk of her much since Madeline never knew her. She died in childbirth."

Livingstone, Brownedyke, and Croft each uttered something incomprehensible. "What is this about?" Jason said, taking in their excited glances. "Is this about Madeline or her mother?"

"Her mother. We need all the information we can get about Martha Alleyn and her activities covering especially the last nine months of her life. Do you have any records? Did you keep anything?"

"I've kept all of Madeline's things in boxes." He looked at his watch. "Let's go have a look."

Chapter 21

Livingstone inscribed a large circle with his right arm. A tunnel appeared, dark and with a strange iridescent, purplish light around the edges, crackling with energy. A moment later they were standing in Jason Wight's living room in the town of Forest Hills in Queens, New York. The house appeared drab, cluttered.

A few minutes later, Jason brought to them several boxes full of records. "Sorry for the mess. I'm not around much. Mind telling me what you're searching for?"

"I don't mean to pry," Brownedyke said, "but every bit of information, no matter how small, is important. Why did Madeline leave you? Were you fighting? Did she just give up? After all, the marriage was only six months old. She may have thought this wasn't for her before too much time elapsed to make it more difficult."

"I thought of all that. I've had nearly eighteen years to think about those last two days. Always the same conclusion. We loved each other. I have no doubt about that. And, look at this place. It's crammed full with her mother's collections. How could she just walk away from that? Here are some other things of her mother I've kept." He pulled some items from the box. "Her mother was Irish, and I think some sort of scholar…archeologist, I believe."

Brownedyke and Livingstone exchanged knowing looks.

"I've kept these hidden away, but don't ask me why because I really don't know. I also have a few pictures, here." He handed them several old pictures showing Martha with her husband and several of her alone. There was no doubt then. Tears came to Livingstone's eyes as the past pain rushed back in. He held the picture of Martha and unsuccessfully tried to blink back the tears.

"You knew her well, Professor?" Jason said, surprised.

"Very well. She had quite a reputation in the Community."

"Wait, she was a member?" Jason said, standing.

"*Puzur* class," Brownedyke said.

"What?" Jason fell back into the chair. "That would make Madeline a member, but she never let on." He hesitated. "Wait a minute. She was so surprised that night." He shook his head. "I-I can't believe it. Madeline couldn't have been a member. We had talked the night before she disappeared. I was finally talking about myself. You know, about my heritage. But, that seemed to disturb her a great deal, so I didn't say more. I even explained Tarkus to her, but it was no good, so I decided to drop it for a better time. She was obviously upset over something. The next day I went off to work and came back home and waited for her, but she didn't return. The house has been just a shell ever since."

Livingstone put a hand on his shoulder. "We didn't mean to upset you, my boy."

"No, Professor, I need to talk about this. I remember calling everyone I knew, and then I turned to the local authorities. Nothing turned up. Her body was never found—nothing."

Jason quieted for a while and then as if coming out of a dream, he said. "Wait, your first name is Lucian. There's a letter in here addressed to a Lucian. I've read it several times." He found it at once and handed it over to Livingstone.

"May twentieth, two days after the other note," Livingstone said to Browndyke. He scanned it once quickly and then reread it more slowly, then aloud for the others.

" 'May twentieth:

" 'Dear Lucian, John and I are happily awaiting the birth of our baby any day now, though the doctors have assured me that it wouldn't be for another two weeks. As I expressed in my earlier messages to you, I want to see you before the birth so that I can begin to plan for my work as soon as possible thereafter. Thank you for agreeing to see me. I hope the hints enticed you and gave you an air of anticipation. This find may be important, but we have to study it fully. You know my theories, how I believe the fathers would not have left us alone, as it had seemed so for all our history. I think my discovery will open our minds, and I do think now they will confirm some of your own theories. All we need is the proper technique, which I think the runes may supply. I'm too tired to go on now in this letter. I hope I have the energy to see you in two days. I feel the birth is closer than the doctors suspect. Martha.' "

"May twentieth," Livingstone said again, "the day of her death. Labor probably prevented her from mailing it."

Brownedyke patted him on the shoulder. "We all

miss her still. Look at this. It seems to confirm what you were saying, but it alludes to some other information contained on the stones—even relating to your theories."

Livingstone was silent for a long while, then he said, "This is a direction I didn't expect. It's more urgent now for us to recover the rune stones."

Cyril Croft pulled something else out of a box, a scribbled note that matched John McCormick's handwriting.

"Professor," Croft said, heavily. "Have a look at this."

Livingstone scanned it. "It seems Martha's husband suspected murder. He must have been writing this to someone, but never mailed it—look." He handed it to Brownedyke.

"Do you remember any controversy around Martha's death? Even our records say natural causes. Cyril, when we get back to the office do some checking to see if John McCormick ever filed a complaint with the local authorities."

"Right."

Livingstone had moved to the far side of the large den, deep in thought. "She was healthy," he finally said, turning toward them. "I remember thinking at the time that the cause of death revolving around a difficult childbirth didn't seem right. Her work was important. I should have connected her death to it. The coincidence is striking, but I was distraught. I never even talked to her husband. What could he have seen or heard? He took off without even naming the child for the records. Why?"

"But the motive," Croft said. "What could it

possibly be?"

"There is every indication the stones were valuable in more ways than mere monetary value, judging by this second note from Martha. There is enough motive there for murder, I dare say."

Livingstone turned on Jason. "Why was Madeline so upset with your conversation that night? You say she was deeply in love, but I tell you some emotions run deeper and along a far more primal area of our psyches. Fear, for instance."

"But what could she have been afraid of…not me. I was always very gentle with her. We loved each other." His eyes had become nearly frantic.

"Think," Livingstone said. "It seems that her father suspected foul play—murderous play. He ran with his new daughter. He knew of the Community. I'm sure Martha revealed herself to him. He may not have had a full-orbed understanding of us, but he knew enough, and her death scared him. He instilled that fear in his daughter. And then she marries you, but with a skewed understanding of who we really are. You then reveal yourself, frightening her. It begins to make sense, Jason."

Jason sank back into the chair.

Livingstone went on. "She became as scared as her father and fled—like him. I think she was already aware of the Community, maybe tangentially, but was raised *barakara umia bar* or of *Atah* class, even though she was first born. She had only her father's opinion and understanding." He pointed a long finger at him. "Did you demonstrate for her?"

"Yeah, o-of course, mild telepathy." Jason ran a shaking hand through his hair. "I should have known."

"You couldn't have known unless you had purposefully peered deep into her mind, but that would have been intrusive, unless you were granted permission. Don't blame yourself, son, and forgive my forcefulness. Her father brought her up to fear us. That's the answer. By chance, she meets and marries a *Puzur* class member of the Community. She ran, Jason. She was terribly afraid, enough to leave all these precious items of her mother and her love for you."

"Why did he suspect murder?" Brownedyke asked.

Livingstone growled something unintelligible. "If she was murdered, then maybe his picture of the Community wasn't skewed at all, was it? They were only together a short time, and alone in their love for much of that. He never had an opportunity to see us, really see us. He was perfectly right to do what he did, to protect his only child. Jason, do you remember the day she turned up missing?"

"It's etched in my mind forever, the worst day of my life. I've thought about her every single day since. I still imagine she's alive. I wonder what she's wearing, what she smells like after one of her runs in the rain. I can't forget her. I-I haven't even remarried. The last couple of years, with Sarah's help I've been better." He settled himself forcibly and looked at them.

"She was taking the day off work to run errands. She was pretty vague about this, as I remember."

"Preparing to run," interjected Croft, with a huff.

"Let him continue," Brownedyke said.

"Yeah...well, I've gone over it a million times."

"Was there another man?" Livingstone said.

Jason stared past Livingstone. "I've asked often, but I always come to the same conclusion. She was very happy with everything. We were making plans. She loved her job at the museum."

"What museum?" Livingstone said quickly.

"The American Museum of Natural History."

"Now that's a coincidence," Brownedyke said.

"Yeah," Jason said. "I think it made her proud to think that she worked at the same place as her mother. Her master's degree was in ancient history, and she was thinking about doing the doctorate. She was quite a scholar, could read Greek and Latin well. But she never went back there. She never even picked up her last check. I finally got it—it's here somewhere. All her clothes are still in the house. It's like living in limbo. All her things—still here." Lost in thought now, he looked up, and said, "Sorry." Then he continued.

"I was just going to get rid of it all as Sarah suggested. Put it all behind me for good. If she just ran, she must have had help from someone to start over. You know, I did receive a phone call from her friend at the museum the day after, wanting to talk to her about one of the appointments she had. I asked weeks later, but she claimed not to remember. Later, when it became clear Madeline wasn't coming back, I contacted the friend again, but she didn't have any more information."

"Do you remember her name, my boy?" Croft asked with a pen and pad he had withdrawn from his pocket.

"Yeah, Charlotte Gentry—I remember her name."

"We'll try to find her," Croft said. "I'll get on that right away." He moved off a little way and began working the cell phone.

"You discussed the prophecy with her,"

Livingstone said.

"Yeah. I was determined to get into it all so she could be a part of my life in the Community. I felt guilty that I hadn't tried harder to talk to her about these things when we were dating. It felt good to get it off my chest. But, you know, I can't say that I ever really believed in Tarkus' vision. It was just something we knew and talked about—obsessed over, really. It was never a big deal with me."

"How did she react to the prophecy?" Livingstone said.

"Well, I explained all the theories. You know, it's hard for me to believe she knew any of the things I was telling her, or else she was a very good actor. And I know she wasn't *Puzur* class. That would be impossible to conceal from me."

"You're right," Livingstone said. "Her father may not have known about the prophecy. However, he knew enough other things to scare her. Talk of her mother's murder, you can imagine. Go on."

"It took her by surprise all right. It would be hard to fake the reaction I got."

"Did you explain the three factors?" Livingstone said.

"Yes."

"And how much of the third?"

"As much as I knew."

"Fully?"

"Yeah, I'm sure of it."

A look of understanding came over Livingstone. "Jason, was Madeline pregnant?"

At first, Jason was puzzled by the question, then a look of horror swept over his face. "No!" he said firmly. "I'm sure of it. She would have said something."

"Maybe that appointment was a doctor's office visit," Croft surmised.

"No, th—they never called," Jason said weakly.

"She certainly did a good job of disappearing," Croft said. "Kind of like her father."

"Pregnant," Jason said. Then it dawned on him. She was tall, so the recent weight gain didn't really show much on her, but extra jogging didn't correct it. Her appetite had also grown precipitously.

He looked up. "She had put on a few pounds." He put his face in his hands and began tearing up. "Why did she do this?"

"Jason, there is a chance that Madeline is still out there, that she ran because of fear," Livingstone said. "She learned something the day after that made her run. She didn't run from you, but from others. If her mother was murdered, you can imagine how her father would have prejudiced her against us."

"The prophecy?" Jason said, his voice strained. "It scared her, but how, why?"

"Precisely, but we can only speculate. If she is out there with a *Puzur* class child, she will need us, need you. And she may have more information about her mother's discovery that we can use."

"After all these years, I-I still love her, but how can I forgive her? What she did is…terrible. Can she really still be alive?"

"Yes, I think so, son," Brownedyke said. "But if she's still alive, you'll have to find forgiveness within yourself. Put yourself in her shoes, and I think you'll be able to." He concentrated and within seconds two others appeared in the room in a single tunnel—Agents Reggie Reynolds and Sarah Duckworth of SAL's enforcement office.

"Give them a complete description," Croft said to Jason. "Go over your story with them in detail, more than we've been through, everything, no matter how small or insignificant. They'll draw it out of you. Give them her background, friends' names, everything you know. They'll get to her if she's alive."

"Reggie—Sarah, report back to my office," Brownedyke said. "Take all the time you need."

Jason looked up as the two agents approached him. He knew them both well.

Sarah caught his eye. "What is this, Jason? What's happened? What's wrong?"

"You'll find out in a second," he said, as he met her anxious gaze with eyes rounded by uncertainty.

Chapter 22

Miss Vivian's tunnel reopened at one of the second-floor transport loci SAL headquarters contained. These locations, variously spaced throughout the second-floor central hall, were the only places most *Puzur* class individuals could tunnel into this very special building without the proper clearance. Security demanded this. Without this precaution, any renegade *Puzur* with a murderous bent could tunnel discreetly into any spot of the building unannounced, do great harm, and then tunnel away before being caught. The building was too heavily trafficked not to limit access, so a quantum block device had been installed.

Vivian's paperwork for the clearance she needed to expedite her added responsibilities in the Transport Authority was still days away. Without clearance, she couldn't go directly to her intended target, the director's office.

Exiting the tunnel transport terminal, she marched directly over to the office of Dr. Darius Brownedyke. She hadn't told him earlier what she and Bert suspected, but it was probably for the best. What she and Bert had witnessed was beyond strange, and it had her stumped. It was so farfetched she had let it drop. And now after visiting the mother of the little beauty with the perfect tunnel, she suspected the woman had lied to her.

And what of the other two children she and Bert witnessed. They couldn't all be the tall redhead's children. It wasn't possible to have three *Puzur* births in one family. Vivvy had come to that conclusion on the way to Bulgaria. The woman was obviously covering something up, probably for another family member. A cousin perhaps. Whatever their motivation, she would have to get to the bottom of it. Anyway, Browndyke had been out on some important errand, and she never got the chance to tell him about the unusual activity at that shabby little backyard shed.

She was furious at the rude behavior the tall redhead had exhibited on the doorstep. Still mad about it, she didn't stop to be announced by Brownedyke's administrative assistant. As she pounded the floor with determined steps, she quickly scanned the office and knew instantly that Darius was in. She also sensed Lucian. His presence didn't matter. In fact, it was perfect. She burst through the door and into the room and was promptly greeted by Buster. But she was too angry to cuddle the diminutive hound or to be coddled by her male companions.

"Vivvy," Brownedyke said. "Was the trip to Ithaca successful?" He then noticed her rancid demeanor and frowned.

"I need a brandy," she moaned, and the crystal top floated off the cathedral cut brandy decanter across the room. The decanter tipped on its own, and the brown liquid poured into a matching crystal glass, which then floated directly into Miss Vivian's outstretched hand. She took a large gulp of the ginger brandy she preferred before answering.

"Successful? Hummfp! If you call a door nearly

flattening your nose successful. The wench. Why, I never saw rudeness like that down home. Oh, Darius, this makes me long to spend more time in Virginia. I'm getting too old for these indignities."

"Sorry to hear, Vivvy, but you'll have to keep trying. I take it you never got to discuss the matter."

"Not even close. The wench wouldn't even give me her name. She sent her daughter away to her room. She seemed frightened, like she knew of us already. Why don't you accompany me back there now? I'm sure she'll talk to you."

She took the last gulp of her brandy and looked longingly in the direction of the decanter before Brownedyke took the glass and placed his arm over her fat shoulders, angling her to the door.

"Afraid I'm in the throes of something at the moment, Vivvy. Perhaps Bert could help."

"She'll run for sure if she saw him. Oh, well, I feel better now anyway." She licked her lips. "I'll try again tomorrow. She's obviously on edge about something. There is something unusual I'll have to talk to you about first, but it can wait until tomorrow if you're busy." She glanced at Livingstone. "I'll go back and apologize for interrupting her, but only after I see you first. Then she and I will have a nice long talk."

"Sounds like a good plan, Vivvy. Lucian and I are tied up at the moment. I may be able to help then. Just let me know when you've gotten her ready to sit down and hear us out."

"Poor dear. You know, originally, I thought the other two girls with her were just friends of our target. Then the woman says they're sisters. Can't be. She's covering something up. Appears there are multiple families involved.

Browndyke wasn't listening.

"Why, no wonder she's frazzled, poor thing. Yes, I'm sure it'll be better tomorrow."

"That's right," Brownedyke said, smiling and edging her still closer to the door.

"Wait till you see this one, Darius. She makes a perfect tunnel and such a beautiful girl, long flowing black hair, striking green eyes."

Brownedyke moved her out the door.

"Absolutely perfect tunnel. And the redhead produces the most unconventional—"

The door closed before Vivian could finish the sentence.

Chapter 23

As night deepened in Manhattan, the lonely figure of an old man looked up from the front walk toward the grand entrance to the American Museum of Natural History. He had been inside the museum numerous times, overtly and covertly. Each time he had failed in his mission, and each time the involuntary tremble in his hands started anew. Failure was unthinkable because the consequences would not be pleasant. He knew his master desired a report and he was finally ready to give him one.

"Master," he probed and in the next instant thoughts from far away flooded his mind as Erazmos entered with staggering force. To keep from falling, Rasmusun sat down on the steps to the museum, pulling his long overcoat around his old knees against the night chill.

"You are overdue. Why did you keep me waiting?"

"I haven't found the stones yet. The place has changed drastically, and they haven't kept good records. I will not be able to do this alone. I need someone on the inside to help me find them."

"Then find someone."

"I have. She's confirmed many things. We must find those lockers we used if they still exist."

"How likely is that?"

"Hard to say, Master. It has been nearly forty

years. I fear the lockers may be gone."

"And with them, the stones." Rasmusun cringed at these words. "When will you try again?"

"Tomorrow," Rasmusun said. "I think, maybe...yes, I-I believe tomorrow—early."

"Very well, but I desire periodic reports whether good or bad. Is that understood?"

Erazmos didn't wait for an answer. Instead, he sought to reinforce the lesson. The pain was immediate and intense as the strength of the transmission began to grow. A violent scream escaped Rasmusun, echoing through the lighted streets. He clutched his head with both hands, pulling at his hair he writhed on the museum steps. A young couple walking a few yards away noticed his agony. They exchanged startled glances, but when they turned to help him, he was no longer there.

****

Jason Wight sat in his house in Queens, the one he and Madeline had bought together more than eighteen years past.

"Do you think it could be true, Jason?" Sarah asked. "Could she really still be alive?"

Their questioning was over and Reggie, off duty now, had left to be with his family on the West Coast. With no family of her own, Sarah remained alone with Jason in his living room.

She looked at him with probing brown eyes, eager for understanding. She was learning more of his past, that brief interlude that was his marriage. He had rarely spoken of his life with Madeline in the two years he and Sarah had been seeing one another. She had known of his ill-fated marriage—but this possible outcome no one had suspected.

Sarah had also lost a spouse five years earlier to the clan warfare that was ever before them. But this was undoubtedly different. Her husband was dead, irretrievably dead. In his case, apparently, the dead sometimes return.

"You're trembling," Sarah said, as she took his hands in hers. "Could she?" she asked again more softly, fixing her searching eyes onto his.

Jason could hardly speak. This topic had always been difficult for him, and he spoke sparingly of it even to his family and never in detail to her. He swallowed hard.

"She could be. I mean, it's possible if Professor Livingstone and Dr. Brownedyke think so." He looked away from those probing eyes and the inevitable question she wanted to ask but then decided to face it. "If she's alive then that means she left me, doesn't it? And in a terrible way. Sarah, I could have a child out there. What kind of person would do that? A child," he whispered, but it was more like a groan. "How could I still love her after that?"

"But you do, don't you? I see it as much as I feel it in your trembling hands."

"No, Sarah," Jason said, pulling his hands away. "It's been too damn long. I lost hope long ago and now today, out of the blue, it's all come back. I don't want to have to go through it again. I can't conceive that she could still be around. I won't think of it."

Jason took her hands in his and fixed her gaze. "This changes nothing between us." He put her hands to his lips. "Eighteen years is too long, even if she is still out there. It's just been too long."

"Good," she said, after studying him for some time more. She came closer and laid her head on his shoulder. "Oh, Jason, I think it's time for us now, don't you?"

"Yeah—yeah, I do too."

But Jason hadn't kept the emotion from his voice. He hoped she hadn't noticed. Truth be told, he didn't know what it meant. He loved Sarah, but this was Madeline they were talking about, his wife, not some long-lost high school fling. And from what Professor Livingstone said, the spin he put on it, made it seem Madeline may have had a good reason to vanish, that even in doing so she could still love him. But how could she do it? Why did she?

He stared across the room at some of Madeline's possessions they had pulled from the boxes, ancient figurines she loved. He thought of the Claddagh marriage symbol Madeline had probably taken with her. Because of that, he knew the answer to Sarah's question. She was still alive, somewhere. He had been blind not to have seen the answer before. It was her favorite piece, and it had turned up missing once he began clearing her things away a few years ago. He'd thought he had misplaced it somehow, but now he knew otherwise. She was alive. His heart beat faster thinking that one thought over and over.

He didn't share this with Sarah. He couldn't. But she was right. He should move on. Finalize things with her. They were in love, were lovers. They both needed stability. They were right for each other, and Sarah would never leave him. He should think of the future and the loyalty she'd showed him. But in spite of himself, the only person stuck in his head was his long-lost wife. Her red flowing hair over white shoulders. A face stuck in time in memories *Puzur* class individuals could bring up at will. Whatever her reasons, whatever her fears, it seemed to him that she needed him. He couldn't stop thinking of her, didn't want to stop. And he couldn't turn away, not if she needed him.

He sat there holding Sarah's hand, thinking hard about the meaning of that Claddagh marriage symbol, what he'd lost, and possibly could never get back. Could he have it with Madeline again? He sighed, his mind in turmoil. She had made her choice; he had one to make now. He looked down at Sarah, kissed her on the head, nuzzled her, held her tighter, and felt nothing in doing so. Not with Madeline looming over his thoughts.

Chapter 24

Murderers, war mongers, sorcerers, her father had called them to Madeline's face, not seeking at all to soften his words for his young daughter's sensitive ears. And now these people were here in her town, knew where she lived. She had been found, but maybe not yet identified, not that she knew anyway. The old woman at the door hadn't known her name, and she wasn't about to tell them, but how to stop them, what to do?

Refusing to answer her daughters' many questions, she locked herself in her bedroom and paced the floor. From what this Vivian Turnpike person said, two things were clear. One of her girls must have inherited the abilities from her husband, but which girl? The old lady had mentioned the beautiful one, and while the three of them were attractive, Rhea stood out.

Whatever Rhea was doing could be tracked. Her activity had led them to their home. But the woman hadn't referred to the others. Could Phoebe and Dione have these abilities as well?

And what were those words the woman used, *Puzur* and *Atah*? Madeline recognized the language from the phenomena she witnessed a couple of nights before.

Sumerian.

How odd for the dead language to be in everyday usage in modern times by an otherwise ordinary person? Madeline had its lexicon. *Puzur* meant secret protector and *Atah* meant helper. Were there really two classes of individuals in this Community of theirs?

Madeline searched her memory, frantic for any tidbit that might help. Her husband had spoken of a prophecy implicating the birth of multiples. A set of three, mentioned prominently. A birth. The implication of triplets. A great conflict arising. The three would experience the *dirig ed*, the change, and ascend to a class within the Community that relatively few held and never more than one per family.

Puzur.

Jason told her these things in passing, finally ready to reveal himself as he never could prior to their marriage. Or was it that she had never let him? Always averse to the mysterious, she was sure that she'd blocked out many signals. She'd loved him so much. Could it be she simply refused to heed the inner warnings? Her antennae pointed unwaveringly at shadowy things to help her avoid them, but had she suppressed it for romance, for him? She remembered these things now, hoping beyond hope that it was not so, that it was only Rhea, that Phoebe and Dione couldn't be a part of this, too. This prophecy of theirs would be nullified if that was the case. They could still be safe from all the implications Jason had spoken of.

Madeline was still pacing the floor of her bedroom when her hair rose on end. She heard a faint crackling of static electricity as aqua green electric flashes filled the room. Her daughters stepped out of a large black hole parting the air in her bedroom. They had guilty looks on their faces.

As usual, Phoebe spoke up first. "We have to talk

to you, Mom."

Madeline plopped down on the bed, her legs too weak to stand. "Oh, honey, why didn't you come to me before now?"

"We should have," Phoebe said. "We know why that lady came here today. I looked inside her head and found out before she left."

Madeline closed her eyes, a heavy pressure building around her. "You too?" she sighed. But before Phoebe could answer, Madeline looked at Dione, not wanting to hear the inevitable answer.

Dione gave her mother that smirk of a smile. "I can't do much, but I'm getting better."

Madeline nodded, trying to understand how it had come to this. The planning, the precautions, all for naught. More of the prophecy burst into her mind from that awful night. Jason's thoughts. Multiples. Impossible for the Community. It had never happened in an unbelievably long history. But then it had happened. To her and Jason. She had carried three babies. Three beautiful girls, all with *Puzur* chromosome Z. *Puzur* triplets.

Only firstborns in a family could normally inherit the Z genetic signature, but more than one per family was supposed to be impossible. He'd explained these fun facts, as he put it, thinking she would be interested, surprised no doubt, but able to cope. He was wrong.

It was an immutable dictum. Triple births. More than one *Puzur*. It was all laughable to most members of the Community, even to those who held to the prophecy with cult-like devotion. It flew in the face of facts that had several millennia of attestation. The *Puzur* birth principle was a biological certainly so deeply ingrained in the collective consciousness of the Community that it was unchallengeable, like the law of gravity.

But the great Tarkus, as Jason called him, had spoken, given his interpretation and people accepted his word as dogma. Fanatics fought over these seemingly harmless things. *Puzur* class firstborn triplets would come. The third factor would be individuals, would match up against the second factor, and a great war would follow.

Madeline should have been happy, but, instead, news of the coming births had been like the sea crushing her in its dark depths.

Rhea spoke to her, breaking her thoughts. "Why did that lady want to see me?"

Madeline shook her head. "You don't have to get involved. We won't."

"Why? What's the deal, Mom?" Rhea asked.

"These people are dangerous," Madeline snapped. She caught herself. Anger wouldn't help.

"That's why you left our father," Phoebe said.

Madeline felt naked before her own daughters, her soul laid bare. "How did you know that?"

Phoebe's piercing, hawk-like eyes bored in on Madeline. "*It started happening last weekend,*" she said telepathically. "It's easy now for us to read minds, even from miles away. But I don't know how we do it."

Madeline cleared her throat and opened her mouth. Closed it again. She could find nothing to say.

Phoebe placed a hand on her mother's shoulder. "We should have come to you sooner."

Madeline shook her head. "It isn't your fault. I should have known this would happen. Your father tried to tell me, but I panicked."

"Does it have anything to do with our grandmother being murdered?"

"Or the rune stones she discovered?" Rhea asked.

"How did you—No, no don't tell me. I know already."

Phoebe shrugged. "It wasn't really by our powers. We've been poking around the closet in your study and found that box you have. There was a note in it. It was our grandmother writing to someone named Lucian, but the name on the piece of paper was McCormick. We didn't recognize that."

"It's my birth name," Madeline confessed, flinching as all her secrets were spilling out.

Phoebe nodded. "We read the note. She was an archeologist and had made a discovery."

"My father was very proud of her accomplishments. It's all I really knew of her growing up. She's why I became a professor. I wanted to—I felt I would be closer to her if I became a scholar and studied some of the things that interested her."

Dione cleared her throat. "We found out you've been studying magic and runes. We think what we do might be magic."

"And that would make us witches," Rhea said.

Phoebe gave her an expectant look, but Madeline shook her head, tensing at their misunderstanding. "You mustn't make those kinds of connections. My research is more complicated than that." She stopped, trying to find the right words. "I don't have your abilities, but they are inherited. Your father told me that night that no one understands how the group came to be. I get the feeling these people grapple with trying to understand that one thing. In fact…" Madeline stood, a new thought entering into an old dilemma. "Maybe that's what my mother was so excited about. Finding their origins. But then something scared her, some kind of threat. My father said these people were dangerous, and they—" She put her hands to her mouth, afraid to say the words.

"They murdered her," Phoebe said. "I know that's what you believe, because I read your mind."

Madeline just looked at her, accepting this as a new normal in her life. "I believed what my father believed. He took us far away when I was only hours old. Eventually, we came back to New York to settle down when he thought it was safe. I grew up in the city. I don't believe I ever told you that. In Queens. But he was always nervous, unsettled. It took many years off his life, and he just gave up and died very unhappily, when I was twenty."

The girls went to her, and they all embraced.

"Don't be afraid," Rhea said, her lips quivering. "We won't let anything happen to you."

Madeline wiped her eyes. "I can still hear your grandfather saying, 'Don't trust those damn people; they murdered your momma,' with his face going so red. He said much worse things too. These people may be sorcerers. I can't even believe I would say such a thing in the twenty-first century, but it's true."

Phoebe drew closer. "Why did you abandon our dad?"

"Oh, honey, abandon is too strong a word. It all scared me so much, but I was willing to listen to him. I trusted him. I knew he was a good man."

"Then, why?"

Madeline shook her head. "I don't want to tell you." Then she looked at Phoebe. "You probably know already, don't you?"

"I saw something about a prophecy. He was telling you something about it."

Madeline nodded. "The next day is when I got the news from the doctor. I panicked, and, in the next two hours, I planned out the rest of my life to protect you from these people. I've obviously failed."

"We don't need protecting anymore," Phoebe said.

"But now we've been found. They know about Rhea, but maybe not you and Dione."

"No, not about Di and me," Phoebe said. "I didn't see it in that woman's mind. But why is this prophecy important?"

Madeline shook her head at the question. "We can't let them find out that you and Di have it too. Do you understand? It's the very thing they're looking for to stop the prophecy before the conflict."

"They want to kill us?" Phoebe said, wide-eyed.

"For different reasons, I think. That's why I left New York. They're violent, and I didn't want anything to happen to your father or you. I *had* to get out. All I saw was my poor mother at the hands of these monsters. I didn't want that to be me or you. You have to understand, Phoebe. It's you three they want."

Madeline could see Phoebe thinking behind those piercing, perceptive eyes. She knew her daughter well, knew it would gnaw at her. She wouldn't let it lie.

"Maybe all of this is related," Phoebe said, nodding. "I mean, our grandmother's murder and this prophecy thing that we're connected to."

Madeline remembered something. "The other

morning as you slept, there was…I don't know…a phenomenon in the house. I became aware of it as I tried to wake, but then I thought it was all in my head, like I was losing my mind. It was too strange."

The girls looked at one another. "We had a dream with these weird words in it."

"It's true then. It did happen." The confirmation didn't relieve her. "The words were Sumerian."

"We know. We looked some of them up in that book we found in your office."

"I caught a few of them. *Ligin* means tablet or maybe a school text. Come to think of it, that word could refer to the stone tablets she found. What others do you remember?"

They went over the words they had dreamed. All seemed to Madeline to be connected except for the ones that indicated stone pillar and circle. She was brought out of her concentrated thought by Dione.

"Where are the rune stones now, Mom?"

"It's not important." Madeline gave each of them hard looks. "None of you should use your powers again until we figure out what we'll do next. I don't think that lady will be back for a couple of days, but even if she comes back tomorrow, I may be able to put them off again."

But Phoebe was shaking her head. "One little peek inside your mind."

Madeline nodded, understanding what she meant. "Then we'll have to move to a hotel room for a few days until I'm able to rent a house."

"We can't leave," Phoebe said. "We just can't. Wait! That guy, Lucian, our grandmother mentions. She trusted him. Maybe he's still around. We ought to talk to him—get him to help us."

"What about our father?" Rhea said. "He can help."

"Yeah, they could all help us now!" Dione's eyes, more red now than blue, were flashing wildly.

Madeline listened to them, trying for their sake not to panic. "They know where we live. It'll just be for a little while then we'll come back." She knew differently, but she wasn't going to admit it. They would have to leave town for good, abandon everything, disappear like she and her father had once done. "Promise me you won't use your powers anymore until we contact someone. You'll be found that way."

"But we ought to find our father," Phoebe said hopefully. "He can help."

"We'll see," was all Madeline would say.

A decision had to be made—tonight, the next day, she couldn't put it off. Jason had convinced Madeline he was no zealot. She believed him and thought for the first time that there might be more like him. Like Phoebe said, maybe they could get help.

Having allowed the girls to remain in her king-sized bed, she began pacing again after switching on the small television set, for once needing the distraction. A news program was just winding down. A reporter with blonde hair and full red lips was near the end of a segment. She seemed to have a sound grasp of the science behind the disturbances.

Apparently, this same report had been broadcast at the five o'clock hour. The local Ithaca affiliate had carried it then and decided to rebroadcast it now at this hour. Madeline hadn't seen it earlier, but it held her attention now. She remembered all the telescopes people were buying in New York.

Linda Wheil was saying toward the end, "...the orbit of the moon now appears to be declining steadily. LIDAR measurements are being made every few hours at select locations around the world. To put this in perspective, the moon is now twenty-four thousand miles closer to the earth from where it is supposed to be. Reports from around the globe are showing various amounts of tidal disturbances. Five hundred deaths have already been attributed to these events.

"That concludes this week's special report, but before I sign off, another unrelated matter has come to my attention. It is of utmost importance that the daughter of Martha McCormick contact the newsroom at KABC in New York City. The number is at the bottom of the screen. Madeline, if you're out there, please respond as information of utmost importance believed to be in your possession is needed. This is Linda Wheil saying thank you and good night."

A buzzing sound invaded Madeline's mind. What she heard didn't quite register. The girls sat up, looking at their stunned mother.

"Did you hear that?" Phoebe asked. "That woman said our grandmother's name, and yours. How could that happen?"

A glass of water slipped from Madeline's fingers and crashed to the floor, splattering its contents. At first, she hadn't realized she dropped it, then her mind clicked.

"Please!" she said to them, "Help me with this mess!"

An internal struggle of Jupiter-sized magnitude

ensued as Madeline receded into a twilight zone between realities. Why contact her in this fashion when they already knew where she lived? Then she remembered that Vivian Turnpike didn't know her name. Could this be a separate, independent attempt to locate her, made by Jason perhaps, but why this way and why now after all these years?

The older lady on the doorstep did seem harmless enough, and, as Madeline had told her girls, she hadn't run from her husband out of fear of him, but more of what could happen to him, to them all. The new facts seemed puzzling. That old lady was mostly harmless. But Madeline's father had painted them all as monsters. The truth must lie somewhere in the middle and not on an extreme as she had been taught. Maybe she should just relax.

But how could her mother possibly be connected to what was happening with the moon? Why had this reporter mentioned her when she was an archeologist, not an astronomer? And why would they employ this seemingly reputable reporter in this fashion? What if this was somehow connected to the lunar disturbances? It would be irresponsible to ignore this plea to call in.

She remembered the prophecy again, and her mind took a dark turn. Unrelated matter, the news reporter said. Madeline didn't think so, not to the Community.

She debated for nearly forty-five minutes, her girls awake and watchful. Finally, she marched over to the phone and placed the call after retrieving the scribbled number. Relief flooded her when she got a recording that kept her on the phone for about a minute, explaining the situation. The recording referred her to another number to call during regular business hours, which she also jotted down.

She realized she could sleep on it and decide later if this, indeed, was the right course of action. She could change her mind tomorrow.

Madeline sat down on the bed, frazzled, out of sorts. The world she inhabited felt foreign, belonging to a different reality where the physical laws she had known to be true were false. Trusted ways of being were worthless. A new paradigm had set in, stripping off her old understanding of things, of self, replacing it with nothing. She felt like a child, worse than that even, an infant, needing nourishment and nurturing, needing to be taught new lessons.

****

Maybe it was self-defense, a way the mind has of protecting itself from psychic injury. Phoebe didn't have any answers, but she did know that as her mother sat down, she seemed to lose touch with reality. She lapsed into a state that scared Phoebe. She didn't seem to know they were still there. Phoebe got off the bed and stood before her mother. No change. A total blank.

She waved a hand in front of her face. No response. Yet her mother remained upright and seemed to be conscious, able to control her posture.

Her sisters came closer. They needed to help their mother, but what could they do?

"Mom," Phoebe said, barely squeaking out the word. She touched her shoulder. Nothing. Her eyes were glazed.

"Go ahead," Rhea said. "It's the only way."

For the second time, Phoebe entered her mother's mind. She wasn't fully conscious, which somehow made it easier to scan through to levels Phoebe had found before. Nothing interested her much, yet something had to be causing this.

Then she saw the barrier—a compartment or room, with a door. Locked. Phoebe took a deep breath and tried to barge right in.

An electric shock went right through her, and she convulsed. Her vision blurred with afterimages of her mother's memories revolving around her mind. Then something in that room spoke, and there was a mental push.

Phoebe cried out. She'd been thrown from her mother's mind.

She fell, landing on her butt, her head slapping the wooden floor at least five feet from where she had been standing. Stars danced before her eyes.

Her mother still sat there, motionless.

"What happened?" Di and Rhea yelled. They each grabbed an arm and pulled Phoebe to her feet.

Phoebe rubbed her tailbone and the back of her head while they walked her to a chair in a corner. Their mother continued to study the opposite wall, unblinking.

What had just happened? It wasn't her mother doing this. Something else was in there. It didn't frighten Phoebe, but she wanted to know what the hell it was and why it was there. Coming out of her daze, she said, "Not enough power."

She looked at Dione and knew instinctively what to do. "I'm going in again. This time I won't be surprised. The moment you see me fighting, I'll need help. Don't hold back."

"What do you mean? I-I can't even—"

"Yes, you can," Phoebe corrected her, grabbing her

by the shoulders, squaring up with her. "Remember what's been happening? What happened behind the shed? I need you to do that but do it consciously and with control this time. You can do it, Di. I need you."

Dione nodded, and Phoebe hoped she got it, because if she had been right about Dione, she really did need her.

"Whatever is in Mom's mind is pretty strong. I'm going to go in slowly this time, and when I get to that door—"

"Door?" Rhea asked.

"A barrier or something, a mental thing that's blocking me. When I get there, I'm going easy and let resistance build slowly. But I know I can't do it alone, so that's when I'll need you guys to help."

"Okay—we're ready."

Turning back to her mother, Phoebe stood silently for a moment, thinking about what she needed to do. She returned to her mother's mind with more of a strong telepathic presence this time, like walking into a new place as if she owned it. The superficial layers were easy to navigate. Thoughts were all around her, and she perceived some of the information they had recently learned.

Phoebe went deeper until the door, or whatever it was, stood right before her. Dark, a mental image of a strong force she knew without a doubt was too much for her to overcome alone.

She collected herself then with tentacles of thought, she began probing the barrier, skirting over it, searching for cracks or openings, anywhere this thing might prove to be weak. But there were no weaknesses, only imponderable strength. This wasn't her mother.

This had been placed there, but by whom or what and when?

It probably wouldn't work, but it had come to Phoebe's mind so suddenly, she went with it. She whispered audibly, "Mom, it's me, Phoebe."

No weaknesses presented themselves, only an impenetrable barrier. Then something came to her that froze her blood. A presence.

Swallowing hard, her heart dancing in her chest, she began an even deeper probe, and the resistance was immediate and fierce, tearing at her mind like a starving panther bringing down its prey. But this time she was ready, and she fought it almost to a standstill.

Almost.

Sweat beaded on her face, and she had to take one mental step backward, then two, then with separate thought tentacles she called out to Dione and Rhea.

"Now!" she gasped, aloud this time.

Phoebe felt them at her back, as if they were holding her upright. It wasn't hands she felt, but their energy, their will. And the support was strong. Dione had understood.

Phoebe easily regained the position she had lost. She could feel Dione flowing into her with awesome power, raw and untamed, power enough to break down the barrier. Linked to Dione's mind, Phoebe glimpsed near infinite reserves of an unquenchable tap, a living fire. And that link allowed her to control it.

From Rhea came suppleness. Phoebe could move about in a mental form, flowing like liquid, stronger than a raging river. It created an ease of knowing, such a flowing sensation that, on this plane, her mental patterns were able to rush here and there as if effect happened before cause.

The barrier couldn't keep up.

As she examined it with this newfound power, there came to her a susurration. Words were being whispered, not in English but in Sumerian, familiar words now, the same words they had heard before in their dream—*enun* (innermost room), *dimma* (instruction), *kul* (heavy), *barag* (open or spread), *nir* (valuable stone), *dim* (post or pillar), *ni karkar* (circle around). Phoebe heard these and others, but none of it made sense. They seemed disconnected, random.

The power relaxed her. There was no need to hurry, so she glanced sideways at her sisters. Rhea smiled, sensing the same thing. Dione, however, was in that trance, her hair many times brighter, as were her eyes. Arms extended, she looked like a statue of a punk rocker frozen in the middle of performing, hair flowing in spiked swirls, lips parted, eyes wide and wild. The wind and crackle of energy coming from Di filled the room.

Phoebe did the only thing she could. She stepped into the barrier, and it dissolved instantly around her, pulling back like a veil being swept aside, as though a long-forgotten memory had suddenly been found and freed.

It was amazing. Other images flashed by in whirlwinds of thoughts, making it hard to orient herself and digest what was happening. Expecting some sort of fight to protect her mother from some unseen force that had somehow entered her, she was stunned to sense nothing of the sort.

Instead, there was peace and the overwhelming sense of a welcoming presence, of love, a mother's love. That thought surprised her.

A presence, someone else was there, and she knew instinctively that the thing would follow her out if she led the way.

Phoebe backed out and the psychic link between the sisters dissolved. In the next moment, their mother came around, blinking, dazed, disoriented.

Rhea and Dione threw themselves on her, but Phoebe turned to face whatever it was she had freed. It wasn't dangerous. She had sensed a protective influence, pure and untainted love.

A distortion in the air appeared. Writhing and thickening, it finally congealed into a woman who looked just like her mother, maybe a little younger. Lifelike, but not alive, it was wraith-like in appearance, a psychogeist. She had seen that word once in the book of myth they owned. The dream woman had red hair and a few freckles across her nose exactly like their mother and Dione.

Ghost-like, but not a ghost in the classical sense, sharper, more real. The woman stood, waiting like a teacher expecting the full attention of her class. Recovering quickly and seeing Phoebe's distraction by this, whatever it was, her mother rose from the bed followed by Rhea and Dione. They came alongside Phoebe, glaring at the smiling apparition. No one said a word, but none of them were afraid.

The woman appeared to be talking to someone. Then, resolving further into more detail they saw that she held a baby, speaking to the newborn in whispers and in a variety of languages. Their mother smiled because she understood them all.

Sumerian words flowed easily from their

grandmother's lips. She held their mother to her breast, kissing her. A moment later, though, the image changed, resolved again into another form.

The apparition looked at them, still smiling. It began to speak in a mild Irish brogue.

"Madeline, my lovely child."

Their mother gasped, and the blood left her face. Staggering, she stumbled back to her bed and sat down hard, but she couldn't sit still. Bouncing up, hands to her mouth and tears flowing, she walked back to where her daughters stood, looking into the beautiful face of her mother. The figure said nothing for a few seconds, as if anticipating the effect those four words would have. Phoebe and her sisters were waiting, gazing at their grandmother from head to toe, awe and wonder etched on their faces.

"Don't try to speak to me. The image you are looking at cannot respond. Listen attentively. I am so sorry it had to be this way, my beautiful daughter. You're wondering how and why, two questions there is no time to explore here for there was only so much power I could give this quantum trace as we call it. But if my premonitions are true, I am also standing before my triplet grandchildren as well, though I cannot know whether they be boys or girls or a combination. And since I am here before you, I can only assume they have come into their power, for only they could have released me from your mind. There is so much I wanted to tell you and could only do in moments before passing from this sad world. I knew my time was short—that something was terribly wrong. You can now recall these words, Madeline, thanks to the children opening the trace through their combined powers.

"Where to start, how much to go into? Unfortunately, there is no time here for a long explanation. Search your dreams. They will provide the answer after this message has gone. If the dreams weren't clear before, they will be now. You will remember them in detail. I have given you the talent you will need. My own talents. My gift to you. The stones must be protected, and the runes must be interpreted. If he lives, search out Livingstone and trust him. Dear Lucian will help you in your efforts.

"Remember that I love you always and that I wish I could be standing at your side now, my children, if things had only been different." She hesitated as though forgetting a long-lost thought. "Remember, there is always time enough to capture lost moments."

A pained look came across the apparition's face, and the image resolved again to an extreme close up, encompassing just her head and shoulders. She appeared to be lying in bed. There was a hospital gown, and a baby could be seen. But in the next moment, Martha's head sagged as in death, and the image dissipated abruptly.

Phoebe turned to look at her mother who had broken into a wide smile. Phoebe had never, ever, seen her smile quite so big. Her mother's eyes looked clearer than they ever had. They radiated brilliance and knowledge, replacing the despair and depression she had known all her life.

****

The merriment Madeline felt was real. Like a summer rain, it sprinkled hope down on her, something she had never felt. Yet, tears were still flowing freely, tears of joy this time, for, in that moment, miraculously, she remembered everything her mother had whispered to her as an infant. She could see her mother's face as if she were still there in her arms being cradled. Such a gift.

"I know how to get the stones," Madeline gasped. "The information has been with me, locked inside." She looked at Phoebe, "You understand this, don't you?"

Phoebe smiled and nodded. "Once the barrier came down, I saw how."

"Mom, what did she mean, 'search your dreams?' " Rhea asked.

"My dream—yes," Madeline said. "I almost forgot." She closed her eyes. "Her face...clear now...I see it clearly. And the Sumerian word *Barag*, to spread or part. I've been dreaming that all my life and could never quite understand or see her face."

"But what does it mean?" Dione said.

"It's the key," Phoebe said, looking intently at her mother, "and so is this." She extended her arm, and, still looking at her mother, the Claddagh came floating through the doorway to Phoebe's outstretched hand.

This time Madeline was unfazed at the display of power.

"Yes, it seems to be. I see the instructions clearly, but you must promise me not to go after the stones. We have to make contact somehow—elicit help."

"From our dad!" Dione said excitedly.

"Yes, honey. I think perhaps you're right. It's time."

Phoebe went up to her mother and placed a hand on her arm. "I know we have enough to think about with this group and trying to get the stones, but there's something else."

"What?" Madeline said, unsure whether she could take any more revelations.

"Professor Wick and that shop owner, Haldane, the one on the commons. They're after the same thing, but I don't believe they know what just yet."

Dione spoke up first. "I told Phoebe we shouldn't go in that weird shop! Those men are nuts."

"They think we're witches," Rhea said.

Madeline shook her head and frowned. Wick and his cronies shouldn't know about the stones, but anything was possible after the last several days. "You opened yourself up unnecessarily by doing something I've said repeatedly not to do."

The other girls hung their heads, but not Phoebe. "And you lied to us about our father and other things."

"To protect you, yes. But no more. I won't lie again."

Phoebe nodded. "Well, I don't think they know what they're doing, but they think you're up to something. They had a plan to run us over with a cart to put one of us in the hospital and clear the house out to search it."

Phoebe saw anger in her mother's eyes.

"I'm glad you told me. These men may be dangerous, but they're not like the others. You understand?"

Phoebe nodded. "We found out their bindrune was crap. And there's something else. We captured a nosy reporter. Dryer. He's trapped in the shed. I've got him in stasis. He stole your mother's note and gave it to Wick. He's being punished for it.

****

Later, with everyone in their own bed and after

301

checking on the sleeping reporter, Phoebe looked into her mother's mind and knew a change had come over her.

"Mom seems to be better," Rhea said.

Holding the Claddagh, studying it, Phoebe said, "Yeah, I think she is."

Dione said, "We're going for the stones, aren't we, Phoebe?"

Phoebe didn't answer right away, but she didn't need to. "Did you study the maps, Rhea? Think you can get us from here to New York City to the museum?"

"Sure, it's not harder than a trip through our woods."

"All right," Phoebe said without hesitation. "We need to know what all this is about, and those stones will help. Tomorrow night when Mom's sleeping, we'll go get them, and we're bringing Dryer."

"How are we gonna keep him for a whole other day?"

"I'll think of something."

Chapter 25

Friday

Sherman Rasmusun had been trying for days to find the lockers he remembered so well now from constantly thinking about that time in his life. The stones were always kept in the same unit and in precisely the same part of the locker. Nearly every day before Martha's actual work started, he would take them down for her, always in her presence, and she would work for an hour or two. It was always the same monotonous routine. Martha had insisted on it. The repetition helped keep the stones safe, and since no one knew of them, they weren't hard to hide.

Searching his memory over the last three days, he finally succeeded in recalling most of that sad period in his life where the path he'd chosen then had led inexorably to the person he was to become. Forced into this unwanted exploration of his memories, he hadn't slept much, nor eaten much, and with each passing day, his misery and desperation increased. With each passing day the absurdity of this situation grew clearer. The task was impossible. After almost forty years, the stones would simply not be in those lockers any longer. The lockers were probably long gone. They and the stones, forever gone, probably years ago. But how to explain that to his master?

Rasmusun shuddered, just picturing the response. It would be nothing like the beatings he had endured at the hands of his father. The scars on his back could attest to them. The younger Erazmos wouldn't leave any scars. The son would go inside his mind and do real damage. Nerve endings all over his body throbbed just thinking about it. If he couldn't find them, he would hide, close his mind off, and run away, far away. Any continent would do, except maybe Europe—not far enough.

Reflecting on the demonstration his master had given on the island, his shudder became an involuntary tremble. He wouldn't be able to hide forever, and then the pain would be great indeed, death a welcomed respite.

Confident that the old janitor he had just incapacitated would be down for hours, he walked out of the office he had inadvertently tunneled into. The outer room was a large storage area with a high ceiling—the one he had been caught in before by Charlotte Gentry and her guests.

The room was well ordered, unlike the others he had searched. As he walked, looking at storage crates, cabinets, and lockers that appeared to be from roughly his approximate time, he remembered his work routine with Martha as if it were only yesterday.

His responsibility was never great, far less than that of a true colleague, but he hadn't complained. He needed her company. He would retrieve the stones from the top shelf of the lockers while she maintained visual and mental surveillance of the area. Closing his eyes just now, he could easily put himself back in that time, climbing up on the footstool because he was too short to reach them otherwise. One by one, taking them down and unwrapping the velvet cloths she had used, all of this taking place in the early morning hours when just the janitors were around. It had been easy to be covert right under the very nose of the head of the division who had agreed to sponsor her other research activities but knowing nothing of these artifacts.

As if in a trance he lifted his arms ten times, once for each stone, going through the old familiar pattern. He delighted in her scolding him in that charming Irish brogue, admonishing him to be careful. Opening his eyes and turning his head to the right, he half expected to see her standing there, tall and beautiful, red hair flowing to white shoulders, supervising his activity, chiding him for his ineptitude.

His arms would ache. One by one he would carefully stack them on the workbench behind him. Ten stone tablets of great workmanship, each less than a half inch thick, grayish in appearance, but of various shapes and dimensions with tiny markings etched with substantial cuts in neat rows on the front and back.

Recalling his usefulness to her made him almost forget that terrible thing he had done. Almost.

The stones were now in his mind's eye, a long-forgotten memory. Eyes closed again, he could almost feel their edges, each cut with exacting detail, looking as if they were the work of a twenty-first century artisan, not that of someone who had lived five thousand years before. The etchings were extremely neat and finely carved as if produced with a modern lathe.

"Why does the master desire these now?" he whispered to himself. "After all this time?"

Remembering their smoothness, he moved his hands as if caressing them, but thinking of her, running his fingers over the fine markings as if over her porcelain skin.

Incredibly, a tear came to his eye, and dropped onto a workbench where it retained its globular form. Like a window to the past, he could see her face and brilliant red hair in the droplet as he bent over examining it. Funny, he hadn't shed any tears all those years ago—why now?

Suddenly, this sign of weakness disgusted him. He should have been braver and more mannish, then and now. He couldn't change who he was, but if he had been so, he could have won her heart instead of her scorn. Why did she have to resist his advances, awkward though they were? He hated himself for even thinking about her again.

With his flashlight in hand, he began walking through the windowless room, deep black if not for the weak beam. He noticed long work benches arranged in rows perpendicular to the walls, benches vintage to his time here. At the sight, hope rose in his heart, but then the lights came on, and someone gasped behind him.

Cursing himself for being distracted and in a dangerous mood anyway, he spun around and saw Charlotte Gentry walking up to him.

"I was just wondering if I would catch you doing something like this again. How did you get in? And why did you come down here when I told you this is not a public access level? If you don't want me to call security, you'll have to—"

She couldn't utter the last word because Rasmusun had raised his hand. Charlotte stood there wide-eyed, clutching her throat, getting redder by the second, but not from lack of air.

Rasmusun released her. She would have turned to run, but something was preventing this. "What—how—" she managed to say before her vocal cords seized.

"You will not speak, nor will you call out," he said. She nodded and he released her again, but as he did so, she blacked out. She woke a moment later entirely passive, her former agitation gone.

"Show me the lockers," he said, smiling now that he knew he was close because he could see in her mind that she had come back to this room last night and had gotten excited about the prospects of finding them.

"Over there."

She led him down another long walkway. They took a left turn and walked straight over to a wall where stood the lockers Rasmusun knew so well, but were these the right ones? He walked to the end, looked up, and smiled. At about shoulder height he found small letters he had cut into the side of the cabinet, rather childish for a man who had been twenty-five at the time. It read *SR + MA*. These were the right lockers, but this was no fond memory. She was his superior in more ways than mere seniority. He should have heeded his instinct.

Walking back to Charlotte at the middle door of the three-door cabinet, he found it to be locked with what looked to be the same one he had once used. He moved her gently over to one side. She responded with a nonsensical, "Thank you."

With a concentrated effort, he projected his mind throughout the entire floor, and found normal activity and not very many people. He then screwed his face and projected a minute kinetic energy wave through the hand holding the lock, meaning to trigger the locking mechanism. Some used their hands in peculiar ways to shape waves of various sizes and strengths. The kinetic blasts could also be imbued with other properties depending on the talent of the person developing it or released at various levels of force for the desired effect.

Instead of disengaging the lock, something curious happened. The quantum discharge ignited a quantum flux, brief in duration, but very wide. The whole cabinet, about ten feet long, two feet deep, and six feet high, seemed to absorb his minute blast and radiate an eerie glow.

The glow didn't dissipate readily, but lingered, the sound reverberating in the cavernous room like a deep gong, but oddly discordant with the size of the energy input the lock had received. Waves of distortion erupted from the locker and engulfed them, spreading outward in a three-hundred-sixty-degree pattern. It had no effect whatsoever. Rasmusun didn't know how far out of the room the distortion wave would carry. It had gone right through the wall at the far end.

He thought awhile and then tried it again, this time with a blast that had a little more kick to it, but not much more. At first, nothing happened, but then the cabinet began glowing again and as the seconds ticked off the glow intensified. There was also a slow building vibration which ended in the cabinet violently shaking. Rasmusun looked at Charlotte, hoping that this was all there would be to the manifestation, but, in the next instant, another quantum distortion exploded from the locker.

Rasmusun and Charlotte were blasted across the

aisle where they crashed into a parallel set of cabinets. They crumpled to the floor, dazed.

Charlotte got slowly to her feet, no longer under his control. She stood, groggy and disoriented.

"What was that?" she asked, forgetting her former fear, now more afraid of the locker. Rasmusun rose on creaky legs.

"Some type of quantum resonance," he said, his old legs shaking. "This locker has been tampered with, probably by Martha, but for it to remain patent all these years…"

His voice trailed off as he remembered Martha's talent. He never realized just how talented she really was. "I doubt if even my master could open this. More force would be ruinous—exponential feedback." He was muttering now. "We would likely need the right frequency to open a gateway right through that door." He pointed his finger as he said this.

He began wringing his old hands, a persistent habit when nervous. He walked back and forth in front of the locker, muttering, cursing. Then: "So close—the stones are in there—I can almost feel them." He ran his hands over the door, his longing almost indecent.

Turning, he said, "You there, Charlotte."

"Look, mister, I don't know why you're here or what you're after."

"But you do," he said. "I told you several days ago, remember?"

"Yes, but I-I can't help you get inside that locker. It looks like it could have some sensitive research material in there, causing the reaction I saw. I'm sure my boss, Dr. LaPierre, can help. Why don't we just go upstairs?" She said all this while backing away from him.

Too quick for his age, he grabbed her wrist, roughly this time. "We're staying right here."

With force, he entered her mind again, more thoroughly this time and she fainted. He caught her, easing her descent to the floor where he spent the next few moments looming over her, examining her.

"Daughter?" he said suddenly. This puzzled him. "But not your daughter."

And then he had it. Madeline's history, her educational background, all the things Charlotte knew about her friend, including their recent conversation. Ecstatic, he induced wakefulness in Charlotte and pulled her to her feet. She stood before him in a daze and had no idea he'd gotten information he hadn't counted on, information she wouldn't have willingly revealed.

"Maybe the firstborn daughter of Martha Alleyn can help me."

Charlotte gasped. "How did you know that?"

Not answering, he began pacing again, wringing his hands, muttering. Finally: "I need her address—*Now*. Do you have it? And don't lie to me. I'll know it!"

"Y-yes, but—"

She was helpless to stop him. He didn't wait for an answer but entered her mind a third time. "Ithaca," he said. "Good—good, Two-Fourteen Woodlawn Drive—West Hill. Master will be pleased."

Turning back to Charlotte from his frenetic pacing, he said, "This woman you know, Madeline Alleyn. I need her help. You're her friend. I see that much in your mind. You'll come with me to Ithaca, and we'll bring her back here."

"T-to Ithaca, but that'll take hours, all day." The woman groped for her cell phone. "I-I could call her first—prepare her f-for our arrival."

Rasmusun stopped his pacing and looked at her. "Yes, that sounds like a good idea, but I'll be listening closely." Then remembering his orders, he said, "But first I need to report to my master. This will take only a moment."

Remaining still while looking at Charlotte, he said, "*Master, I have a report.*" He felt rather than heard Erazmos enter. Flinching, he went on. "*There is some interesting news. I believe I have found the daughter of Martha Alleyn, my old colleague and the discoverer of the Stones of Sumer.*"

"*Why should that concern us?*"

"*S-she may know how to get them. She may know many things and be persuaded to help our cause.*"

"*Have you found the lockers?*"

"*I have the lockers but have not opened them yet. I believe the stones are there.*"

"*How do you know this?*"

"*There is a quantum phenomenon around the lockers...a...a kind of lock, a trace, I believe. It rebounds exponentially to a factor many times the initial kinetic probe I tried. They are quite impossible to open.*"

"*I see,*" Erazmos said. "*Can this woman help?*"

"*Surely her daughter can. She is probably Puzur, and she also has a past with this museum.*"

"*Where is she?*"

"*Ithaca. I gleaned it from my contact's mind.*"

"*In Greece?*"

"*Oh, no, no, in New York, a city, hours to the west, in the middle of the state. I will go there shortly to retrieve her. The address is Two-Fourteen Woodlawn Drive. Do you want me to get the daughter, Master? I'm ready to go.*"

"*No, that is not your mission, but this is welcome information. I'll send another. You have served me well. Stay where you are, and do not fail me in your retrieval of the stones.*"

Chapter 26

Two-thousand islands comprised the Greek archipelago. The Évripos strait, a narrow waterway west of Evvoia, separated the island from the Greek mainland. To the east lay the Aegean Sea, to the north Bulgaria, separating Greece from the rest of southern Europe.

Situated at the southern end of Evvoia sat the Okhi Oros mountain range and nestled along its eastern slopes sat an enormous compound just north of the small city of Karystos. The compound was owned by Prometheus Erazmos and besides the mansion, it consisted of many other smaller dwellings for his men and their families, stables for his horses, barns for the various animals of the sprawling ranching and farming operations, and training facilities for his recruits.

The families and other hired help were all of clan *Saĝtuku*. They tended his acres of olives, grapes, and wheat. They also worked his magnesite and lignite mines on the island and elsewhere in Greece. His marble quarry was especially valuable to him, its product spectacularly displayed throughout the mansion. But his wealth was based on much more than this, primarily tied to the sea and shipping.

Buffered from surrounding neighbors by the twenty thousand plus acres on which it sat the compound was the fortress from which Erazmos controlled his vast empire. For much of the year, he could be found sitting on the large, east-facing veranda, looking out over the Aegean in the distance. This was where he was today, brooding, plotting his next move.

He liked this spot above all for it smelled of the seas from which the world would come to him, a world he believed he would someday rule. In his mind, the prophecy said it was so, and he would make it happen. Reveling in the salty breeze blowing from the northeast, he sat there contemplating the future destiny had in store for him. This was his time and place. The world would soon discover his name.

Thinking of these things again, he removed his dark sunglasses, stood, and lifted both arms as if paying homage to some other god, but by this act, he was merely taking in a fuller portion of the salty breeze. He could hear the waves crashing on the rocky coastline and his large flock of sheep baaing in a north pasture nearby. His dogs at his side strained to run, but he held them in place by the force of his will.

"Victor," Erazmos said coldly, "call for Dimitri. He is even now busying himself with the mundane, but I have need of him."

He began stroking his twin Greek sheepdogs, Phobos on his right and Deimos on his left. They had eaten half cooked steaks from the hand of their master and were now anxious for work with the sheep. They looked up at him expectantly. He then smiled the smile he reserved only for his children and released them. They sprinted off and would be with their keepers in moments.

The old *Atah* shuffled off the veranda into the nearest receiving room and pressed an intercom button.

He knew Dimitri must be near. A stark black tunnel opened next to Erazmos.

"I felt the extra gravitational increase weeks ago," he said nonchalantly to Dimitri, "long before its effect on the moon was discovered this week. It is intensifying. I see it in the very seas around our beloved homeland. I have been contemplating these events and their relationship to the prophecy ever since."

Dimitri Primolov, Bulgarian-born member of clan *Saĝtuku,* was Erazmos's age. Much less physically imposing than his master, Primolov stood under six feet tall, but his stocky build gave him gargantuan strength.

His family had immigrated to Greece from the Khaskovo region of Bulgaria when Dimitri was nine. He and Prometheus had attended the Tarkus Academy for Extraordinary Youth in Athens at the appointed age. They had quickly become friends and together terrorized for five years the other children.

Though of equal age, their relationship had gradually become one of master and servant when Dimitri went to work for Erazmos's father after boarding school. Neither attended university, finding no use for such ordinary education. When Erazmos's father died mysteriously only five years after the friends left the academy, Prometheus found himself, at twenty-two, the inheritor of a vast fortune. What the two were able to do next was truly astounding. With Dimitri serving as Erazmos's enforcer, the Erazmos fortune had doubled by the time both were thirty.

Dimitri proved his worth many times over in unspeakable acts of violence. His loyalty didn't go unnoticed or unrewarded. These facts, however, didn't mean the two men were friends any longer, as they once were, for the master/servant relationship became ever more pronounced as both men reached the age of thirty and continued to denigrate to its current status today. Dimitri lived to do the bidding of Prom, as he had once called him, and as Erazmos's arrogance and power grew, their long friendship slipped into one of servitude.

"Yes, Master," Dimitri said obediently.

"Are these signs heralding the prophecy or will we be, yet again, disappointed, as has happened so often in our history?"

Erazmos smiled as Dimitri froze at the question. A test. His friend hated questions, as it wasn't his nature to be a thinker, only a doer to be relied upon when decisive action was required. He had never been known for his intellect, and that certainly wasn't his worth to his master. The test now before him was one of loyalty and trust, an opportunity for him to demonstrate belief in his master's identity, but his dim mind understood this too late.

Erazmos demanded undying devotion from his people, and no one was more central or needed than his oldest friend. Erazmos wanted confirmation of Dimitri's loyalty, yet Dimitri appeared double minded, and his answer showed it.

"What is your feeling, Master?"

Erazmos's smile didn't give away the disappointment he felt. He looked down at Dimitri, eyes narrowing, studying his old friend, trying to arrive at the measure of the man.

Perhaps it was just that Dimitri was slow on the uptake as he had amply demonstrated many times. It would be overlooked this time. Dimitri would have the opportunity to recover later. Dimitri lowered his head under his master's reproachful stare.

"Have faith, Dimitri," Erazmos said, turning away from him to stare out to sea. "We will not have long to wait now, and you will see my destiny come to pass." He wished his dogs were still at his side as they alone of all his devotees gave him unwavering loyalty.

"I have not seen the three," Erazmos said after a minute or two. "But I felt them earlier—far off across the water. I felt the onset of their power, but I do not yet know their capabilities. They are a puzzle still. We are set to begin as soon as this third factor is disposed of. Would you like to observe them?"

"Them? Master, you mean to say they are people— live people?"

"Live, yes," he said, laughing at Dimitri's stupidity. "Does that surprise you? I have always taken Tarkus literally on this point, and now we will finally see. Come, observe them with me, and see for yourself."

"Yes, Master."

"You may stay, Victor," Erazmos said, as the old *Atah* started to walk off.

Composing himself and remaining still as was required by the technique, whispery vapors, some light colored and some dark, materialized in front of the three men and for a brief instant remained suspended in the air. The vapors began to whirl, slowly at first, then faster and faster until finally settling to form shapes in three dimensions.

There appeared a quiet residential street, a sidewalk with houses. A car driving by. The scene began moving as if a camera rolled along the sidewalk.

A corner turned. The front of a small bungalow with yellow siding and dark green shutters with moon and star cutouts.

Another car passed, and then the voices of girls talking. They came into view, carrying a box, eating doughnuts out of it. The three girls turned up the front walk leading to the little bungalow.

"There—you three, yes you." It was the man whose eyes had recorded the scene. "May I have a word?"

The three girls turned and approached him. Two had black hair: the short one, shoulder length, with curls, and the other, longer and straight with a satin sheen. They could be twins, yet they were dissimilar as well, not identical, obviously siblings. The third teen was taller with bright red hair and a modest dash of freckles spread across her nose and upper cheeks.

"Do you live here?" the young man asked, smiling.

"Yes," the tall dark-headed girl said, the one with bright green eyes and long, luscious hair. All three appeared nervous, as if they were doing something wrong.

"Where do you go to school?"

"Ithaca High," the redhead said.

"You're seniors or something?" he said with apparent interest.

The redhead nodded.

"We're not supposed to talk to strangers, though," the smaller, dark-haired girl said with authority in her voice. She adjusted her glasses and frowned at him. She appeared to be the leader of the little troupe. "We're going now," she said, looking disapprovingly at the others.

318

They started to walk off, but the man's voice suddenly became sharp. "No, stay. I'm not done."

Erazmos could tell he had penetrated the shortest girl's mind. Dimitri leaned in closer as Erazmos had done when he first saw this little scene. The short girl staggered a step or two. The redhead put out a hand to steady her.

What the boy found was a deep, lucid mind, as clear as a perfect note from a pristine instrument. Through his contact with her, the boy had passed many things onto Erazmos. The three seemed to have limited experience with telepathic communication. The short one had been startled at the power of the boy's test, like daggers had been driven into her mind. Intrusive. Unclean. It frightened her and amused Erazmos.

Then the most interesting thing of all. She resisted with a single counter thought that came up subconsciously from deep within. The word was, stop, but it wasn't the English word she used. It was Sumerian, *Batiltu*. Apparently, this girl had no idea how she knew this word. Curious. It was all so curious.

The counter command hit the young man with a force that nearly felled him. He staggered like a drunkard, as if a nail had been driven through his skull. He fought to maintain his focus, though he was well-trained in such combat, and she was just an insignificant, American teen. This startled the young man, and he broke off, but the single thought had come to him in the brief time he had been in contact with the girl.

Settling quickly while the girls backed away from him, a look of shock on their faces, he said shakily, "Triplets—you three are triplets—aren't you?"

He could only look at the girl who had driven him out, astonished at the burst of power she had just unleashed. His eyes were still unfocused, but he was strong and was already beginning to regain some composure.

The girl who had stopped him said, "Back off," and she started to walk away again, leading the others. As they were turning, he entered the minds of her two sisters simultaneously. In that brief moment he learned the other part of the puzzle.

Puzur. All three.

This fact at first confused him, but then comprehension spread across his mind like a towering wave and the meaning pounced upon him with sudden fearsome understanding.

Dimitri looked sideways at his master, the fear in the young man evident through his master's projection. The young man began backing away from the girls. He opened a tunnel. With their hair dancing, the three teenagers ran to their house as the images blinked out of existence.

Dimitri stood still, staring blankly at Erazmos, who said, "I send my spy to search for a ruby, and he instead brings me a diamond—the largest, most precious diamond on earth."

"Whose mind recorded this, Master?"

"Our man at SAL," he said, laughing. "My spy has infiltrated their vaunted security, but his identity is immaterial for now. This incident happened an hour ago, around eight o'clock their time in the city they arrogantly call Ithaca in the American state of New York. We were merely tracking the activity of our enemies who it seems are also after the rune stones. My spy was sent to confirm information I received about the mother of these children who may be valuable to us, but he instead stumbled upon a far greater prize—the children."

Erazmos could hardly contain himself, and again, he let out a short, malevolent laugh. "We will pull this prize out from under the nose of Livingstone, that pig-loving, would-be protector, before he even knows what he has."

"Do they know about the children yet?"

"Our spy says he doesn't believe so, though he has heard rumors of a search. I know now that SAL searches for their mother. They will neither find her nor her children. But when you go, use extreme caution. Our man is sure they are onto something, and it probably won't be long before they have her, but I want her first."

"Master, this girl…our man seemed to be forced out with ease. How was this possible?"

Erazmos smiled. "I felt her power through what he shared with me. It must have actually been many times greater. A teen—yes—I would welcome the combat, but I have no time to play with children. Can you not deduce who, or what, these three are? Their power comes on at the time of the first factor, Dimitri. Are these merely coincidences?"

"But, still, how can you be sure these three are the ones, master?"

"Of course, I cannot be absolutely sure yet, but I am giving you an opportunity to confirm what I know is correct. You saw and I felt the power in one so young. And they are *Puzur* triplets, something that surely even you must know has never happened in our history."

"*Puzur* triplets," Dimitri said, puzzled. "And her use of the ancient tongue, how can that be?"

Erazmos nodded. "I do not believe this one was even consciously using it. Your contact with them will be interesting, I am sure, but I am confident in your abilities my old friend."

"*Puzur* triplets." The thought mesmerized him. "I can hardly believe it. I mean, the prophecy is impossible."

"Impossible? Tarkus was your clansman. Our clan has always remained faithful to his word and that will be our greatest advantage. The rest are filled with doubters, unbelievers. They will soon feel the true strength of *Saġtuku*."

"Yes, Master, but what do you desire of me?"

"Tell me, Dimitri, have you not read the New Testament gospels, the part about King Herod?" He looked at Dimitri through his dark glasses and saw how he was taken aback by this question.

"No, Master," he answered truthfully. To lie would not have been wise.

"Really, Dimitri, you should read more. You would like King Herod's style." Erazmos chuckled at this. "Herod, too, had enemies, like me, but unlike my situation he could not yet pinpoint his enemy's exact identity. Also, like me, his enemy was a child who he believed would grow to supplant him. What do you think King Herod would do to rectify this situation?"

Dimitri contemplated this for a while, and then smiled. "If he could not pinpoint the threat, he would simply destroy all those he believed had the potential to be the right person."

"Good—good, my old friend, you think like the

kings of old. Of course, my situation is not exactly like Herod's. Do you understand this?"

"Yes, I do," Dimitri said.

"We do not need to kill all three, do we, my friend? Just one will do, one dead girl and Tarkus's ancient prophecy will be shattered, the third factor broken."

Erazmos broke into an almost uncontrollable laughter. Dimitri grimaced and backed away. As Erazmos's maniacal laughter ceased, he removed his glasses, stood, and looked deeply into Dimitri's eyes, unimpeded by the dark lens.

"Is your faith not deeper now, my friend—deeper than it was minutes ago when you doubted the prophecy, doubted me? Do not disappoint me, Dimitri, and do not attempt deceit if you fail, lest I plumb the depths of your mind to learn the truth. Bring back evidence of the act." As he said it, he forcefully penetrated Dimitri's mind to give him the global coordinates of the children's residence.

Dimitri bowed low and trembling, said, "I will not fail you."

"Kill one or all, I care not, but bring the mother to me unharmed."

Chapter 27

Madeline Alleyn had been found. The news had come to them an hour ago. SAL agents had sorted through hundreds of calls, finally confirming the presence of four people in the little house on Woodlawn Drive. When they verified the homeowner as their target, Livingstone and Brownedyke were informed immediately.

This unconventional attempt to contact Madeline had been a long shot at best, like looking for the proverbial needle somewhere in that haystack of humanity. They had readily approved Sarah Duckworth's idea. No one had been sure she was still alive, but Jason was sure of it, surer than he had been about anything in his life. He didn't tell anyone of his rock-solid certainty; he knew it in his bones, the missing Claddagh pretty much confirming it for him.

With little sleep the night of their attempt, Jason had been summoned immediately once they had her identified. They were all in Brownedyke's office at SAL headquarters for a strategy meeting. Jason stalked about, his nerves on an extremely thin edge.

After getting the exact coordinates of her residence, Jason could have tunneled there any time he wanted over the last hour. He had almost done it so many times since receiving the telepathic message from Livingstone.

"When can we go?" Jason asked angrily, not caring to watch his manners.

"Please, my boy, we don't want chaos. Vivian was just there yesterday on an entirely different mission, and the reaction she received wasn't good. Let's think of them. She ran once; now it's time to put our best foot forward."

"Lucian is right, dear. The little lady is quite scared. She knows she is found, though possibly not by you. I wish I had known yesterday. Good gracious, what a coincidence."

Jason didn't answer but instead increased his peripatetic pacing. He stalked the perimeter of Brownedyke's office like a caged lion, his eyes displaying a fury not native to his emotional makeup. He could understand their reasoning, but then he couldn't. Eighteen damn years was a long time to wait to introduce yourself to your own children. That was his right. He should be the one to say when, but—

"Okay!" he finally said. "I guess I see your point, but when?"

"*Lirim Ne* are watching them now," Brownedyke said. "They're not going anywhere."

"I was just thinking we ought to confront Madeline first—tomorrow," Livingstone said. "When she's had time to adjust to our presence—to you, Jason, and talk to her girls. We could go for another visit, perhaps even later in the day or the next. We should let her say when."

Their ploy had worked easily it seemed. Could she have wanted to be found? She probably didn't know yet that they were very near to discovering her, didn't know that her running was coming to an end, that Jason knew she lived and was out there, close.

"Okay," he said. "The last thing I want is to scare her—put demands on her."

The thought that he had triplet daughters hit Jason unbelievably hard. They were all stunned. Livingstone and Brownedyke were anxious to get there, but being older they knew the benefit of patience. They would take it slowly.

From Vivian, they already knew that at least one girl was *Puzur* class, but Vivian had given them a good deal to suspect the others as well. Jason's pride swelled even more at this news. There was no doubt in Jason, but he kept that to himself. Why else would there be triplet firstborns in the Community if not to fulfill the vision Tarkus had left for posterity? This brought the prophecy into razor sharp focus for him. It suddenly loomed over him like a charging bull elephant, and he felt incredibly humbled. He remembered the brashness he had exhibited all of his adult life. The way he had always been ready to tell anyone who would listen that he didn't believe in the prophecy. It was obsolete for the modern age, an anachronistic icon that they all should just get over. As he looked admiringly at Brownedyke and Livingstone, two staunch believers, he was highly embarrassed, but fear ate at him like a canker.

"*Puzur* class," he mumbled to no one in particular.

Livingstone looked up from where he had been sitting. "I wonder," he said. All eyes turned to him. Though Jason knew he had effectively closed his thoughts off to this group, he also knew of Livingstone's significant talent. "Could they really all be *Puzur*?"

"If you only saw what I saw," Vivvy said. "Felt what Bert and I felt?"

Jason suddenly found it hard to control himself, so he walked to the far end of the office, far enough so they wouldn't see him trembling. The fact of the triplets and the implications they presented were staggering. He was angry and excited, sad and happy at the same time. *Puzur* class individuals were taught to compose themselves because of the terrible power they could wield, but he was finding this difficult. What he needed most of all was to meet his children, and look to the future, a future that for them looked dangerous.

Three daughters, all *Puzur* class, an impossible idea. The prophecy of Tarkus. How in the world was he going to protect them? He waited and paced, waited and paced. He could do nothing else until Livingstone made up his mind.

****

The triplets spent the rest of the day inside, mostly in their bedroom. That guy who had stopped them as they returned home from a doughnut run had shaken them. They wanted to tell their mother about what had happened as they returned home but didn't think she could handle it. Why had he come around? And the way he'd left so suddenly after trying to get inside their heads. What did it mean? Could he have been part of the group their mother had contacted? The timing was right, but something felt wrong. They were being watched by people like them, but something was different about this guy. Phoebe had been in the old lady's mind, and it seemed like she was all right, but not him. It wasn't right what he did to her.

How many more could there be like them? The

question nagged at them all day.

"I saw things," Phoebe said, "especially when I told him to stop. People bowing before a tall man with black hair and dark glasses, kissing the ring he wore, a red stone with bright yellow gold around the base. Then there were those eyes. Black eyeballs. A man and woman screaming. The man dangling in the air like a puppet. Dead."

"What's the man's name?" Dione asked, taking Phoebe's hand. "The one inside that boy's head."

"I didn't catch it."

"Could this be the result of the call Mom made?" Rhea asked.

Phoebe didn't want to scare them, but they had to know. "I think there are two sets of people searching for Mom."

Rhea's eyes widened. "This isn't good. One's gotta be bad news. When did Mom call the second time?"

Dione answered, "Before lunch."

Phoebe nodded. "I was keeping track of her. She's been scared, but a different kind of scared than before."

"You think we should tell her?" Dione asked.

Phoebe shook her head. "She'd want to run again, but I don't think she could escape this time. We should give this Lucian man a chance to contact us. We can hang on until then." She grabbed her favorite stuffed bear. "Mom's got a lot of people pissed at her. Professor Wick and his cronies. The group she ran from. And then there's the laughing man. How does he figure in?" She gave each of them a hard stare. "I'm thinking he's the head of the bad group."

"That murdered our grandmother," Dione said.

Phoebe nodded. "These things can't be a

coincidence. First that woman shows up, then the TV person last night. Mom calls, and then this guy shows up today. They're related."

"It all has to do with those dumb stones our grandmother found," Dione said.

"It's the key to everything. We're gonna get them back, and then we're gonna find our father. He'll take care of Wick and his cronies and help us with the others."

"What about Dryer?"

With their mother's permission, they had been managing him all day, and now Phoebe had him in stasis again. He knew too much. When they could, they would turn him over to the group and let them sort him out. Their mother had said the group was secretive, and Phoebe knew why. They had been developing a growing sense that they should keep their abilities hidden. It was better that way, much better.

That was the main energy behind their thoughts the rest of the night. Find the stones. Find their father. He would help them. Phoebe clutched the Claddagh and seared these two things into her brain. Nothing else mattered. Holding tightly onto the Claddagh, she finally nodded off.

Chapter 28

As the night progressed on West Hill, the watchfulness of the *Lirim Ne* waned. By midnight there had been long stretches, as much as a half hour, when no one stood guard over the shitty little house on this most insignificant of American streets. Dimitri Primilov had even counted the progressively lengthening periods when agents were absent. Sloppy and undisciplined. Those in his charge caught in such shameful performance would have been immediately and severely punished, maybe even executed outright.

It began to dawn on him what this possibly meant. Could it be that SAL was unaware that the woman had also been found by his master? That must be the answer for the light surveillance.

He smiled. This would be easier than he thought.

As he observed his adversaries from his hiding place, their sloppiness disgusted him. They weren't discrete but were out there for all to see. One loitered at the opposite end of the street from where he stood in a small, wooded thicket in someone's front yard. Another strolled directly in front of the house in question. Another walked the sidewalk on his end of the street.

The problem must be an ill-choreographed changing of the guard. Americans—pampered, undisciplined, inexperienced. He hated SAL, but he especially hated the Americans in it.

Dimitri had to exercise extra caution on approaching the house because he knew *Lirim Ne* would be quick to react to the coming violence. Those he could see didn't bother him, but there was also the possibility of those he couldn't see. Like him, they might be anywhere, enclosed by their tunnels and, with their minds closed off, not easily detected. So, he closed his own mind and waited to commence his attack.

These agents wouldn't be able to respond to him in time to stop the slaughter. The women didn't concern him at all; he wouldn't make any special effort there. But he preferred to avoid confronting *Lirim Ne* since his assignment wasn't to kill them, so he waited and watched with his legendary patience. Uncertainty was there, but also thrilling possibilities for combat, pain, death.

The house contained four occupants—one adult, three teenagers, exactly as he had been told. Earlier, the woman had been working at a keyboard, but now, nearing midnight, she was also in bed. He sensed her tiredness. They were all sleeping. Easy.

The night had turned black as clouds rolled in, blocking the stars and hampering the moon's eerie gaze. Though much closer to the earth than it had ever been, the moon had advanced beyond its full phase. Its light thus curtailed, a dark figure dressed in black could stalk the streets with impunity.

He planned to time his attack when the agents were fumbling with their change of guard. Having established the timing precisely, he waited. The black silk made him imperceptible; his light skinned face covered with black paint totally blotted him out. Black silk was also worn over his clipped blond hair.

Impossible to see in the anemic light. The large yard effectively separated the house a good distance from the neighbors. Good. There were no dogs within several houses of his target, another good sign.

Primilov's habit was to assign the jobs he had been given to one of Erazmos's lesser servants, his prerogative as Erazmos's number one henchman. But this job couldn't be trusted to just anyone. Because of the prophecy, this job was the most important of his career, far more important even than kidnaping the daughter of a Sage.

He would do it alone. Stealth dictated a silent and efficient attack. Erazmos wouldn't accept failure, and in turn, Dimitri would receive all the acclaim without sharing it with lesser men. He would be remembered as the destroyer of the prophecy, the conqueror of the vaunted third factor. He could almost smell the acclamation he would receive, the looks from others, the envy of lesser men. Women would beg to mate with him then. This produced another smile and an insatiable hunger.

When the man walking in front of the house suddenly vanished, Dimitri acted.

****

As a distant clock tower struck the note for midnight, Dimitri Primilov entered the house unbidden. The woman lay sleeping in her bedroom, her children on the other side of the one bath a little way down the narrow passageway.

A stark black tunnel opened near the two bedrooms. Loose floorboards creaked as his full weight transferred to them. The crackle of energy was imperceptible, and the black electric flashes weren't visible in the equally black passageway. Dimitri produced a small quantum discharge about the diameter of a quarter, guiding it with his open left palm. He knew where he was by sensing the presence of the three girls in the room farthest down the hall. A simple scan told him that the mother was dreaming, which produced a smile. It was about a man with dark hair and a deep tan.

He broke off the connection, amused, and then felt gently along the walls with his meaty right hand until he got to the girls' doorway. He extinguished the light and felt down the door to the knob. He turned it slowly. The door swung inward noiselessly. He crept forward but stopped just inside to get his bearings. Separate beds. The closest only about three meters away.

He smiled again. Now to pick.

He would normally have chosen one victim, done what he had to do, what he had done many times before and gotten out, but these were not regular *Puzur* class members and certainly not normal young women. The result was that, for the first time in his career, he underestimated his prey.

He turned toward the nearest bed where the pretty one slept and, in a moment, would have blasted it with a force so terrible a grown elephant wouldn't have recovered. But as it turned out the girls were not sleeping a regular sleep. He stopped, puzzled. He sensed an oddity, an infusion of psychic energy, linking them. It puzzled him and then it was too late.

The little one woke...or was she still sleeping? Her mind seemed to be neither asleep nor awake. Then a clear thought came to Dimitri, planted by one of the girls, the intelligent one, the one he had observed hours before.

Why are you here? Leave now. The last two words were in Sumerian, a language all *Puzur* class had studied, but never used with regularity.

Pag adal—leave now—the girl said again with greater clarity and strength. It penetrated deep into his mind with a force he had only felt from his master. Her mental probe clawed at his psyche with staggering power. Like a drunkard, he stumbled forward into the room.

Hesitant, confused, staring at the little one, still not sure whether she was awake or asleep. Her mind was in a curious state, one he had never perceived before. The other two were sitting up in bed now, and he could sense the three of them conversing. He tried to break into the conversation as curiosity overcame his order to murder. A rush of thoughts leapt through his brain, some in English, but most in ancient Sumerian.

Aba zae (who are you)—*Taka* (abandon)—*Anaš* (why)—*Halam nen ešhur* (forsake this plan).

The mental assault was like entering a dreamscape. Strange colors and shapes floated in and out of his subconscious with words and phrases coming gently to him—probing, inquisitive, discerning. Thought worms probed his mind, examining him down to the core of his being.

This wasn't good, because he knew himself. He'd never been equipped for this kind of assault. Then suddenly the tender, almost sublime, feeling changed. The words became intense, delivered in harsh tones. They pounded at his mind, coming to him in a strange mixture of English and Sumerian. Other phrases were there as well, tearing at him with numbing force, producing a babble of maddening thoughts.

He reeled from the onslaught and lunacy would have ensued if not for his disciplined training, which began to penetrate through to his consciousness. He took two backward steps, his mind in agony. He tore at his skull with his hands and would have screamed, but he conquered the impulse. The room seemed to be closing in on him, a squeezing pressure. Any moment his brain would dissolve into a gelatinous pool of mush.

To break the attack or spell or whatever it was they were doing, he instinctively acted with brute force. Through forced concentration and clenched teeth against the psychophysical onslaught, he crouched low and leaned forward as though facing gusts of tropical storm strength and aimed a kinetic killing blast directly at the beautiful one with the long, luscious hair.

The house shuddered in protest. He heard the woman cry out and, a moment later, she entered the room. She flipped the light switch, only a meter or two away from Primilov. She tried to scream again, but he had been too quick. He grabbed her and held her at arms-length with one hand on her throat, her voice suddenly frozen.

But it was no good. The fucking girls were locked into his mind and anticipated his moves. He couldn't break out of this mind combat. The pretty one, Rhea, he had gathered from the other's mind, had tunneled to the middle of the room, easily avoiding the blast that destroyed her bed and nearly punched a hole through the exterior wall of the house. All three girls were now on their feet, still in a trance-like state.

Their psychic union was unlike anything he had ever heard of or studied. The prophecy came to him then. The third factor. Their brains would be unique even beyond the usual quantum neuroscience paradigm Community scientists had established.

The two brunettes were advancing on him, moving in creeping steps, bodies erect, daunting, unafraid. It impressed Primilov, but what could their ultimate aim be? He took a step back. Only Dione, the skinny redhead, remained behind, standing like a statue, immobile with arms extended at her sides, palms open and facing forward, fingers spread. Her dancing hair gave the dark room an eerie fluorescent glow. Two red dots peered at him from behind the other girls.

A thought came to Dimitri, his thought, not one planted there. These girls were barely old enough to be considered women. They were teenagers, mere children still. Act now. But how?

He felt inferior to the three. His vast training and power seemed to have been eviscerated by them.

Act.

He fell to his knees and face, dragging the woman down with him. She plummeted hard to the floor and a gasp of pain escaped her. Head bowed; he feigned surrender.

****

Coming into her right mind, Phoebe saw the broad face staring at them, smeared with foul blackness. She still held the Claddagh. Rhea held her other hand, and together they said, "Mom?"

In the dimly lit room, as Dione's strange glow faded, the intruder started grinning, looking right at Phoebe. Before she could react, he erected himself, still on his knees, still holding their mother in his right hand, he sent another killing blast, this time at Dione.

But Rhea was quick. She pulled Phoebe into the black hole and directed it at Di who was half-pulled, half-blasted into it. The three girls were whisked away with their mother still in the clutches of the madman, her screams echoing through Phoebe's brain.

****

Primilov managed to connect his mind to the redheaded girl before they disappeared. What he found pleased him. No brain activity. She had faded away, evidence enough for his master.

Still on her knees before him, the woman looked up, her face wet with tears. Primilov released her, stood proudly, and said, "The sacrifice of such a life is a small down payment for the world."

He then penetrated her mind with force, stripping the last vestiges of consciousness from her, and produced a deep, lingering coma.

He carried her back to her bed and departed, confident in his victory over the third factor, but hungry now for more battle. He felt humiliated that his master would see how he had won, by deception, a mere trick over insignificant teenagers. This angered him into a slow building rage he knew would only increase. He wanted his rage to build. Needed it white hot.

Sensing Rhea's quantum echo, one death would not be enough. He would show his master utter victory, unsullied and brilliantly executed, and then he would come back for the bitch and snatch her out from under the lazy grip of the vaunted *Lirim Ne*.

Chapter 29

Drawn by the strange force engulfing the Claddagh figurine and knowing the general direction she had to go, Rhea corrected her path after leaving the bedroom. Phoebe didn't know how she did it, but Rhea had also extended the black hole thing, like reaching out with another arm, and yanked Dryer out of the shed. In another moment Phoebe and Rhea were standing in a cavernous room in the basement of the Natural History Museum. Dione lay unconscious on the floor, her mind almost completely shut down, but not dead. Dryer had been handled so roughly it broke the hold Phoebe had on him. He groaned after hitting the floor and managed to sit up, groggy.

Rhea bent over Di, caressing her hair, whispering for her to wake, to be all right, to live. When Phoebe gently entered her mind, Di woke.

"Are you okay?" Rhea asked, sobbing the words out.

Dione blinked and tried to get to her elbows but couldn't. "This floor is hard." She groaned and fell back down. Rhea pulled her to a sitting position. "Where are we?"

"After you were hit and we escaped, I told Rhea to take us to the museum—like we planned all along."

"But—Mom—that big man." Dione groaned again and tried to lie back down. Phoebe held her up.

"I know his plan, Di, and I told Mom we were okay. She'll be fine."

"He thinks he finished me, doesn't he?"

Phoebe nodded. "He's gonna follow us, though. I had to lead him away from Mom. He wants to kill all of us, and he wants to capture Mom and take her away. That's what I saw in his mind. They're looking for the stones. They think Mom can help them, but they're here—right in there." Phoebe pointed to a group of lockers. "We've got to hurry and get them and then get back to Mom."

Di grimaced and settled against a row of lockers. "How'd you know to come here?"

"This old figurine helped, and Rhea said she could get us to the museum, but right before we left, I planted a thought in Mom's mind that everything was going to be all right. When I made contact with her, I saw that she knew where the stones were. She knew about this room. Someone named Charlotte has been helping her. She and Mom were just here, looking around this very room."

Di started to say something, but Dryer groaned again, and she saw him for the first time. "How'd *he* get here?"

"I did that," Rhea said. "We were gonna use him to help us, so I thought it better be now."

Phoebe didn't have time to debate the idea. She looked down the row of lockers. "Can you feel that? It's coming from the stones right inside there."

Dione sat up cross-legged and rested against Rhea, kneeling behind her. With difficulty she raised her hand toward the locker and what had been invisible for nearly four decades began to faintly pulsate in the visible spectrum. It presented a dazzling array of colors dancing wildly as if enlivened by Dione's mere presence. There was a perceptible vibration coming from it and a humming sound, very faint.

Dryer felt it, too. He'd overheard everything. "So, they've been here all along." He looked at Phoebe with expectant eyes. "That's great for you." He stood, still fighting the effects of the state Phoebe had kept him in.

"Well, thanks for bringing me back to the city. You made me miss my return flight, you know." He hesitated and looked at his watch, glanced back at Phoebe. "You've had me for close to thirty hours?"

Phoebe nodded. "We've taken care of you, gave you water. You don't remember because I sort of swi—"

"Shit!" he said. "My boss is going to kill me." He looked around. "It's been fun, but I have to—"

Phoebe lifted her hand. "You're not going anywhere. Time to pay up."

"You've cost me my job!"

"And you stole from us and said you'd help. Now's the time."

"Shhh," Dione said before Dryer could protest more. "You hear that?"

Phoebe and Rhea glanced at each other. "No."

"Never mind," Dione whispered. "It's beautiful."

It was a low murmur they finally heard after listening close enough. It seemed to be calling to them with an urgency they began to feel.

Phoebe understood immediately. "The information was planted in Mom by our grandmother. It was like I could speak directly to her, though she's been dead so long. Di, I think she knew things about this prophecy.

She thought she would be the one to have us, or children like us, triplets. But instead, she had Mom, and it was her instead. And she's helping us now. It's in this Claddagh and the word Mom remembered. We're the only ones who can get the stones. Our grandmother fixed it that way."

"But, how?"

"I don't know how. I just know it's true. But it's really just you. Rhea and I don't have your power. You're the one who can get through those doors, just like we got through that barrier in Mom's mind, but this is much bigger, stronger. It's been dormant so long. We must have just activated it. Can you feel it?"

"Something's around that locker. Look at it glowing."

Dione held her hand up against the fluctuating quantum trace. Phoebe had picked up these words from her mother's mind. It was what they'd faced already; another barrier of some sort, but this one was much stronger. There was a thickness in the air around the locker and it stirred one way then another as the strange glow undulated. The large room was now backlit by the eerie glowing miasma, shadows playing off the walls and ceiling in tune to their grandmother's quantum trace, like spirits dancing in wild ecstasy.

"Do you think you can get up?" Phoebe said to Di. "We have to do this quickly before he comes after us."

"Too late," Rhea said, rising and looking over her shoulder as a dark tunnel popped open across the cavernous room, darkening rather than lighting it.

Phoebe followed Rhea's gaze. *Di, you rest here. He thinks you're dead and I want him to keep thinking that.* Phoebe turned to Dryer, and whispered, "Stay with her and keep out of sight. If you do something stupid, I don't know if I'll be able to protect you."

She placed the Claddagh in Dione's hands. It began to radiate softly and seemed to whisper to her.

"But you need my help," Di said, ignoring the Claddagh.

"Not this time," Rhea said quietly as she turned to face Primilov, walking slowly and confidently toward them.

"Who's that goon?" Dryer asked, but there was no time for an answer.

****

Jason Wight jumped to his feet from the chair where he'd been sleeping. Not knowing who had summoned him, he acted by following the dim echo of the dissipating thought worm and arrived on the sidewalk in front of Madeline's bungalow. He had opened his tunnel next to the agent on duty.

"What the—" the startled agent said, but Jason immediately quieted him.

Jason turned toward the house. The faint echo had vanished. "I have to go inside," he said, struggling to understand what was happening.

"We were told not to bother them."

"I know—contact Livingstone and Brownedyke—get them here. There should be four people in that house, but there's just one."

"What—that can't be—"

"There's no time!" Jason bellowed. "Get them here."

Jason turned to the house, sure he had just been summoned by his *Puzur* class daughter, but he wasn't sure how that was possible. In no mood to argue, Jason tunneled into the house. He flicked on the lights as he moved cautiously room to room.

****

Dimitri Primilov laughed as he saw the two brunette sisters stand then turn to face him. They were attractive and, for the first time he thought perhaps there was time enough to have fun with them before following his orders. The third one was nowhere in sight. Dead, he knew, the third factor conquered. They were now just two ordinary *Puzur* teens, women really as he looked more closely at their forms. Yes, he would delay their deaths a bit.

He could sense directly the aura of the intelligent one, the one who had given him so much trouble before. He liked her dark curls. This time there was no strange psychic flow coming from her, from them. There was no odd mixture of the Sumerian and English filling his thoughts, no trance-like appearance. He was free to do battle on his terms. And they seemed scared, as well they should. He would make these young American brats pay for his earlier humiliation. Then he would turn them into whores before finishing the job.

But they were next to the locker he suspected was the one Rasmusun had mentioned. He could see the strange glow, could feel the force of the thing surrounding it as he reached out with his mind to touch it. When he tried to penetrate farther into the miasma engulfing the girls, something rebuffed him, some ill-defined unwholesomeness that made him cringe.

He backed off, feeling sullied. The glow and the susurration felt evil. His master would have to deal with it when he brought the mother back, but he wasn't worried about it now. He didn't know how the teens could have found their way here, but Rasmusun had warned him of the lockers, to exercise caution.

"Come away from there," he growled.

The two dark-headed girls were bathed in the glow. He sensed it was some form of protective force surrounding them. He called out to them again and they obeyed.

Primilov lifted his head. Whispers filled the air, a voice speaking words in a guttural dialect. As they came closer to him, he could see tentacles following them, writhing bands of energy. Sweat dropped from his forehead as he eyed the floating spirits dancing eerily on the far wall.

He sensed disdain toward him, but it only made him smile. It was curious and beyond strange, but it didn't remain that way for, in the next moment, a change came over him, building quickly to a strong and terrible pang of dread. Where curiosity had been, doubt now ate at him and for the first time in his life, he became afraid of someone else besides his master.

They finally pulled completely away from the dense fog surrounding them. He could see them clearly now for the first time. Young women. Their bodies pleasing in the torn night clothes they wore. Beautiful and dangerous. He shook himself as if discarding a bad dream. The perspiration of fear that had begun dried and, having conquered himself, he quickly regained his composure.

****

As long as this ugly man was here their mother would be safe. He wanted to kill them. Telepathy didn't tell Phoebe that. His eyes did. They were narrow and mean. And she knew he had other, more unpleasant, plans for them.

"Normally, we are polite and give our enemies a chance to join our side," he said, trying to sound magnanimous.

"You killed my sister," Phoebe lied. "We wouldn't join your club even if I believed your offer was real."

"Perceptive of you. There will be no offer. You must be sacrificed so my master's way to power is unimpeded. Tell me. What is that foul thing?" He pointed to the roiling disturbance surrounding the lockers and still engulfing Di and Dryer.

Phoebe turned to look where Dione was sitting quietly just out of the madman's line of sight. She looked weak in the smoky disturbance, dread etched across her delicate face. Dryer was bent over her, his hand on her back. *Good, he's obeying.* Then Dione noticed her and smiled, but the smile didn't last. It faded as she stiffened into an involuntary trance, head thrown back, face blank and expressionless, her mouth a narrow slit.

Phoebe felt the raw power flow into her and turned back to their attacker.

****

The words came upon Primilov suddenly. Sumerian words. Not what he had at all expected. Nor was he as ready for it as he thought.

Before his eyes, the beautiful and tall black-headed girl seemed to become insubstantial. She appeared to be in many places at once as if tunneling instantly from one location to the next as any *Puzur* class individual could do. But this was so different. Vestiges of her physical form lingered here and there around the room. She was moving so fast he couldn't get a fix on her, so he concentrated on the intelligent girl instead. But again, his curiosity slowed him, and before he could act with force, he had his answer.

Amagal ib šedu, the little intelligent one said to his mind with fearsome force that caused his ears to explode out. Before he could collapse a whirlwind took him up. It was something the other one was doing. It took him into the air where he hung, momentarily suspended, ten feet above them, held up as if he were a puppet. As he began falling twin tentacles from this strange force protecting the girls twined around him and held him aloft. There he stayed, consciousness slipping from him, but still alive.

****

Phoebe stared at him, dumbfounded. He was dangling like a rag doll in the air as she came back to herself.

"What did you tell him just then when he asked what that was?" Rhea said.

"The truth," Phoebe said, "that the spirit of my dead grandmother was mad at him."

****

Immersed once again in the miasma of the quantum trace protecting the stones, Dryer helped Phoebe pull Dione to her feet. He seemed perfectly fine now because his reporter instincts had finally kicked in. He had pulled a small note pad and pen from his pocket and was scribbling on it, apparently having decided that maybe he had a story to tell, after all.

"Who was that?" he said.

"We'll talk later, Mr. Dryer, I promise. And thanks for helping with Di." Phoebe looked at Rhea. "We really appreciate it."

"What do we do now?" Di whispered, too scared to talk any louder with Primilov dangling some twenty feet away. "This thing is shaking so much it's making my fingers numb."

The Claddagh was vibrating violently as if an angry bee trapped inside was trying to get out. The Sumerian words of their dream were emanating from it, clearly spoken by their grandmother. Phoebe glanced at Rhea and communicated the idea that the stream of words was no longer random but were being spoken in whole sentences. They had no idea what it was trying to communicate, but there was one thing.

"It's reacting to you, Di." Then Phoebe suddenly said, "*Barag.*"

It was the word to open the trace. Nothing happened, except there seemed to be even more pressure building and the quantum trace was no longer as pleasant for them as it had been. Something was happening to it. The pressure had greatly increased. It seemed to be inside them, inside their heads.

"You say it, Di," Rhea moaned as she put her hands to her ears. "Hurry!"

Dione looked frightened and would have run if she could. She swallowed hard and held the Claddagh out at arm's length, the vibrations worsening. "*Barag,*" she said clearly.

There was a loud moan as if the Claddagh had breathed its last breath, finally glad to be free of its responsibility and ready to rest after holding its secret so long. It cracked in several places and crumbled out of Dione's outstretched hand.

"I broke it," Di gasped, looking in horror at the pieces lying on the floor around her. "Mom's gonna kill me."

"No, she isn't, silly. It was probably meant to do that. It's done its job."

Dione didn't hear these words. Instead, she sagged against Phoebe as power escaped her. Dryer held her up before she could drop in a pile. Not unconscious, but not fully awake either, Dione began muttering incoherently, as weak as a newborn.

Phoebe thanked him with a thought as the pressure relented and the miasma that had become even thicker slowly cleared. But the susurration, this time coming from the locker, increased in intensity.

Before their stunned eyes a round hole appeared in the locker. It was like the opening of one of Rhea's black holes except much larger and with fluorescent scarlet flashes around the edges. Whispers coming from inside called for them to enter.

Dryer entered and sat Di down in a corner to continue his note taking.

"What next?" Rhea said, her voice quavering.

"I guess we have to go in there, too."

Rhea looked stunned but didn't say a word.

There was nothing for it. As they walked through the opening, the locker, or what it had become, opened into a large room, a kind of other dimensional space, a quantum compartment. Phoebe somehow knew the term from her mother's veiled memory. It was much larger than the mere two-foot-deep cabinet they had been standing near. The room was even larger than their big kitchen at home, probably half as large as their entire house.

"Go get them," Dryer said, "and let's get the hell out of here before more goons show up.

The room was black and with the same red flashes flickering everywhere, making their hair rise and their skin tingle.

"Look!" Phoebe said.

Against the far wall held up by what appeared to be those same weird tentacles were the ten stones of ancient Sumer.

Not wasting any time, they ran to them. The tablets were each a different size and shape, ragged looking and thin, the thickest about a half inch and the thinnest no more than an eighth of an inch. The largest was about eighteen inches at its widest point and the smallest about ten inches. They appeared to be sandstone chiseled out of a larger piece and smoothed over to make a neat writing surface.

Phoebe took down the smallest and examined it. The tablet was covered with small runic symbols in rows on its front and back surface. Phoebe placed it back in its original position and gave Rhea a hug.

Rhea smiled at her. "We really did it."

The stones would explain who they were and why they were able to do this magic or whatever these powers were. The stones would also help their mother as they were obviously put there for her to find. They were just about to gather them up when their grandmother began speaking.

The psychogeist finished forming as Phoebe turned. There she was, tall and proud. She appeared to be in her late twenties, beautiful and with scarlet hair that came down to her shoulders in wavy swirls. Probably the way she looked just before her death, except the psychogeist didn't show her pregnancy.

"Since this trace is opened, at last, you have found

the Stones of Sumer. Congratulations, my children, for only you three could have done such a thing. I can't know in what circumstances you find yourself or whether your mother even still lives. I can only now proceed as if she has had the kind of life I would have wished for her and the kind of education I would have given her myself. But I induced John, your grandfather, to provide a proper education for her, in case anything happened to me so that these peculiar runes could be properly translated in the fullness of time.

"If she is not here, you must take the stones to her. Only she can finish my work. With just a little study, she will be able to begin. Our clan will be happy indeed and certainly the whole people, the *Gu Umia*, as we say, will welcome what the stones have to teach them. If he still lives, tell Livingstone that I am happy he will see our dream fulfilled. And I am also happy for the contributions he will no doubt make to that end for the survival of our people.

"Now for you three. If you haven't already, you must seek out Livingstone. He will guide you concerning the prophecy and advise you in the coming conflict. Trust him as you would me and trust to your own abilities. Be brave, my little *Puzurs*, and fulfill your destiny."

As Martha began those last words Phoebe reached out to her, but of course not her; only a semblance of her real grandmother was there. She started fading and, in doing so, this short, old man standing behind them at the door to the compartment cried out.

****

At a quarter to seven, Rasmusun was beyond anxious, his pacing frenetic, his mumbling incoherent.

He couldn't imagine why Primilov hadn't contacted him. Looking at Charlotte, who had remained as mute as a priest listening to confession, he decided to act. As he shuffled over to her, she shrank back from him but couldn't get away. He grabbed her arm and pulled her erect, and then they were suddenly in the cavernous room of the museum, which had been turned into a den of terror.

"Who're you?" the shorter of the two girls asked as she spun toward Rasmusun and Charlotte.

"I was just about to ask you the same thing, girl, but I've no need of that, do I?"

Charlotte suddenly gasped as she saw a third girl lying silently beside her. Turning his head, Rasmusun saw her too and recognized the family resemblance.

"The triplets—of course. Dimitri wasn't entirely successful, I see."

One appeared to be dead, but Rasmusun wasn't taking any chances. He was well past his prime and was never disposed to battle, so he began backing away as the tall, pretty one yelled, "You're with him!" She pointed to Dimitri, still dangling some feet away.

The short girl, the one with the piercing eyes, entered his mind, throwing Rasmusun to his knees before them. Her examination was quick and thorough, and then she discovered something she hadn't counted on, a secret not even his master knew.

"Murder," she breathed in barely a whisper. "Murderer," she said again, more dangerous this time.

The realization of who this man was shocked her, and in her youthful inexperience the connection that held him in place broke. Taking advantage of her surprise, Rasmusun jumped to his feet and cleared the opening in two quick steps. Momentarily forgetting who he was, instead of using his talents he used his old feet and ran blindly into the now darkening room. But he ran right into Primilov still being held by the weakening quantum trace, now dangling only a foot in the air.

Rasmusun fell over him and together they crashed to the floor, their bodies tangled, the collision reviving Primilov from his stasis.

In a moment, Primilov was on his feet, his faculties restored. He saw them and his rage blossomed. In one furious growl, he turned fully toward the American girls who were gawking at him from the entrance to the strange quantum compartment.

Chapter 30

Saturday

Livingstone and Brownedyke arrived at Madeline's house moments after being contacted. They were briefed in seconds and Livingstone's purplish tunnel opened in the living room of Madeline's bungalow on the other side of the front door where they found the house well lit, but no one in sight.

At one glance, they took in the essence of her home. Everything seemed to have been placed haphazardly; the furniture didn't match but was thrown together regardless of design. The room was fiercely decorated with books, mostly professional volumes related to Madeline's work, which meant they were all of three broad categories—linguistics, history, and historiography with the occasional esoteric volume on runology thrown in. Two large Alexandra style cherry wood bookcases held most of these, but others were scattered throughout the room, placed randomly about. Floor to ceiling bookshelves contained an eclectic mixture. Fiction of various kinds covered two other walls.

The house seemed to be in order—no movement, only a pervasive quietness. As they walked through the menagerie of books, Livingstone said telepathically, "*Jason?*"

"First bedroom down the hall, Professor."

****

Earlier, Jason had found Madeline sleeping peacefully in her double bed, on her back, half uncovered, her nightshirt torn, breasts exposed. The emotions that assaulted his mind were almost unbearable. Legally, this was still his wife, but this was not his bedroom, and he had no right to be standing there, looking at her.

It was like the intervening years had melted away, and tears came to his eyes, anguish mixed with anger mixed with happiness. He thought she looked exactly as he remembered her, older, but not that it spoiled her beauty. She seemed larger than life, an elemental force, her scarlet hair brighter now than he remembered, her white skin glowing in the soft light sneaking in from the hallway.

Jason touched her gently on the shoulder and called her name. She didn't stir. Her skin was cold, so he covered her fully, purposefully pulling the covers so as to rouse her. She remained deadly still, her breathing even and slow. Her unresponsiveness made him uneasy, and as he looked at her apprehension flooded his mind. Something wasn't right. A wild shiver crept into him as he feared the worse.

Livingstone arrived at that moment and was at her side instantly. After a minute he had the problem diagnosed.

"She's been tampered with," he said softly, continuing to probe her mind. "She's all right, but before I bring her around let's have a look at the rest of the house. Jason, go to the other rooms down the hall. I'll stay with her in case she awakens. Darius, search

354

the other areas—quickly."

Moments later, they heard Jason's anguished cry. They found him kneeling on the floor of the girls' room, his eyes wide and tortured. "My children," he kept saying.

The devastation was terrible. One half of the room was destroyed including two beds and what could have been a chair. One wall was broken through, and the ceiling was cracked in that corner. The children weren't there, but there were no physical signs of injury.

Brownedyke had his agents search the other rooms more thoroughly along with the entire yard. The children were gone without a trace.

After what seemed like hours, Jason got up and went back to his wife's room. Livingstone and Brownedyke found him holding a picture frame showing the development of his children from early infancy to what looked like present day. The resemblance of the two brunettes to their father was striking, but even the redhead had a pale resemblance of his nose. He looked up at the other two, smiling weakly, and said, "My girls," holding up the pictures for them to see.

"Come, let's revive Madeline and get to the bottom of this," Livingstone said with noticeable strain in his voice.

They discussed the best way to proceed to reduce the shock. Livingstone could tell her semi-comatose state had been induced. He brought her to a state of controlled consciousness. In minutes, he had her awake and sitting up in bed, her mind fighting to regain control. It took several more minutes to bring her to the next level and then Livingstone released her.

Jason sat next to her, holding her hand. Brownedyke and Livingstone stood alongside. She came around to full awareness, looking up at the men. Livingstone had prepared her well. There was no panic.

"J-Jason?" she said thickly, as though she had spoken to him only yesterday and every day prior going back eighteen years. "How are you—why—where—"

"Someone attacked you."

"What?"

"We can talk later. Right now, we have to tell you something. This is Professor Lucian Livingstone and Dr. Darius Brownedyke, my associates, and good people. They want to help you—and me."

"The girls—Jason have you met—" She tried to get up. "Wh—what time is it?"

"Not yet. They're not here—"

"Oh, th—they must be at school. Wait till you see them."

Jason turned to Livingstone for help, pleading with his eyes. Livingstone just nodded his approval to continue. He turned back to her. "Madeline—listen. You didn't oversleep. It's barely past one o'clock in the morning. Saturday morning. Something happened here. We've only just come and discovered you unconscious. The girls are gone."

"Gone?" Madeline said, still not comprehending. "Where?"

"Did you hear anything earlier?"

"Earlier? I-I slept soundly." She did sit up this time. "Where are my girls?"

Jason took her hand. "There was a struggle, but we don't see any signs that they were injured. They're not here."

Fully awake, comprehension dawned. She overcame Jason's resistance and jumped out of bed. Before they could stop her, she had run into their room where she stopped, both hands over her mouth.

"What happened?" she sobbed.

Jason didn't know what to do, so he let the years of anguish and his recent anger melt away. He wanted to comfort her, but he paused as she turned to him. She hesitated, too, but only for a moment, and the look on her face was enough to break him all the way down. He stepped closer, and she fell into his arms, sobbing on his shoulder.

Livingstone and Brownedyke walked somberly to the kitchen and began brewing coffee.

****

After quieting her, Jason led Madeline back to her bedroom where he left her behind to dress. He placed an agent at the door. They had clearly been attacked, but why hadn't the agents on duty noticed? Jason was furious with everyone, but especially with himself for agreeing to take the slow course. How had his family been found so quickly by the enemy?

Entering the kitchen, he refused to acknowledge the looks of Livingstone and Brownedyke. He turned inward, waiting for Madeline to come to them, barely listening to Brownedyke giving instructions.

He had already organized a search. He now had SAL focused singularly on one task—find the triplets. But this was impossible. They could be anywhere in the world or all three could be dead or in Greece if they were captured. Miss Vivian had versed them on her findings and how Rhea could produce a perfect tunnel from what she had seen and recorded with

Livingstone's quantum flux detector. They had its signature recorded. If she tunneled, they would have her location instantly. Then there were the other two and there was no longer any question—the three were *Puzur* class, and at least one of them was producing quantum distortions off the charts.

Using Ithaca as an epicenter, every agent they could muster began a detailed circular search pattern. They could move great distances in a short time so the circle began enlarging quickly, but this would prove a fruitless exercise.

Madeline then entered the room looking ragged. Her world had crashed and burned.

****

The idea of Jason, always close to the front of her mind, was almost as much a shock to her as her missing children now that he was physically present. His great strength gave her hope, but she was embarrassed and at the same time glad for the help he could provide.

Livingstone thought it a good idea for the four of them to talk together. He had a plan, but he needed information.

"Tell me exactly what you remember," he said calmly.

"That broadcast Saturday night—I-I responded to it about an hour after I heard my mother's name mentioned. I debated what to do. I finally called but got a recording."

"We had you located at that point," Brownedyke said. "Unfortunately, we think our men were being followed by the enemy. We're trying to find out how they became aware of what we were doing."

Livingstone patted her hand. "Madeline, our reason

for wanting to find you had to do with finding information about your mother. It was by chance that we discovered your existence and your marriage to Jason. You can imagine his shock. He thought you were dead, as you wanted, I might add." She looked at Jason with a sick feeling. She wanted to explain and tried to begin, but Livingstone cut her off. "You and your husband obviously have some issues to discuss, but that will have to wait. What do you remember from last night?"

"After I didn't get through, I was relieved. I decided to sleep on it and try again in the morning if I continued to think it was the right thing to do. I called again and got another recording. The rest of the day and night I tried to put it out of my mind. Then the girls and I went to bed, and...I guess I overslept."

"But you didn't. Whoever came had induced a kind of comatose state. You would have struggled out of it eventually. I merely helped speed up the process. It's still the middle of the night, Madeline."

"Oh," she said weakly, looking at Jason again who now had turned away completely, staring out of the large kitchen window. She turned back to Livingstone. "Thank you."

"How do you feel now, my dear?" Livingstone asked.

"For some reason I feel calm—shaky, but calm. Phoebe said they were escaping and would be all right, so that helps."

Madeline said these words nonchalantly but looked up with surprise as soon as she did. "Wait, what did I say?"

Jason turned from the window, full of expectation.

"Madeline, if you please…"

And she felt a floating sensation but came out of it almost immediately.

"Quite remarkable. I think that we can say that we have at least two *Puzur* class children, and I suspect that all three are," Livingstone said.

Madeline nodded. "I know. They revealed it all to me after that woman showed up here. I remembered what Jason said about the prophecy, and I discussed it with them."

"What do you remember of the prophecy?" Livingstone said.

"Jason had explained everything to me. The next day I learned of my pregnancy." She turned to him, tears building in her eyes. "Oh, Jason, please forgive me. I was so scared—my mother—"

Before she could go on, she started to sob. Jason didn't hesitate. He came and held her hand.

"Phoebe planted a message," Livingstone said, breaking in. "Escape is the operative word, but there is more. Madeline, Dione was hurt, but I can't tell how serious it is. But still more—I find from Phoebe's mind that her attacker was very pleased. The enemy would only need one to die for the prophecy to be broken, you see. We've always thought the third factor works in concert. He was never after all three, necessarily. He thinks she's dead, but I believe he's wrong."

Madeline instinctively clutched Jason's arm and didn't let go.

"It seems that Phoebe thought she was all right. You witnessed the attack, but the attacker, Primilov, who I know by reputation, induced a state in you that had your mind suppress it, but I've drawn it out. Do you see now? Do you remember?"

She could see the attack now. "Dione is not dead, then?"

"I don't believe so," Livingstone said. "The girls did the only thing they could do and that was run. Jason, please, you look—privacy, you know."

Jason turned to Madeline. "I need to pull out completely what you witnessed. I can do this without your permission, but our codes don't allow such intrusiveness, not even in married couples. I wouldn't want to look into your private life. Do you understand?"

It was an awkward moment, but Madeline held his gaze. "My life is open to you. I haven't done anything I'm ashamed of since the day I left."

He nodded and she felt an immediate floating sensation. She closed her eyes as if resting.

****

Jason held her gaze a moment, contemplating these words, but then entered her mind using a soft probe. As he probed, he saw the detailed account of the attack from the moment she had entered the room. He marveled at the strange demeanor of his girls. It was all clear to see from Madeline's perspective, but he saw something else that began to soften the hard edge he had felt coming on since they found her.

Her motives, her fears. He was able to look back at his Community from the eyes of an outsider and see that all was not good. In fact, there was outright danger there, and it frightened him.

But he saw even more. She had thought of him, often it seems, and in not a bad light. He saw sadness, and much longing that had been squelched for the sake of their children and, it seemed to him, for his own safety. He saw that she had made an ultimate sacrifice for them and given up on a chance for happiness for herself in things that mattered to adults. She hadn't hated him at all, but she had loved her children more than herself and had done these things to protect them all.

Madeline opened her eyes, and he held her steady gaze. A change had come over him. It had been hard for her to look at him. He felt her embarrassment, her shame for abandoning him.

He knew one thing. He was incomplete without them, but he didn't know if he could capture ever again the family he had begun so many years ago. He had let it all slip through his fingers, but the woman he had once loved and wed was sitting there, her shining eyes locked onto his.

Chapter 31

Primilov pursued the two girls to the opening of the strange dimensional compartment. He had sent off blast after blast from the hands of his awful power. Several rows of lockers were blown apart in the violent display and the wall behind the compartment cracked down the middle. Sirens could be heard outside on the street. The blasts and the building alarm had alerted the police.

Rasmusun had seen the stones. They were in easy reach, but those girls were in the way. Several of the stones had been dislodged and had fallen to the floor. He could only watch the display of Primilov's fury, but then one of Dimitri's wildly aimed blasts hit the opening of the quantum room directly and, though the trace had faded significantly, Rasmusun could tell it would begin to resonate and rebound with exponential strength in wildly exaggerated proportion to the blast it had absorbed—a powerful blast.

"Stop!" Rasmusun screamed to Dimitri, but he couldn't hear over the carnage and his rage.

Cowering in a corner, Charlotte began making her way to the entrance of the cavernous room, seeking her chance to run, no doubt. The two dark girls could barely stay on their feet. They ran back to the dead girl and dragged her to a far corner of the room. Rasmusun saw a man with them, probably a museum employee. The three of them stood in front of the dead sister.

"Do something!" Rasmusun heard the pretty one say. She had been blocking fragments of flying wood using her telekinesis to build a shield. Impressive.

They crouched behind it, but they weren't safe. The resonance had built slowly but inexorably. Great rings of distortion waves spread out from the epicenter near the door in a three-hundred-sixty-degree pattern. Dimitri was at the door now in the center of it all.

A great gonging sound emanated from the quantum trace. The room they were in began to vibrate, the quaking making it difficult to stand.

Quantum effects manifested as wildly undulating ribbons of color exploded from within the room in ever widening circular bands. As if replaying the immediate past, the quantum distortion produced a temporal display—two girls and a man dragging a third girl through the opening door.

"What is it?" Rasmusun screamed above the vibrations.

The scene repeated itself the same way each time. The two dark-haired girls left the man with their sister and ran to the stones.

Dimitri entered the room, but the ghostly images disoriented him. He swung his arms wildly at the images, his rage taking on a purely physical dimension. He lost his balance and fell over.

A terrible scream escaped him as he vented his rage against the ghostly figures. He realized his folly only after Rasmusun planted a thought in his head about what he was seeing. This halted him, and standing, he quieted himself, searching for his enemies.

The little man flung himself at Dimitri just as he sent another killing blast at the children. This time the small girl was hit but being inside the quantum flux the energy of the blast had dissipated greatly, absorbed by Martha's trace.

Dimitri cursed violently at this, but it was too late for another try. The pretty one had collected her sisters and the man as another blast tore toward them.

"They're gone!" Rasmusun wheezed. Primilov had grabbed his throat. "We...must...go!"

He struggled to breathe. His small hands clutched at Primilov's meat-hooks, but Primilov's rage was slowly abating, control reasserting. He released his companion and began casting around for some sign of the teens.

"We'll be killed," Rasmusun screamed."

Dimitri looked around, the strange apparition scene still playing out before him, quantum distortions building, pressure coming down on them as though they stood at the bottom of the Atlantic. The fire in his eyes finally dimmed.

"The whores," Dimitri said weakly. "Must finish— the job."

Rasmusun pleaded with him. "You've obliterated the prophecy. This is a great victory for our master."

"Their mother then," he growled, trying hard to regain his senses.

"We don't need her any longer. We have the stones. See!" Rasmusun held up an arm full of the tablets he had just taken down. "Now!" he cried, "before it's too late!"

The throbbing of the quantum distortion was getting louder with each passing second, the sound penetrating their bodies, seemingly arising out of the very fabric of space-time. Rasmusun raised his one free hand to his ear trying vainly to block it.

"Now!" Rasmusun screamed again.

Dimitri reacted by grabbing the rest of the Stones of Sumer. As he retrieved the last of them, the quantum compartment dissolved. Suddenly it was a mere locker again. They stood in the aisle before it. The locker pulsed just as their transport tunnel closed their ears to the explosion that followed.

****

Rasmusun's tunnel opened on the same veranda from which he had departed. They placed the tablets on the table beside the ornate outdoor chair. The old man promptly sat down, exhaustion washing over him, his adrenaline high abating slowly. Primilov stalked off into the mansion.

He looked out over the Aegean where a beautiful sunrise presented itself. He was content to sit and stare, reflecting on his night's work. The morning sky, bright with mystery, somehow added to the inscrutability of the orders he had received, of the odd scenes he had witnessed. The red disk rising out of the east remade the sea into a vast bed of molten copper.

Yawning copiously from lack of sleep, he admired the red sun beginning its ascent over the beautiful Aegean. It illuminated the shimmering blue early morning sky with a translucent pink sheen. Sparse, white billows streaming overhead were painted with a tinge of the red rays. But the glory of the picture couldn't assuage his weariness. His head began to nod when his master surprised him.

"*Are you comfortable, thief?*"

The strength of the communication was like a tractor rolling through the depths of his mind. His hands flew instinctively to his head. The man's father had been far easier to deal with.

"Master. Y-you startled me."

"With your mind, buffoon!"

"Yes, yes, I forgot."

"I see that you have them."

"Yes, they're here."

"Good, bring them to my study in the west wing."

Muttering to himself, he lifted the ten stone tablets wearily and half-staggered through the expansive mansion seeking the west wing.

Luckily, Victor hobbled up to him and showed him the way, grinning at his labor and warning him not to drop them, but doing nothing to help. The marble floors echoed his footsteps throughout the vast interior as Rasmusun sped along clumsily, following Victor.

When they were placed before him, Erazmos examined them one by one. "Made by the hand of *Saĝtuku* himself," Erazmos exclaimed reverently. "I do not remember that my father ever had a scholar's interest in such things. Quite the contrary, the only thing he was ever interested in was making money. Isn't that right, Victor? You knew him better than anyone."

Victor nodded. "But he had other reasons to be interested in this and the means to acquire the information he was seeking. The other nine clans, even those who think themselves most noble, can be bought, you see. One member must have heard something about an unusual discovery and informed him for a handsome price, I am sure. But I am old now and do not remember why these may be so important."

"It's easy—the answer, I mean," Rasmusun

stammered, still breathing heavily. "I remembered while at the museum that my colleague was onto something that would have intrigued the whole Community. It was some kind of important information your father wanted buried. But what it could have been I don't know."

"But why?" Erazmos asked, puzzled. "If you worked closely with this person, could you not tell us the purpose of the work?"

"Actually, no—she was secretive about the translation, and she certainly didn't confide in me. She never really got started in earnest on the work before her accident."

"And who might she be? This person you mentioned, the stones' discoverer."

"Martha Alleyn. A very well-known archeologist and a very talented linguist. A member of clan Zid, if memory serves."

"I see. Victor said your previous work with the stones was incomplete. Could you not complete the translation now so we can all know what it was my father wanted buried?"

"Yes, well, it never really was…uh, what I mean to say is that I had little understanding of the inscriptions. It was really her work, you see. This wasn't my area at all."

"But you were her assistant," Erazmos persisted.

"Yes, but not in the translation work, Master, and I doubt there is anyone alive today that can do this work. The runes are not normal. As I remember now, she believed they were an oddity, an aberration. They don't follow the usual conventions. I was told at least this."

"Then the meaning of these inscriptions is lost to

us forever if what you say is correct," he said, frustrated.

"I'm afraid so, Master, but perhaps the daughter may yet be of use."

Erazmos looked at the stones admiringly—such precise work, beautiful markings. He passed his hands lightly over them as if trying to make a connection through the millennia to *Ad Saĝtuku*, his clan's founder, one of the ten ancient fathers of the *Gu Umia*.

"What I would not give to have the information they contain. The status that would bring me would make easy my rise to power." Erazmos sighed. "It is just as well. We do not need to think about anything else but the prophecy, do we, my friends? My father was probably right to keep this information, whatever it is, buried."

"Yes, Master."

"You are dismissed for now, Rasmusun, until I need you further. Victor, usher the others into the room."

Just before Rasmusun's tunnel closed, three figures dressed in black entered, one of whom was Dimitri. They approached Erazmos quickly and with great deference. Each in turn then dropped to a knee, but Erazmos bade them rise. He then beckoned the three worshipers to an alcove in the study set about with comfortable chairs. Rasmusun's tunnel then closed and he was gone, the hair on the back of his neck risen with lingering fear.

****

The alcove had been set with a splendid breakfast for at least ten—black sketos coffee, hard-boiled eggs, olives, feta cheese, and cinnamon koulourakia. Erazmos promptly beckoned Dimitri to report.

"I have completed my task—" He smiled. "—successfully."

"Good, good, my old friend—show me," Erazmos said.

At Erazmos's command, Dimitri became extremely still, and began to project from his mind directly in front of them the encounter with the children in the form of a holographic animation, complete with sound. This was the encounter in the bedroom only, but it showed Erazmos what he wanted to see, the proof he expected. The events that had occurred only an hour or so previously were played out again before the men seated there.

"Only one, then," Erazmos said, slightly disappointed. "No matter, but what of our enemies Livingstone and Brownedyke?"

"No one was there, Master."

As he looked again and again at the replay, examining the attack, he marveled at his clansman. "You fought with tactics to deceive. I am surprised at you, Dimitri."

"I found a way. These teens are strange. They are not regular *Puzur* class, and they have no training, but would have defeated even me."

"They are amazing, yes, quite amazing…maybe one day…" Erazmos's voice trailed off. Then he composed himself.

"But your fulfillment of my orders is only partial. Where is the woman?"

Dimitri hesitated. His master was right, of course. "It was Rasmusun. He bade me to forget her as we would have been destroyed by the explosion. I can go back."

"And now it is probably too late." Erazmos paced before him. "There will be other opportunities." He clapped his hands. "Come, the time is at hand, at last, my old, faithful friend. I have already summoned our people to begin planning."

Erazmos said this while pivoting and welcoming those with outstretched arms who were at that moment arriving in transport tunnels popping open around them. Dimitri stood there surprised at the quickness of the response.

"Dominion is now within our grasp." And turning again to Dimitri he said coldly and in a deep gravelly voice so that all could hear, "The Prophecy of Tarkus has failed."

And one by one the men who had arrived came near to him, and bowing to one knee, each kissed the ruby ring of Alexander Tarkus.

Erazmos smiled at Dimitri and thought now that he detected no doubt in his oldest comrade who was now more servant than friend.

Chapter 32

"I have it, professor," Jason said, clearing his throat, his voice husky and flat. "But my daughters...they...it's strange, their behavior during the attack. There was no fear. I sensed absolutely no fear where there should have been. Hell, I wouldn't have stood up to the attack half as well. They appeared to be semiconscious until the very end."

"Interesting," Livingstone said. "The prophecy concerning the third factor contains mysteries no one can possibly know. We're seeing their further development, probably forced on them because of the threat. We can use this information to throw the enemy off—confuse him, but your children and you, Madeline, will continue to be in danger. I believe they are out of danger for now and safe. They're talented to have escaped the one who attacked them."

Madeline looked from Lucian to Jason, her eyes wide with fear. "Oh, I feel so stupid...about everything...and now they're—"

Livingstone took her hand. "They concealed their abilities from you quite well. My dear, they've been developing powers for at least several weeks, probably longer, even unknown to them until recently."

"But how? I-I never knew until they confessed to me last night." Madeline looked at Jason. "I never knew."

Jason placed a hand on her shoulder. "It's okay, Madeline."

Livingstone motioned to Brownedyke. "Darius, we need to go." As he said this, Sarah Duckworth appeared beside them in the kitchen. She eyed Jason and Madeline holding hands and cleared her throat.

"*There's been a development,*" she said to the three *Puzurs* present. "*An explosion moments ago at the Natural History Museum down the street from headquarters destroyed about half the structure. The ordinary authorities suspect terrorists. We've been monitoring their communications. An eyewitness has been saying some wild things about being kidnapped and appearing and disappearing, about seeing two men and three girls blow up the museum. And,*" she said, motioning to Madeline, "*mentioning her name.*"

"*Nothing more of the children?*" Jason asked quickly.

"*Afraid not, Jason,*" Sarah said, staring at him and then at his hand still holding Madeline's. "*I was monitoring the situation here in Ithaca when I heard about the explosion—sorry.*" Her eyes darted back to Madeline's hand in his.

He didn't remove it, and Sarah turned away from them.

Madeline had been tracking their faces. "What is it, Jason, what's she saying?"

Jason took her other hand in his. "It seems the children were just spotted at the Natural History Museum. There was an explosion, but we don't know any more than that."

Madeline slumped against him.

"Who was this witness?" Livingstone asked.

"A woman. Seems she works there…her name's—"

"Charlotte Gentry," Madeline said softly. "She was helping me locate my mother's stone tablets. It must be her. There was an unsavory character she told me about. I saw him, too. They must have found the stones."

"Have they recovered any—" Livingstone began but stopped.

"Bodies?" Sarah finished. Madeline groaned. Sarah turned back to Livingstone. "Not yet. They've only just started the process." She put a finger to her temple. "Others are there now interviewing some witnesses. My people say they're talking to the press." She looked at Madeline again. "Your name keeps coming up. A Dr. Mark Harper and the curator of a section of the museum have confirmed your possible involvement."

Madeline groaned again.

"Darius, ask Vivian if she traced the child's tunnel with the quantum flux detector," Livingstone said quickly.

A moment later, Vivian Turnpike appeared in the room, her eyes puffy from lack of sleep. She acknowledged Madeline with a concerned smile. "My dear, I expected our next meeting to happen under much better circumstances."

"Not now, Vivvy," Livingstone interrupted. "How has the monitoring gone tonight?"

"As you know, we don't monitor in real time, but the machine records all the activity on all continents. We've been checking often. I'd finished reviewing the last hour's activity and, sure enough, I found her little darling's tunnel signature. It departed this house about an hour and a half ago, arriving at the museum a moment later. It began as a different morphology, though, but soon settled into her normal shape. It had four people in it."

Madeline looked at Jason, "Four?" And then she remembered. "There was a reporter here asking questions. He broke into the house while I was in Manhattan. The girls captured him. They must have taken him with them when they escaped. But why?"

Jason turned to Vivian. "And leaving the museum?"

"Two other tunnels were traced there. Primilov's we recognized, but the other is not known to us. We have no record of anyone leaving before the explosion."

Madeline hugged herself and Jason put a hand on her shoulder.

"But," Miss Vivian said quickly, "we also picked up a tremendous quantum distortion that would have obliterated all echoes of any tunnel leaving. I believe that distortion is what blew the place up. I would examine the recording if I were you, Professor. I've never seen anything like it before—such power. It built and grew until it began to fade and then there was a spike. Then the explosion happened. The timing of it coincided exactly."

"So, they could have gotten away," Jason said.

"Yes."

Madeline looked hopefully to Jason. "I have to believe they escaped again," he said squeezing her hand. "They're all right. I know they are."

She smiled at him and nodded.

"Our enemies have the stones," Livingstone said, his kind face transformed to something raw and hard.

Brownedyke said, "Sarah, you and Reggie drop your part in the search for the children and monitor the situation with the building. Tell us the moment bodies are found—if any are found."

With one look at Jason, which he returned fleetingly, Sarah was off in her own tunnel.

The two older men got up and prepared to leave, explaining to Madeline that she should prepare for a quick trip to Manhattan and the Society's headquarters.

"When I return, I will have to prepare both your minds with my girdle technique for my deception to work."

Madeline looked uneasy, but Livingstone went on. "You ran years ago, but circumstances have caught up to you and your children. You will not have to bear this alone. This burden is now fully upon you and your little family, and you must not falter. You must look to the strength you possess to protect your children, to no longer forsake your husband and the Community of which you are a member by birthright, as was your mother's family back through many millennia. Let us help you. You two must understand that you have a greater responsibility to the world around you. This is unfortunate, but true. You will have to make more sacrifices now. You can no longer run."

"What sacrifices?" Madeline said.

Professor Livingstone leaned forward, took Madeline's hands in his, and said, "We must not place your children in jeopardy again. We *must* protect them at all costs. They're too important. We have an advantage while he thinks one is dead, and we must encourage him in that misconception. He will not act too quickly, preferring to plan accordingly, and at a leisurely pace in his arrogance. The best way to protect and save your children is to keep them secret when we find them. This place is no longer safe. When I come to you again, I'll prepare you for a meeting at which you will be challenged by those who can gaze into your mind. You must feel real loss. And this sense of loss must be sustained. Only then will the deception succeed, and only then will they remain secret and, therefore, safe once we find them."

"Jason, I-I can't lose my children—not now."

Jason turned to her and embraced her gently. "And I have to gain them. You kept them from me. Now let me keep them safe. These people may try again and maybe succeed if we don't do this. They're bent on world domination, and they believe the children are the key to achieving it. They can't find out they've failed."

Livingstone stood over Madeline. "They won't be out of your lives entirely. We can create…circumstances…whereby you can see them. However, we will need to create and maintain in you a sort of mental and emotional distance from them. I'll disposition your mind to this end tomorrow morning. We will try to maintain the pretense of this supposed death. And we will find them as soon as possible."

Livingstone stopped, took Madeline's hands, and looked deeper into her blue eyes. "My dear, you are so like your mother. She would have been enormously proud of you. Know that you have friends in the Community, friends who loved your mother and all she stood for. We want to help you, Madeline. Don't shun that help, for your children's sake."

"I won't," she said. Then Madeline remembered her mother's words from the previous night. "I saw my mother last night."

Jason, Livingstone, and Brownedyke glanced at each other, but none dared comment on this revelation.

"She came to us. She spoke of you, Professor. Lucian. She said to trust you—that I have a task to do. Because of her, I'm not nearly as frightened as I have been."

Livingstone's heart swelled at the mention of Martha, and his resolve hardened. He would help this little family even if it killed him in the doing.

****

Not much later, having packed as much and as quickly as she could for an extended stay of indeterminable time at Jason's house, Madeline found him staring out the picture window facing her expansive backyard. Though waning in its cycle, the moon was now so much closer to the earth that it still dominated the night sky, hanging over the woods bordering Madeline's property like a huge, shadowy wraith.

She came alongside him, hesitated a moment, but before she could place her hand in his, he took the initiative. She had longed for this moment, dreamed of it, but knew in her heart they would never be together again. Yet, suddenly, here he was, the father of her children, the man she had run from to protect him and her unborn girls.

Fear remained—for herself, her girls, for Jason still—but there was resolve she hadn't felt all those years ago. She had always thought her father's paranoia had been transferred to her, but something more had been in play. Now she knew her mother's veiled presence, released from her mind by her daughters, had directed her. Somehow her powerful mother had given her that strong protective impulse, the overwhelming urge to run, guiding her steps, saving them all for this day. But now, finally, she had been found, and her running was over as Lucian Livingstone had said.

"I'm ready," she said in a small, firm voice. "Ready to go home." She didn't know how he would take the implication of her words.

He simply nodded but didn't say anything for a long moment. "They're out there... somewhere." His voice was husky and trembling with emotion. "I'm going to find them. I promise."

"I know, Jason." She wanted to draw nearer to him, but it was enough to be this close for now. "I-I don't know why, but I believe they're okay. They have to be." He looked down at her. She lifted her eyes to his and forced herself not to turn away, her shame over what she'd done to him nearly overpowering her again. "Please forgive me for ruining our marriage. I was frantic. I needed to—"

He put a finger to her lips. "I understand, Madeline. And I've already forgiven you. There's no more to be said. It was my fault as much as yours."

She nodded once, her lips quivering, but she forced back the tears welling up. No more crying until her girls were found. She turned back to the window, her chest growing tighter as fear entwined her heart. Her girls weren't safe. This prophecy. The frightening threat to the planet. Her mother's murderers still out there. Her family still a target even after all these years. Despite her reservations, she drew closer to him, dreading his response, needing him to accept her. She sighed when the tension seemed to drain from him.

"What will become of us, Jason? What will become of the world?"

He released her hand and put his arm across her shoulders, pulled her closer. "I don't know, Maddie. I really don't know."

"Maddie?" she asked, glancing up at him.

He had rarely called her Madeline before or after their marriage. His use of her nickname just now after all this time felt...right. Normal. And she knew then that she wanted him back, for her girls certainly, but also for herself.

While packing, knowing they were alone in the house, it felt so right, but that would have to wait.

He gave her a weak smile, his eyes sparkling, but the sadness she also felt was in them.

She moved even closer to him. "I suppose no one can know. And the girls are definitely a part of this prophecy, according to what you told me the night before I ran."

He grimaced and nodded agreement. That had been the real trigger to her overreaction. Talk of the prophecy, of these strange people they were all connected to, had frightened her far more than her father's rants and warnings ever had. And she knew her reticence to all things weird had been placed there by her mother. But now she needed to hear all of it.

She gently shrugged his arm off her shoulders and turned to him, her back to the window. "Tell me about it, Jason. I need to know." He didn't seem to be following her, so she said, "The prophecy...you only told me bits and pieces. You held back. Tell me all of it this time."

He sighed and turned away from her. When he

turned back, it was with a determination she could plainly see on his face. "It won't help much, but…" He hesitated, and before Madeline could speak up, a misty, smoky substance began to form around his head. Separating from him a moment later, the smoke began to form words. They appeared high overhead, an ephemeral tableau. The message lasted long enough for her to read every single word.

Earth will rise in that day to forge dominion,

Yet three, remote within its circle, will contest Earth's claim.

—Fire, Water, Air—

Father's pride, Mother's bane, Born as one

In the day Jupiter fades, in the month the Moon threatens

Earth groans, Fire ransoms

Death, Death, Oh Death;

Yet glad will be the whole people!

Madeline tore her eyes from the words as they began to fade. She turned away, her hands covering the sobs she wouldn't let escape. Before her children were born, months after running from her marriage, she hadn't let his brief description of this prophecy affect her. How could it? Who believed in such things anymore? But for years afterward, she hadn't thought of much else because of her mother's note, and that had kept her determined and away from him, hidden, safe. She thought so.

But now, seeing the very words floating before her, seeing the connection to her daughters. *Death…in triplicate.* Her daughters would have to die.

She felt him at her back, a tentative hand touching her, taking hold. "It doesn't mean anything, Maddie.

Believe me; it doesn't have to mean what you think."

She heard his words, understood them, their sentiment, trying as he might to allay her fears, but she began sobbing anyway.

Chapter 33

Three girls and a man crashed to the ground in a tangle of limbs. Phoebe groaned, rolled away from the thing poking her in the back, and reached up to the knot forming on her throbbing head. The pain was a good thing: it meant she was alive. But alive where?

Rhea had gotten them out, but not nearly far enough, barely across the street and down the road a bit from the museum. Moments later it had exploded and in that awful moment all hope of getting their grandmother's discovery back had ended. Phoebe had sensed those men escaping a moment before, had wanted to follow, but Rhea hadn't listened, and no amount of argument could convince her. She was done. And Di was definitely done.

There they waited and watched while on the street. She didn't know how long they remained there in the open, vulnerable. It didn't matter. No one came, and in the chaos all around them no one cared about four people watching from a safe distance. But they had to move so Rhea deposited them near their home in upstate New York.

Maybe.

Phoebe glanced around the gloom—woods, a forest. Even some strange, savage land would be okay if that crazy man they'd barely escaped hadn't sensed them and turned back.

Phoebe reached out into the dark with her mind. Could these be the woods they had often visited growing up? The National Forest near Seneca Lake was big enough to get lost in. And then there was that story of the wild man living there. An urban legend. Phoebe wasn't sure. Weird that Rhea would bring them here. She reached out with her mind again. No one.

Nothing seemed broken, so she got to her knees and saw Dione lying flat on her back a few feet away. She looked paler than usual, like death. Steven Dryer lay sprawled to the left. She studied his still form, regret bubbling up in her. He'd discovered the triplets by accident. Hadn't known of their power but had gotten a good taste of it since meeting them. Too bad for him. They'd captured him and with their abilities forced him to help. It was a debt he owed after stealing from their mother. There was no way he could escape them, but he'd slowly come to understand his purpose in all this. He was meant to help their family, and because Phoebe had gazed into his mind, she knew him, all his predilections, every nuance of him. She knew he would keep helping even without her control. And because of this knowledge it wasn't much of a gamble to trust him. He'd come through big time and been brave in the face of that bastard's attacks at the museum.

Only Rhea seemed to have managed a smooth landing. Phoebe reached out with her mind, feeling for Rhea's aches and pains. She knew then that her knees had taken a beating. She'd been thrown to the ground with enough force to break them, but Rhea seemed okay otherwise. The four of them were still alive, and that was the only thing that mattered. Not their tattered nightclothes or soiled appearance.

Phoebe managed to stand on shaky legs and tried to get some sense of the direction they'd taken, of the length of time they'd been borne aloft. It was useless. She doubted even Rhea would know. The disturbance that had been their grandmother's quantum trace and the explosion that had destroyed the museum had eliminated such sensory perception.

She managed to shuffle to where Rhea was bent over Dione, crying. Di was unresponsive, the result of the attack earlier that very night. Phoebe went to Dryer next and tried to stir him with a mental probe but gave up soon after. Her skills were still new. She wouldn't risk damaging him.

Then the full realization of their predicament descended on her as she noticed more of their surrounds, the noises of the forest spooking her at every turn. Though dark, these woods seemed familiar. That sycamore with the Z-shaped scar shining in the moonlight off to her right. The familiar sound of a nearby stream. Somehow Rhea had managed to bring them home. It was their woods.

With the tree as a landmark, Phoebe turned in the direction her house should be and let her mind drift out. People were there, and then they weren't. She shook her head, trying harder to clear thoughts that seemed glued together like they were stuck in mud.

Her mother should be there but try as she might she could not sense her.

Then her heart froze, and she knew the throbbing in her head was caused by more than the spill they had all taken. She had been sensing the opening and closing of those weird black objects, the same thing Rhea had used, just managing to save their butts before the explosion at the museum.

Their enemies were here. They'd been followed.

Her mother should be home but wasn't. They'd obviously taken her, but where? Before she could chase those thoughts very far, Phoebe glanced aside at Rhea who returned a frightened look. Dione moaned and Rhea turned back to her.

"We failed, Phoebe," Rhea said, sobbing over Di. She shook her sister's shoulder. "We failed our grandmother. We didn't get the Stones of Sumer, and now those men have them. We can't do what she told us."

Phoebe acknowledged all this with a stiff nod no one saw. What Rhea said was true, but it was no longer important. The stones would have to wait. Their mother was gone. These people had her. Her family's mortal enemies. She'd have to tell her sisters this soon enough. It was the only thing that mattered anymore. They had to get her back.

Phoebe shivered in the cold March air, her bed clothes failing to keep out the night chill. Suddenly, an owl called somewhere out in the darkness. A rush of wings and Phoebe jumped to her feet, looking into the canopy. Dancing shadows everywhere, swaying branches, but not a hint of wind. The bird hooted again, and this time Phoebe saw him glide onto a nearby limb. It looked at her and hooted a third time. She turned away and pulled the thin fabric tighter around her, terrified and wanting to move from this spot.

An irrational hate suddenly permeated the place. It seemed to be coming from…

They were in a tiny clearing, encircled by trees. Phoebe looked past them into the gloomy shadows.

Something was there, a watchful presence, but nothing physical. It exuded anger. Phoebe thought of the haunting laughter that had come to her days ago. She let her mind expand out again. Without warning, the trees began swaying as if in a furious enchantment.

Phoebe backed up to where Rhea was, trying to warm Dione as best she could. She reached out to Di's mind. No use. It still seemed like a blank, dead thing. It didn't worry her just yet. Di's talents weren't like her sisters'. That trance-like state she would fall into, the energy bands she would throw off were beyond strange.

The night sky dazzled over them, sparkling with a trillion stars, the almost three-quarter moon much too close, filling the sky like a giant ephemeral scythe, cutting the stars loose from their mooring.

Phoebe sagged, hands on her knees, the weight of all that had occurred crushing her. She was cold and wet, but she had Rhea. Di would be of little use this time; the two of them would have to manage alone.

She turned her mind to the house again, but it was no use.

Oh, where is she?

What she felt for her mother was like a deep empty place in her heart. Their enemies would be able to look into her mother's mind, and not gently as Phoebe had once done. She wanted to shout and curse at the outrage, but she kept a cool head, kept her thoughts to herself. Full of sorrow for her dead grandmother and the stones they had failed to retrieve. Full of hatred for her grandmother's murderer and their attacker. Her fists clenched. Her eyes watered.

Those people have my mother.

Rhea could move them from here easily enough,

but that wouldn't do with their mother missing. Her head throbbed again, and she finally reacted to it by reaching out with her mind. Someone had suddenly appeared in her backyard. A sentry, probably sent to wait for their return.

Phoebe's fists clenched tighter, and the man crumpled to the ground, unconscious.

It startled her, the power she now had to affect people with just a thought. It was something that could take her over, remake her into something she wouldn't recognize or want to become. But it felt so good. The power. This idiot deserved it. All these people did. They would all get the same when she found their mother. She'd make damn sure of that.

She realized the sentry hadn't been followed by others, so she looked into his mind. A low-level soldier, he didn't even know about her mother. Phoebe searched farther—through the house, down the street. Nothing nefarious. Nothing at all. Should they enter the shed at the back of her yard, operate from there for a little while? She shook her head. She couldn't chance staying on the property, not with these jerks coming and going. They didn't have much time. It was either the shed or...she didn't know just yet. Maybe Steven would have an idea.

Phoebe had been pacing around Di and Rhea without realizing it when she suddenly stopped. They needed a plan to get their mother back. These thoughts dominated now more than any other. Get even with the pricks that had done this to their little family, then get the hell out of Ithaca and start over somewhere else. She hated to do it, but the house and property were just too dangerous right now. They'd have to find someplace close from which to work. She told Rhea this without using her voice. Rhea nodded and soon she had collected Di and Steven and they were gone once more with Rhea's black hole flashing those aqua green sparks. The same color as Rhea's bright eyes.

A word about the author...

Nothing fascinates me like writing, creating stories, or sub-creating as JRR Tolkien referred to it. And, of course, to write and write well, one must read widely. It started early in my life and continues to this day. But long before I began writing stories, I worked long hours as a college professor, squeezing in time whenever I could to work my hobby. I'm from a small Cajun town of Plaquemine, Louisiana. My early heroes were my parents and especially my older brother, Harry. Then I started reading Marvel Comics and my list of heroes grew exponentially. Realizing I didn't have the right stuff to be a superhero myself, I concentrated on academics and took my first post as a college professor at The University of Mississippi. After many scientific publications and several textbooks, the call of storytelling was overwhelming. So, here I am today. You can find out more of what I've written at my website: spbrownbooks.com.

Thank you for purchasing
this publication of The Wild Rose Press, Inc.

For questions or more information
contact us at
info@thewildrosepress.com.

The Wild Rose Press, Inc.
www.thewildrosepress.com